A WINTER OF BLOOD

THE DCI COOK MURDER MYSTERY SERIES
BOOK 1

JACK CARTWRIGHT

A WINTER OF BLOOD

JACK CARTWRIGHT

PROLOGUE

Christmas Day

"If anybody else puts another log on that fire, I'm going to pass out," said Thomas, much to the amusement of Jeff, his eldest brother, who dropped to his knees beside the wood store and selected a particularly fat log. "Don't do it, Jeff. It's hot enough."

"Ah, come on," he replied. "It's freezing outside."

"Yeah, outside," Thomas replied. "It's practically tropical in here. Honestly, I think Dad's lemon tree thinks it's summer again and is ready to bear fruit."

"Will you two just stop arguing?" Janice said. "You've been at it all day. Honestly, no wonder the kids have all gone upstairs to play on the Xbox. It's supposed to be a holiday. If I wanted an argument, I'd have gone to my in-laws with my own kids."

"Your sister's right," their father added from the far side of the room, where he manned the open plan kitchen wielding a pair of tongs and wearing his grubby apron over his threadbare Christmas jumper. "All this arguing isn't doing your mother any favours."

"Don't bring me into it," Mum said. "I'm sitting here minding my own business." She was curled into her armchair with a glass of sherry in one hand and the latest Kevin Banner novel in the other, and she smiled across at Susie, Jeff's wife, holding the book up. "This is a good one."

"Ooh, I'm glad you like it. I wasn't sure what it would be like since he had that thing with his mother-in-law."

"Yeah, but he wasn't involved, was he?" said Mum. "That's what I heard anyway."

"I don't think we'll ever find out the truth," Susie replied. "I read on social media that the neighbour did it, but I heard somebody in the garden centre say that he was involved, his wife too."

"Well, he writes a damn good murder mystery," Mum replied.

The scene was as idyllic as Christmas could be. The huge open planned living space had been meticulously decorated by Janice's mother, with a slightly over-the-top nativity scene from carved wood on the sideboard, garlands draped over the doorway and mantelpiece, Christmas trinkets such as little nutcrackers and sleighs subtly placed beside the framed photographs that were there all year round, and of course, the tree. It wasn't a giant, by any means, but it had clearly been decorated with a tender loving hand. It reminded Janice of the trees one might see in a garden centre filled with baubles, bells, stars, and even pinecones to the point where there was barely a space to add anything else. It was so over the top that it was perfect.

It was a scene of festive opulence, and a shameless demonstration of wealth, which Janice presumed was more for Susie's sake than anybody else's.

"Is the King doing a speech?" Jeff asked as he slumped down beside Susie on one of the sofas.

"Not on our telly," Dad replied from the kitchen, then snapped his tongs twice as if to reiterate his hatred of the monarchy.

"I'll watch it on the player thing when he's gone to bed," Mum said quietly. "He'll be sound asleep by seven o'clock."

"Ooh, I wouldn't mind watching it," Susie said, then glanced up at Dad in the kitchen. "He won't be asleep that early though, will he?"

"Does it every year," Thomas replied, standing with his back to the bi-fold doors to cool himself. "He'll give a speech at dinner, usually about how grateful we should be that the family business is still going, then he'll eat too much, then drink too much, then after a few farts and inappropriate jokes, he'll fall asleep. It's like clockwork."

"Then he'll apologise in the morning in case he offended anybody," Jeff added. "Which is when we like to make up things that he did but can't remember. That usually entertains us until Boxing Day lunchtime."

"And then we start it over again," Thomas said, grinning. "The kids love it. They find it highly amusing that he can recollect absolutely nothing about their favourite day of the year."

"So when do you do presents?" she asked.

"After dinner," Thomas replied. "We all get to choose one present to open in the morning and then we do the rest once we've eaten."

"Blimey and the kids are okay with that?"

"I suppose they have to be," Thomas said. "That's where the one present thing comes in. It softens the blow a little."

"It's because Dad used to work on Christmas Day," Janice said, feeling the need to give Susie a little more of an explanation. "It just kind of became a habit that we got used to."

"Blimey, there would have been an all-out war at my house if my parents had suggested that," Susie replied.

"Oh, we've had our wars," Janice said, then lowered her voice. "Some of them are ongoing."

"Righto," Dad called out, as he opened the oven door and fanned the steam from his face. "Can someone get the kids down here? I'll be serving up in five minutes."

"Five minutes?" Thomas said. "I need the loo first."

"Same," Jeff said

At this, Janice shook her head and whispered to Susie, "That's the same every year too. Dad announces dinner and these two suddenly need the bathroom. They do it when everybody's eaten too, to get out of helping the clean-up."

Thomas and Jeff glanced at each other in a panic. Then they shot from the room in a race for the downstairs cloakroom, meeting at the door and struggling to squeeze through first, leaving Janice talking to Susie and Mum still reading her new book on the armchair.

"They've done that for the past thirty years," Janice said, bored of the same old rigmarole.

"I think it's lovely," Susie replied. "It actually makes me think of my own family Christmases as being quite, well, boring if I'm honest."

"I'd settle for something a little more sedate," Janice said. "You'd better make the most of it. When Gareth gets here, the fun will plummet."

"I haven't met him yet," Susie said and glanced at Mum to make sure she was still engrossed in the novel. "I hear he's quite a strong character."

Janice smiled the comment off, deeming her reply as not conducive to a happy family Christmas. There would be arguments later. It wasn't worth starting one just yet.

"He's focused," her mother said, without looking up from her book. She sipped at her sherry and set it back down on the arm of her chair. She gestured at Dad, who was filling serving bowls with the sides. "Gerry used to be like that before he retired."

"Yeah, and Gareth inherited the ball and chain," Janice said.

"If you're referring to the family business as a ball and chain, Janice, then perhaps we should return your presents, seeing as it was the business that paid for them and it's the business that employs you all."

"Oh, you know what I mean, Mum," Janice said. "I'm not

ungrateful. It just seems to be at the centre of everything we do. It's like everything revolves around Dickens and Sons."

"Everything apart from your husband and children, you mean?" her mother said, her tone sharp, but not as deadly as it could have been.

"It's Richard's parents' turn to have Christmas at their house, Mum," Janice said. "Like I've explained already, a dozen times or more."

"It would have been nice if they could have come here is all I'm saying," she replied. "I told you to invite Richard's mum and dad. We've got the space. They could have had the annexe."

"They wanted Christmas in their own home, Mum. What was I supposed to do, get them in a headlock and tell them the mighty Dickens family insists on their attendance?"

"Have you spoken to Gareth, dear?" Mum called out to Dad, ignoring Janice's comment, which in itself was a sign of whose side she would take in the inevitable forthcoming row.

"He's two minutes away," Dad replied, as he set the last of the dishes on the huge table. "Let's get everyone seated, shall we?"

Being new to the family, Susie was the first to the table, where she paused to take the scene in. Janice had to admit, her parents knew how to put on a show. The centrepiece was handmade from holly and ferns. The silverware was placed as if Carson from Downton Abbey had popped by with his ruler and white gloves. And the matching dishes were adorned with a floral pattern that tied in with the serviettes and even the crackers. It was a sight to behold. But Janice dared not mention how impressive it looked for fear of feeding the family ego.

"Where shall I sit?" Susie asked.

"Dad will sit at the top," Janice said. "Gareth will sit at the other end. The rest of us mere mortals will sit in between, hoping they'll throw us some scraps."

"That's enough," Mum said and ushered Susie into a seat. "I thought you could sit here, dear, so you can have the children on either side of you. You never know, it might inspire Jeffery and you to have some of your own one day."

"Whoa, Mum, give her a break," Janice said. "They've only been together a few months."

"No," Susie said. "No, it's okay. We've already spoken about children."

"Already?" Janice said.

"Marriage too," Susie said, grinning from ear to ear. But then her grin faded and she looked fearful. "But don't tell him that I told you that. I wouldn't want to ruin his surprise when he finally pops the question."

"Oh, I wouldn't worry too much about that," Janice told her, as she took a place near the middle of the table, where she could be as far from her dad or Gareth as possible. "We all had you pegged as married, laden with kids, and grey just from the fact that he hasn't chucked you after one month."

"Really?" Susie said, her brow furrowed with concern.

"Don't pay any attention to her," Mum said. "She's just bitter and twisted."

Janice leaned forward across the table to speak quietly to Susie.

"That's how I've survived for so long. If you want to survive, then you should try it."

"Is it that bad?" Susie asked.

Janice checked that Dad and Mum weren't looking, stole a crispy roast potato, and then took a bite.

"In case you haven't noticed, the company name is Dickens and Sons. Not Dickens and Daughters."

"I hadn't thought of that," Susie replied, to which Janice raised her eyebrows.

"If you've got a pair of tits in this house, then you'd better grow a pair of balls."

"We'll have less of that," Mum said, then glared at her when she saw the half-eaten potato she was trying to conceal in her hand.

It was a sharp move by Mum, to place everyone where she had, ensuring herself a seat beside at least one of the grandkids, from where she could manage them as she saw fit. Susie took her seat, just as Jeff and Thomas returned with the two young boys in tow.

"Over here," Susie said, putting on an excited tone to hopefully inspire the kids, who were obviously a little disgruntled at being torn away from the Xbox.

They both walked to the table and knelt on two chairs opposite their grandmother to inspect the food. It was only when little Harry reached for a roast potato that Mum showed her darker side, the side that had corralled the family into place when Dad had been at work. She rapped his fingers with a serving spoon and then wagged a bony index finger.

"Wait," she told them both. "We say grace once per year. After that, you can eat as much as you want."

"Come on, boys," Susie said, clearly a little disturbed at the sight of the reprimand. She looked up at Janice who simply replied with a knowing look.

Mum coaxed the boys onto the chairs she had earmarked for them and then took the one beside young Harry. Jeffery and Thomas occupied the last two side seats, leaving just the two end carvers free.

Dinner had been timed with a perfection that only seven decades of being a total control freak could garner. There was only one person capable of dashing his moment; a person whose ego emanated from every pore in his skin, and every word he spoke. Just as her dad had placed the turkey on the table initiating a small chorus of oohs and ahs, Gareth appeared at the doorway like a hero home from war, standing there waiting for a reaction.

"The door was unlocked," he said, as their mum, who could

barely conceal her glee, rushed from her seat to hug her eldest son, and then led him to the seat at the end of the table.

"You sit there, dear," she said. "You deserve it."

"This looks great, Dad," he said, taking his seat, and then finding his two sons staring up at him. "Have you been good for Nanny and Grandad?"

"They've been an absolute joy," Mum told him, as she upturned his glass and filled it with red.

From where Janice was sitting, she observed the whole charade as if she was just a spectator. She had often played the game of saying nothing until she was brought into the conversation to see how long it would take, but usually, she was proven right and ignored for the most part.

Susie, however, was observing Gareth. It was the first time the two had met and, Janice noticed, he hadn't even introduced himself, or welcomed her – a sure sign that his feet were well and truly embedded in Dad's footsteps.

"You must be Susie," he said eventually as if Janice's thoughts had somehow reached him. "What do you think of the house?"

It was an odd question to ask, even by a Dickens's standards.

"Oh," Susie said, a little taken aback. "It's lovely. I haven't seen much of it yet, but–"

"Jeffery will take her for a walk in the grounds tomorrow," Dad said. "The ponds are nice at this time of year."

"The ponds are a quagmire," Janice said. "I hope you brought your wellies–"

"We have spare," Mum added, with a quick glance around the table to make sure everybody had a drink.

"How was work, today, Gareth?" he asked, a question which, in Janice's opinion, could have been asked in private, before or after dinner, but clearly had been intended to reiterate the fact that they wouldn't be there if it wasn't for Dickens and Sons.

"All right, Dad," he replied. "I let them go early."

"That was big of you," Janice said, taking a sip of her soda water and meeting his glare with a carefree stare of her own. "They must have been queueing at your office door to pay their respects."

"That's enough," Mum said. "I'll not have any arguments at the dinner table."

"Actually, I do need to speak to you," Gareth said, gulping at his wine as if it were Vimto.

"Oh?" Janice said.

"Nothing important," he replied. "Just a bit more streamlining, that's all."

"Streamlining?" Dad said. "Let's not dress it up with colourful language, Gareth. Let's give it the brutal reality the word deserves. Redundancies. You're talking about destroying people's lives."

"I just want to thin out the support functions and some of the operations team," Gareth replied. "We don't need three IT guys, and if we re-arrange the shifts, we can probably do away with the nighttime security firm. You know? Make it a twenty-four-hour operation."

"That's a bit drastic. We're talking about peoples' livelihoods here," her dad said. "Should we talk this over?"

"I've already made the decision. We already have a plan," Gareth replied. "Do you want to hear it?"

"Maybe not on Christmas Day? And not at the dinner table?" Janice suggested, which was completely ignored.

"It's nothing to worry about, Dad," Gareth said. "A lot of businesses are doing the same thing. It's the whole Covid thing. We're lucky to still be running in the first place."

"Well, as long as you know what you're doing."

"I do," Gareth said, smiling his way out of the hole he had been close to digging.

"You've handed the reins over to him now, dear," Mum said, to which Dad seemed mildly appeased.

Finally, with a subordinate smile, she took little Harry's hand in her left hand, and little Arthur's in her right.

The rest of the table followed suit, each of them holding hands with the people on either side. Janice took Thomas's hand in her left and Jeff's in her right. Dad waited a moment to ensure he had their full attention before he closed his eyes and began.

"For what we are about receive, we are truly grateful," he began. "And for everything around us, we are truly proud."

Thomas gave Janice's hand a gentle squeeze, a silent sign that he too had recognised the ridiculous ostentatiousness of what was supposed to have been a verse or two of sincerity. She opened her eyes and looked his way, and he rolled his eyes with a bowed head.

"And for the year ahead," Dad said, "we promise to create opportunities so that others less fortunate than ourselves may benefit."

"Amen," Gareth said.

"Amen," all but two of them chorused.

CHAPTER ONE

The little two-bed house that John Gregory called home stood at the end of a terrace of stone cottages on Heighington High Street. It was modest in every way, but functional, and with the addition of the double glazing he'd had installed, plus several hundred pounds' worth of loft insulation, the heat from the log burner permeated almost every inch of the home. The investment had been a tough decision to make. He had used every penny of the holiday fund and more. But when he stepped through his front door, felt the heat on his face, and saw his two young children warmed enough to frolic in just t-shirts, he felt it had been the right one to make.

Sinatra's warm and calm tones filled the silence from the little speaker in the kitchen, along with the aroma of roast chicken with stuffing. The fairy lights on the tree pulsed gently. The incessant Christmas pop hits that the factory radio had played all day had tried to bring it to life, as had the flashing lights in the windows of the houses along the streets, but nothing could create the wonderful feeling that home could.

"Happy Christmas, John," Penny said, taking his coat and reaching up to kiss his cheek. She wore her apron over a knee-length, floral dress, and on her feet were the slippers he had bought her the year before.

"Oh," he said. "When did you start hanging my coat for me?"

She hung it on a hook, smoothed the creases out, and then bit her lower lip to conceal the depth of her happiness.

"It's Christmas Day," she told him. "We've missed you."

"Well, I'm home now," he replied, as he dropped into the sofa beside Emily, his eldest, who lay with her legs hanging over the arm and a book held above her. "All right, kiddo?"

She pulled the book away from her face so she could see him, revealing a beaming smile that only the innocent are capable of.

"Hello, Daddy," she said.

He placed his hand on her forehead and smoothed the wild and wispy hairs that were too short to stay in place.

"Are you having a nice day?"

She nodded and held the book cover for him to see.

"Aunty Fiona got me this," she told him.

"Oh, that's nice," he replied, and before he could say anything else, Penny started.

"I said they could open one each," she said. "I had to keep them busy."

"That's okay," he said. "You should have opened them all. I would have."

"We wanted to wait for you, Daddy," James, his youngest, said. He was in a similar position to Emily but in the armchair nearest the fireplace, and in place of a book he held the games console they had given him for his birthday. It had been an extravagant gift by their usual standards, but one which had been necessary to match the computer they had bought for Emily to do her homework on.

"Well, thank you," he told him. "What did you get from Aunty Fiona?"

"A new game," James replied. "Turbo Racer."

"Turbo Racer, eh? Is that a driving game?"

"It's rated for ages four and up," Penny said as if some justification was needed.

"Well, maybe you can show me how to drive after dinner?" John said. "When you've opened your other presents."

"Really?" James said, rolling onto his side. "We can have a race."

"A race? Well, I'd better not eat too many of your mum's roast potatoes then."

"I'm going to have ten," James said, returning to his previous position and resuming his game.

"Speaking of dinner, is there anything I can do?" he said to his wife.

"You just sit there. I'll get you a beer," she replied and disappeared into the kitchen.

He heard her open the fridge, then the clinking of bottles, and he stood before she could return, finding her with his back to the kitchen door working the bottle opener. He slipped his arms around her and nuzzled into her neck, then removed her hands from the bottle.

"Merry Christmas," he said, and gently forced her hips to sway to the rather apt tune of Sinatra being home for Christmas. "Let's have some wine."

"I thought we were saving it for when Mum and Dad come tomorrow?"

"We'll get some more," he said into her ear. "Come on. We deserve it."

"What with, John?" she said, turning in his arms and reaching up to his shoulders. "We're into the overdraft—"

"Sod the overdraft, Penny," he said. "If I can't share a bottle of wine with my beautiful wife on Christmas Day, then what's the bloody point?"

"But Mum and Dad will be here in the morning. Dad will want a glass, and I don't want them to know we're struggling. You know what they're like. They'll think we can't manage—"

"I'll drive down to Satish's in the morning. He's always open on Boxing Day," John said. "What else do we need?"

He glanced around the kitchen, still holding her in his arms. The eclectic collection of serving dishes was ready to be filled with the delights that were boiled, roasted, and baked in and on the oven. He looked across at the little dining table she had prepared. All four seats had been set with their usual dinnerware, plus the addition of the paper serviettes they had bought the previous year. The centrepiece was a single candelabra which had been cleverly adorned with tinsel.

"No crackers?" he said, holding her away to look her in the eye. "I thought we bought some?"

"I was saving them for tomorrow," she said sadly. "Mum will notice if we don't have them, and I can't tell her that I've forgotten because she kept going on and on about what she needed to bring."

He leaned forward and kissed her forehead.

"I'll get some," he said. "Put whatever we have out for tonight, and I'll pick some up tomorrow. I know Satish has some. I saw them when I was there for milk the other day."

"John, we can't afford—"

"Put them out," he told her. "Those two kids in there are going to have a lovely Christmas. You too. And me. We can make cutbacks in the new year if we have to, but I'll not have them remembering half-baked Christmases like I had to. They shouldn't have to go without just because times are harder than they once were. I'll talk to Janice to see if there's anything that can be done. Extra shifts or weekend work."

"You're already working every hour under the sun, John—"

"Then I'll ride my bike to work to save petrol. I don't care what I have to do, Penny. I want those kids to have a nice Christmas. We might not be able to get them everything they want, but they'll have a Christmas to remember."

She closed her eyes and rested her head on his chest. So, he pulled her away and saw the tears in her eyes.

"You're such a good dad," she told him, to which he shook his head.

"Christmas isn't about money," he said. "My dad told me that once. I was young, so of course for me, Christmas was about presents. But when I look back at those times, do you know what I remember?"

"No," she said softly.

"It's not the presents. I remember the big ones, like when I got a bike and when my aunt bought me a little Casio keyboard. But the thing I remember most is the times. You know? The games we played after dinner. My mum a little tipsy from the wine. And my dad, who on every other day of the year was a bad-tempered, old git, wearing a paper hat from a cracker. That's what I remember. So put the bloody crackers out so I can wear a hat. And open the bloody wine."

"So you can get me tipsy?" she said, her face aglow with what he could only describe as Christmas.

"Am I that transparent?" he said and winked at her. He clapped his hands three times for the kids to hear. "Right then, let's get this party started. How long until dinner?"

"A few minutes," she said.

"Good," he replied, reaching for the little speaker to crank up the volume. Emily and James appeared in the doorway at the commotion and he ushered them to the table, seating each one in chairs at the ends of the table.

"This is your chair, Daddy," James said, laughing. "Where are you going to sit?"

"In your chair, dear boy," John replied, in a mock well-spoken accent. "For you are the master and your sister the mistress for the evening."

"Has Dad been drinking?" Emily asked her mother, who laughed as she handed him a glass.

"No, sweetheart. He's just happy."

"It's Christmas," John exclaimed in his own defence, then lowered his voice as he raised his glass, and looked each of them in the eye. "And you three make me the luckiest man alive."

Penny began placing the dishes on the table, leaving the chicken until last, after which she handed John the carving knife, and then pulled the little box of Christmas crackers down from the top cupboard.

She took her seat opposite John and they each reached for the hands of their children. Penny waited for John to say a few words.

"Close your eyes and bow your heads," he told them. "And think of those less fortunate than us."

They did as he asked, and before Penny followed suit, she smiled at him, offering every ounce of faith she had.

"I'm going to make you all a promise," he told them. "This year has been difficult. We've all had to go without some of the things we want. We've all had to compromise. But I promise you this. Next year will be better. I'll see to it that you have what you want, what you need. But we are where we are right now and I'm going to make this a Christmas you never forget."

"Amen," Penny said, letting go of the children's hands and reaching for her glass, which she held up to John, her eyes moist and proud.

"Amen," he told her.

CHAPTER TWO

It might have been any other weekend on the ground floor of Lincoln Police HQ, which, for Detective Chief Inspector Charles Cook, was absolutely ideal. If he had his way, he would hide in the station until New Year had passed. Sadly, the powers above him, with all their snowflake agendas, monitored and measured each officer's downtime.

There was a time when Charles had been a young, uniformed officer strolling Lincoln's streets, that they would have rewarded voluntary attendance. But these days, it was almost as if they didn't want him loitering around for fear of disrupting the balance of shifts, which somebody who had likely never even worked a shift had created, and who likely had a family to go home to, a roaring fire, and a fat turkey to feast upon.

"Night, guv," the custody sergeant called out as Charles passed the desk to head out into the car park. "When are you back?"

"Oh, in the new year, I think, Sergeant Barrow," Charles replied.

"Lucky you," Barrow said. "I've pulled the short straw this year."

"I'm on call," he said. "But I doubt they'll consider me if

something comes up. Apparently, I've accrued too much holiday, which seems like a ridiculous concept."

"Too much? How much have you taken?" Barrow asked, to which Charles grinned.

"None," he replied. "Aside from a couple of days last March when I was having a new bathroom put in."

"Blimey, it's a shame they're not paying out this year," Barrow said. "I remember last year, they gave us the option of cashing in outstanding annual leave. Paid for Christmas, that did."

"I remember the days when we could pick and choose our shifts," Charles replied. "Everyone knew everyone else and if you wanted a week off, you arranged it with your colleagues. Nowadays I don't recognise half the faces in here. Still, I suppose progress is progress, and who am I to argue?"

"You're on your own then, are you? At home, I mean, guv. No family?"

"You know very well I've no family, Barrow."

"I meant brothers or sisters, guv. I wasn't being impertinent."

"I have a brother in Inverness. Too far for me to drive, so I'll be alone," Charles said, as he made for the exit.

"Just the way you like it, I suppose," Barrow said, which seemed a curious thing to say.

Charles stopped at the door to fasten his overcoat before remembering his manners and looking back at the young custody sergeant.

"Let's just say that it's the way others like it," he said. "You're off soon, aye?"

"Couple of hours, guv."

"Well, Merry Christmas," Charles said. "Enjoy the time with your family while you can."

"Same to you, guv," he replied, and Charles walked down the few concrete steps into the car park.

The night was cold, but not so cold that he hurried. The headlights of his Jaguar flashed once and when he pulled the door closed, the world outside seemed distant. He mused, as he drove, on the other drivers. Christmas was one of those times of the year when the roads were near empty, and the few cars he did pass were likely to be either shift workers, families going home after dinner with relatives, or single dads dropping their kids back to their mothers.

He knew the latter wasn't accurate and was presumptuous, yet it reflected the life he had once known. It stirred the bitterness that had taken root like ivy, which once established, was almost impossible to eradicate.

The drive home to Bracebridge took less than five minutes, long enough for the car to warm up but not long enough for the windscreen to clear entirely. As was his habit, he reversed onto the drive, which made getting out in a hurry faster. As per the advice his father had given him decades ago, it also made dealing with a flat battery far easier. Not that flat batteries were as common as they were all those years ago. In those days, the street they lived on was filled with the sounds of Austins, Morrises, and Fords coughing into life like sixty-a-day smokers.

Charles sat on his driveway for a moment watching a young couple pass. Their arms were linked and the girl seemed to lean on him as they hurried along, her heels clicking up the road. In pitch darkness, his house seemed far less appealing than the station had been. He could have had his feet up in the social room and saved himself a few quid on heating. He might even have had a chat with some of the less fortunate officers who couldn't be with their families on Christmas Day.

He closed the front door behind him, setting the latch as he always did, and once he'd hung his coat and scarf on the old hat stand, he wandered into the kitchen to pour himself a drink. Brandy was his drink of choice. Cognac, to be precise. Poured over ice in a short, cut-crystal tumbler. He was too late for the King's speech, and if he was honest with himself, his desire to avoid it this year was stronger than the habit of watching.

The living room was large enough for a family with three or four children, and it seemed to swallow him. Despite only ever having lived in the house alone, he'd still furnished it with two sofas. It was a balance thing, he supposed. Everything in life was a balance. The healthy vegetables he ate balanced the junk food. The money he squandered on frivolities balanced the amounts he deposited into his pension. And the time he spent alone with only his thoughts as company balanced the time he spent chit-chatting with colleagues.

The clock in the hallway gave a single chime for half past six and he kicked off his shoes before reaching for the radio beside him. BBC Four was his favourite. No music, just idle chit-chat, some of which made him chuckle. The rest of it, he could tune out, unlike the television which would no doubt be awful, and even if he did find a film to watch, it would no doubt be interrupted halfway through with an obligatory Christmas phone call. There was nothing quite so irritating as missing five or ten minutes of a film and losing the plot. He always imagined the caller, be it his only surviving cousin, or his only surviving aunt, ending the call and then rejoining a throng of entertainment, oblivious to the fact that they had just ruined his evening.

Dinner should have been on his mind, but for the life of him, he couldn't face standing in the kitchen. Beans on toast seemed quite appealing, or even beans on cheese on toast, but even that seemed an effort. He sipped at his drink instead. Perhaps the drink would wake a hunger. At least he wouldn't wake up to a stinking, greasy pizza box on his lap. But then, he supposed, that somewhere would be open on Christmas Day, and willing to deliver him some dinner.

Exactly as he had thought, it was the phone that interrupted him.

Had he been a betting man, he might have wagered on it being his cousin Iain. Aunt Julia would call later when the family had gone home.

"Evening," he said, wishing he'd poured himself a larger glass.

He always enjoyed talking to Iain, but seeing as he lived on the other side of the country, he rarely had the opportunity to see him. They both liked gardening and shared similar views on politics; both deemed themselves to be neither left nor right winged, adopting a more common-sense opinion on how the country should be governed. They had spent an entire fifty-nine-minute call recently discussing the illegal immigrants who came to Britain on little boats, risking their lives in the process. The call had been fifty-nine minutes long, as Iain had some kind of deal with his provider, which gave him free landline calls under an hour, after which they simply hung up and dialled again.

"Dad?" the voice said.

It seemed to stop time itself, a voice Charles hadn't heard for nearly a decade.

CHAPTER THREE

Nobody wore the paper hats that had tumbled from the John Lewis Christmas crackers, along with keyrings, little magic tricks, and in Janice's case, a metal bottle opener. She had given it to Thomas, who had slipped it onto his keys.

"That'll come in handy," he told her.

"Dad, that was excellent," Gareth said, leaning back in his chair and patting his stomach, which was as flat as a billiards table, and knowing how much her brother worked out, probably just as hard. "You knocked it out of the park this year."

"Hear hear," Susie said, raising her glass, to which nobody responded, not even Jeff, who in Gareth's presence lost his alpha male fight and adopted more of a subordinate character, always seeking to please either their eldest brother or their father.

Janice took it upon herself to ease the girl's embarrassment and she held her soda water up, at which Susie smiled sweetly and gratefully, albeit a little red-faced.

"Can we open our presents now?" little Harry asked, and Janice noted the lack of excitement that kids' voices should be filled with, reminding her of her own subdued childhood, where she grew as a sapling in the shadow of her brothers. But unlike many saplings, she had fought for the daylight. Not for her father's attention or her mother's love, but for daylight, for choice, and a life outside of the family.

"Yes, we can," she said before any of the others could delay the children's joy any longer.

"Well, I thought we'd wait–" her mum started.

"Oh, come on," she said. "The poor kids have been waiting all day."

"But what about the clearing up?"

"I'll do it," Susie said and then shrank under the attention. "I'll help anyway."

"We'll do it together," Janice said. "The boys can get the games ready."

"Games?" Gareth said.

"Yes, Gareth, games."

"Risk could be good," Jeff suggested. "Do we still have it, Mum?"

"Risk? Really, Jeff?" Janice said. "With the kids?"

"It's a game."

"What about cards?" Mum said. "We used to play Newmarket when you were young. I'm sure I've got some pennies somewhere."

"Cards could be good," Janice said. "What else? Susie, what do you normally play with your family?"

"How do you know she plays anything?" Gareth said.

"Because it's Christmas, Gareth, and most families play games at Christmas. Most normal families anyway."

"What's that supposed to mean?"

"All right, all right," Mum said, then fell in with what Janice was suggesting as if trying to make her feel welcome had been her idea. "Susie, dear, what do you normally do with your family?"

Clearly not a fan of being in the limelight, Susie shrank in her seat.

"Well, my step-mum likes poetry. She sometimes reads one or two."

"Oh, for God's sake," Gareth muttered, ignoring Janice's glare.

"And then we sometimes play Who Am I?"

"Who are you?" Jeff said.

"Who Am I?" Susie said with a shy laugh. "It's the one where everyone has a sticky note on their forehead with the name of a famous person on it and they have to ask yes or no questions to find out who they are. Haven't you ever played it?"

"Do we look like the type of family that enjoys each other's company?" Janice said.

"It's a good game," she replied. "And easy too. We just need some sticky notes and pens."

"We'll play that then," Janice said. "Anything else?"

"Charades?" Susie said with a shrug. "Karaoke—"

"Hold on, hold on," Dad said, who until now had been watching them all quietly as he often did. "I draw the line at singing."

"Oh, come on, Grandad," Harry said.

"No," he said. "No singing."

"We could always play dance-off?" Susie suggested, then when everybody looked at her blankly, she felt compelled to explain. "You know the one where you have to dance and mime to a song and the rest of us score you on effort and accuracy?"

"Bloody hell, it gets worse," Gareth said. "The sticky note thing is fine. Charades maybe. But I'm not prancing about or singing. I've been at bloody work all day and I'd like to put my feet up with a nice drink."

"Please don't swear, dear," Mum said.

"Right, that settles it," Janice said, as she began gathering the empty plates. "Susie and I will sort this lot out. Either, Thomas, Jeff or Gareth can find some sticky notes and get the presents ready."

"What about us?" Harry said.

"You can distribute the presents," Janice told him. "I want to see nine neat little piles of presents besides the sofas."

"I want to see eight neat little piles and one *huge* pile," Thomas said. "The big one being mine."

"Right, get to it," Janice said, as she began the first trip to the kitchen.

"Who made you the boss?" Gareth said, making no effort to move. "I don't take orders from you."

She set the plates down on the kitchen island and contemplated letting it go. But he needed telling.

"Why do you always have to turn everything into a power play?" she asked. "It's okay. We all know who has their tongue furthest up Dad's arse—"

"Hey," Dad snapped. "I won't hear that type of vulgarity in my house."

"Oh right," Janice said. "Is that because it's true or because the words came from my mouth and not his?"

"Janice, what on earth?" Mum began.

"Okay, okay," Jeff said, taking control of the situation. "We're all a bit tired. It's been a long day, let's not ruin it. Come on, Gareth. You can show me where to find sticky notes."

"You know where to find them. They're in the study."

"Just come with me, will you?" Jeff said. "Susie, are you okay in here?"

"She'll be fine," Janice said, letting the two oldest brothers leave the room.

The two young boys, with the help of Mum, began sorting the Christmas presents into piles, while Thomas made a break for the bathroom. Dad just sat there, watching everything happen around him. He topped up his wine, then set the bottle down beside him, all the while barely taking his eyes from Janice.

"Do you want to wash and I'll wipe?" Susie suggested.

"Sure," Janice replied, leaving her father peering after them. She ran the hot water to fill the sink while Susie scraped the plates into the bin. "We'll wash the greasy pans. Everything else can go in the dishwasher."

"Gotcha," Susie said, and they settled into a rhythm. "So, Jeff tells me you run the HR for the firm. How do you find it?"

"They gave me the HR Manager title," Janice replied. "But it should have really been skivvy. I run most of the operational staff, aside from the finance team. Gareth likes to keep an eye on them. He couldn't give a toss about the rest of them."

"Oh," Susie said, and quite rightly didn't know where else she could take the conversation.

"Sorry. I'm being bitter. Let's talk about you. Jeff said you work in a school. Do you teach?"

She gave a little laugh.

"No, I'd be a terrible teacher. I man the front desk and do most of the admin."

"Do you enjoy it?"

"I love it," Susie replied. "I mean, the pay isn't great, but the teachers are mostly nice and the rest of the team all get on, apart from the caretaker. But I don't have to deal with him, thankfully."

"That sounds like my job," Janice said, as Susie loaded the last of the plates into the dishwasher. She peered up quizzically as if prompting Janice for an explanation. "Mostly, the people I work with are okay. It's just one or two that really get on my tits."

"Right," Gareth said, as the two men burst into the room. He slapped the pack of sticky notes onto the cleared dining table, and Jeff slid a few pens beside it. "Sticky notes and pens. Can I sit down and put my feet up now?"

"And there they both are," Janice said quietly to Susie, who turned away from the men and lowered her voice.

"I thought you and Jeff got on well?"

Janice gave a little laugh, as she rinsed the dishcloth and hung it on the mixer tap.

"I get on with Jeff better than Gareth," said quietly. "In much the same way Winston Churchill got on better with Stalin than he did Hitler. I trust neither of them."

Susie seemed a little disheartened at her new boyfriend being spoken of in such a way, but that was her issue to deal with. She'd learn the ways of the family if she stuck around long enough.

"You two took your time," Janice called out. "Don't tell me you're still afraid of the dark, Jeff."

"Ignore her, Susie," Jeff said. "She's just doing what she always does."

"And what's that?" Janice asked.

"Being jealous," Jeff told her.

Janice snatched her glass from the counter and then claimed the only free armchair before Gareth could, and when her move had been successful, she gave a hearty sigh and set her wine down on the floor beside her.

"Are these mine?" she said, pointing to the nearby pile of presents.

"No, Aunty Janice, these are yours," Harry replied, pointing to the pile that had been positioned in front of the centre seat of one of the sofas. "Look they've got your name on."

"I thought you could sit with Susie and Jeff," Mum said. "Those gifts are Gareth's."

"I'll sit here if it's all the same to you. I'm feeling a bit hot after all that cleaning."

"But the gifts, Janice," Mum said. "Don't start messing things up—"

"Harry, be a darling and slide them over to me, will you?" Janice said.

"Harry, leave them be," Mum countered, then clicked her fingers. "Janice, move."

Janice was used to being treated as the black sheep, but having fingers clicked at her was something else entirely.

"I'll move," she said, snatching her phone from the armchair and shoving herself out of her seat. "I'm going to bed. Enjoy your Christmas."

"Oh, come on," Thomas said. "Mum, just let her sit there, for God's sake."

"No, forget it," Janice said, grabbing her glass from the floor and the bottle from the table. She stopped to admire their expressions: three were shocked, one was disparaging, two were beaming, while her father's expression was impassive, to say the least. "Do you see what you've created, Dad? Can you see how abnormal this family is?"

"I've created a dynasty, Janice," he replied, his voice cracked and throaty. "Jobs for life, for you, Gareth, Jeffery, and Thomas, not to mention the grandchildren. But if that lifelong security means nothing to you, then you're free to seek employment elsewhere. Nobody is holding you hostage at Dickens and Sons, just as nobody is holding you hostage here."

"You should be careful what you wish for," she told him, and with a cursory glance around the room, she ended on a statement to drive her point home. "You forget how much I know about the business and how my loyalty wanes every time you take sides with your precious sons."

He stared at her, just as she had seen him appraise potential suppliers and even staff, with barely a shred of emotion on display.

"Have a think about that," she told him, before addressing the room. "Merry Christmas, Dickens and Sons."

CHAPTER FOUR

"Penny, that was delicious," John said, leaning back in his chair and rubbing his belly. His plate was clean, as was both Emily's and James's, aside from the smudges of leftover gravy.

Penny's plate still had a few pieces of chicken that she had pushed to one side, and she saw the three of them looking at the tender morsels.

"I'm saving them so I can have a sandwich later," she told them. "So you can just put those tongues back in your mouths. Besides, we have Christmas pudding."

James's face lit up at the mention of pudding.

"With ice cream?"

"Custard," she told him, repositioning her paper hat, which had fallen to one side.

"Custard is my favourite," John said. "We can have ice cream any time of the year. But custard, now that was made to go with Christmas pudding."

The lack of ice cream had done little to dilute James' excitement and he rocked in his seat at the prospect.

"Can you two help Mum clear the table?" John said.

"Oh, Dad," Emily began.

"It's okay, I don't mind–" Penny started, but he held up his hand. It wasn't often he asserted his authority, but when he did, he liked to think it was for a good cause.

"Just help her, please. Your mum has worked hard today, the least you two can do is clear the table," he said, as nicely as he could. His words and tone were a far cry from the orders he had received from his own father after dinner, but as differing as the deliveries were, the sentiment remained. He stood from his chair and placed his napkin on the table. "Go on. I need a few minutes alone."

"Is everything okay?" Penny asked as she ran the hot tap to fill the bowl with water.

"It's fine, dear," he replied, hoping that she saw the appreciation in his smile, and then he slipped into the lounge.

It was a small, cosy room offering no more than the bare essentials. Penny had lovingly placed the Christmas tree in front of the window, between the TV and the front door, and judging by the decoration, she had enlisted the help of the kids.

Penny had hung his coat on one of the hooks on the wall beside the front door, and after a quick check to make sure nobody was looking, he fished in his inside pocket, removed three envelopes, and then tucked them into a spot between the kids' presents. While the family cleaned up the dinner things, he made himself useful by tidying the lounge so they could make a fresh mess opening their presents. But it would be a fun mess, and he was excited to see the looks on their faces as they tore the paper from the gifts.

He put James' games console on the bookshelf along with Emily's book, making sure to slip her little Disney bookmark in place before doing so. The fire was burning low, so he added a few logs, enough to keep it going for an hour or so longer, and then collected the random items of clothing that had been strewn about the place during the course of the day. Lastly, he collected the empty glasses and cups, finding a coffee mug down the side of Penny's chair, where she left it every morning.

Without disturbing them, he leaned into the kitchen to place the glasses and cups on the side and then slipped away. They hadn't noticed him. Penny was too busy listening to Emily's retelling of the Christmas Carol play they had put on at school, and how she might be an actress when she 'got bigger'.

The room was ready. All he needed to do was light the candles and dim the lights, which he considered to be one of the joys of opening the presents so late. With the flickering flames from the fire and the candles came dancing shadows, warmth, and a romance that would be hard to match during the cold winter mornings. But the moment he most looked forward to was when the children were in bed and Penny would snuggle into him on the sofa. Those were the moments that mattered, those were the memories he longed to make, and those were the traditions he longed to build.

"Pudding's ready," Penny said from the doorway. Emily and James came to her side, with the latter itching to get at his gifts but torn by the promise of pudding and custard.

"Fantastic," John said, pushing himself to his feet and then crouching to look into his son's eyes. "They'll still be there after pudding."

He ruffled the lad's hair then ushered him back into the kitchen where they took their seats.

"I'm afraid I had to use some of the brandy," Penny said, as she placed the pudding onto the table, ablaze with a gentle blue flame. "I hope it's okay."

"Well, I was saving it," he replied. "But now I can't think of a better way to have used it."

He took up the knife, and with a few careful cuts, he divided the sponge into eight. Then, serving his wife first, he dished the pudding out, allocating himself two pieces of the eight.

"Hey," James said, his mouth full of dark brown pudding and

brow furrowed as if he was arguing with his sister, about to let loose the infamous claim of something being unfair. "You've got two bits."

"Have I?" John said in mock confusion. He spooned the pile of sponge into a soft mix, so they became one. "No, I haven't."

"You just mixed them up."

"No," John said, covering his crime with a healthy blob of custard. "No, you must be mistaken. I mean, would I do a thing like that?"

James' mouth hung open, aghast but unable to articulate his emotions, and John took a large mouthful.

"Oh, this is delicious," he told Penny. "Absolutely spot on. What do you think, James? Is it good?"

Pudding and custard lined the boy's teeth when he grinned his response.

"Emily? Do you like it?"

She swallowed her last mouthful and sat back, much as John had after the main course.

"I couldn't eat another thing," she said.

"Oh, that's a shame," John said, turning to his wife. "I suppose we'd better hide those chocolates."

"What chocolates?" James blurted out, spitting his pudding onto the table.

"Oh, it's not important now," John said. "It's just that Mummy and I bought you some chocolates. But if you're both too full to eat them—"

"I'm not," he said, tugging at the waistband of his pyjamas. "Look, there's loads of room."

"I don't know," Penny said, adding to the boy's torment. "I mean, you've had a big dinner and pudding, not to mention all those sweets you ate earlier."

"I only had three," he said, pleading with them both.

"What do you think, Mummy?" John asked, offering her a sly

wink. "Do you think they deserve chocolate? I mean, did they help you today?"

"Well, if I'm honest, no. They wanted to play by themselves all day."

"I would have helped if you'd asked, Mummy," Emily said, her expression one of utmost hurt.

"All the same," Penny replied sadly. "Here I was, toiling all day over a hot stove, scrubbing the floor on my hands and knees—"

"I didn't see you scrub the floor," James said.

"And you prepared most of the food yesterday," Emily added. "You told us, you did."

"Well, that might have been a little white lie."

"So do we get chocolate?" James asked, beaming suddenly. "Do we?"

John studied his children and the empty bowls before them.

"Let's see," he said. "Come on, let's see what Santa has brought."

"What about the dishes?" Emily said.

"Leave them. You can do them tomorrow," he replied, leading the way into the lounge, where he claimed a spot on the sofa so that Penny might join him. "Come on, hurry up, hurry up."

The children ran in and dropped to their knees in front of the tree. But then they stopped just as Penny sidled up beside John, and their expressions sought permission.

"Actually, how does everyone feel about opening the presents tomorrow?" he said, to the children's audible dismay.

"No way," James said.

"Oh, Daddy, no," Emily added.

"I just thought it would give us all something to do, that's all," he said.

"But. Daddy—"

"Oh, go on then," he said. "Dish them out."

The children needed no further prompting and they had the

presents sorted and in small piles beside their respective seats in under two minutes.

"You are a tease," Penny whispered.

"I'm creating memories," he told her quietly. "I'm just creating memories."

"What are these?" James said, holding up the three envelopes, the last of the gifts to be distributed.

"Oh, it's just a little something for each of you," John said, and Penny pushed herself away to study him, a bemused expression on her face. But John gave nothing away, just clapped his hands for them to begin.

"Can we open them first?' Emily said, holding her envelope up to the firelight as if seeing through it might offer a clue.

"Can we, Daddy?" James said, copying his big sister by holding it up to the light.

"Well, I was going to save them until last," he told her. "But you might as well open them. Pass Mummy hers, won't you? I want you to all open them at the same time."

"What are they?" Penny said quietly, appearing slightly hurt that she hadn't been included in whatever secret he had devised.

"You'll see," he said, watching as they each took a different approach to opening the envelopes. James was being overly careful by ripping along the top, Emily was trying to unstick the envelope, while Penny had inserted her little finger into the gap as if it was the electricity bill and was tugging her way along, which of course meant that her envelope got opened first, but she held it closed until the kids were ready. "Okay, are we good to go?"

"Ready," James said, peeking inside.

"All right then, you can see what's inside," John said, and he sat back in his chair, reached down for his wine, and savoured the mixed expressions that formed on their faces.

"What is it?" James said, holding up a slip of thick paper.

"What's Virgin?" Emily said.

"These are flight tickets," Penny said, doing her best to

suppress a smile while fighting with the urge to talk about the financial aspect. "To Florida. What the... Where did you get these?"

"Florida? No way," James said, and then immediately looked at his mum for help. "Where's Florida?"

"It's in America, dumbo," Emily said.

"America, whoa," James replied, holding the ticket up like he was Charlie with a golden ticket. "We're going to America? Really?"

"Dad?" Emily said, wiping a tear from her eye. "Are these real? They're not one of your jokes, are they?"

He reached forward and grabbed onto her hips, dragging her so she could perch on his lap.

"It's not one of my jokes, I promise," John said, ignoring the stare from Penny that bore into the side of his head. He took a long swig of his drink, pleased that the reactions had been well beyond what he had hoped for. "Well, to be precise, we're going to Disneyland."

"John–" Penny began, but she struggled to find the words. Then he pulled James closer, so the four of them could huddle. "I told you we're going to make memories and I meant it. We're going to Disneyland, and it's going to be a holiday we'll never ever forget."

CHAPTER FIVE

Charles was reeling. His throat dried in an instant and his mind went into overdrive as he thought of a hundred or more questions he could ask, or perhaps should ask, along with some that he shouldn't.

"Dad? Are you there?"

"I am," he said, then cleared his throat. "Oh God, Vanessa, you caught me off guard, there. Sorry I, erm–"

"I thought it might surprise you," she said.

"How's your–"

"Dad, don't," she said, cutting him off. "I just called because... well, because it's Christmas."

"It's been Christmas eleven times, Vanessa," he said.

"Listen, if you're going to start–"

"Sorry, sorry," he said. "I shouldn't have said that. I'm pleased to hear from you. Truly, I am. I don't know. I'm just not ready–"

"You're not ready?"

"I mean, I'm just unprepared, that's all. But honestly, it's great to hear your voice. Where are you?"

"Dad, you know I can't tell you that."

"Right," he said.

"Maybe it's best if I ask the questions," she said, at which he smiled. He could picture her, as he remembered her way back.

"Can I ask one?" he said.

"Dad, if it's about the family—"

"It's not," he said. "I promise, it's not."

She paused while she thought, as a suspect might consider a strategic response to a question during an interview.

"Go on," she said, with equal hostility as the suspect. "Just one though, Dad. Please don't try to pry the doors open."

"No prying," he replied. "Scout's honour."

"Okay."

He inhaled, long and deep, then settled on the question at the forefront of his mind. One that would allow him access to the memories he had tried so hard to put to the back of his mind for so many years.

"Do you still have your long, blonde, curly hair?"

"What?" she said, almost laughing.

"Do you?" he said. "That's how I remember you."

She paused again as if she was trying to work out if he was being serious.

"I do," she said. "I've tried changing it, but nothing seems to work. The curls just keep on breaking through."

"Just like me. I had curly hair in my day. You know that, don't you?"

"I didn't, no."

"Oh, come on. You must have seen photos."

"We don't have many," she said. "Not of back then at any rate."

The words were like a dagger in his heart and he swallowed hard to keep his voice strong. "Well, anyway, thank you," he said. "Now I can see you, at least."

"Sorry?"

"In my head, Vanessa. I can picture you," he said. "Do you remember when I did your hair before that school play?"

"Dad, you've had more than one question."

"I know, but—"

"Now it's my turn," she said, leaving him room to prepare himself.

"So you didn't call just to say hello," he said.

"I need to see you," she told him, leaving him scant room for argument. "Urgently."

"Urgently? Is everything okay? Is it—"

"I'll tell you when I see you. I can get to Cambridge. Can you meet me there?"

"Cambridge? Is that where you've been hiding?"

"I can get there, Dad. That's all you need to know."

"I can't come now. I've had a wee drink, Vanessa. I could come tomorrow. Should I bring something? Do you need money?"

"Tomorrow's fine, and no, but thank you. I don't need your money. I just need to see you. There's something you need to know."

"Tomorrow then," he said.

"Tomorrow. Midday at the botanic gardens."

"I think about you. You know that, aye?"

She hesitated for a moment and he felt the mood plummet.

"Not yet, Dad," she told him. "Let's talk tomorrow."

He held his breath, fighting the deflating feeling in his chest.

"Okay," he said eventually. "I'll see you tomorrow. I love you, Van—"

But she ended the call before he could finish, leaving him holding the handset for a moment, staring at it, in case the whole episode had been a dream.

He stored the number she had called on, doubting that it was her actual number. It was most likely a Pay As You Go sim in an old phone. She'd always been a smart kid, he thought, as he replaced the handset and sipped his drink, savouring the burn in his throat briefly before sinking the whole thing and pouring the second of many more.

CHAPTER 6

December 26th

The open-plan lounge and kitchen bore all the telltale signs of a party, one in which the guests and hosts alike had all retired, either planning to clean up together in the morning or that the only one without a hangover would do it all.

"That's not going to happen," Janice said quietly to herself.

In the shoe cupboard, she found a pair of her old trainers that she kept there, and she slipped into them, pulling her jeans down over the tongues.

The kitchen island was a mess, littered with beer bottles, two empty whiskey bottles, and a plethora of others – gin, vodka, tonic water, and even Jagermeister, which Janice presumed was Thomas' contribution. He always liked to hit it hard.

The east, south, and west elements of the house all consisted of floor-to-ceiling glazing, affording a view of her father's property almost in its entirety, save for the extensive driveway and small pond. Lincoln Cathedral, once the tallest building in the world, peeked above the skyline in the distance, but closer still, two red kites hung in the near-still air against an almost perfect, blue sky.

It was one of those mornings where the view from a window belied the actual temperatures outside. It might have appeared balmy and welcoming, but the reality was that any exposed skin would feel winter's numbing burn within a few minutes.

Her father's study might have held all the secrets of the Dickens and Sons' empire, but Janice wasn't interested in those. What she needed could be found in her mother's writing bureau which stood against the internal wall, though she'd never understood why her mother had needed a desk, seeing as all she ever did was shop and meet friends for coffee.

She found her mother's stationery – a pad of off-white paper and the Mont Blanc fountain pen that Jeff had bought her one birthday – then took a seat in the old Chesterfield captain's chair.

It wasn't as if she had to compose a heartfelt letter. Everything she needed to say could be summed up in a few words.

26th December, 2023

To Dickens and Sons,

With immediate effect, please accept this letter as formal notice of my resignation. I find I can no longer pursue a career led by individuals who care so little for their employees, and for a business so buoyant on a river of blood.

Janice Dickens-Brown.

On a second sheet of paper, she composed a far less formal note, albeit more delicately considered.

Mother,

I'm sure that one day when Father is gone and Gareth has led the family to ruin, you will be free to follow your own path. I know there is some good in that heart of yours, even if you allow it scant daylight in which to bask. I know it is there, and I believe it can be resurrected.

My position within this family has passed me by, so that as each day passes, I find I have to shout louder, yet for all my yelling and calling, I remain unseen and unheard.

Gareth is on the path to destruction. Sadly, I feel that when that happens he will take Jeffery and Thomas with him. I cannot be a witness to this, but I know that only his demise will lift my spirits. I long for the day he falls, a sentiment he has nurtured through cruelty and the inherent cold blood that fills his venomous veins.

When that day finally comes, when the family is on its knees and all other avenues of rehabilitation have been closed to you, as I know they will, my door will be open.

Until then.

Your daughter,

Janice.

She clicked the lid onto the pen and arranged the letters side by side so that her mother would find it as soon as she opened her desk, which shouldn't happen until the family had left, which would be days away. Then she slid the lid closed.

Her bag was where she had left it beside the front door in the hallway, and as she bent to pick it up, she took one last glance at the house she had known forever and loathed for an eternity. It was a strange sensation to have so many memories attached to a place which she should have loved.

But it seemed as if every exposed brick was a part of those memories. They were, individually, fragments of the family's strength, yet collectively, they formed the walls that divided them, and every pretentious photo that hung upon them was a stain the family had left on the pristine landscape.

Quietly, she opened the front door and was met with a cold lick of air across her face as she stepped out onto the raised porch steps. She turned to close the door as quietly as she had opened it, but a soft voice stopped her, and she pushed it open to find the source standing on the stairs in his pyjama bottoms.

"Where are you going?" he called out, far louder than Janice would have liked him to. She put her finger to her lips and offered a reassuring smile.

"I'm just popping to the shop," she said. "I won't be long."

"Can I come?" he said, descending the wooden stairs barefoot, which in the near silence sounded like he was wearing heavy boots.

"No, sweetheart, it's too cold."

"I've got my dressing gown," he said. "And my slippers are down here."

"Shh," she hissed, pleading for him to keep quiet.

"Please," he said. "Dad won't be up for hours. He got all tipsy last night. I'll wait in the car. I won't come in. Not if you don't want me to."

"Okay then," she said, her plans being struck down at the first hurdle. "Get your slippers. And be quick about it."

The boy ran through the house making no attempt to keep quiet, then returned a few moments later with his Spiderman slippers slapping against the wooden floor.

"Come on," she said, ushering him out of the door. "You'll have to get in the back, and don't forget your seatbelt."

She clicked the button on her key fob and the Audi's interior light came on softly. Once she'd helped him in, she glanced up at the house, and once she was sure that nobody had seen her, she climbed into the driver's seat.

"What do you need to get?" Harry asked from the back seat, and she found him in the rearview mirror, innocent beyond any means that Janice could measure herself by.

"Oh, just something for Nanny," she replied. "Something to say…"

"To say what?"

"To say thank you," she told him, finding the response a suitable exchange. "I just want to show my gratitude, that's all."

"Like a thank you card?" he asked. "Mum always made us write thank you cards, before she…"

His voice trailed off. The poor lad had been through more than most people Janice's age had and yet somehow found the strength to control his emotions.

"I tell you what," she said. "Why don't you help me choose the card?"

"Really? Can I get her one too?"

"Of course you can," she said. "We'll write them out in the car, and then I'll drop you back here at the end of the driveway."

"Aren't you staying today? I thought everyone was staying until New Year's."

"Oh, I am coming back," she said. "I just have a few things to sort out, that's all." She put the car into gear and caught his eye in the mirror. "Are you ready for our adventure?"

"Yes," he said, waving his little legs with excitement. He pointed forward between the car seats like a general leading his troops to battle and screamed. "Let's go."

Fearful that somebody might hear his yells, Janice put her foot down and roared to the end of the driveway. Without stopping, she turned into Acredyke Lane and guided the large, powerful car along the quiet and narrow tarmac.

The sudden burst of speed had, at first, thrilled the young boy in the back seat, but the narrow lane with all its dreadful potholes seemed to scare him, and his smile soon succumbed to a terror-stricken grimace.

She eased off the accelerator, all the while keeping an eye on her phone on the passenger seat, waiting for the moment the screen would light up. The question on her mind was, which of her deranged family would it be?

The convenience store at Heighington was open, exactly as she had hoped, and she pulled the car to a stop a few metres past the shop. The clock on the dashboard read seven forty-five, yet the road ahead was so quiet it seemed as if time had come to a standstill.

"Right, then. We need to be quick," she said, shoving her door open so she could let Harry out. He ran into the shop with the tails of his dressing gown flowing in the cold breeze, and she took a moment to check the street for any sign of somebody coming, somebody who might recognise her. But she found the street empty and followed Harry inside.

He was standing at the little rack of cards, turning the stand to view them all.

She reached over his shoulder and picked two random cards, both of which bore a picture of some flowers and the words *Thank you* in some kind of stylish but flamboyant font, exactly the type of thing that she would baulk at.

"These'll do," she said, and then placed them on the counter, adding to the little stack of local newspapers.

"Can't I choose one?" he asked.

"No time," she replied, as Satish, the man who had run the little convenience store since she was a child, emerged wearing a tired but pleasant grin.

"Good morning," he said, his accent still thick despite decades in the UK. "Just this?"

"Just this," she said, fishing a twenty-pound note from her pocket. "Here. Happy Christmas."

"It's too much," he replied, hitting buttons on the till as if he were hurriedly trying to find her change.

"Keep it," she said. "Put it in the charity box if you don't want it."

"Well, I–"

"Come on, Harry," she said, gathering her purchases and opening the door. But Harry was ogling the magazine and comics hopefully. "Fine. I'll just be outside."

CHAPTER 7

With all the effort that Penny had put into Christmas Day, it was only right that John should make an effort on Boxing Day, his day off.

Instead of the instant coffee they usually had in the mornings, he dug out the jar of ground coffee from the back of the cupboard, the one they kept for when guests stayed. The cafetière was hiding at the back of another cupboard, and by the time the kettle had boiled and he had spooned a few teaspoons of coffee in, he heard the first footsteps on the creaky stairs.

Peeking from the kitchen into the lounge, he saw Penny making her way downstairs, wrapping her heavy dressing gown around her.

"What are you doing?" she whispered, joining him in the kitchen. "It sounds like you're playing the drums down here."

"Well, I was going to bring you coffee and toast in bed," he replied, to which she softened.

"With the good coffee? I was saving that for Mum and Dad. You know how Dad hates the instant stuff."

"Well, I can pick some more up," he said. "I'm heading down to the convenience store in a bit."

"What? Why?"

"I told you I'm going. We need some wine and I was going to get some bacon."

"Wine? It's only quarter to eight."

"He'll serve me," John said. "He's all right is Satish. He knows me well enough."

She took over making the coffee, but her silence spoke volumes, loud enough to put John on edge.

"John, don't get me wrong. I love that you're trying to make Christmas special. But, we're literally on a shoestring here. By the time the mortgage comes out in a few days' time, we'll have about forty quid to see us through."

"I told you not to worry about that," he said.

"How can I not worry? The kids go back to school in two weeks and if we keep buying bacon and wine, and God knows what else you have in mind, I don't know how they're going to get there, let alone eat."

"I've got it all in hand, Penny," he said.

"And as for the holiday," she cut in, shaking her head but trying her hardest not to appear ungrateful. "How are we going to pay for that? Do you know how much Disneyland is? It's not like a regular all-inclusive holiday. It costs an absolute fortune."

"But they'll remember it for the rest of their lives, won't they?" he countered.

She turned to look at him, a new expression forming: concern.

"John, is there something you're not telling me?" she said. "Are you sick? Am I missing something here?"

"I'm not sick," he said and moved across to hold her. "I just want to give the kids what they deserve. And you. You deserve a holiday, don't you?"

"I'm not sure Disneyland was at the top of my list," she said, then sighed. "Can you at least tell me how you're going to pay for it?"

He let his arms drop to his sides and stared her in the eye.

"Do you trust me?" he asked, to which she shook her head.

"Of course I do. I just don't understand what's going on."

"You don't need to. All you need to know is that things are going to be better from now on."

"Have you had a pay rise?" she said. "Has that tight-fisted bastard actually recognised how hard you work, finally?"

"Just trust me," he told her. "We're not rich, but I'm hopeful you won't have to cut the green bits off the kids' sandwiches anymore."

"I wish you'd tell me what's going on," she said, unable to conceal the smile that was slowly taking command of her face, banishing those worry lines back from where they had taken pride of place for far too long.

She handed him a coffee, and to her credit, she made it far better than he would have done.

He took the cup, cradled it in both hands and then leaned on the kitchen counter.

"Are they awake?" he said.

"James is pretending he's not and playing one of his games, and Emily is reading," Penny said. "We'll give them a slow start."

"If I'd have known that, I might have stayed in bed for a while longer," he said.

"That will have to wait, I'm afraid. At least until Mum and Dad have gone."

"Ah," he said. "Of course. We can't let your mum and dad hear us enjoying ourselves, can we? I mean, you're only thirty-six."

"Oh, stop it," she replied. "My mum wouldn't mind. It's our house, and we've got two bloody kids. But I don't think I could look my dad in the eye if he heard us."

"No," he replied. "I mean, it's not like they did it, is it? I imagine when you were conceived, he gave your mum a sherry, then—"

"Oh, come on," she said. "I don't even want to think about that."

Footsteps bumped on the ceiling above them, cutting their fun short.

"Well," he said, holding his index finger up to emphasise the point, "just remember, you've got a night of wild passion in the bank. All right?"

"An entire night?" she said with a laugh, as he made his way to the door, where he was pulling on his coat.

"Well, twenty minutes then," he said, to which she still seemed to disbelieve him. "Okay, okay. Ten minutes, a couple of pints down the Turks Head, and a kebab. How does that sound?"

She grinned that childish grin of hers, which she shared with Emily.

"That's how we ended up with two kids," she said, as he opened the front door.

"Back in a bit," he told her and raised his finger again. "It's in the bank, all right?"

"Go on with you," she said, and he pulled the door closed behind him.

The shops were a few minutes' walk away and there was something quite surreal about the peaceful street. It wasn't a particularly busy road anyway, but on that fine Boxing Day morning, not even a mouse stirred.

Until, somewhere in the distance, he heard a loud diesel engine being driven hard. John caught himself tutting, just as his dad used to, at the ignorance of some people.

He turned the corner onto Heighington High Street just as a young boy walked out of the shop wearing a dressing gown. But it wasn't until he stepped off of the pavement onto the road that John really paid attention. Just as the boy's barefoot hit the tarmac, the rear lights on an Audi that had been parked outside the shop, lit up.

It was as if the whole thing was playing out in slow motion, but still too fast for John to react. He hadn't even processed his thoughts when the car lurched backwards. In his mind, John wanted to call out to the young lad, but he couldn't. He was paralysed.

He could only watch in horror as the car and the boy collided.

CHAPTER 8

"Thank God that's over," Charles said out loud.

He was lying in bed by himself, as he had done for more than a decade. The alarm radio was on, gradually getting louder with every passing minute, on which a man was talking about God and how we should let Him guide us, how by letting Him into our hearts He can steer us through life. Charles leaned over to silence the chatter.

It's ten past eight, for crying out loud. Far too early for all that nonsense.

But it was when he rolled over that he felt the consequences of the previous night. The front of his head throbbed and the dim lights on the clock radio seemed to burn his retinas. He groped inside the top drawer of his bedside table, found the packet of Paracetamol, and popped two from the foil shell.

The next part was the hard part, but he did it knowing that procrastination, in this scenario at least, would only heighten his discomfort. He forced himself from the bed to the bathroom, where he took a mouthful of water along with the tablets, and waited for the pain inside his head to catch up.

And it did. It was as if he had angered a demon that thrived on the remnants of memories, stirred up by the Scotch, and now its fury was evident. It writhed inside his skull.

Water was the answer. Hydration. Which in the case of Charles Cook, came in the form of coffee, which he knew was wrong. But nothing else even felt remotely close to doing the job of waking him up.

It was a rare occasion when Charles drank enough to rouse that writhing beast, and as he grew older, it seemed to grow angrier every time, which was the reason why, like nearly every other adult human in existence, he muttered the global lie as he held onto the kitchen counter.

"Never again."

With his coffee downed, and having done little for his headache, there were only two more things he could do to ease his suffering – his morning ablutions and a shower. He performed them in that order, and by the time he was standing in his bedroom deciding what to wear to see Vanessa, he felt nearly human. The demon was slow to die. It was like one of those baddies in a movie that the viewer thinks is dead, but then they appear just when you think everything is going to be okay.

A smart pair of tan corduroys seemed most suitable, paired with a light blue shirt and his brown Hush Puppies. He laid them out while he fished some underwear and socks from their respective drawers, dressing as he always did, with his socks first.

He was about to pull on his underpants when he heard a buzzing, which at first he thought might be that injured demon rousing itself from where it lay. But then reality hit home, and he caught sight of his phone screen alight on his bedside table.

His initial thoughts were devastating enough for him to hesitate. Was she cancelling? Had she changed her mind? Perhaps one of the family had learned of the meeting and had put a stop to it?

But the number that flashed up on the screen said otherwise.

"DCI Cook," he said, then cleared his throat so that he sounded a little less like he'd only just woken.

"Sorry, guv," the voice said. "Sergeant Barrow."

"Ah, you're back in. Or haven't you left yet?"

"Seems that way, guv," he replied. "Got something for you. Hit and run. Small boy on Heighington High Street. We've got uniforms at the scene and an ambulance, and there's an eyewitness who saw it."

Charles checked his watch, which was one of those irritating fitness devices that told him to stand every hour, berated him for not doing any exercise, and then had the audacity to need charging every night, which he hadn't.

But the clock on his bedside table, a reliable plug-in device that performed one simple task, told him it was eight forty-five. Time enough to attend the scene, gather a statement, and then head down to Cambridge.

"I'm on my way," he said, automatically fishing a pair of dull, grey trousers from his wardrobe, along with a dull, white shirt and an even duller, dark brown tie that he'd bought on sale from Marks and Spencer, probably because nobody else had wanted a tie that was seemingly made for people who wanted to remain invisible.

"You won't be going it alone on this one," Barrow said. "Detective Chief Superintendent Collins asked me to get you some help, so you'll be met at the scene."

"By whom?" he said.

"Devon, guv," Barrow said. "Detective Constable Devon."

"All right," Charles said, pleased to learn that the tasks that lay ahead of him might be diluted with some effective delegation. "And the boy? How is he?"

The sergeant hesitated and then exhaled, his breath rattling the phone's speaker.

"Not good, guv," he said. "He died at the scene. It's a bloody tragedy. He can only be seven or eight according to my man on the ground."

"And the parents?"

"That's just it, guv," he replied. "He was on his own. Makes you sick, doesn't it? How some parents can let an eight-year-old boy wander the streets in his dressing gown all alone."

"I'm sure there's a reasonable explanation," Charles replied thoughtfully. "Although God knows what that might be."

CHAPTER 9

It wasn't hard to find the scene of the accident. The street had been closed off at both ends. A flash of Charles's warrant card gained him access and the circus was just a few hundred yards further along. The ambulance was still on the scene, as were three liveried police cars. Charles parked some way off, allowing him a short walk to take in the scene and prepare some kind of plan.

At the forefront of his mind was the help Collins had provided. He'd never heard of a DC Devon before and wondered how experienced he might be. Making DC was an accolade in itself, but that didn't mean he'd dealt with the death of a child or informing the parents. That little nugget was thankfully a rare occasion, but one that formed a lifelong memory.

Charles could count on one hand the times he'd had to deliver the news of a child's death. More often than not, the victims of accidents were adults, children being so well protected these days. But he could recall every one of them, and moreover, he could recall the reaction from each of the parents.

The uniformed officers were huddled outside the convenience store, seemingly awaiting direction. A brief glance at their shoulders directed Charles to the most senior of them, a male sergeant who introduced himself as Hammond.

"How are we all doing?" Charles said. "Are we bearing up?"

"Best we can, guv," Hammond replied. "You'll be looking for DC Devon, I suppose?"

"Well, I was expecting to see a body, if I'm honest," he replied, noting the cordoned-off area containing a patch of drying blood and some tyre marks.

"He was moved off the street, guv. Paramedics pronounced him dead, and given the location, DC Devon thought it best to move him."

Charles noted the faces at the windows of the houses not twenty metres away and grumbled his agreement.

"And where is he?" he asked. "DC Devon, I mean."

"Inside, guv," he said. "Talking to the shopkeeper. Very difficult to miss, guv."

It was an odd comment backed by a smug grin and one which incited a few stifled chortles from the other officers.

"All right. Let's get knocking on some doors, shall we? Two on each side of the street," Charles said. "I want to know if anybody saw or heard anything, and if any of the houses have those camera doorbell things. One of them might come in useful."

"I thought as much, guv," Hammond replied, turning to his colleagues and giving them the nod to execute an instruction he'd already given.

"Very good," Charles said, with a grateful nod of his head. He pushed into the little shop, which appeared much as any other high street convenience store with nearly every inch of space occupied by goods ranging from newspapers and magazines to cheap children's toys, greeting cards, and confectionery.

"DCI Cook?" a voice said, female and confident. It seemed to come from nowhere until a stout young woman stepped from behind the central racks and held out her hand for him to shake. "DC Devon, guv."

"You're Devon?" he heard himself say, recognising the surprise in his tone, and then countering it with something far more personable. "Nice to meet you. What do we have?"

She searched his eyes for a moment but said nothing of his initial tone and surprise.

"Satish Kumar, guv. He's the shopkeeper. He didn't see the accident but served the woman who was with him."

"What woman?"

"The woman the boy was with. She came in with him, grabbed a couple of cards, and a newspaper, then left without him."

"She left them here?" Charles said and then looked up to find the shopkeeper leaning on the counter. Behind him, his most expensive products were on display – cigarettes, alcohol, and scratch cards.

"Is this right?" Charles asked him. "The boy was accompanied by a woman?"

"That is correct," he replied, his heritage evident in his accent. "The boy was looking at the magazines. She called him, but... Well, you know what children are like. I think he was hoping she would buy him something."

"Perhaps," Charles said. "And she left him here? She just left him to his own devices?"

"I thought she was just putting her things in her car and that she would return for him. She bought a newspaper and a few other things—"

"She had her hands full. I see," Charles said, looking around the shop's ceiling and spying what looked like an antiquated CCTV system. "I don't suppose these work, do they?"

"All working, guv," Devon said. "It's an old system, but I've got the tapes."

She held up her bag as if to accentuate the fact that she had already made progress, and perhaps to demonstrate her competence.

"Well, let's get that to the station pronto, Devon. Have somebody analyse it and report back. We don't have time to sift through the footage ourselves."

"I'll ask Sergeant Hammond if he can get somebody to run it back to the station, guv," she said.

She was squat, and he was dubious as to whether or not she would pass the force's fitness requirements with ease. But he had to hand it to her, she was efficient and focused, and with only a couple of hours to play with, that was what he needed.

"Thank you, Devon," he said. "Anything else?"

"One eye witness, guv," she said, then opened her notebook. "A John Gregory. One of the villagers. Apparently, he'd come down here to grab some bacon and a few other bits. He saw the car's reversing lights come on and he saw the boy step out into the road behind it."

"Dear God," he said. "Poor chap. Is he okay?"

"I've sent him home with one of the uniformed officers, guv. He was a bit shaken up."

"I bet he was. Did he get the number plate?"

Devon shook her head.

"What about the car?"

"A grey Audi. Four doors. Possibly an A4, but he couldn't swear to it."

"And the driver?"

"Afraid not, guv. He was too far away, and his concern was more for the boy than the car. He did say it sped off immediately after. The driver didn't even get out and was facing away from him."

Charles walked over to the shop window to study the scene and formulate a plan. That selfish part of him would have preferred for there to have been no eyewitnesses given his short window, but logic and experience told him otherwise.

"We'll need CSI," he said. "There are tyre marks on the road."

"They're on their way, guv," she said, checking her watch. "ETA is nine-thirty."

He turned to look at her making no attempt to conceal how impressed he was. But he said nothing and then looked back at Mr Kumar.

"I don't suppose you remember anything about the woman, do you, Mr. Kumar?"

"She's local," he said. "She's been coming here since she was young, but I don't know her name or where she lives. Faces are all I have."

"Could you describe her?" he asked.

"Shoulder length, brown hair. Pretty, I suppose," he said. "Just an average woman. Mid-thirties, maybe?"

"How was she dressed?" Charles said.

"Smart jeans, brown jacket, and dirty trainers. I remember her dirty trainers because they didn't seem to match her outfit. Like she had just thrown them on to walk a dog."

"Or just to pop down to the shop," Charles said. "Did she pay by card?"

"Cash," he said, holding up a twenty-pound note and shaking his head.

"May I?" Charles asked, and before he could fish an evidence bag from his inside pocket, Devon held one up for the shopkeeper to slip the note into.

"Thank you, Mr Kumar," Charles said, and began leading Devon away towards the door.

"Do you want me to stay and see what CSI have to say?" Devon asked.

Charles checked his watch and considered the wheels that were already in motion and those that had yet to set off.

"Come outside," he said, holding the shop door open for her. He followed her out and walked the few steps to where the tyre marks were still fresh on the ground. "Let's recap what we know."

"We've got a woman in her mid-thirties who takes her eight-year-old boy to the shop. For some reason, she leaves him in the shop. The boy comes out just as she's reversing up."

"And she hits him," he finished for her. "But why speed off?"

"Drink driving?" Devon said. "Maybe she was still drunk from the previous night?"

"Maybe," he said, not disagreeing but not quite agreeing either.

"I've asked uniform to go door to door," she said. "With any luck, one of the houses will have a doorbell camera."

"Very good," he said, suddenly seeing through the nod Hammond had given his men. "Plus, we have the CCTV from the shop."

"What we really need is the number plate, guv," she said. "And none of the shop cameras face outside."

"How about the pub?" he asked, peering down the road at the Turks Head.

"Already checked. Nothing. There's one in the car park but that faces the door."

"So there're no cameras on the road?"

"It's a small village, guv," she said.

"But we do know she turned right at the top of the road."

"Which leads us to the new bypass. I know for a fact there are cameras there."

"I'll get onto the station," she said. "The accident occurred at around ten minutes to eight, so I'll have someone check from seven forty-five to quarter past. If no grey Audi shows up, then we'll know she turned off before then."

"We might as well get ANPR on the lookout for the Audi as well," Charles said. "Sadly, my guess is that if she's local, she's gone to ground somewhere."

"What about the boy?" Devon asked.

"I'll get to him in a minute," Charles replied, then looked at her. She had a round face and wore next to no make-up, letting her large eyes, button nose, and full lips shine. "What would you do if you reversed into your son, Devon?"

She gave it little thought. "I wouldn't run, guv."

"But you're a police officer. What would you do if, say, you were a civilian, a housewife for example?"

"Excuse my French, guv, but I'd be bricking it."

"Would you drive off?"

"I don't think so. Not unless I had something to hide, and even then I'd at least check on the boy. I'd like to think so anyway."

"That's what I'm thinking," he said. "Do you have children?"

"No, guv. Not really my scene, if you know what I mean?"

"One day, maybe," he said. "I didn't think I'd have any either. I wasn't an active parent for very long, but even so, if I reversed into my own child, not even the threat of prison would tear me from their side."

"Guv?" she asked, clearly sensing he was lost in his thoughts of something other than the problem that faced them.

"We need to talk to the eyewitness. Maybe they saw something else. Trauma has a way of drip-feeding the facts," he suggested, snapping Vanessa from his mind and checking his watch once more. He looked along the street to where the ambulance was still parked. "But before we do that, I'd like to see the child."

They walked slowly, neither of them particularly keen to see the body of a child, but as they passed the shop, Charles pushed the door open. The shopkeeper looked up from behind his counter.

"Mr Kumar," Charles began, "I wonder if you could tell me what type of greeting cards the woman bought?"

"Type, sir?" he said, with a little shake of his head.

"Were they Christmas cards, birthday cards, or something?"

"Ah," Mr Kumar said, a little confused as to why he might ask for such a detail. "They were thank you cards."

"Thank you cards? Both of them?" Charles said, receiving a nod in reply and then letting the door close. He stepped over to where Devon was watching him. "Why would somebody buy a thank you card on Boxing Day?" he asked, meeting her inquisitive gaze.

"And more importantly, why would they buy two of them?" she replied.

"My thoughts exactly, Devon," he said thoughtfully. "And that is exactly what I intend to find out."

CHAPTER 10

The police officer accepted the cup of tea and set it down on the hearth while John sat on the sofa opposite with James and Emily on either side of him. Despite them not understanding why the policeman was there, and wanting to go and play with their new toys, he held them tight, staring into thin air as the scene rolled over and over in his mind with one of them as the victim each time it played.

"Have a cup of tea, John," Penny said.

"I'm fine," he said, hearing his sharp tone but finding scant energy to apologise.

"What about a coffee?" she said. "The good stuff."

"I said I'm fine," he snapped, and this time he felt the sting of his tongue a little overzealous. "Sorry, I'm just—"

"It's not unusual to feel on edge, Mr Gregory," the officer said. "Something to calm your nerves, maybe?"

"If I wanted your bloody opinion, I'd ask for it," he replied.

"Right, kids," Penny interjected, "come on. Go to your rooms for me, will you?"

"They're staying with me," John said.

"They don't need to see this," Penny replied, standing before him with her arms outstretched ready to help each of them off of the sofa. "Come on, you two. Up to your rooms."

Reluctantly, he let them go, then watched them run up the stairs without looking back.

"I'm sorry, officer," he said quietly, his gaze still firmly fixed on the empty staircase. He tore his eyes away to look the man in the eye. "It's been a bit of a morning if you know what I mean?"

"You don't have to apologise to me, sir," he replied. "Friday nights in town. That's when the real verbal abuse happens."

"But still, I shouldn't have snapped like that."

Penny dropped into the seat beside him and lay her hand on his knee, which he grasped with a trembling hand.

"Maybe you should have a lie-down," she suggested.

"I can't," he replied and looked to the officer for support.

"The senior investigating officer will be here shortly," he said. "He'll want to take a statement."

"For God's sake. He's just..." Penny began, then quietened her voice to a whispered hiss for the sake of the children who, although upstairs, were still within earshot. "He's just watched a young boy get killed. Can't they wait?"

"I doubt it," he replied, then seemed uneasy to say much more, but chose his words carefully. "The driver left the scene. The SIO will be keen to find them as soon as possible, and so far, your husband is the only witness."

"Well, afterwards then," Penny said. "You should have a lie down afterwards."

"I'm fine," John told her. "I just need a bit of space, that's all." He gave her hand a reassuring squeeze. "How about that coffee, eh?"

The smile that she gave him was weak but true, and she searched his eyes for some sign that his words were an accurate reflection of his feelings.

"I'll just be a moment," she told him, just as somebody knocked on the front door. "Oh God, that's them."

"Leave it," John said, as the officer stood. "Just leave it, dear. It won't take long. I'm sure they'll just want me to run through what I saw."

"Well, if you're sure—"

"I am," he said and gave the officer the nod to open the front door.

The officer stood to one side to let the two newcomers in, the first of whom was a man in his fifties with a full head of grey hair. He was tall and lean and wore worn trousers, comfortable shoes, and a heavy parka over his white shirt and brown tie.

The second could be described as the exact opposite of the first. Female, early-thirties, and as his father might have described her, cheerfully rotund with a very pleasant face.

"Mr Gregory?" the man said, showing his warrant card. "I'm DCI Cook, and this is DC Devon. How are you coping?"

John didn't stand, although the well-mannered man he had been raised to be suggested he should do so, but on this occasion, he considered himself exempt from good manners.

"I'm fine," he said.

At this, the older of the two male officers looked at the younger. "Thank you. I think your sergeant will be needing you."

"Very good, sir," the officer said, then leaned into the kitchen. "Thank you for the tea."

Penny mumbled a reply and the officer took his leave, pulling the door closed behind him.

"May I?" Cook said, indicating that he would like to sit on the armchair that the uniformed officer had vacated.

John nodded and then gestured for the woman to take a seat too.

"I'm afraid I can't tell you much," John said. "But I'll tell you what I saw."

"From the top, if you don't mind," Cook replied, then looked to his colleague as if to say something, but found no need when she held her notebook up for him to see. "DC Devon will take notes. With your permission, we'll have your statement typed up for you to sign."

"Fine by me," John replied. "You don't think it'll go to court though, do you?"

"Why? Do you have any objection to giving evidence?"

"Not an objection as such. It's just, well, I don't have much time, that's all," he replied. "I work, see? Long hours."

"Well, I'm sure arrangements can be made–"

"I work every hour God gives me," John said. "Times are hard and money is tight."

"I see," Cook replied. "Well, let's cross that bridge when we come to it. Now, why don't we start from the top? You were heading to the shop. Is that right?"

"It is, yes," John said. "We needed some coffee and a few bits. Satish is always open on Boxing Day morning. He's good like that."

"And how did you get there?"

"How did I get there? I walked, of course. It's only down the road," John explained. "I was about two hundred yards from the shop when it happened. I saw the car lights come on, the reverse lights, that is. Then I saw the little boy come out of the shop–"

"Alone?" Cook asked, to which John nodded.

"Then saw the car lurch backwards and..." He stopped to let the silence explain the hardest part of his story. Then, when he deemed that enough time had passed for the details to be understood, he commenced. "The car sped off. Wheel spins, you know? And I ran to the kid. He didn't look hurt. I mean, he wasn't bleeding much. But he was just lying there with his dressing gown open and his bare feet on the road."

"It's okay, we've just been to see him," Cook said. "Tell me, did you see anybody else? Was anybody else either going to the shop or coming from it?"

John shook his head.

"That was the thing. The road was dead quiet. I remember

thinking that time had come to a standstill. Except for the van, that is."

"The van?" Cook said, with a glance at the woman.

"There was a van," he replied. "I heard the engine."

"You saw the van, did you?"

"Well, no. But it wasn't a car. It was a van or a truck or something. It might have been the newspapers being delivered to the shop."

"And this was after the incident?"

"No, before. I heard the van, then I turned the corner, and then I saw the reversing lights on the car, and then the boy. In that order."

Cook seemed to digest the information but his face gave nothing away.

"And this van," he said, "did it turn left or right at the top of the road?"

John shrugged.

"I didn't see it. I just heard it speeding off."

"But you saw the car?"

"I did, yes. It turned right towards Lincoln."

"Towards the bypass?"

"Yes, that's right."

"Did you happen to see the number plate, Mr Gregory?" Cook asked, to which John shook his head.

"Sorry, I was focusing on the boy. I've got two kids of my own, you see, and, well, you can't help but imagine, can you?"

"No," Cook said. "No, I share that sentiment entirely. One of the drawbacks of parenthood, I'm afraid. Perhaps you recognised the car? Mr Kumar suggested the driver was a local woman. Does anybody around here have a grey Audi that you know of?"

Again, John shook his head.

"Plenty of Audis around here, but I'm afraid I tend not to covet nice cars. I find the more I look, the more I want one, and, well, that's out of the question."

"Aye, I know what you mean," Cook said, reaching into his inside pocket for one of his cards, which he handed to John. "When somebody witnesses a tragedy, which I believe this awful episode is, the brain can often put up walls. It's a defence mechanism, not a weakness."

John took the card from him and read the details.

"Should any of those walls come down, I'll be sure to get in touch," he said, to which Cook smiled his gratitude.

"Well, we shan't keep you any longer," he said, pushing himself to his feet. "I hope you can enjoy what's left of Christmas, for your children's sake, if nobody else's."

"Thank you," John said, as the man led his colleague to the front door, where he stopped and peered down at the telephone table.

"Disneyland, eh?" he said, peering up at John holding one of the children's tickets in his hand.

"Next year," John replied. "The kids haven't been on holiday for years. Not a proper one, anyway. They deserve it."

"Lucky them," Cook replied, replacing the ticket on the table. But then he looked as if he had thought of something. "What is it you do for a living, Mr. Gregory?"

"Call me John, please," John said. "I work in HR. Nothing glamorous, I'm afraid."

"You enjoy it, aye?"

"Not really," he replied. "But it pays the bills and it's not forever. Nothing's forever, is it?"

"No, Mr Gregory," the detective replied. "No, it is most certainly not."

CHAPTER 11

The incident room was exactly as it was on any other day of the year, save for a few on another team who had decided that wearing a Santa hat would lift everybody's mood.

Charles claimed the use of the table furthest from everyone else, and Devon dropped her bag onto one of the chairs.

"Back in a bit," she told him, and she waved the tape from Mr Kumar's convenience store in the air to tell him where she was going.

He was glad of the respite and made use of the time to drag a whiteboard over to their table, then hunt for a few pens, which he found on the whiteboard at the far end of the room.

The other officers hushed when he approached, and he felt them exchanging stares, which he ignored, as he usually did.

"Merry Christmas, guv," one of them said, DS Hannaway, who had been blessed with a full head of thick, curly hair that looked as if it had never seen a comb.

Charles stopped and turned to look at him, deciding if the greeting was actually an underhand insult that the three of them would laugh at when he turned his back.

"The same to you," Charles said and met each of their stares. "The same to all of you."

"You don't seem like your normal cheery self, guv," another said, whom Charles knew only by face and had yet to work with closely enough to get to know.

"Hit and run," Charles told him flatly. "An eight-year-old boy is on his way to hospital as we speak. What do you want me to do, do a wee dance or ring my jingle bells?"

"Sorry guv," he replied, his expression suggesting the apology was genuine.

"Need a hand?" Hannaway asked.

"Not yet," he replied. "But when the time comes that DC Devon and I need help, I'm sure we'll be allocated the resources we need. At the minute, we haven't even got a name for the victim, let alone a suspect. So we're pretty much at a standstill until we can identify the body."

"I'm sure you could make a few enquiries, guv."

"That would be against protocol," Charles said. "Without a positive ID, we can't do a thing. Surely you know that, Sergeant?"

Hannaway leaned forward to speak with some discretion, although he made no attempt to lower his voice.

"We all know the first twenty-four hours are critical," he said. "Nobody would hear it from me if you were to say, run some name checks or check ANPR."

He finished with a wink, in which Charles found it hard to find any sincerity.

"I'll keep to the rule book on this one," he said.

"Just let us know, yeah?" Hannaway replied.

"Are you at a loose end, Sergeant Hannaway? You seem to be rather free with your offers of help."

"I wouldn't exactly call it a loose end, guv. But then, I wouldn't exactly say I'm run off my feet either."

"Reports to type up, I suppose?"

"You know how it is, guv. They have a tendency to pile up while your back is turned. Before you know it, you have a stack on your desk high enough to block out the light. It's like they multiply."

"Do you want some free advice?" Charles asked, to which the over-confident Sergeant nodded. "Never turn your back."

He returned the insincere wink then turned away, heading back to his table with a check of his watch. If he left in the next thirty minutes or so, he could reach Cambridge, which meant that he would need to set Devon up with as many leads as possible. So by the time he returned, there should be at least one thread to pull on.

A thread to pull on. A line he'd heard somebody say once, which had never truly made sense. A thread to pull on would mean to unravel something, a garment or something material. The position he was in now offered very little in the way of material substance, and if anything, rather than unravel what he had, he wanted to stitch the pieces together.

On the whiteboard, he wrote a single word. *Boy.* He circled the word and then drew a line to another single word. *Audi.* To one side of the board, he began a list of possible lines of enquiry. It was a short list, far shorter than he would have liked.

Doorbell cameras.
Eye witness – John Gregory.
Shop CCTV.
ANPR – Audi.
Forensics.

With any luck, the list would grow, or at least he might be able to expand on one of the items. He checked his watch again, just as Devon shoved her way through the incident room door.

"Guv," she said. "We've had a call. A misper."

"A missing person?" he said. Something in his gut reminded him both of his commitment to his daughter and the investigation, while something else toyed with the damage the Scotch had done to his insides. It was like his stomach was a ball of wool and he'd swallowed a kitten.

"A young boy," she finished. "Eight years old."

Kittens, he thought. *Plural*.

"Do you have the address?"

She held up a slip of paper. "Branston Booths. Five minutes from Heighington."

"Do you think you can handle it?" he asked, realising how much of a cop-out it sounded.

"Sorry, guv? You want me to go alone?"

He imagined Vanessa sitting on a bench waiting for him, studying every man that walked into view then feeling that pang of disappointment.

"No. No, I meant, do you think you can handle the family's reaction? But of course, you can," he said, which only served to excite the litter of playful kittens. "Have you given the video to the boys in tech?"

"I did, guv," she replied. "And *she* was very helpful."

The emphasis on the word *she* suggested that Devon was of the younger generation, but more to the point, was a reminder that Charles was of the waning older generation.

"That's good," he said, doing his best not to dwell on his faux pa. "It might be helpful if we had a still of the woman in the video. The family might recognise her—"

She held up her phone to silence him.

"Already done, guv," she said, unsmiling but somehow still smug.

"Well, you are efficient, aren't you?" he replied, then heard his voice weaken. "Meet me in the car park, will you? I just have to make a private telephone call."

Devon didn't move. Instead, she watched him with what he could only describe as curiosity like she was reading him and making a judgement.

"I didn't think you had one, guv," she said quietly so that only he could hear. "A family, that is."

"Who told you that?"

"Oh, you know how it is. Word gets around."

"Well, the next time word gets around to you, Devon, I suggest you bat it to me," he replied and turned his back to find Vanessa's number on his phone. But he felt Devon's inquisitive stare as if she was enjoying the sight of frolicking kittens. He looked over his shoulder at her. "Car park. Two minutes," he said. Then he added with rather more venom than he had intended, "And I'm driving."

CHAPTER 12

Two raps of the door knocker marked the end of a terrible silence, during which only Jeffery's mother had spoken, a few mutterings of reassurance that Gareth had ignored. Instead, he chose to stare out of the floor-to-ceiling windows at how oblivious the wild rabbits seemed to be to the family's tumult.

It was Thomas who, after nobody else even vaguely acknowledged the disruption, eventually stood and marched out to the generous hallway. The heels of his shoes clacked on the hardwood floor then stopped, and immediately, despite Susie only being able to hear a mumble of distant voices, she perceived the tone as formal, if not regretful. Her perception had been accurate, as just a few moments later, Thomas arrived in the doorway searching for whom best to direct his announcement.

In the end, it was his mother, a woman who Susie was finding it very difficult to connect with. She spoke, being in a position to see past Thomas out into the hallway.

"Invite them in, Thomas," she said. "I suggest we give Gareth and the officers some space. I'll stay, but the rest of you should go."

"It might be best if you all stay together," one of the visitors said, a man who, although wearing a shirt and trousers, did so with obvious reluctance and very little flamboyance. He edged past Thomas, who then stepped aside to allow the man's colleague to enter, a woman who quite clearly invested far more effort into her appearance than her friend, though a little make-up wouldn't hurt. "At least, while we can understand exactly what happened."

"What is there to say?" Gareth mumbled, turning his head to look at the man for the first time.

"Are you the boy's father?" the man asked, to which Gareth gave a slight nod.

"Okay. I'm Detective Chief Inspector Cook, and this is Detective Constable Devon. "Before I begin, do we have a photo of the child?"

"Harry," Gareth said. "His name is Harry."

"As you wish, sir," Cook replied and seemed to be waiting for somebody to action his request.

It was Gareth's mother who stood and directed the detective to a sideboard, on which a plethora of framed photographs had been neatly arranged. She selected one of Harry's school photos, in which his beaming smile revealed a missing canine, then handed it to him.

"I'd like this back," she said coldly.

He studied the photo and then showed it to his colleague, Devon. They exchanged looks as if confirming that they had both lodged the image in memory and then handed the photo back to Gareth's mother.

"Here you go," he said, and she accepted it with obvious confusion, then hugged the photo to her body.

"Shall I make tea?" Thomas suggested, making a move toward the kitchen.

"Not for me, thanks," Cook said with practised politeness.

"I'm fine, thank you," Devon added, and Thomas seemed to loiter there for a moment, unsure of what to do.

"Well, I want one," he said eventually, then proceeded to fill the kettle from where he could watch the drama from afar.

Cook to a few steps into the room, coming to a stop in front of Gareth, who barely even acknowledged the man's looming presence.

"The boy's name," Cook began, retrieving his notepad from his pocket. "In full, please."

"Harry Abbott Dickens," Gareth said.

"Abbott?" Cook replied. "Two Bs and two Ts?"

Gareth nodded.

"It's his grandfather's name," Gareth's mother explained, gesturing at the head of the family, who had watched the proceedings in silence from his armchair. "Abbott Dickens."

"Which makes you the boy's grandmother?" Cook asked, and she replied with a taut nod.

"Elizabeth," she said, and he made a note of the names, before looking around the room at the other faces, his eyebrows raised in expectation. "That's Jeffery, his partner Susie, and Thomas is making tea."

"Your sons?" Cook asked, scribbling down names as fast as she muttered them.

Elizabeth nodded again and seemed to sense that Devon was studying her. She met the younger of the detective's gaze with a defensive stare, which Cook caught but did little to stop.

"Is anybody upstairs?" Cook asked. "I thought I heard something as I came in."

"That's Arthur," Elizabeth replied. "Harry's little brother."

"And we were all here last night, were we?"

"We were," Elizabeth said.

Cook didn't look up from his notepad, reminding Susie of a doctor reeling off questions to a patient, from which the answers would steer him to a conclusion or diagnosis.

"And when you woke up this morning, Harry was gone?" Cook said finally. "Is that correct?"

"It is," Elizabeth said, but Cook seemed uninterested in her responses and waited for Gareth to catch on that it should be he who provided the answers.

"We put them to bed at around nine p.m.," Gareth said, his voice monotone and distant. "I was up at eight-thirty. Arthur came down at nine-thirty, so I asked him if Harry was still sleeping, and he said he wasn't in bed."

"We looked everywhere," Elizabeth said, to which Cook didn't reply, turn to look at her or react in any way shape or form. But she wasn't one to be ignored or pushed to one side. "Thomas and I have searched the grounds. Jeffery searched the outbuildings."

"I drove up and down the lane," Susie added. "In case he'd wandered off, you know?"

The detective did at least acknowledge what Susie had to say, and he replied with a brief but polite thank-you smile.

"Which leaves the father and grandfather," Cook said, addressing to two eldest men in the family. "How did you assist in the search for Harry?"

Abbott's face remained completely impassive, not a single line in his ageing face moved, deepened, or formed. Gareth, however, simply let his head fall onto the headrest.

"We waited here," he explained. "Dad can't walk too far, and I... Well, I was hopeful Harry might show up. I thought he might have been hiding or something."

"Why might he have been hiding?"

"Oh, you know what kids can be like," Gareth said. "Always seeking attention, somehow."

"He's a troubled boy, Inspector," Elizabeth said. "Ever since his..."

She was silenced by a glare from Gareth to contain herself, which Cook saw and pried open.

"Is there something I should know?" he said. "We are here to help, after all."

The exchange of concerned looks ran through the family, beginning with Elizabeth and ending with Gareth.

"Their mother died last year," Gareth said finally, when he realised there was no escape from discussing Marie, who as far as Susie knew, was almost never discussed.

"I'm sorry to hear that," Cook replied. "I now understand why your mother suggested that Harry might be troubled."

"He wasn't troubled," Gareth said as if he had taken the comment as a personal insult. "He was adjusting, that's all."

"I see," Cook replied, sharing a quick glance with his colleague, who up until that point, had said nothing. "Anything to add, Devon?"

She pocketed her notepad, clicked her pen closed and then slipped it into her bag, before stepping forward to stand beside the much older Cook.

"I do, as it happens," she began and cast an accusing eye at each of them in turn. "If you don't mind my saying, Mr Dickens, you seem very calm."

"Calm?" he said, and Susie noticed the difference in tone to that which he had used with the male detective.

"I'd agree," Cook said. "Do you know how many missing persons reports I've followed up on in my career?" He aimed the question at Gareth initially, but with a casual glance around the room, invited the rest of them to hazard a guess, which nobody did. "I don't know either. But it's in the dozens. Dozens of distraught families, husbands, wives, children, grandparents, and even lovers who, from the moment I walk through the front door, are almost inconsolable. Inconsolable, Mr Dickens. Tears, wailing, grief. Nose blowing, hugging, and hollow mutterings of consolation from friends and family, reassuring them that everything will be okay and that the missing person will turn up."

"What are you saying, Inspector?" Abbott said, his voice quiet with confidence and cracked with age.

"I'm saying that your son reported your grandson missing this morning," Cook continued. "Your family has searched the grounds, your son's partner has driven up and down the lane, yet you and your son haven't moved. You didn't even stand to welcome us into your home. I have seen no bouts of hysteria, no warmth from any of you, and no emotions save for the indignation of the inconvenience caused by having us in your home."

"It's a difficult time," Elizabeth started.

"It's unusual," Cook said, and he turned on his heels as a sergeant major might perform an about-turn, before starting into a thoughtful pace. But he'd only walked a few steps, his hands linked behind his back, when he stopped and turned again in the same military fashion. "In fact, I'd go as far as to say there's something you're not telling me."

When nobody responded, and the melee of expressions the family had shared came to a silent halt, each of them seemed to withdraw into themselves, leaving Cook the possessor of the family's attention.

"There is a pair of women's Dubarry boots by the front door," he continued. "I saw them when I came in."

"You saw and heard a lot when you came in," Gareth said.

"A curse of the job, I'm afraid," he replied. "They're a size six at least, while you, Susie, are a four or a five at most, and you, Mrs Dickens, are also a four or a five. So perhaps before we go any further, somebody could explain who those boots belong to, and why the dining table has nine placemats yet there are only seven individuals here, plus the one individual who has been reported missing?"

CHAPTER 13

"They belong to my sister," a voice said from the kitchen area of the open-plan living space, and he steeled himself against the dagger-like glares the rest of his family fired his way. "The boots, that is. They're Janice's."

"Ah," Charles replied, as he unbuttoned his coat, slid it from his shoulders, and hung it carefully over one of the dining chairs. "Now we're getting somewhere."

"We're getting nowhere," Gareth spat, still unmoved from his armchair. "All you've done is come here and made us all feel like—"

"Like?" Charles said, and Gareth Dickens quieted, perhaps sensing he had revealed too much in his emotional outburst.

"I just get the feeling you're accusing us of something when you should be out there looking for my boy. He's been gone three hours now. Three bloody hours."

"I can leave now if you wish, Mr Dickens," Charles said. "In fact, I can leave now and knock on every door from here to Lincoln Cathedral if you so wish. However, that might take some time. Perhaps if you could be a little more forthcoming with information, then you might point us in the right direction."

"I don't know what you want me to say," Gareth said, and he

gestured to his brother Thomas that he'd have a tea after all. "What exactly will it take for you to get out there and look for my boy?"

"When did your sister leave?" Charles asked. "The mud on her boots suggests she arrived either during yesterday's rain or shortly after, and the placemat tells me that she at least stayed for dinner."

"You're very intuitive, Inspector," Gareth said.

"I disagree. The facts are there for anyone to see, however, I'm struggling to understand why she isn't here now, and why every time your sister is mentioned, you all seem to hush. Is there something you're not telling me?"

The kettle was one of the old types that rattled angrily before it whistled, and as Charles delved deeper into the fog, the rattle began. Steadily, it would climb, and Charles gave himself until the whistling had begun for one of them to reveal whatever it was they were hiding.

"She was an outcast," Thomas said, daring once more to brave the steely daggers.

"She was not an outcast," Elizabeth said. "She's as much a part of this family as the rest of you."

"But she found reason to leave, did she?" Charles asked, and Elizabeth looked to her husband for support.

"Janice had a bit too much to drink," Elizabeth began.

"Oh, come on," Thomas said, as the kettle entered its whistling phase. "You're not honestly going to put it all on her, are you?"

"Thomas, I'd think very hard before you say anything else," Abbott added.

"Why? In case I insult the family? In case I let you all down?" He said, then turned to Charles. "In case you hadn't realised, this isn't a happy family."

"I'm yet to find one that is," Charles replied cordially, and he gestured for Devon to come closer. "Do you have the image taken from the footage in Heighington, please, Devon?"

"Sure," she replied, fishing her phone from her bag. It took her a few moments to accomplish what it would have taken Charles the best part of a shift to do, and she held the image up for Thomas to see.

"Is this Janice?" Charles asked, to which Thomas rolled his eyes, stared at his family for a moment then nodded.

"That's her," he said. "And that's Harry in the background, too. Is that Satish's shop?"

"And does Janice drive a grey Audi?" Charles asked, very aware of the peaked interest from the seated members of the family.

"She does, yes," he said. "Why? What does that have to do–"

"What? What is it?" Elizabeth called out, and Gareth shot from his seat to have a look.

"That's enough," Charles muttered quietly to Devon, who took the hint and pocketed her phone before the image became a Boxing Day sensation.

"Was that her?" Gareth said. "And my boy?"

"Thank you, Thomas," Charles said, taking himself away from the growing crowd of family members and finding space near the doors where Devon joined him. "Go outside and call the station," Charles told her quietly. "Ask for DS Hannaway and get him to run the name through the police database. We need the number plate of that Audi put through ANPR, and we need any local units on the lookout. Think big, Devon. If her credit cards are used, I want to know. If her car passes through an ANPR camera, I want to know. and if her mobile phone is switched on, I want to see it on a map."

"What's happening?" Gareth said, breaking from the group who were interrogating Thomas on the details of the image. "Do you honestly think my sister has taken him?"

Charles steeled himself for a difficult conversation. If the questioning up until this point had been an uphill climb, then what lay in store was Ben Nevis.

"Mr Dickens, I'm sorry to be one to tell you this, but this morning we were asked to attend a hit-and-run incident. The victim was a small boy, approximately eight years old."

If the discomfort in his gut had earlier been kittens, then they had evolved into lions. Gareth Dickens was, on the outside at least, strong and resilient, perhaps mimicking his father's stoicism. But even before Charles had completed the opening line of his statement, the man's face had broken like hard wax melting and sagging under its own weight.

"I believe it's Harry, Mr Dickens," Charles added. "I'm so sorry."

CHAPTER 14

"I'm going upstairs to be with Arthur," Elizabeth said quietly when the two detectives had left. She held Gareth's arm for a moment but averted her gaze, unable to meet him eye to eye.

Susie sat down on the sofa, pulling her legs up beneath her, feeling the pull of her own family who she had, for the first time in her life, not spent Christmas with. She dragged the fleece-lined blanket that had been draped over the back of the sofa across her feet, more for comfort than warmth.

It was then that Abbott finally pushed himself from the armchair, holding onto the arm for a second while he caught his balance.

"Gareth, my study," he said, gesturing at the door that led to the hallway and his study.

"I think we should stay—"

"That wasn't an optional invitation, Gareth," Abbott grumbled. "Jeffery, Thomas, that means you too."

He ambled from the room, the best years of his life clearly having taken their toll on his body. One by one, his sons followed, obediently and without uttering a word. The only one to display any rebellious instinct was Thomas, who simply shook his head and placed the kettle down harder than necessary.

That left Susie alone. Alone in a room that was bigger than her entire house. Alone in a world where she clearly didn't belong, with a man whom she would have hoped would put up some kind of resistance to his father, or even demonstrate that he cared for her, before dutifully obeying his father.

Her coffee had gone cold, but she didn't make another. She dared not even make a noise. It was just her, a vast empty room, and the frolicking rabbits outside, whom she envied for their ignorance. The only sound was the cooling kettle and its metallic clicking, and the rumble of voices from the room next door.

Abbott's study.

Susie had seen the room, a large six-metre-by-six-metre space with a brick fireplace, an oversized partner desk inlaid with green leather, and a wall of books on every topic imaginable. It was a veritable gentleman's study with Chesterfield parlour chairs for his guests and a luxurious captain's chair at the helm. Brass candlesticks added a splash of sheen to the hundreds of leather-bound, matte spines. A wooden barometer hung on the wall beside the door, the old style for people who either hadn't realised the internet could provide the same information, or didn't want to know.

She pictured the three subservient boys, as they were clearly not yet men, all standing around the desk with their hands crossed before them and their heads bowed as they listened to the old man speak from the comfort of his chair. Perhaps Gareth would be sitting, she thought. Perhaps he might dare, or even be held in regard high enough to fortune him a moment of comfort while his father grumbled some kind of opinionated oration.

But her interest had been piqued. Exactly what was to be said that the old man deemed too delicate for Susie to hear? But even by focusing on the baritone grumble, the words were vague. Syllables were clear and even the intonation caused by heightened emotions, but the detail was far too vague for her to comprehend.

She found herself padding across the living room to the door. She felt her anxiety rise and her heartbeat not quicken, but deepen, like the thudding wheels of a distant train passing over a join in the tracks.

Pa-dum, pa-dum.

Pa-dum, pa-dum.

But even from the doorway, which was only a few metres from the study, the voices were still an orchestra of rumbles, as if she were standing outside the Royal Albert Hall, hearing only the extremities of the instruments. Abbott, of course, provided the unwavering baritone beat, upon which the three sons laid their melodies – Gareth, the depressed bass, Jeffery the obliging tenor, and Thomas – the only one who seemed to dare venture from his father's rhythm – the daring alto virtuoso that danced and rose and fell. And then the whole piece stopped. With the bang of a hand against the mahogany desk, like the deafening boom of a bass drum, the ensemble came to rest.

If it was indeed an orchestra, then the conductor waited for the notes to fade, and for the audience to recover, teasing their desire for more with a practised silence.

And Susie did want more. Not just more unintelligible noise from her spot outside the auditorium, but a spot in the front row, and if such a seat could not be procured then a place in the wings would suffice, a box, as it were, which she discovered with her ear pressed flat against the solid oak door and her hands gripping the doorframe ready to shove herself off should she be discovered without a ticket to the performance.

"I will not tolerate emotional outbursts, Thomas," Abbott said. "We need to stay calm, we need to pull together, and if you feel you can't do either of those, then I suggest you leave."

Susie pulled away, then froze, listening for footsteps coming toward the door, but Thomas, with a little more control over his emotions, spoke.

"I just think we should give her the benefit of the doubt, Dad," he said. "That's all I'm saying. She's our sister, for God's sake. You're all talking about her like she's just a disgruntled employee. This is Janice we're talking about. Janice."

"I'm well aware of who she is, Thomas," Abbott replied.

"Harry is dead, Tom," Gareth said, his voice breaking into a whine. "My son. You heard the man."

Susie imagined the stare that accompanied the three succinct statements, and the softening as the brothers, regardless of how they felt about each other, empathised.

"We don't know that for sure," Thomas said. "At least not until the viewing has been arranged. But if it is him, and it's a big if, you can't for one minute think that Janice would have done it. The detective said it was a hit-and-run. What was she supposed to have done, lined him up in the road and mowed him down—"

"Enough," Abbott said, this time without the thunderous fist striking his desk. "We all saw and heard Janice last night. We all know the frame of mind she was in. I think we have to accept that she's no longer a part of the business or this family."

"Oh come on, it's Christmas. Show me a family that doesn't argue at Christmas," Thomas said. "She's done it before. It's all talk. It's the only way she can get her point across."

"Not this time," Abbott said. "This time she's out. Even if she does come back, she's out."

"Out of the business, or out of the family, Dad?" Thomas asked, which incited a few moments of silent reflection.

"Both," Abbott replied, his voice a low and murmured grumble. "I never want to see her face again."

"I do," Gareth said, which Susie imagined raised a few eyebrows in the room. "I want to see her face when she's standing in the dock and the judge slams his gavel down before sending her away. I want to be there. I want to look her in the eye as she's led down the steps."

"You're a callous bastard, Gareth," Thomas said, and almost immediately, there was a scrape of chairs as Susie imagined the eldest son making a move.

"Stop it," Abbott said, raising his voice louder than she'd heard before. She could picture him staring at all three of his sons as they smoothed their clothes and settled back down. "Now, we are faced with some serious decisions. Serious enough that the four of us need to make them together. We're a family, that's what makes us strong. That is our armour and we can ill afford any more fractures to our armour."

"Sorry, Dad," Gareth muttered, which was followed by a short pause before Abbott continued.

"I can only assume that Janice made some kind of error whilst in a state of emotional unbalance," he said. "And, for the sake of her mother and the sake of appearances, we must assume that, should she have inadvertently knocked Harry down, then she did so with no preconceived notion of revenge."

"What?" Gareth said. "You can't honestly believe—"

"What we believe and what the police and the public think we believe are two very different things, Gareth," Abbott said. "It is very likely that Janice panicked and fled the scene, in which case the police will find her and deal with her accordingly."

"I don't know why we didn't just tell the police where they could find her," Gareth said.

"Because the fact remains, Gareth, that Janice knows enough about Dickens and Sons to destroy every single one of us," Abbott replied. "So, for the purposes of mediation and damage control, we must demonstrate compassion. I'll arrange a press statement, during which your mother and I will plead for her to give herself up, and that we believe her actions to have been entirely unintentional. In the meantime, Gareth, you need time to deal with what's happened. You need to follow the detective's instructions to the letter. Let your mother deliver the news to Arthur–"

"But, Dad–"

"I said you need to follow the detective's instructions to the letter, Gareth. View his body, then grieve if you must, but grieve here. We stay together. I don't want this to be an invitation for the police to delve into the business, and if they do, then I want us to be under the same roof where I can control matters. Do I make myself clear?"

"Yes, Dad," Gareth said.

"Jeffery, when we're done here, I want you to send Susie home. She has no part to play in this."

"What? I can't send her home. Her family have all gone to Scotland. She'll be on her own for Christmas."

"This is going to get harder before it gets easier, boy," Abbott said. "I'm sorry, she's a nice girl, but you need to decide which is more important to you, the family or some cheap floozy who only wants your money."

Susie's mouth fell open. She wanted to burst in and tell the old bastard exactly what his sons were too afraid to. But Jeff spoke and the words were razor-sharp points to her laden womb.

"I'll speak to her when we're done," he replied subserviently.

"Good," Abbott replied. "After that, you and Thomas are to go to the office. If Janice decides to open her mouth, I want nothing in that office that will substantiate any claims she might make."

"Okay, Dad," he replied.

"And Jeffery?" Abbott said. "When you send your floozy packing–"

"She's not a floozy, Dad," Jeff said.

"Make it permanent," Abbott replied. "Until this is over, we let nobody in. Just us. We keep it tight."

A fire burned at the back of Susie's eyes and a warm tear began its downward journey. Her throat seemed to tense and close, and her mouth became the desert in which she found herself alone.

"Okay, Dad," Jeff said softly. "Okay, I understand."

Susie felt herself slip from the doorway and back into the living room, an alien world in which she was no longer welcome.

She collected her shoes from where they sat beside one of the bifold doors and pulled them on with no socks. She considered going upstairs to collect her bag but deemed the risk of the meeting finishing whilst she packed too high, and the last thing she wanted was to face the spineless coward.

But she had to have the last word. She had to leave on her terms. So, she found herself standing before Elizabeth's bureau. Carefully, so as not to make a sound, she raised the lid in search of some paper and a pen.

And then she saw it.

CHAPTER 15

The doorbell made a joyous sound that, in the light of the morning's events, seemed out of touch with reality, weirdly reminding John of a scene from *Only Fools and Horses*, where the Trotters turn up to a funeral wake wearing a Batman and Robin outfit.

"Who's that?" he asked Penny from the sofa.

She leaned into the lounge, her face a picture of concern.

"That'll be Mum and Dad," she replied, then paused for thought. "Should I ask them to leave? They'll understand."

"No," he said and inhaled some energy into his bones. "No, let them in."

"Are you sure?" she asked, already untying her apron strings. "I mean, after what you saw..."

"I said that we're going to make memories," he told her. "And memories we shall make."

She smiled weakly at him then ducked out of the apron loop.

"Well, if you need some time alone, just pop upstairs. I'll explain it to them."

"If there's one thing that this morning has taught me," he

replied, "it's that we should treat every day as if it's our last. Who knows where we will be next year?"

She considered his closing statement and the doorbell rang again, so he added a supporting nod at the door.

"Let them in," he said. "Let's allow some life into this place, shall we? Besides, I'll need to pop into the office in a bit and I don't want you to be alone with the kids. Not on Boxing Day."

"The office? Oh, John, you said you'd be off—"

"And I *am* off," he told her. "I just want to check things are okay. The last thing I want is to go back to a disaster. I want to make sure everything is tickety-boo."

"They don't pay you enough," she said. "And they don't deserve you."

The doorbell rang again, twice this time, and she opened the door before he could answer.

"Mum, Dad," she said, flinging her arms out to hug them both. "Merry Christmas. Here, let me take your coats."

Never, in all the years John had been married to Penny had he seen Violet wearing anything but a floral dress, a large friendly smile, and enough Chanel No. 5 to sedate a horse. She drew her arms back for Penny to pull her coat off and then peered into the kitchen.

"Where are the bairns?" she asked.

"They're upstairs," John said, and Violet appraised him. She took a few steps with her short, stout legs and then held his hands as if seeing him for the first time.

"How lovely to see you, John," she said. "I hoped you'd be home."

"It's Christmas, Violet. I wouldn't miss it for the world."

"Where do you want these?" Les asked, holding up his two arms laden with bags.

"In the kitchen, dear," Violet said without looking. "I'll be in shortly to get started."

Penny led her father from the living room, leaving just Violet and John in the quiet space.

"You know Penny would have loved to cook for you," he told her.

"And I would have enjoyed every morsel," she replied. "But what have I left if I can't cook a meal for my family? You never know, it might be my last."

"Or mine," he said with a smile. "Why don't you pop upstairs and see the kids?"

"I will," she replied, taking a step back to study him from head to toe. "Once you've told me what's on your mind."

"Sorry?"

"I'm a mother, John. I might not be yours, but I'm a mother. We know these things." She glanced over her shoulder at the kitchen door. "Tell me."

"Nothing's wrong," he whispered. "Nothing at all."

"Well then," she said, seeming disappointed. "Where are these bairns then?"

"Now then," Les said when John entered the kitchen. Penny was unloading the bags of shopping onto the worktop and her father occupied the seat at the head of their small dining table. "How's that job of yours going, John?"

"Oh, you know, Les. A boring job is like life, isn't it? The only thing worse is the alternative."

"No job at all?" Les replied.

He was a lean man, which was an incredible feat considering he and Violet had been married for decades. His hands were splayed on the table, accentuating his long, bony fingers, and after a brief glance around the kitchen he gave a quick and knowing nod, then caught his daughter's attention.

"How about that tea then, love?"

"On its way, Dad," Penny replied, as she sifted through the bags. "What has Mum bought?"

"You know what she's like, love. She didn't know what you have in your cupboards."

"She's here every week. She probably has a better idea of what we've got and don't have," she said, pulling out a large tub of ice cream and holding it up for John to see. "At least the kids will be happy."

"I'm going to head off," John announced, reaching for a cup of his own and placing it beside the one Penny had prepared for her father. He cleared his throat, leaned against the counter, and waited for her to provide an argument.

She said nothing, of course, but he could see by the way she held her head, with her chin high, her eyes downcast, and her lips thinned to a faint smear of darker flesh, that she might very well do later, perhaps when they were in bed, out of earshot of her parents.

"Where are you off to?" Les asked. "I thought we'd be having dinner, the six of us."

"It's just for a while," he said. "I just want to—"

"Make sure everything is tickety-boo," Penny said, turning to her father. "He's diligent and loyal, to the detriment of those who care for him the most."

"I'll just be an hour," John said, more to his wife than her father, although he watched the old man's expression with intent.

"Well, mind how you go through the village, John. It's closed off down by the shops."

"Still?" John replied, then realised the old man was ignorant of the full facts, and he sighed at having to retell his account of the morning. "There was an accident down there this morning. A young boy was hit by a car."

"Oh dear," Les said, as he accepted the tea from his daughter. "That's ruined somebody's Christmas. Hurt bad, was he?"

"Dead," John said, then softened his voice. "He died. At the scene, I believe."

"Good Lord," Les said, setting his cup down. "Well, that does rather shine a different light on it. Local, was he?"

"We don't know," John replied, taking a sip of his own tea. "All we can do is be grateful for what we have, as little as that may be."

"You're right there."

"And take care of it," John added.

"Hence your visit to the office?" Les asked, to which John nodded.

He slipped into the living room, grabbed his jacket from the hook, and pulled it on. He re-entered the kitchen as he fastened the zip.

"I might not be a rich man, Les," he said, taking a mouthful of his tea. "Not in financial terms. But, in every other sense, I am a millionaire."

He kissed Penny on the cheek and winked at her, leaving them both with a final nod of goodbye from the doorway.

"I'm doing this for you, you know that, don't you?" he said to Penny, and she looked up at him from where she stood by the shopping bags. "Everything I do, it's all for you."

"I know," she replied softly and glanced at her father as if his comment had embarrassed her. "Just be back for dinner."

"Oh, I will," he said. "This year will be different, Penny. I know it will."

CHAPTER 16

I thought it would be different this time.

Eight words. None of them emboldened, in caps, or underlined. Just eight words carrying enough bitter venom to articulate disappointment and regret.

Charles clicked the button to reply to the text message, and nearly two minutes later, his thumb still poised over the keyboard with not a single character typed, Devon spoke.

"Everything okay, guv?" she said, and he clicked the button to lock his phone, slipping it into his pocket with a weak smile.

"All good," he replied, then turned off the engine, before he stared through the windscreen, which was smeared with winter grime. "Are you married, Devon?"

"Guv?"

"Are you married?" he replied, turning to watch her compose her response, finding her seeking the same distraction through the windscreen as he had only moments before.

"It's not for me, guv," she said finally. "I'm not really the relationship type."

"Oh? I wasn't aware there was a type."

"I'm too..." she began, then faltered and shook her head, as if to dismiss the conversation.

"Are you trying to tell me that your career is more important, Devon?"

She continued to gaze through the windscreen, feigning indifference the way a suspect's eyebrows might raise a little when, from the far side of the interview table, Charles presented infallible evidence.

"Dad was a copper," she said eventually. "And his dad before him. Seemed only right that I should be."

"Were either of them anybody I'd know?"

"Not unless you served in Sunderland, guv."

"Ah, Sunderland. I knew it," Charles said. "I've been trying to place your accent since we met."

"Why didn't you just ask?"

"Well, it's not polite, is it?" he replied. "Besides, we had a dead little boy to deal with, to which the origins of your accent pale in significance."

She laughed softly, politely even.

"I suppose," she said.

In the few short moments, since he had switched off the engine, their combined breaths had begun to fog the inside, masking the road grime and even the leaves that were tucked under the lip of the bonnet.

"I suppose we should go," Charles said, reaching for the door handle. "Are you familiar with the local pathologist?"

"I'm not," Devon replied, as she too climbed from the car. "But I've heard she's good."

"She is good," he replied, joining her in the walk towards the hospital's main entrance, then muttered to himself. "Sometimes I only wish she wasn't so good."

"Why's that?"

"Oh, you know how it is with these home office pathologists," he replied. "Their minds work quite differently to yours or mine."

"You mean, she doesn't always tell you what she's thinking?"

"Quite the opposite," Charles remarked. "Quite the opposite indeed."

"What about you?" Devon asked as they crossed the little hospital road. "Are you the relationship type?"

"I was," he said. "I still am, I suppose. I don't think I've changed. I'm older, I guess. More set in my ways than I perhaps was, but I like to think I'm still quite the catch for the right person."

"You hold yourself in high esteem," Devon said, as he opened the door for her.

"Well, if I don't, then who will?" he replied, following her inside.

They walked in silence to the pathology department, which, despite all the changes to the hospital over the years, hadn't really altered. He watched Devon as they walked, observing quietly as she took in all the signs, studied nearly every individual they passed, and tuned into distant conversations. He was almost glad when they reached the double doors that led to the pathology department, where there were few signs for her to read, no people to study, and no sounds save for the clacking of their heels against the painted concrete floor. It was then that her active mind sought a new occupation, much as he had expected it to.

"So, you never married?" she said as if the chance for him ever to do so had long since expired. "You strike me as someone who would be."

"Oh?"

"I don't mean anything by it," she said. "But you just have that look. You know? The look of a married man, confident, experienced."

"Tired?" he suggested, to which she gave a little laugh.

They stopped at the security doors and he reached for the buzzer.

"Brace yourself," he said, purposefully avoiding the conversation of his private life.

Thankfully, he heard the swish of the heavy, insulated doors from inside, and moments later, one of the double doors opened to reveal the pathologist, who stared up at him, saying nothing. She wore a white tunic with a multicoloured pen in her breast pocket and a pair of blue scrub trousers. On her feet, she wore a pair of dark blue Crocs, and reaching up from the confines of her tunic was the tail of a great Welsh dragon.

"Detective Constable Devon, meet Doctor Pippa Bell." He presented the doctor with a sweep of his arm. "Pip meet Devon. My new partner in crime."

"Partner in crime?" Pip replied, allowing Devon to bask in her melodic Welsh accent.

"For the time being, at least," Charles added, then gestured inside. "May we?"

"You may," Pip replied, stepping to one side. She glanced up at the little digital clock on the wall. "You're a few minutes early."

"Mr Dickens isn't here yet, then?" Charles asked. Then he added, "Are we all ready for him?"

Pip opened one of the cupboards in the little reception room, where, to Charles's surprise, she checked her reflection, and lifted the collar of her tunic to cover the dragon tattoo. She gave a few deft sweeps of her bobbed hair to straighten it out, then closed the door and turned to him.

"The boy is as presentable as he could be, given the circumstances. Thankfully, the injuries were mostly internal."

"And the cause of death?" Devon asked before Charles could.

Pip looked at her curiously but directed her answer to Charles. "Internal bleeding. Splenic rupture," she said.

"Ruptured spleen? Anything else?"

"A few broken ribs, one of which punctured a lung. Two broken fingers and some damaged teeth," she replied, then completed the picture in Charles's mind. "In short, the poor lad was hit hard. Didn't stand a chance. I haven't seen the crime scene, but given his injuries and the associated bruising, he was hit from behind and landed face down. Thankfully the driver must have stopped before the wheels rolled over him, but I'm afraid that's the only positive."

"It could have been worse, you mean?" Charles said.

"The outcome? No, that could never be worse. But the boy's injuries could have been."

"So Mr Dickens will see his body as he remembers him?" Devon asked.

"If that's how you want to put it," Pip said, rather catlike in her tone.

Thankfully, the awkward silence that ensued was cut short by the door buzzer, and each of them took a breath to ready themselves. Charles opened the door and met a grim-faced Gareth Dickens, alone and looking as far from the confident and arrogant young man he had been only a few hours earlier.

"Mr Dickens," Charles said, hoping his dull tone and sombre expression offered some kind of respect.

"Cook, wasn't it?" he replied, to which Charles nodded. Gareth Dickens peered inside the room, finding Pip and Devon waiting patiently, each of them with their hands folded in front of them.

"Mr Dickens," Pip said, clearly far more practised in the scenario than Charles. She stepped forward and offered her hand. "I'm Doctor Bell. I'll be beside you the whole time. Now, before we go through, if the identification is positive, then you'll be allowed some time alone."

"Right," he replied, appearing very much as a father in his position should be – anxious and worried.

"We'll wait in here," Charles offered. "DC Devon and I. To give you some space."

"That's very much appreciated," Dickens replied, although the good manners felt rather forced.

"Shall we?" Pip said, leading the way through a small door on the far side of the reception.

Charles gave him a supporting nod as Dickens followed her through, and it was as if a pressure valve had kicked in when the door closed behind them.

"God, that's hard. I don't know how she does it," Charles said, dropping into one of the couches. "It's bad enough having to relay the news to grieving parents, but to hold their hands while they view the body?" He shook his head at the prospect. "That's a different ball game altogether."

"I like her," Devon said, peering at the door through which they had left. "She's odd, all right. But I like her."

"Aye? Well, let's hope she likes you," Charles replied. "For your sake."

"He's been knocked down a peg or two, hasn't he?" she replied, taking the seat opposite him and lowering her voice. "Bloody awful business if you ask me."

"How humbling death can be," Charles said. "It just goes to show, that it doesn't matter who you are, death touches us all."

"You sound like you're speaking from experience."

He smiled at the comment but offered nothing in the way of a reply.

"Based in Lincoln, are you?"

"Newark, guv," she said. "Transferred a few months back."

"A few months? I haven't seen you around."

The comment clearly caused some discomfort or unease, as for the first time since he had met her, she stared at the floor, then at the wall, anywhere but his eyes.

"They tucked me away in a back office, processing statements, developing CPS reports, that sort of thing."

"Who did you report to?"

"DI Standing, at first."

"Standing?"

"He's not with us anymore. He transferred back to a rural station. North Kesteven, I think."

"Which left you..."

"High and dry, guv. For the past few months anyway," she replied, finishing the statement for him. "I doubt even the top brass know I exist."

"I very much doubt that."

"Ask them," she said with confidence. "I'm one of those people who can't seem to make friends."

"Hence you volunteered to cover the Christmas shift," Charles said, recognising the motive.

She looked up at him, cornered with all angles of escape or distraction covered by Charles's knowing expression.

"I thought some of the others might appreciate it," she said. "You know? The ones with families."

"And did they?"

"Like I said, they don't even know I exist, guv."

The silence that followed was, for Charles at least, filled with a resonance of himself in his younger years before age had hardened him and life had made him bitter.

The door behind her opened and the awkward silence halted as abruptly as a caesura in jazz, where every instrument rests in perfect time and the listener knows the music will continue at any moment, but the tease is delightful, joyous, yet unbearable in equal measure.

Pip's robust and short stature filled the bottom half of the doorway, and as she stepped aside to let Gareth through, she nodded once at Charles.

They stood, Devon and Charles when it was clear Gareth was suffering, and Charles offered the grieving father a seat with an outstretched hand.

"Please," he said, as softly as he could.

The father was tall and lean, with shoulders that sagged under the weight of what he'd just witnessed. Under any other circumstances, his presence would have been formidable. It would have been he who guided Charles to a seat, controlling the room. But such were the consequences of death, and the process of healing had barely begun.

He perched on the edge of the couch, holding his head in his hands and letting his fingers find their way through his thick, dark hair, like tentacles groping for a purchase on its prey.

"I want her found," he said quietly, without raising his head. "I want that bitch found and I want her punished."

"Gareth, we're doing—"

"Find her," he spat, his head snapping up and his hands falling to his knees to reveal a terrible anger in his eyes, which paled with loss, taking with it his venomous tone. "Just find her. I want her behind bars."

Charles let the man's emotions settle and cleared his throat with a cough.

"I'm sorry," Charles said.

"Why is this happening to me?" Gareth continued. "Why?"

"I don't know," Charles said.

"It's like..." He paused to allow his thoughts to assemble and then stared Charles in the eye. "It's like I'm being punished for something I haven't done."

CHAPTER 17

The view from the gates of Dickens and Sons fortuned the viewer a timeline that illustrated several centuries on a sprawling site that hugged the River Witham. From the abandoned eighteenth-century farm buildings at the furthest point to the red brick, Victorian factory buildings beside them, to the two-story office building closest to the gate, which had been erected less than three years previous. It was an ugly, modern sparkle of glass and steel, a graffiti on the memorial, a stain on the old world, from where the Dickens family could view their dynasty, change lives, and watch their employees endlessly toil.

The security guard, a contractor of African descent whose eyes glowed with the red scars of fatigue, leaned from his little cabin to view John's pass, then raised the barrier before slipping back into the radiant light of a small television.

John eased the accelerator down, noting the disparity between the two car parks before him. Seventy or eighty of the spots designated with blue signs for the factory workers were filled, which was the same for most days of the year, while the dozen or so spaces in the foreground of that modern stain of glass were all empty. All empty, that is, save for one. A sleek BMW that was parked in the spot bore a white sign with the name *Jeffery Dickens* in the company's primary colour – dark blue.

It was as if the signs for each parking space denoted the collars of the individuals they were for. White text on a blue background for the blue collars, blue text on a white background for the management. He found himself noting things like that more often, internalising his remarks on those little segregating details, and although his desk was housed in the glass building for the purposes of efficiency, he spent most of his time with the workers in the factory.

John still clung to his blue-collar heritage. They would have to tear that from his cold, dead hands before he aligned himself with the likes of the Dickens. This sentiment had been acknowledged by Gareth Dickens who'd assigned John a space in the blue car park, from which he was forced to walk through the wind and rain to the ugly, glass stain.

"There simply aren't enough spaces for middle management," Gareth had announced after the opening of the building. But what John had heard was, *I'm not having the riff park their heaps of junk beside my car.*

The clouds were high. The sky beyond was a bright winter blue. Yet the air was cold, like death, and the wind off the river had an edge as keen as the flint tools found along the river, discarded or dropped by fairer hands thousands of years before.

With his hands firmly entrenched in his pockets, John pulled his jacket close and braved the fierce breath, avoiding the sporadic puddles and doing his best to keep to the allotted footpath. Heaven forbid he strayed onto the landscaped grass that surrounded the office building and tarnished the fur-like lawn with his boot.

To his joy, however, a breath of warm air greeted him as he pushed into the reception, and by the time he had ventured through into the middle management office on the ground floor, a veneer of sweat had formed on his back.

He dropped into his seat, switched on his PC, and while the operating system booted, he ventured over to the coffee machine, which was so old and temperamental that, had it been in the old Victorian factory, it might have been considered part of the building's heritage, like the ornate cornices or the brick-arched windows.

The machine, for once at least, appeared to be in working order. The lights were on and the little LCD screen suggested it was ready for him to make his selection. However, the Christmas holidays seemed to have let standards lapse, and the little plastic column in which the cardboard cups were usually stacked was empty, leaving him no alternative but to venture upstairs to where there were sets of bright white china cups for the senior management team and visitors. They wouldn't miss one, and only Jeffery Dickens was in, a man who was famous within the middle management team for rarely leaving his office.

John took the stairs, deeming the pointless lift and its cheerful chimes too much of a risk. The last thing he needed was for Jeffery, the second of Abbott Dickens's sons, to poke his head from his office and enquire as to why he dared to trespass on the first floor.

The space at the top of the stairs was, in John's opinion, a waste of real estate, designed to convince visiting customers to sign on the dotted line in one of the spacious meeting rooms. The first floor had its own reception, which was usually manned by a pretty, young thing named Victoria who almost never even offered a hi or goodbye to any lowly servant who dwelled at ground level. She manned the first-floor desk on most days, overseeing the cleaning of the executive washrooms and making coffee in the little kitchen which was situated just behind the reception desk.

It was as John was entering the kitchen that he heard the first of the raised voices, causing enough intrigue for him to brave a peek through the little window into the corridor. He knew the layout well enough from the few times he'd been summoned up the stairs. Aside from the meeting rooms, which were on the left of the aisle, there were just a few large offices. Janice Dickens's office, then Thomas', and Jeffery', and finally Gareth Dickens's at the end, affording him a view over the Dickens estate and the river, with historic Lincoln in the distance.

John knew enough of the layout that when he saw Jeffery's office door closed, and Gareth's open, his curiosity got the better of him. So much so that he found himself pushing open the door to the corridor and, against every sensible bone in his body, he made his way towards the end office.

"It's got to be here somewhere," a voice said, Thomas's perhaps, although his car wasn't outside. "Where would he keep it?"

"I don't know. I doubt even Gareth bloody knows," Jeffery replied. "The only thing we do know is that it's in here somewhere, and if we don't find it, Dad's going to blow a gasket."

"What does it look like?"

"A folder. I remember seeing it once before Dad retired. It's a black folder filled with old papers. I couldn't even read the handwriting, but Dad could. He'd probably memorised it. You know how fixated he can get on the past."

"If he thinks this folder can take us down," Thomas said, "why bloody keep it?"

A drawer slammed closed and John heard the slap of papers hit the carpet. But there was a silence that John imagined was Jeffery conveying some kind of severity.

"It's our history," he said. "Without it, you and I would be like every other mug out there, slogging our nuts off for pittance, making somebody else rich."

"On the ground floor, you mean?"

"There wouldn't be a ground floor, Tom," Jeffery said. "The factory would have been knocked down or converted into warehouses or something. It's our bloody heritage, Tom. Like it or not, it's our heritage."

"But not one we can be proud of?"

"Oh, Dad's proud of it, and I dare say Gareth is too, but not in public."

Quietly, John took a step back, but bumped into the wall behind him in his haste, and the noise from inside halted in an instant.

"Who's that?" Jeffery said, and John winced at his error. With no way of going back to the reception without being heard now, he reluctantly nudged the door open.

"Pardon me," he began, seeing the two men on their knees before a mound of paperwork and folders. "I heard noises, that's all. I was just checking everything was okay?"

"What the bloody hell are you doing up here?" Jeffery said. "How dare you?"

"Like I said, Mr Dickens," John said, "I heard noises. I thought there might be intruders."

"Do we look like intruders?"

"Well, no," John said, eyeing their task before them. Jeffery followed his gaze.

"What are you doing in anyway? I was under the impression that only the factory was in today."

"I just wanted to get a few things in order," John said, then glanced at the paperwork on the floor again. "Is everything okay?"

"Everything is fine," Jeffery said, standing up and striding across the large office towards him. He reached out to close the door. "Now, if you'll excuse us–"

"I just thought..." John said, and Jeffery Dickens gripped the door, giving him a few seconds to finish. "I just thought Janice might be in. I have a few things I'd like to run by her before the new year. Some ideas, if you will."

He stared at him, and over his shoulder, John saw Thomas avert his gaze.

"I suggest you keep hold of those thoughts for the time

being," he said. "Janice has gone away for a while. Emergency leave."

John heard the words but read in the man's eyes a meaning altogether different.

"I'm sorry to have disturbed you. I was just being vigilant." John said, and then he nodded, smiled graciously, and turned on his heels.

"It's John, isn't it?" Jeffery called out, stopping John in his tracks. "John Gregory. Is that right?"

"Yes, Mr Dickens. That's right."

The second son of Abbott Dickens stared hard at him as if reading his thoughts, or at least trying to.

"I'd appreciate your discretion," he said.

"Discretion?" John said. "With regards to Janice being on leave, you mean? Of course, I won't tell a soul. Is she okay? Has something happened?"

"And this mess," Jeffery said, and he nodded over his shoulder to the papers on the carpet, completely ignoring John's questions.

"What mess?" John replied, after a pause for thought.

"Good," Jeffery said. "Now go home and enjoy the rest of your Christmas."

CHAPTER 18

The gloom of the formal identification still loomed over Charles and Devon like a dark cloud that fed off their darkest thoughts and empathy.

"It's this one," Devon said, breaking the silence and pointing to a large property on their right. "There's an SUV on the driveway, but no Audi. But then, I suppose she's hardly likely to leave it out for everyone to see."

"You'll be amazed at what people are capable of in a panic, Devon," Charles replied, as he drew the car over to the kerb. "I attended a house once, way back when I was still in uniform. The neighbours had reported screaming and shouting. We did that then, you know? Attended those sorts of reports. Couldn't do it now. We wouldn't have the time to do anything else."

"Times have changed, guv," she replied but made no show of hurrying him along. In fact, she rather enjoyed listening to his accent. It wasn't harsh like the way poor comedians portray the Scottish, but soothing, somehow.

"The husband answered the door. He did his best to behave normally, of course. But you get to know the signs, don't you? He couldn't look me in the eye, couldn't even lie convincingly when I asked him if anybody had been shouting or screaming."

"What happened?" Devon asked, to which Charles simply shrugged.

"I asked to speak to his wife and he said she wasn't home. So I told him that the neighbours had seen her arrive home, and then suggested we speak inside to avoid the twitching curtains. That was the key, you see? To be invited inside amicably. I noticed his shirt tails were untucked, and a woman's coat had been tossed onto the chair by the telephone table."

"The what? Sorry, was this in nineteen-thirty?"

"No, it was not," he said. "It was still a thing back then. Everyone had one. Everyone with a telephone, at least. We didn't have mobile phones or even cordless phones. We had to sit in the hallway if we wanted to make a call, and anybody and everybody could listen in." Charles shook the tangent off with a shake of his head. "Anyway, I followed him through to the kitchen, and while he was filling the kettle up, I had a little nose around. Peeked inside the bin, I did."

"The bin? What for?"

"Just nosing, that's all," Charles replied.

"And you found something?"

"A broken coffee cup," he said. "And some old rags. That was when I started to look closer at things. He was talking with his back to me. Telling me how his wife had left that morning and everything had been just fine."

"And all the while you were looking in every nook and cranny?"

"Surreptitiously," he said. "I noticed a breeze coming from a door on one side of the kitchen. It was ajar, you see. So I wandered around to see if I could see inside."

Charles studied Devon's face. She had intelligent eyes, but there was a sadness to them. A sadness he recognised, and empathised with.

"And what did you see?" she asked.

"Nothing. Nothing, he saw where I was heading and shut the door before I could see inside."

"Why?"

"I remember it well," Charles said, ignoring her question. "I had an idea he was hiding something, and he had an idea that I wasn't falling for his story. But neither of us was going to be the first to say anything."

"So, then what?" Devon asked, her confident voice almost childlike in intrigue.

"Then nothing," Charles replied. "I said nothing and he said nothing. We both just kind of stared at each other. He, a sweating, nervous wreck, and me a PC, completely out of my depth and on my own. I tell you, if he had decided to whack me, I'd have been done for."

"But he didn't?"

"No, of course not. He slid a cup of tea towards me, then laid his hands on the work surface. He waited for me to take a sip, and then eventually he raised his head and spoke."

"But what did he *say*, guv? If you don't mind, you know how to drag a story out, don't you?"

Charles gave a short laugh and then switched the engine off.

"She's in the garage."

"He said that she was in the garage?"

"In a wheelbarrow," Charles added. "He was going to bury her in the garden when it got dark."

"And he just confessed? Just like that?"

"Sometimes, Devon," he replied, "it's best to just stay quiet. The guilty will always speak eventually."

He reached for the door handle and climbed out, straightening his coat and taking in the large house before him.

"I'll bear that in mind," Devon said, as she came to stand beside him.

"Of course. It doesn't always work," Charles said. "Sometimes they take a little more convincing." He gestured at the house with a slight nod of his head. "Shall we?"

"But it worked that time," she said. "And you were just a PC?"

"Be careful how you say that," he said. "There's no such thing as *just* a PC. We all have our roles to play. It just so happened that, on that occasion, I was the one who was sent to investigate." He stared up at the house, remembering the days that followed that incident and how different his life might have been if he had remained in uniform with more of a scheduled work routine. "That was when I was first noticed," he said.

"Noticed?"

"By my chief inspector," he said. "I don't even think he knew I existed before that investigation."

"You mean, that was when you decided to move into plain clothes?"

"I mean, that was when he and everyone else realised I was more than just a socially awkward, quiet, young constable who nobody ever spoke to and was the butt of everyone's jokes."

He smiled at her, knowing that his words had resonated, even if it was just a little. She was smart enough to see what he had inferred.

"And all because you chose to say nothing. Because you waited for him to speak first," she said. "That's how you found your path to DCI?"

"That and a few other factors," he said, nudging her up the driveway politely.

"Like what?" she said, as he reached up to ring the doorbell. He dropped his arm to his side and sighed, before finding her staring at him, utterly enthralled, her eyes filled with hope.

"Like putting my job before my family," he said weakly and thoughtfully. "And the two other women they found buried in his garden." Her eyes widened in horror and her mouth fell open in shock, it was all he could do to smile back at her in the hope it might lift her spirits. "I imagine that probably helped my case."

"Mr Dickens?" Charles said when a smart-looking gentleman opened the front door. He wore a V-necked Kashmir sweater, corduroys, and moccasin slippers, and gave little more than a cursory glance at their warrant cards before narrowing his eyes.

"Yes? Can I help?" he said, his voice deep and professional but not unfriendly. Charles said nothing but held his stare long enough to convey the seriousness of the issue. "Is something wrong? Is it the kids?"

"I was hoping to speak to your wife," Charles said. "It's Janice, isn't it?"

"That's right. But I'm afraid you're out of luck," Mr Dickens replied. "She's at her family's house for Christmas."

"That's just it, Mr Dickens. She's not there."

"Sorry?"

"She's not at her parents' house. We were rather hoping to find her here."

"Well, she's not," he replied, with a quick check of the driveway for her car. "What's going on?"

"Perhaps it's best if we speak inside, Mr—"

"Richard. It's Richard Dickens."

"You took your wife's name," Charles said. "I admire that."

"I had very little choice in the matter," Richard replied, as he stepped aside. "Anyway, that's another topic. Come in, please. I'll get the kettle on."

"Oh, it's okay," Charles said, as he followed Richard inside. "We won't be here long enough for tea. I really need to speak to your wife. Is there somewhere she might have gone? Somewhere other than her parents' house?"

With a casual wave of his hand, Richard invited them both to the bar stools at the breakfast bar, then leaned against the large RangeMaster, folding his arms in thought. Behind him, glazed, burnt orange tiles formed a splashback which cascaded down to a single course surrounding the butler sink. The floor was an oak-effect laminate containing hues of reddish brown. A range of copper Le Creuset pans hung from a wooden pot rack, which in turn was adorned with black, wrought-iron fittings and a rather wonderful nasturtium that seemed to thrive on its perch with its tangle of branches entwining the wood.

"Why do you need to speak to her?"

"I'm afraid we can't really–"

"I have an idea of where she might be. But you'll need to give me something first," he said, then waved his index finger at them both. "I can see by your expressions that this isn't a pleasure visit. You haven't just popped in to see how she's doing."

"Your nephew was knocked down this morning, Richard," Charles said, which served its purpose and silenced the man, dousing his confidence with all kinds of possibilities. "I'm afraid he died from his injuries."

It took a moment for Richard to digest the news, during which time he studied each of their faces for any sign that the whole thing was some kind of sick prank. But after the ordeal with Gareth Dickens only an hour before, Charles was anything but jovial and as far from playing tricks as he could have been.

"My nephew?" Richard said.

"Harry," Charles added, for clarity, to which Richard simply whispered his response.

"Harry? Bloody hell." It took a few moments for Richard to gain some kind of perspective, and when he had, he looked up at Charles curiously and spoke with trepidation, as if he already knew the answer. "And why do you want to speak to Janice? What does she have to do with all this?"

"Because a grey Audi was seen speeding from the crime scene," Charles told him. "She does drive a grey Audi, doesn't she?"

"No, I do," he replied. "The Audi is mine. That's her Volvo on the drive."

"Oh?" Charles replied, offering Richard the chance to explain a little further.

"We swapped. I had the kids for Christmas Day, you see?" he said, then disregarded that tangent with a shake of his head. "What do you mean? Are you trying to say you think she knocked Harry down? And then what? Did a runner?" He shook his head again, either in complete denial or utter disbelief. "Jan wouldn't do that. If you knew her—"

"I thought Christmas was a time for families," Charles said before he entered into a rant about how saintly his wife was. In Charles's experience, those kinds of recitals were rarely accurate and mostly biased. "Why were you apart?"

"It was my turn," he replied, after a pause for thought.

"Your turn?"

"Yeah, you know? She gets the kids one year, I get them the next."

Charles felt Devon glance at him as if she wanted to ask the exact question that he did.

"You're not separated, are you?"

"Separated? Me and Jan? No, of course not. It's just something that families do, isn't it? Spend Christmas Day with one family one year, and then the next year..." His voice faded with his enthusiasm when he saw the blank expressions on both their faces.

"That's not how it worked in my family," Charles said. "My wife gets the kids every year. But thank you for the insight into how normal families operate."

"Normal families?" Richard said. "Have you met her family? They are not normal. They are anything but normal."

"Is that why you chose to be with your own family, Mr Dickens?" Devon asked, speaking up for the first time. Charles looked across at her, noting how she was slouching, which pushed her blouse up into her neck, forcing the loose skin beneath her jaw to hang over her collar. "Because you don't get along with her family?"

Richard laughed once and shook his head.

"You really don't know them, do you?" he said. "It's not just me who doesn't get along with them. Nobody does. The only people who truly like the Dickens are the Dickens, and even then their loyalty is questionable."

"What does that mean?" Devon asked.

"It means, that the old man—"

"Abbott?" Charles said, for clarification, and Richard nodded.

"Abbott is a control freak. He might be retired and his kids might all be grown up, but trust me, he rules that house with an iron rod, much the same way he ruled his business before he retired, that is."

"Thank you, Richard," Charles said, pushing himself off of the bar stool and flicking his eyebrows at Devon for her to follow suit. "We'll need to talk to your parents if you don't mind. It's a formality, I'm afraid."

"My parents? Why?"

"Because the car belongs to you. We just need to make sure you were where you said you were."

"Bloody hell—"

"But first, we'd like to find Janice," Charles added. "So where do you think she might be?"

He shoved off of the RangeMaster, straightening his sweater. He was a lean man who clearly watched what he ate. Unless he was one of those lucky so-and-sos who could eat what they liked and never put on a pound. He stepped over to the doorway as if silently inviting them to follow him.

"If she's not here, and she's not at her parents' house, then there's only one place she can be," he said over his shoulder, as he opened the front door. "The lion's den."

"The lion's den?"

"Dickens and Sons," he replied. "The office. It's down near Washingborough, beside the river."

"The big place?" Devon said. "The one that's been there for years?"

"That's it. That's the Dickens family business," Richard said. "That's where you'll find her. Bowing and scraping like the good daughter that she is."

"You don't hold the Dickens family in very high regard," Charles said. "Is there something else we should know? Something you're not telling us, perhaps?"

Richard straightened his sweater again, adjusting his collar this time, while he considered his response.

"I would have thought a man of your intelligence might have worked it out already, Chief Inspector," he replied, his expression one of intrigue and curiosity. "But in case you haven't, then I'll make it easy for you."

"Go on," Charles said. "Let's hear it then."

Richard leaned forward, stooping down to Charles who was standing on the doorstep in Devon's shadow.

"They're monsters," he whispered. "Greedy, blood-sucking monsters."

"Thank you, Mr Dickens," Charles said after a reflective pause. "We'll be in touch with your parents."

"And if you find her? Should I help look for her?"

"No, no," he replied. "You just keep an eye on those wee bairns of yours. If we find her, I'm sure she'll be in touch."

"But you'll arrest her," Richard said. "Should I call a solicitor or something? She'll need help."

"Aye, she will."

"But what do I tell the kids?" he asked. "Is she coming home?"

Charles stopped at the doorway, allowing Devon to leave before him.

"That remains to be seen, Mr Dickens," Charles said. "I suggest you keep it to yourself for the time being. These things have a funny way of being blown out of proportion."

CHAPTER 19

From the passenger seat of Detective Chief Inspector Charles Cook's car, Devon admired his profile as he drove in silence, a myriad of thoughts evident in the slight twitches of his brow, his lips, and ruffling of his nose, which, from the side, was crooked or hooked. From the front, however, it was flattened at the bridge as if somebody in his past had got the better of him, although Devon deemed him not much of a brawler. In fact, the prow of his forehead suggested he was a man, as Richard Dickens had suggested, of great intelligence, which gave her cause to consider how his nose had become so.

"I thought we were going to her office?" she said, as he indicated and slowed to turn into Acredyke Lane, the single-lane track that led to the Dickens house.

He said nothing in reply, clearly lost in thought. He drove as if he had only recently passed his test, with his hands at ten to two, his back ramrod straight, and his eyes flicking from side to side as if he expected somebody or something to leap from the trees onto the lane at any moment.

"Are we popping back into the Dickens house?" she asked. Again, he said nothing. "The lion's den?"

"I thought the lion's den was the factory down by the river," he said quietly. "According to Janice Dickens's husband, anyway. And yes, in answer to your second question, we're going back to the Dickens house. Something isn't sitting right with me."

"What about Janice Dickens? Shouldn't we be going after her?"

"She won't get far," Cook replied. "You did have ANPR alerts set up for the Audi's number plate, didn't you?"

"Of course," she said. "It might be his car, but it's registered to Janice."

"And have you heard anything?" he asked, as he nosed the car into Abbott Dickens's lengthy drive, slowing to handle the bumps in the gravel, which were both deep and plentiful.

"I would have said if I had."

"In which case we can assume she's gone to ground," he said. "And the only way we'll find her is if somebody close to her gives us a clue."

"What about her phone?" Devon asked. "We could always have somebody get in touch with the carrier to see where it was when she last used it."

"Be my guest," Cook said. "But in my experience, that approach rarely leads us anywhere. If she has any sense, she'll have turned her phone off."

He turned the car in a wide arc and then reversed into a space beside a small pond that held some sort of huge plant with leaves that sagged under their own weight. In the summertime, she imagined, the plant would have been magnificent, but just like the recent summers had pushed the limits of heat, the winters were harsh and cruel enough for anything but the hardiest of lives to perish.

"She'd need somewhere to go," Devon said, musing as she studied the large, brown leaves. "A house or a flat or something."

She turned to find Cook following her gaze.

"*Gunnera manicata*," he said, then smiled shyly at her bemused expression. He nodded at the pond. "The plant. It's called Giant Rhubarb."

"It doesn't like the cold," she said.

"No," he agreed. "No, it doesn't." He exhaled heavily as he switched off the engine. "And you're right. She needs a roof over her head. When we're done here, do whatever it is you need to do to find the mobile phone, and then see if she has access to any other properties. The family has money. It stands to reason that she has somewhere to go."

"Got it, guv," she replied, as they climbed from the car.

A bitter chill found her exposed ears almost immediately and she dragged the hood of her Parka up to cover them. Cook, however, seemed not to feel the bite of the season's north-easterly wind. The tails of his coat flapped wildly as he approached the front door, where a small box sat on the doorstep, wrapped in newspaper with a length of gold ribbon tied in a bow.

"What's that?"

She bent to pick it up and read the little card affixed to the ribbon.

"Bah, humbug, kiss, kiss, kiss," Devon read aloud. "Bah humbug? What the—"

Cook knocked on the door before turning on his heels to scan the nearby lane, but there was nobody in sight and they hadn't passed a soul on the way in.

"Bah humbug?" she said again, and then Cook smiled to himself, as footsteps approached the door from the inside. "What?"

The door was opened by Thomas Dickens, who, as far as Devon could make out, was the youngest of the three brothers. His expression wasn't exactly welcoming when he opened the door, but somehow it slipped into something far more frigid when he recognised them both.

"Now then," he said, a typical Lincolnshire greeting that conveyed a multitude of meanings differing only by tone.

"Mr Dickens," Cook began, then as an afterthought, he held out the gift.

"Is this supposed to make us feel better?"

"Sorry, I... that is...we found it on the doorstep," Charles said. "Can I take it Gareth has broken the news?"

Thomas stepped outside, pulling the door behind him.

"My mum's taken it pretty badly," he said, then glanced at the upstairs windows. "Gareth is up there with Arthur."

"And your father?" Cook asked, to which Thomas appeared slightly sheepish.

"Dad doesn't really do emotions, unless they're the angry type, of course. He's quite free with those," Thomas said, clearly remembering an occasion in particular. "No, Dad likes to keep his emotions in check. He's in the garden. It's his peaceful place."

Cook glanced back at the front door and then settled on Thomas.

"I was hoping we could go inside," he said. "Perhaps somebody knows something that could help us."

"Such as?" Thomas replied and then sighed. "Look, if you go in there, you're in for a rough time. I can't guarantee that my family will be polite."

"If you mean that we'll be on the receiving end of those emotions you spoke of, Thomas, then I can assure you we're well-versed in being told that we should be out there working on the investigation instead of sitting in people's homes chatting over tea."

"I hope you don't expect tea."

"I never expect anything, Thomas," Cook said. "I find it's the easiest way to avoid disappointment."

Thomas began to walk the few steps back to the house, but then stopped and turned towards them again.

"Is there anything in particular you want to know?" he said. "I mean, if you don't have to go inside."

Cook handed the conversation over to Devon with an expectant expression and raised eyebrows.

"We were hoping to learn the addresses of the family's property portfolio, Mr Dickens," she said.

"Our portfolio?" Thomas said.

"You're not telling me that a wealthy family such as yours doesn't have some of its capital tied up in bricks and mortar, are you?"

"Well, Mum has a few houses—"

"We need the addresses," Devon said. "And the keys too, if they're to hand. Get us those and perhaps we can avoid causing any more upset."

"The keys are in Mum's desk," he replied, with an obvious drop in his enthusiasm. He stared at the front door, then, as he reached out and took hold of the handle, he looked at them both. And for that brief moment, he wasn't one of the stand-offish Dickens or the brother of a grieving father. He was softer, somehow. "She didn't do it. Janice, I mean. She wouldn't have. She's not like that. She's got kids of her own."

"The keys, Thomas," Cook said, forcing a polite tone. "We're not here to judge."

"If it *was* her, then it was an accident. She wouldn't do that on purpose."

Cook said nothing, even ignored Devon's stare, although there was no doubt he could feel it or see her from the corner of his eye. It was that silence he had spoken of, used for a slightly different purpose, but to the same effect.

"You'd better come in," Thomas said eventually, and he shoved his way into the house. He waited for them to enter then closed the door behind them. The door closed with a thud that echoed off the wood-panelled walls so loudly that surely nobody in the house could be unaware of the visitors. And, as if to prove Devon's thoughts correct, Elizabeth Dickens leaned into the hallway from the living room.

"Ah, Inspector."

"Chief Inspector," Cook corrected her, making no further attempt to engage in conversation.

"Thomas?" she said, offering one of those motherly glares designed to extract information. She emerged from the room, lithe like a lion stepping into the view of its prey, unafraid. "I don't think now is a good time for visitors, do you?"

"They just need—"

"What's that?" she said, eyeing the little, six-by-six-inch box in his hand.

"Oh, it's just—"

"We found it on your doorstep," Devon said, much to everyone's surprise. "We thought a neighbour might have left it for you."

Elizabeth held out her hand but made no move to close the distance. Instead, Thomas took the few steps and held it out for her. She studied the newspaper wrapping with what Devon could only describe as disgust, and then read the tag.

"Bah humbug?" she said, looking up at Cook. "Is this some kind of joke?"

"I suggest you ask the sender that question, Mrs Dickens," he replied. "Now, I don't want to take up too much of your time." He moved his attention to Thomas. "If we could get those addresses and keys, please?"

"What keys?" Elizabeth said, directing the question at her son.

"Oh, they just need—"

"Janice wasn't at her home address, Mrs Dickens," Cook said. "Her husband thought she would be here."

"Well, she isn't."

"In which case I'd like to check any property she might have access to."

"She doesn't have access to any properties, only her own house."

"But she has a key to this place?" Cook asked.

"Of course. She's my daughter. She grew up here."

"So she has access to this house and the keys to your other properties."

Elizabeth stiffened like a dog ready to snap, but then softened with an audible sigh.

"I'm sorry," she said, after a moment or two of reflection. "It's been a hard day. We're all tired."

"I can assure you, Mrs Dickens, you do not need to apologise to me. I just want to find your daughter. We have a process, and that involves searching every property she might have access to."

"Is there a property in particular you want to check?" she asked. "I'll fetch the key for you."

"All of them," Cook said, which seemed to stop her in her tracks.

The statement caused more of a reaction than the old lady was perhaps willing to give, and she looked away while she composed herself.

"We own a few properties locally, plus a villa in Benalmadena."

"Spain," Cook told Devon when she looked to him for a clue, then he shook his head.

"How likely is she to go to Spain?" Devon asked.

"Unlikely," Cook said before Elizabeth could speak. "The car would have been picked up by ANPR—"

"That's Richard's car. The Audi, I mean," Thomas said. "She usually drives a Volvo."

"Which is on her driveway," Cook countered, and then explained. "We spoke to her husband. Besides, if Janice did knock your grandson down accidentally, statistically she'll be handing herself into the nearest police station within twenty-four hours."

"And if she doesn't?"

"Then she's hiding somewhere locally."

"What if it wasn't an accident?" a voice asked, and they all looked up to find Gareth leaning over the landing banister. Tears had swollen the skin around his eyes and reddened the whites, but his expression was anything but sorrowful. His eyes locked on to Cook's as he descended the oak staircase slowly and surely like he had traversed those steps a hundred thousand times, from a child to the angry, soulless man he was now. "Eh?" he said, to break the silence. "What if she meant to do it?"

"Gareth, darling—" his mother interjected but was silenced with a single raise of his hand.

He stepped over to Cook, folding his six-foot-two frame to meet the smaller detective that Devon had known for only a day face to face. "It was her. It was my sister."

"Why?" Cook asked a single fearless question that cut through the anger and emotion.

"Because the bitch knows how to hurt me," he hissed. "That's all she's got. She can't get to me any other way."

"I'm afraid that doesn't constitute a motive," Cook said, appearing genuinely perplexed enough to irritate the already seething Gareth Dickens.

"You want a motive? I'll give you a motive," he said. "Janice, my kid sister, thinks she's better than me. She thinks she's better than us all. She thinks that because she went to university. That somehow it should be her running the company. When in actual fact, she should be bloody grateful I still employ her. She thinks that if she gets to me enough, that I'll break down again, just like—"

"Gareth," Elizabeth said, trying to stop him, but again he raised that hand of his without looking her way.

"Like what, Gareth?" Cook said, his tone soft and unshaken.

"Just like when my wife died," Gareth continued this time adding a shake of his head as if to add weight to his statement. "But not this time. My boy is dead. My sweet, beautiful, little boy was killed this morning, down on Heighington High Street when he should have been here with me and his brother and his grandparents. He was down there with *her*. With Janice. Why? Because she knew it would rile me. Because in her deranged mind, by taking Harry from me, she could have one over on me. Me. Not the family. On me. Do you understand?"

Despite Cook's small frame and modest presence, he remained remarkably calm and unfazed, holding his chin high and his hands folded neatly before him.

"I understand," he said, which seemed to alleviate some of the rage building within Gareth.

"So why don't you get out there and bloody well find her?"

"That's precisely why we're here, Mr Dickens," Devon said, hoping to draw Gareth away from her boss.

"What?" he spat.

"I said, that's precisely why we're here," she repeated. "We have procedures to follow."

"Procedures?"

"Procedures that are built on experience, honed on actual investigations, and that have been designed to bring an investigation to a close. The first thing we had to do, before we'd even begun the investigation, was to obtain a positive identification of your son's body."

"And you did that," he replied, his voice cracking slightly.

"And the next thing we need to do is understand the whereabouts of family members and friends. In this instance, everybody was there except for Janice and her husband. We'll be checking her husband's story when we've found Janice, but to find her, we need to search every address she could have gone to, every building she has access to."

"So do it," he said, looking at his mother for the first time. "What's the problem?"

"There's no problem, Gareth," she said softly, then glanced up at Devon. "This way. There's a folder in my desk."

Thomas was wide-eyed beside the front door, and he gestured for them to follow his mother into the living room, where they found Susie and Jeffery huddled on one of the plush couches. Elizabeth strode over to an old-fashioned writers' bureau and slid the roll-top lid open.

She set the box down rummaged in a drawer for a moment, and then withdrew a yellow, padded envelope, which she opened and peered inside.

"The addresses are in here," she said. "The keys are with our property managers. Their details are inside."

"Mum outsources the property management," Thomas said, trying to be helpful. "She's always looked after them, even when Dad was still working."

"I see," Cook replied, as he examined the contents of the bag.

Devon took the opportunity to gaze around the room. The house was impeccably finished and extremely well-appointed. But it wasn't the Chesterfield couches that caught Devon's eye, nor was it the wall of ovens and appliances behind the kitchen island. What Devon noticed more than anything was beyond the floor-to-ceiling glazed panels: an old man who, only that morning, had appeared bullish and resolute, now hunched on a bench with his hands supporting the weight of his head.

"What's this?" Elizabeth said softly, looking at Jeffery and holding a piece of paper up for him to see.

"What is it, Mum?" he asked, leaving Susie on the couch and joining his mother by her desk. He took the stationery from her and read the scrawled handwriting.

"It's a resignation letter," he said, finally, dropping the note to his side. "A bloody resignation letter."

"From Janice?" Cook asked.

"Yes, from Janice," he said, as a teenager might squabble with his sibling. "Of course, it's from her."

"May I see it?"

"You don't need to see it," Jeffery replied. "It's company business."

"But still—"

"It's company business," he snapped with defiance in his eyes.

He folded the paper and tossed it back onto the desk before retreating to his position beside a shocked and silent Susie. "Well, no prizes for guessing if Janice really did bloody—"

"Jeffery," his mum shouted from where she stood beside the desk. Then her voice softened, and she opened another folded note written on the same stationery.

"What is it?" Cook asked.

"It's to me," she replied, gently, then wiped her eye, folded it and handed it to Charles. He read the neat writing, and felt the tone of Janice's voice, despite having never heard it.

"What does this mean?" he said to Elizabeth, handing the note to Devon.

"It means that she's gone," she replied, the softness gone from her voice and in its place, a bitter snarl. "It means she's sick and tired of this family. Of all of them." She pointed at Jeffery and the rest of them. "And who can blame her?"

"I blame her," Jeffery said. "It's not like she's the victim here, is it?"

She opened the gift and peered inside, and then froze, holding the open box in her hand.

"Jeffery?" Elizabeth said calmly, staring down at the box and wiping a tear from her eye.

"Sorry, Mum," he said, turning his head away. "It's just that we all know she did it—"

"Jeffery," she said again, louder this time, and with far more venom in her voice.

The room fell silent, and calmly, Cook stepped over to Elizabeth Dickens. He took the box from her, having to pry it from her clenched fingers, and then peered inside before looking up at Devon.

"What is it, guv?" she asked.

"We need uniforms," he said, looking down into the box again. "And get CSI down here. We need the whole bloody circus, Devon."

CHAPTER 20

"It's hers," Elizabeth said, her voice quivering with the shock of what she had seen. She was perched on a couch opposite Susie, her knees locked together, and arms wrapped around herself as she rocked back and forth. "That's her ring."

Placing the box down onto Elizabeth's desk, Cook leaned over to examine the contents. On a cushion of silk, presented like a rare, precious stone was a finger. A pinkie, judging by the size of it, with a blue-painted and polished nail at one end, an expensive-looking ring close to the white knuckle, and the grisly, bloodied tissue at the other end.

"We don't know that, Mum," Jeffery said. He dropped into the seat beside his mother and slid an arm across her shoulders. "It could be anyone's."

"I know it's hers. I gave her the ring for her birthday. It was her twenty-fifth."

Her voice trailed away as if she was recalling the time, but the distraction didn't last long before the cloud of grief cast its shadow, just as Devon re-entered the room pocketing her phone. She nodded to Charles, confirming that the necessary teams had been alerted and were en route.

"Our forensics team are on their way. They will analyse it," he said, keeping his voice low and steady to prevent inciting an outburst. "Until they can run some tests, we must keep an open mind."

"We'll need something of hers," Devon added. "A toothbrush or a hairbrush would suffice. Something with her DNA on to provide a benchmark."

"I can go up and get her toothbrush if you like," Susie asked, seeming keen for an excuse to get away and help somehow.

Jeffery gave her a nod, cradling his mother in his arms.

"But what does it mean?" Thomas asked. "I don't get it. If it is Janice's finger, then why?"

The question had been rolling around Charles's mind since the moment he had first laid eyes on the bloody digit, but hearing it being voiced gave him an idea. He dropped to a crouch and then fumbled for his reading glasses in his pocket, with which he began to read the printed newspaper articles that had been selected for the wrapping.

"This is today's paper," he said, and Devon crouched beside him. He pointed at one particular side on which the date was prominent.

"Local business owner donates one hundred thousand pounds to homeless," Devon read, her face now uncomfortably close to Charles's. With the end of her pen, she turned the box to read the next side, squinting at the small print. "OAP freezes to death in poverty."

"Something tells me these articles aren't a coincidence," Charles said to her, as she turned the box once more.

"Job losses forecast in factory cutbacks," she read. "Dickens and Sons an engineering firm based in Washingborough, North Kesteven, is set to increase local unemployment figures in a bid to reduce expenditure and increase profits for its shareholders. The privately owned company has been in business for more than a hundred years, beginning its existence as one of the largest farms in Lincolnshire, moving into engineering in the late nineteenth century, and even aiding the war effort from nineteen forty to nineteen forty-five. More than eight generations of Dickens have steered the family-owned giant on which many local residents rely for employment. A source close to the business stated that more cutbacks are planned for next year and that the survival of the Dickens dynasty is of far more importance to current CEO Gareth Dickens than the wellbeing of its employees."

Charles stood slowly, giving his knees a welcome break, and then turned to face the room. Thomas appeared perplexed, as did Jeffery and Susie. Elizabeth had buried her face in her hands, but at the doorway to the hall, Gareth appeared resolute.

"We get it all the time," he said flatly. "It's just jealousy. They don't understand business and they don't like seeing others succeed."

"Is it true?" Charles asked.

"The cutbacks?" Gareth said, shoving his hands into his jean pockets and walking into the room to gaze out at his father who hadn't moved from the bench. "Dickens and Sons is not a charity, Chief Inspector. Costs are rising – energy, materials, taxes. We have to find the money from somewhere."

"And who knows about the cutbacks?" Charles asked. "Was it public knowledge?"

"Only those in this room," he replied, his eyes never leaving his father. "And one other."

"Janice?" Devon asked, to which Gareth turned his head and gave a slight nod of confirmation.

"And did anybody oppose the decision?" Charles asked, and Gareth tore himself from the window to sit on the back of a couch, from where he could rest his hand on his mother's shoulder.

"This is a family business," he said. "We make decisions together."

"But those decisions ultimately lie with you," Charles said. "As the current CEO, you have the final word."

"I do," he replied. "Just as my father had to make difficult decisions before me, and his before that. Look, are you here to discuss the running of Dickens and Sons? Or are you here to find my sister for what she did to my—"

His voice broke, and he bit down on his knuckle to stem the emotion that had been so close to breaking free.

"That's just it, Gareth," Charles said, taking a few slow steps to compose his thoughts and construct a sentence that would articulate the turn of events in as efficient a manner as possible. "You see, I don't believe your sister had anything to do with your son's death, other than being a dedicated and loving aunt who took her nephew on a ride to the local shop to buy thank you cards for her mother and somebody else, in light of her resignation."

"What are you saying?" Gareth asked, his nose scrunching in disgust at the prospect of his sister being the innocent party."

"If I'm right, Gareth, somebody else knocked Harry down this morning," Charles said. "And if we don't act fast, then you can expect another delivery soon."

"What are you saying? Somebody has taken her hostage?" he said, almost laughing at the idea. "Janice, a hostage? Who the hell would want to do that? And why the bloody hell would they want to kill my little boy?"

"The Dickens family is both wealthy and disliked," Charles said. "So, as CEO, it is your job to understand exactly who might have learned of the cutbacks and who might have acted on them. Unless, of course, you want your dear sister to lose another finger."

"Who's your superior?" he asked. "I'm going to call them and make a complaint. This is absolutely diabolical."

"Chief Superintendent Collins," Charles said without hesitation. "You won't find him in today, but I'm happy to give you his number. I'll need to call this in to escalate it anyway."

"Escalate?" Thomas said, stepping into Charles's view. "To what?"

"Extortion, demanding money with menaces, and aggravated assault, to start with. If I'm right, and considering the perpetrator has gone to great lengths to make you all sit and listen, then Janice is being held somewhere. We can expect more communication to follow, presumably with their demands," Charles said. And before Gareth could interrupt, he added, "I have no idea what those demands might be, but given that the people in this room are the only individuals who know of the planned cutbacks at Dickens and Sons, then I am forced to presume that the instigator of this terrible incident is here."

"One of us?" Jeffery said, jumping to his feet and glaring at him.

"One of you," Charles confirmed. "I would suggest you all think very carefully about who you've been speaking to recently and what you might have said. I'll be conducting voluntary interviews with each of you in turn, starting with you, Susie."

"Me?" she said.

"Yes, you," he replied, then turned to Gareth. "I'd usually do this at the station, but given that we're expecting some sort of communication, I think it's best if we stay. I'll need somewhere private. Your father's study would suffice."

"You can't do this," Gareth said. "We don't have to talk to you."

"You're right, you don't. These will be voluntary interviews," Charles said. "But I'd think very carefully before you refuse. Because right now, your sister's life may be on the line, and so far the only plausible suspects I have, are you and your family, Mr Dickens. Specifically, you."

CHAPTER 21

"Are you sure this is the right thing to do?" Devon asked as she closed the study door behind her. Charles appraised the big, mahogany desk inlaid with green leather. A brass lamp stood in the centre, and before it, a polished, wooden stand to hold a rather decadent letter opener and magnifying glass set. To the right-hand side, a beautiful Mont Blanc fountain pen and ink bottle sat atop a mahogany plinth. One of the walls had been shelved to form a floor-to-ceiling bookshelf, and behind the leather captain's chair, a Hunter log burner was aglow within its brick fireplace.

It was the type of office Charles had always coveted. Being a single man, he had given up one of his four bedrooms as an office but had done very little to the decor save for hanging a cork pinboard, installing a cheap desk and chair, and putting the single bed that used to live in there up for sale. There was a TV, of course, and his father's old wireless, but he rarely used the room, preferring instead to vegetate on the couch downstairs, especially during the dark winter months when he would arrive home too late to put the central heating on. Having the central heating on a timer would be a pointless waste of money. Rarely did he ever arrive home at the same time for two nights running.

Guv?" Devon said, reminding him of her question.

"It is the only course of action we can take, Devon," he replied, as he lowered himself into the captain's chair. He fished in his inside pocket for a pen and then laid his notepad on the desk. "I need some paper. Can you find some, please?"

"Guv, we don't know what this is yet. Shouldn't we wait until–"

"Until another finger arrives at the doorstep?" he asked. "Or perhaps, some other part of Janice Dickens's anatomy?"

"We don't know what's going to happen."

"I do," he said, making his stance abundantly clear. "We have a young boy who was killed this morning in a hit-and-run incident. The father's sister is missing, and her car was seen speeding away from the scene of the crime. It stands to reason that, at first, we considered Janice Dickens as the prime suspect. But given the recent events, most notably the contents of that box, I'm positive this is something far bigger, and little Harry Dickens's death was an awful accident."

"Do you really think she's being held hostage, then?"

"Why else send a finger?" he replied. "A finger with a ring her mother gave her, at that."

"You mean, whoever did this must have known the origin of the ring?"

Charles sat back in the seat, laying his hands on the carved armrests. He watched as she perched a plump cheek on the corner of the desk.

"You're right," she said thoughtfully. "I hadn't thought of it."

"Gareth Dickens said it himself, only the people here and Janice knew about the cutbacks."

"Unless Janice told somebody else," Devon added.

"True. But it strikes me that the members of this family enjoy their isolation. They are united in their success," he told her.

"But we can't deal with a hostage, guv, can we?" she replied, and for the first time since he'd known the woman with intelligent eyes and as few friends as himself, he saw doubt in her expression. "We're not…"

"Not what, Devon?"

"Well…equipped, guv. It's just you and me."

She was a smart girl, and intuitive, and each time she had spoken out in front of the family, she had done so with professionalism. She had earned herself the right to an opinion, but on this occasion, Charles felt compelled to speak with a certain bluntness he usually saved for officers with far less experience.

"We can't do this alone," he agreed. "In fact, we can't do this at all. Without the chief superintendent's go-ahead, CPS would reject the evidence in fear of the defence claiming the correct protocols were not followed."

"So, why are we interviewing the family?" she asked, to which Charles said nothing, instead choosing to smile at her while he waited for those sharp cogs of her mind to click into place. "You're buying time."

His smile turned wry.

"You're buying time while a specialist team arrives," she said, studying his eyes for a clue that she was right.

He inhaled long and deep, and let it out through flared nostrils.

"Will you be seeing your family this Christmas, Devon?" he asked.

"My family?" she asked. "No. No, they're back home."

"In Sunderland?"

"Yes, guv," she said. "To be honest, I was looking forward to spending some time on my own. You?"

"Me?" he said. "Well, I haven't seen my daughters for over a decade."

"A decade?"

"I was supposed to meet my youngest at noon," he added.

"Vanessa. It was to be the first of what I had hoped to be the building of something new."

"But you had to deal with this instead," she said. "That's why you asked if I could handle it alone, wasn't it? Back at the station."

"Duty calls, Devon. Duty calls."

"Have you messaged her?"

"I called. But she didn't answer. I didn't expect her to really."

"Well..." Devon began, then said nothing. "A decade, you say?"

"More than," he said. "Listen, I've been in this game long enough to know that us walking away from here and hoping a team of specialists will turn up in my absence is only going to come back and bite me in the backside."

"So, you're going to give them a handover?" she asked.

"We are going to leave no stone unturned," he replied. "The CSI team is on its way. We'll set them to work on the box and the digit. That reminds me, did Susie give you the toothbrush?"

"And a hairbrush," Devon replied. "Bagged and tagged and in the car."

"Good. I'll make a call to Collins, and while we wait for the specialist team, we'll conduct the initial interviews. When they arrive, we'll hand over. Then you can go and–"

"Have some me time?" she said.

"And I can see if I can salvage something of my aloof family," he replied.

"It sounds like you've got it all worked out," she told him.

"I'm just trying to make the best of a bad situation," he said. "But I'm afraid I do have some work for you."

"Oh?"

"I want you to visit anywhere within a few miles of here that sells newspapers. If they have CCTV footage, then request it."

"A few miles?"

"She won't be far," he said. "This was planned. They wouldn't risk being on the road with her for too long. That should give you Metheringham, Branston, Heighington, and, of course—"

"Washingborough?"

"Almost certainly. And you might want to add Waddington to that list. Thankfully it's Boxing Day, so not many places will be open, but there'll be a few."

"Anything else?"

"When uniforms arrive, I want them to go door to door."

"That shouldn't take long," she replied. "We're in the middle of nowhere."

"Which makes it even more likely that somebody would have been noticed, doesn't it?" he said. "Somebody delivered that box during the time we were out at the hospital and while we were talking to Janice's husband. What is that, three hours? Sometime between noon and three p.m.?"

"Cameras," she said. "Doorbell cameras."

"Precisely. There's a dog boarding place down the road. See if they have cameras, too. Do you think you can manage all of that?"

"I can," she said. "But don't you want me in the interviews?"

He leaned forward on the desk and saw the hope for something more in the way she stared back at him. She could handle the tasks he had set her with her eyes closed.

"Lincoln HQ can't deal with a hostage situation," he said.

"Nearest one would be Nottingham, guv."

"That's an hour away."

"More, by the time they've scrambled."

"What do you think, thirty minutes per interview?"

"Fifteen, if we ask the right questions."

"Would you like to sit in on the interviews, Devon?"

"Think of it as my Christmas present," she said. "Although, you don't really know me, so..."

"And the CCTV?"

"I can do that in my own time," she said. "When you're—"

"Salvaging my family?"

She took a few sheets of paper from the printer on one of the bookshelves and slid it in front of him.

"I need to call Collins," he said.

"I'll rally the troops then," she replied, moving over to the door. But she stopped and turned her back to it, placing her hands flat against the wood. "Do they really not like you, guv? The other officers, I mean."

"I don't know if they like me or not. Being liked has never really bothered me. But if you asked me to count the number of police officers I actually admire, right now," he said. "You could use the finger in that box."

"One?"

"One," he said. "You." She smiled at the comment and seemed to question its sincerity with a scrutinous gaze. He held his phone up for her to see. "Give me five minutes to talk to Collins," he said. "Then we can start."

Her expression returned to its resting state, biting down on her lip, narrowed eyes, and a persistent frown that gave her an angry disposition. She pushed down on the door handle and then turned away, stopping once more, as Charles was searching for Collins' number.

"Guv?"

He looked up from his phone, peering over the top of his glasses.

"Devon?"

"I just..." she began, then stopped and sighed. "Thanks, guv. This means a lot."

CHAPTER 22

"Before we begin, Susie, I should explain that this is a voluntary interview. And as you can tell, it's rather impromptu. But what we hope to gain is some insights into the family. Quarrels between siblings, recent arguments, and, of course, your own movements."

"My movements?" she said and seemed rather nervous.

"There's nothing to worry about," Devon assured her. "Now, shall we begin with your full name?"

"My name?" she said, her breath heavy and fast. "Oh, it's Susie Fraser."

"Middle name?" Charles said.

"Francesca," she replied. "Susie Francesca Fraser."

"And is Susie your real name, or is it Susan?"

"Oh, yes. It's Susan. Sorry, I'm just a bit nervous."

Charles made a note of the name at the top of a clean sheet of paper, then drew a horizontal line across the middle, marking the centre of the line with an X, besides which he wrote *RTA*.

"RTA?" Susie said, peering across the desk at his notes.

"Road Traffic Accident," Devon said.

"Harry?"

Devon nodded, and Charles, keen to press on, explained what he was doing.

"This is a timeline, Susie," he said, marking the left end of the line with another X. "This is the Christmas Eve and this..." He marked the right end of the line with a final X. "Is now. Boxing Day. Four p.m."

"And you want me to fill in the bits in between?" she asked.

"I do. If you made phone calls, then I want to know about them. If you went somewhere, then I want to know. Or anybody else for that matter."

"It'll help us build a picture of everybody's movements," Devon explained, to which Susie nodded.

"I understand. We got here on Christmas Eve."

"We?" Charles said.

"Jeff and me. He picked me up in the morning. Around eleven o'clock, I think it was."

"So you don't live with him?"

"No, not yet. We've only been together for six months. We've spoken about me moving in with him. He has, anyway. But I wanted to keep my independence. For a while, at least. I'm glad I did now."

Charles laid his pen down and interlinked his fingers.

"Is there something you'd like to share, Susie?" he asked, which seemed to unsettle her further and she shook her head. "I don't wish to pry, you understand, but it's imperative I understand the nature of the relationships within the family. Who gets on with who, who has a grudge to bear–"

"A grudge?"

"They may seem like minor details, to you, but I can assure you, somebody in this family is involved in this whole sordid affair and I intend on finding out who that is, and bringing Janice home safely."

She listened well, maintaining eye contact with him as he

spoke, and then finally she made it clear she understood and prepared to speak the truth.

"I'm going to call it off. With Jeff, I mean," she said, and Charles remained still, saying nothing in the hope that she would fill the audible void with some kind of narrative. "I've seen a side of this family. I mean, I don't think I want to be a part of it."

"And when did you come to this decision?" Charles said.

"This morning. After you'd been," she said. "Jeff's dad called a meeting in here."

"Oh? And what was discussed?"

She paused, then averted her eyes.

"I don't know. I wasn't invited. It was just him and his sons."

"I see," Charles said. "So you did what in the meantime? While you waited, I mean."

"What did I do?" she said, then stared hard at the pen on the stand, down and to the left. "I just waited in the living room."

"On your own?"

She nodded.

"In a strange house?" Charles said. "You didn't snoop around? Or make any calls?"

"No. I just sat on the couch. The peace and quiet was nice. I'm not really used to a full house. I prefer my own company. Well, that's what I'm used to anyway."

"I know what you mean," Devon said, raising a brief smile on Susie's face that faded as fast as it had come. "I'm not really much of a people person myself."

"There just seems to be too much ill feeling for my liking," Susie said, then lowered her voice in case somebody was listening. "I mean, I know all families have arguments and whatnot, but you should have seen it on Christmas Day. As soon as Janice got here, it was like…"

"Like what?" Charles said, prompting her.

"Electric," she said. "The air. The tension. I don't know. I can't explain it."

"Between her and Gareth, or somebody else?"

"No, Gareth didn't arrive until just before dinner. He'd been at the office," she replied. "No, it was her and Jeff. He's just as bad as Gareth."

"Not Thomas?"

"No," she said thoughtfully. "No, he seems all right, does Thomas. If anything, he was on Janice's side."

"So there are sides?"

"Not really. But he didn't attack her. Not like Jeff and Gareth do."

"And when Gareth arrived?"

Susie rolled her eyes and shook her head.

"Put it this way, the pecking order is clear in this family. There's no mistaking that, that's for sure."

"Abbott at the top?" Charles said, to which she nodded.

"Then Gareth, then Elizabeth. Jeff and the others fight over the scraps," she said. "And those are Janice's words, not mine."

"Interesting," Charles said. "So, is it fair to summarise, Susie, that Gareth and Janice have some underlying argument, or friction as it were?"

"I would say that's a fair judgement," she replied.

"And just to be clear, you haven't made any calls or been in contact with anyone since you arrived?"

"Oh, I called my mum on Christmas Day, of course. And I messaged a few old friends. I can show you if you want. When Jeff and Thomas left, I was on social media. You know, catching up, the usual Christmas messages."

"Jeff and Thomas went out?" Charles said. "Where?"

"To the office, I think. They were only gone for an hour or so."

"What time was this?"

"Shortly after the meeting," she said. "Gareth went to meet you–"

"To see Harry?"

She nodded again.

"They left at around the same time. They were back before him, though. I can check what time it was if you like."

She pulled her phone from her pocket but Charles held up his hand.

"I'm sure we've got enough," he said. "For the time being, at least. How long will you be staying here?"

She shrugged.

"I suppose that all depends on when I can talk to Jeffery. It's not going to be an easy chat to have, given the circumstances. But I think I need to talk to him sooner rather than later. It's not right to be here when all this is going on."

"I agree," he said, as he completed his timeline and put the lid back on his pen. "Although I have to say, I don't envy you, the truthful path is often longer and fraught with danger, but the destination offers far more freedom and peace of mind."

"Is that some sort of saying that I should have heard before?" Susie asked.

"No, I just made it up. But I can assure you it is based on a lifetime of talking to people and being lied to," he told her, to which she again averted her eyes. "If you could ensure you pass on your details to DC Devon. I wouldn't want to detain you any longer than absolutely necessary."

"So I can go?"

"Like I said," he replied, "I wouldn't want to detain you. Why don't you go and see your family? See if you can salvage some sort of happier Christmas."

The comment clearly pleased her, tickled her even, although something weighed heavy on her mind.

"Thank you," she said, as she stood from the chair and made her way over to the door. "This is confidential, isn't it?"

"Of course," he said. "You've given us a lot to think about, Susie. Thank you for your time."

She left the room, quietly closing the door behind her, and leaving Charles alone with Devon.

"Well, that's the easy one out of the way," Devon said. "Who do you want next?"

Charles watched her, feeling a pang of disappointment at her lack of intuition. Unless of course, she had seen the signs as he had but was choosing not to voice them until she had more to go on.

"Thomas," he said. "Let's give her a chance to have that chat. You never know, by the time we speak to Jeffery he might be suitably riled up to let a few truths slip."

"You're devious," she told him, as she made her way to the door, grinning to herself. "What time did Collins say the team would be here to take over?"

"He's going to make some calls," Charles said. "He'll let us know."

"Well, let's hope they hurry up," she said. "It's dark outside already."

He was about to reply when the door burst open. Thomas stood there in the doorway, breathless and wide-eyed.

"Mum's had a phone call," he said. "It's them."

CHAPTER 23

They found the family huddled around Elizabeth, except for the two family leaders, Gareth, who was pacing up and down the kitchen, and Abbott who must have been back inside at some point to collect a jacket but had returned to the garden, despite the bitter chill carried by the incessant breeze, and the dark. Somebody had thought to switch on the garden lights, illuminating the surrounding gardens and casting him into a statue-still silhouette. Susie was there, although she was keeping her distance, playing the role of supporting girlfriend for the time being.

Jeffery, oblivious to the planned break up, had his arm around his mother, placing him, in Charles's mind, in the position of the doting son. Although stereotypes rarely helped to fight any cause, they did offer an insight into the family dynamics.

Abbott, the grandfather, the wise, old man who had handed the reins over to his eldest son, Gareth, without due guidance on leadership. The two seemed wildly different. The old man who mulled on his thoughts before making a decision and the hot-headed son who so thrived on cracking the company whip that he continued to wield it in his private time.

Jeffery, the second eldest son, dwelled in Gareth's shadow but displayed more empathy than any of the siblings combined. Perhaps he would have been a more likely candidate as CEO and head of the household.

Thomas, from what Charles had seen so far, was altogether different. Perhaps he inherited more of his mother's traits than his father's. He was softly spoken, his voice lighter in tone. But he had an edge. He wasn't afraid to speak out, just like his mother.

His mother. Their mother. The matriarch who held each of those men together held them up, and could very probably destroy each and every one of them with a single lick of her sharp tongue.

"Well?" she said, from her seat on the couch. "Aren't you going to say something?"

"Guv?" Devon said. "You okay?"

"What? Yes, of course. Why?"

He checked his watch, realising he had been staring, and then regained his bearings.

"Man or woman?" he said finally, which did little but confuse the family before him.

"What?" Gareth said, striding over from the kitchen end of the open-plan room. "We just had the bastards on the phone, and after staring into thin air for five minutes, you asked us if it was a man or a woman. Are you out of your depth here, Inspector?"

"Was it a man or a woman?" he said again, as the sickly aroma of Gareth's Scotch-laden breath warmed his face.

Gareth searched his family's faces for some support but found only shock and fear in their eyes.

"Mum?" he said. "You answered the phone."

"A man," she replied.

"Accent?" Charles asked.

"Local."

"Tone?"

"I beg your pardon?"

"Tone," Charles said. "Was it deep like Gareth's or light like Thomas's?"

"Um, somewhere in between, I suppose. It was hard to hear them. There was music playing."

"Music? Was it something you recognised?" Charles asked, and Elizabeth shook her head.

"No. It was that modern music. The type with all the drums and no melody. No singing, either."

"Any ideas?" Charles said, turning to Devon for help. "I'm not really up on modern music."

"Dance music?" Devon asked. "Was that what it was?"

All eyes fell on Elizabeth, who seemed not to know the name of the song until Susie had the idea of playing the type of music on her phone.

"If that's what it's called, then yes," Elizabeth said. "It was repetitive. The same beat over and over."

"You're sure?" Charles replied. "It was definitely dance music?"

"What the bloody hell difference does it make what music was played?" Gareth said, and Susie cut the song off. "My son has been killed. My sister's finger has been sent in a bloody cardboard box, and my mum has just received a call from the man who did all of this. Why aren't you out there bloody well finding him? You've been here all day, and so far, all you've managed to do is piss me off. I'm supposed to be grieving. I'm supposed to be caring for my other son, not down here with this, you moron."

"I haven't been here all day," Charles said, keeping his voice calm and quiet, a tactic to ensure silence while he spoke. "And neither have you. You visited the hospital this afternoon with us. While your brothers paid a visit to your offices."

Gareth glared at his brothers, and then at Susie, who didn't offer any argument and turned away to stare out of the window at Abbott.

"You haven't even asked what they said," Gareth said, this time keeping his voice to a hushed hiss. "There was a threat in there somewhere, or an accusation. Neither mattered. Neither had any substance.

"I know what they said," Charles replied, surprising even Devon, who, to her credit, remained by his side and kept quiet during such a tense moment.

"What?" Gareth said. "How on earth—"

"They didn't ask any questions. They didn't give your mother time to talk. They just spoke. The music was a distraction to capture her attention and possibly to disguise the voice. They wanted your attention, that's all."

"And they have it," Thomas said, from where he stood over near the raging log burner.

"Good. And so they should."

"All right then, Mystic Meg, what did they say?" Gareth said. In the space of a few short minutes, the man had traversed the realms of frustration, anger, humour and disbelief, and now he had resorted to using sarcasm and insults to claim his position as the head of the house. "Eh? What did they say to her?"

Charles stared at Elizabeth until she eventually looked up at him with eyes sore from a day filled with equal measures of grief and fear.

"They told you they would be in touch, didn't they?" Charles said. "That's all they said. Something like, don't call the police, don't talk to anybody, and nobody leaves the house."

Elizabeth said nothing, gently but gratefully extracting herself from her son's embrace. She stood, straightened her dress, and then stepped over to Thomas, squeezing his hand for a moment. And then finally, she moved over to Gareth.

"He's right," she said, studying Charles's eyes. She pulled a tissue from her sleeve to wipe her eyes and then returned it. "Don't talk, just listen. No police. No outside help. Wait for me to call again."

"Wait for *me*?" Charles said. "They used the word *me*, did they?"

"They did," Elizabeth said.

"Do you think it's one bloke?" Thomas asked.

"No," Charles replied. "No, it's more than one."

"So why is that important?"

"Because it means you were talking to the man in charge."

Gareth gave a laugh. Not a belly rolling laugh, or even a laugh from any humour whatsoever. It was a scornful laugh. The type that might escape from extreme fear or extreme terror.

"It's okay to be scared, Gareth," Charles said.

"What?"

"I said, it's okay—"

"I heard what you said," he replied, then inhaled to expand his chest, smoothing the creases in his shirt. "Do you think we're scared? Is that what you think?"

"I would hope you are scared," Charles said, not breaking eye contact with the mother, who bore more wisdom than all of her offspring combined. "If you're not, then you damn well better be."

Eventually and reluctantly, he stared at Gareth to accentuate his point.

The doorbell broke the moment and Devon made a beeline for the hallway, raising her hand to stop anybody else from joining her.

"We've arranged for a team of uniformed officers to go door to door," Charles began. "They'll be asking your neighbours if they saw anybody near this house today, or even heading in this direction. They'll also be looking for doorbell cameras and CCTV. Speaking of which, are there any cameras on the property?"

"None that work," Jeffery said. "They're decoys."

"Do you think whoever did this would be stupid enough to get caught on camera?" Gareth asked.

"I've also arranged for a CSI unit to collect the box," Charles continued, purposefully ignoring Gareth's question. "And finally, a specialist hostage negotiation team will be here soon."

"A what?"

"A specialist team trained in negotiations. They'll guide you through the process."

"And you can't do that?" Gareth said. "You can't talk to this man and see what he wants?"

"Oh, I know what he wants," Charles said, as Devon re-entered the room with a large evidence bag. She snapped on a pair of gloves and began bagging the box, and a breath of cool air rushed in from the hallway. Devon was just a distraction. The family still had questions that needed answering. One in particular.

"Which is?" Gareth asked. "What does he want? Money?"

"Have some respect, Gareth," a deep, gravelly voice said from one of the rear doors, and Charles found Abbott standing there, emerging from his period of grief to lead the family through whatever came next. "He's here to help, not to be insulted. Have some manners."

He closed the back door and stood before the fireplace, warming his hands.

"What is it they want, Inspector?" he asked. "Why are they doing this? It's more than money, isn't it?"

"I'm afraid so, Mr Dickens," Charles replied. "They want to see the Dickens family destroyed."

"And what course of action do you recommend?" he asked, without turning from the fireplace.

"That all depends," Charles said. "How much are you prepared to lose in order to save Janice's life?"

CHAPTER 24

"Violet," John said, as he tossed his napkin onto the table. His plate had been wiped clean, a smear of rich gravy the only indication it had been used at all. "That was astonishing. I don't know what you did to those potatoes, but I know people who would pay good money for them."

"Ah, it's a family secret, I'm afraid," she replied, politely dabbing the corners of her mouth with her napkin, which she then folded and lay neatly down on the table. "One that will go with me to my grave."

"I thought we *were* family," John said.

"We are, and if truth be told, I've been handing down my culinary skills to Penny her entire life. If she chooses not to use them, well, then that's her prerogative."

"I do use them," Penny said. "I made them exactly the same way yesterday, Mum. He's just buttering you up."

"Well, it'll take more than a nice comment about my roasties to get on my good side, John."

"What if I said I'd do the washing up?" John asked, which made the kids' faces light up at the prospect of getting out of their usual duty.

"That would help," Violet said with a smirk. "But I have to say, if I'd known you were going to be volunteering I wouldn't have gone so easy on the pots and pans. I've done most of it already, to help out the kids."

"Well, consider it my contribution to dinner," he said. "Now, who's for ice cream?"

"Me, me, me," Emily said, shooting her hand in the air.

"Can I have some?" James added.

"Magic word?" John said, cupping his ear with his hand.

"Pleeease," they both said together.

John stood and piled the plates, scraping any leftovers onto the top plate along with the cutlery.

"There's a jam roly-poly in the fridge, too," Violet said, and before he ran the hot water, John turned to face his extended family.

"A jam roly-poly?" he said, hoping to drum up even more enthusiasm from the kids. "Jam roly-poly and ice cream?"

"It needs heating through," Violet said.

"Well," John replied. "It's like all my Christmases came at once."

He slid the roly-poly into the oven and set the timer for ten minutes, and just as he set to work cleaning the dinner plates, a familiar scent tickled his senses.

"You're in a good mood," Penny said, quietly, so that only he could hear. "Not that I'm complaining."

"Am I? It is Christmas. I thought that was the idea."

He squirted a heavy dollop of washing-up liquid into the bowl then gave the water a good rummage to get the bubbles going.

"It is, but you weren't exactly full of Christmas spirit this morning before you went out. What happened? Where did you go?"

"I went to the office, darling," he said. "Just like I told you. What's the matter? Can't I be happy?"

She grabbed a tea towel and took the first plate from him.

"Sorry," she said. "I was just a little worried about you, that's all." She glanced over her shoulder at her parents doting on their children. "It's not easy, you know? It's okay to be upset about what you saw."

"I'm not upset," he replied. "I was, but now I've had time to think. Time to appreciate what I have. What we have." He pointed through the window into the night outside. "Somewhere out there, a family is dealing with the loss of their child. If that was us, if we were in that position, would we want others to mourn? Would we want their pity?"

"Of course not," she said.

"And so, while that poor family is prominent in my thoughts, my own family stand before them, and I'll say it again, dear. We need to make memories, and that's what I intend to do."

"Memories?" she said, almost mocking him, but not really.

He placed another plate onto the draining board and then leaned in close to her.

"How can Emily and James ever enjoy a jam roly-poly again without thinking of today," he said, to which she smiled. "The little memories are as important as the big ones."

"Like Disney World?

"Like Disney World," he said, adding a wink for good measure.

"Well, this certainly has been a Christmas I won't forget," she said and gave him a quick peck on the cheek. She bent down and opened the cupboard. "Now then, should I see about some pudding bowls? I think you and I might have to wait until the kids are done. We only have four."

"Oh, don't worry about me," he told her. "I need to pop out, anyway."

"You what?"

He tipped the water away and rinsed the dishcloth, hanging it on the tap, as Penny often did.

"I need to pop out," he said. "Don't worry. I won't be long."

"Where do you need to go? It's Boxing Day, John. We're

supposed to be spending time together. Making memories, you said."

"And we will," he said. "I just have a few things to take care of. Work stuff, you know?"

"But, John—"

"I'll be an hour," he said, holding her by both shoulders. "And when I come home, we can play games. How does that sound?"

She seemed disappointed, and if John was honest with himself, he completely understood why. But there was little he could do about it, not now.

"Don't make a scene," he said. "I'll slip out and be back before anybody has realised."

He leaned down and kissed her forehead.

"An hour?" she said. "You promise?"

"I promise," he said. "And then we'll make some more memories. Good ones."

He gave her another kiss, then wiped his hands and left the room to pull on his coat as fast as he could. It was only when he reached for the front door that she spoke again, loitering in the doorway with the kitchen and the family fracas behind her.

"John?" she said.

"What's up?"

"You're not in any trouble, are you?" she asked. "You'd tell me if you were, wouldn't you?"

His shoulders sagged under the weight of her worry and he stepped over to her, grabbing her by both arms.

"I'm not in any trouble," he said. "I told you that from now on things will be different. And they will. I promise they will. But I have to make that happen. I have to make our dreams come true, and I'm happy to shoulder the burden, but I do need some free rein to do it."

"Some free rein?"

"Some freedom," he said. "Some trust."

"I do trust you," she replied softly. "I really do. I just worry—"

"There's nothing to worry about," he told her. "Now go back inside and enjoy Christmas with your family." She seemed unconvinced but eventually relented, and let her hand slip from the doorframe.

"If you're sure that you're not in any trouble," she said. "I just feel like you're missing out for our sakes."

"I'm not in any trouble," he said again. "Besides, I was never really one for jam roly-poly. I'm more of a sticky toffee pudding type of guy."

He winked, then left her standing there, stepping out into the cold night where his breath formed a cloud and the cold wind found the layer of sweat on his back the way vultures find the carcass of some poor beast in the desert.

It would be a long while before he could leave the house without fabricating some kind of truth. He walked the little alleyway to the side of his house and peered in through the kitchen window. Penny had taken her seat and Violet was dishing out the pudding, but the two kids weren't as joyous as they should have been.

He pulled his phone from his pocket, dialled a number from memory, and then put the phone to his ear, all the time watching his family, dreaming of the days that jam roly-poly would be a regular occurrence, and they'd have more pudding bowls than they would ever need.

"I'm out," he said when the call was answered. "I'll meet you there?"

CHAPTER 25

"Are you trying to tell me that nobody is coming?" Charles said as Devon re-entered Abbott Dickens's study. She took the seat she had sat in during the interview with Susie and made her entries in her notepad regarding the uniformed officers and CSI, whom she had set to work as per Cook's instructions. "I've got bloody CSI analysing a finger, half a dozen uniformed officers going door to door, and a DC who, as competent as she might be, has her bloody work cut out, sir."

He listened for a moment, gesturing needlessly to Devon that he was talking to Collins. She acknowledged the gesture with raised eyebrows and a cocked head, demonstrating that she was interested and that she understood from what she had heard that things weren't going to plan.

"No, sir," he said. "Listen, I've done everything that has been asked of me. I've taken the investigation to a point where a team can come in and take over. It's not like we're washing our hands of it." He listened for a while, his eyes closed in disbelief at what he was hearing, and although Devon couldn't hear the other half of the conversation, she had a pretty good idea of the outcome. "Sir, we don't have the experience."

Another pause, during which Cook began pacing the room to the fireplace and back.

"That was a decade ago, for..." he said, then stopped himself. "Sorry, sir. I just feel that this family need a bit more support than that. In the space of a day, they've lost a little boy in a hit and run, and pretty soon they're going to start getting demands from the hostage takers."

Pause.

"Yes, sir."

Pause.

"No, sir."

Pause.

"It's no longer just a manslaughter case, guv," he said, then lowered his voice in case the family could hear. "They cut her bloody finger off."

Pause.

"I don't know. It'll take a day or so for them to analyse it, but the mother seems to think she bought the ring that was on it for her daughter's twenty-fifth birthday."

He stopped pacing and held the phone away from his ear like a teenager bored of hearing his mother berate him over the phone. Eventually, he put the phone back to his ear.

"So that's it then, is it? We're on our own?" he said, then listened for a moment, shaking his head at whatever Collins was saying to him. "Well, under ordinary circumstances, sir, I'd be thanking you for the opportunity, but as it stands, I'd like to put it on record that I think this is a big mistake."

As Devon's planned 'me time' retreated to some unforeseeable time in the future, she dragged the pile of A4 paper she had given to Charles across the desk and began preparing Thomas's interview, cresting a similar timeline to the one Cook had drawn. Typically that sort of thing would have been done on a whiteboard in an incident room, but given that whoever was holding Janice Dickens captive could call at any time, it made sense to stay on the scene.

"Yes, sir. You have a nice Christmas, too." Cook said, then ended the call and tossed his phone onto the desk. It was the first time she had seen him get worked up. Even when Gareth Dickens had been in his face, he had remained unnaturally calm. "I suppose you got the gist of all that?"

"I did, guv," she replied with a heavy sigh.

He collected his phone and slid it into his pocket.

"Sorry, Devon," he said.

"Oh, don't worry about me, guv. I can have some me time anytime."

"I meant that I'm sorry for you witnessing that. It was unprofessional, to say the least."

"Oh, was it?" she said, then sat back in her chair. "Listen, if we're going to work together on this, then we can't pretend to be different people. I'd like to know I'm dealing with the real Detective Chief Inspector Cook and not some imposter who is trying to make a good impression."

"I'm not trying to make a good impression, Devon," he told her. "And I don't often behave in such a manner, but it just gets my back up when somebody up above doesn't get their finger out of their backside. It's like they can't remember what it's like to be on the ground." He sighed and turned away abruptly. "Apologies. I shouldn't whine. It's been a long day."

"And it doesn't seem as though it's going to end anytime soon," Devon said. "Which means you're not going to get to Cambridge tonight."

"And your alone time is dwindling," he countered.

"My alone time doesn't have a decade of lost time to make up," she said. "You should call her."

"She won't answer," he said. "She messaged me to meet her at eight p.m., followed by a curt *don't let me down*."

Devon checked her watch.

"It's getting on for six p.m.," she said. "You could still make it."

"And what, leave the family like this?"

"Maybe I could—"

"Negotiate with a kidnapper? Advise the family on what to do?" he said. "I don't wish to put you down or cast aspersions, Devon. Lord knows you've proved you're more than capable of your duties today, and I don't give praise like that very often, I can assure you. But we need to face facts. What is required tonight is beyond your duties. It's beyond mine, but..." He paused and feigned inspection of the timeline she had prepared for Thomas Dickens. "That's very diligent of you."

"But what, guv?"

"No buts," he said. "It's good. You can prepare the rest of the interviews if you wish."

"I wasn't referring to the timeline, guv. You were talking about what we have to do being beyond our duties. You stopped mid-sentence."

One half of his mouth curled up, but it wasn't a smile by any means. If his glazed eyes were anything to go by it was quite the opposite of a smile.

"Guv?"

"Shall we see about getting Thomas in here?" he said, blinking his eyes clear and clearing his throat. "It's getting on, and I imagine their resistance to our efforts will grow with every passing hour."

"Are we really going to see them all tonight?

"No. No, I very much doubt it. But we should stay at least until the door-to-door is complete. I'd like to have as many facts as I can to mull over during my long, sleepless night."

"Sleepless night, guv?" she said. "Do you struggle?"

"Not always," he replied. "God, listen to me. My own doctor doesn't even know about that. You must think me very self-indulgent, Devon."

"Not really," she said. "I don't think experiencing difficulty sleeping is unique to you. Half the station probably suffers from it."

"Well, I don't as a rule. Only during these complex investigations," he said. "And usually only at this stage, when the facts are coming in thick and fast and none of them seem to fit together. I often liken it to tipping the contents of half a dozen jigsaw puzzles onto a table. Eighty per cent of what we learn is of no relevance whatsoever. The difficulty lies in identifying the other twenty per cent."

She grinned at the analogy and clicked her pen open and closed a few times in thought.

"Do you think we have any of the twenty per cent yet?"

"I do," he replied, but then seemed to have a thought. "What about you? Of everything we know so far, what do you think offers us a path forward?"

"Which do I think belongs in the twenty per cent pile? That's a difficult one, guv," she said. "But I'll say this. I think Janice left here this morning to visit the newspaper shop. Harry Dickens was wearing slippers, which suggests he hadn't been awake for long. Perhaps he was awake before anybody else? Perhaps he asked to go with his aunt for a little trip out. Kids love doing that, don't they?"

"They do," he replied. "Mine did, anyway."

"If snatching Janice Dickens was planned, then I'm sure they hadn't planned for her to be with her nephew. But if that's the case, then how did they know she would be there?"

"Maybe they followed her?"

"But then how would they know she would go to the shop?"

"And therein lies my conundrum," Cook said. "We need to know if anybody knew that she would be going."

"Okay, okay," Devon said, shoving herself from the chair. She paced three steps towards the fireplace, then turned, her idea becoming clearer with every step. "So, she leaves here taking Harry with her. She's not properly dressed, so she throws on a pair of old trainers or something, leaving her boots by the door. She loads the car with the cards she bought and is about to return to get Harry when she's jumped. They drag her off."

"The van," Cook said. "The witness. What was his name?"

"John Gregory," Devon said.

"That's it. He said he heard a loud diesel engine roaring off. Then when he rounded the corner, he saw the Audi speeding off."

"So there are two people," she said. "One driving the van with Janice in the back and one taking her car, presumably to stash it somewhere."

"The one who took the car reversed out of the parking spot just as Harry left the shop," Cook said. "So either somebody knew she was going to be at the shop, or they followed her."

Devon nodded her agreement.

"How about we get Thomas in?" he said. "I'll message my daughter while you're doing that."

"Guv, are you sure—"

"There are certain things we can control in this life, Devon," he said. "The trick is to understand which they are."

"Perhaps you could arrange to see her when all this is over?" Devon suggested.

"Perhaps," he replied, a hint of sadness in his tone. He gestured for her to go, and then sat down in the leather chair heavily.

"Guv?" she said from the doorway.

"Your concern is endearing, Devon. But, I've made my decision," he said. "My daughter is safe. Janice Dickens is not. And right now, which of the two would be most happy to see me?"

CHAPTER 26

"Right then," Charles said, snapping the lid off of his pen. "Thomas Dickens. Middle name?"

"Abbott," he replied. "We all have the same middle name."

"Except Janice, I presume," Charles said.

"She got Mum's name," Thomas told him.

"Janice Elizabeth Dickens," Charles said, noting Thomas's full name down. "Have you ever been in trouble, Thomas?"

"Me? No. Managed to keep my nose clean, I did."

"Glad to hear it," Charles said and then took a breath. "Okay, so first things first, I just need to know where you've been from Christmas Eve until now. I'm sure you understand. You've probably seen it on the TV or something."

"I get it," Thomas said.

"Good. Well, it's all quite rudimentary stuff, really," Charles explained. "After that, we'll need to get into the nitty-gritty."

"Such as?" Thomas asked.

"Well, like I said, perhaps we can get to that afterwards?" Charles said. "Now then. Christmas Eve."

"I was here," Thomas said, and then he saw the questioning look Charles offered. "I arrived the night before. Mum wanted some help with getting everything ready. You know? She wanted to make a good impression on Susie. Wanted to show her what she's getting into, I suppose."

"Because it was the first time your mother was going to meet Susie?" Charles said.

"Right," Thomas said.

"And since then? Since you arrived here? Have you spoken to anybody outside of the family, called anybody, or..."

"Nobody," Thomas said, pleased with himself.

"You don't have a significant other?"

"You might say that I'm between significant others," he replied. "Having a break from them, if you know what I mean?"

Charles laughed a little, more to make a connection with the young man than anything else.

"I do, as it happens."

Thomas took the bait and his head cocked to one side.

"How long for you?" he asked, to which Charles glanced at a little tabletop calendar on the bookshelf to his left. A picture frame had been positioned beside it, featuring the entire Dickens family, including a woman who Charles presumed was Gareth's wife.

"You first," Charles said.

"A few months," Thomas said. "But it was nothing serious. It wasn't going anywhere."

He sat back, then waited with raised eyebrows for Charles to reciprocate.

"More than a decade," Charles said and watched Thomas develop an expression of both awe and pity. "And it was serious. And it was going somewhere."

"You win," Thomas said, after a few moments of contemplation. "I can't beat that." He turned his head to face Devon, who suddenly appeared uncomfortable. "Are you playing, Devon?"

"No," she said. "No, I'm not in the habit of discussing my private life with..."

"With?"

She hesitated but was bold enough not to break his gaze.

"With families that we're trying to help," she said, and Thomas smiled the smile of a man who was used to having his own way with women as if she was some kind of project or plaything for him.

"You went to the office today. With Jeffery. Why was that?" Charles asked.

"Because that's what we do, isn't it? We work. We provide employment. We serve our customers."

"But Boxing Day?"

Thomas was as laid back as they came. He had an answer for everything, and a confidence that, judging by the little glances in Devon's direction, rarely failed.

"In the words of Gareth, my father, and his father before him," Thomas said, "the business is a ship laden with history. It needs a captain, a helmsman, and a reliable crew. No more. No less."

"But it can never stop," Devon said. "Because it will never get going again."

Thomas sat up in his seat and turned to face her, clearly impressed.

"You've heard the analogy before?"

"No. But it was obvious where you were going," she told him, giving him every signal that his attempts to win her over were failing, but not so cold that she had broken any connection that Charles had built. "Plus, my grandad worked on the docks. That maritime stuff kind of comes naturally to me."

"So maybe I need to work on my analogies," Thomas replied.

"But why specifically today, Thomas?" Charles said. "What could have possibly needed your attention today?"

"Nothing really," he replied. "Only that if we hadn't gone in, then Gareth would have." He looked across at Devon again. "Somebody has to steer the ship."

"Tell me about the others," Charles said, to draw him away from Devon, and he pointed at the photo beside the calendar. "When did they arrive?"

Thomas puffed his cheeks and exhaled, making a show of recalling the individual arrivals.

"Jeff and Susie came late morning on Christmas Eve. Janice arrived on Christmas Day. She doesn't like to spend too long here."

"And Gareth?"

"Just before dinner on Christmas Day. He had a few things to do at the office."

"On Christmas Day?" Devon said.

"Production doesn't stop. We're already behind thanks to the cutbacks," Thomas said. "Gareth seems to think the employees are grateful for the overtime. It's like he's done them a favour."

"And has he?"

Thomas looked him in the eye, unafraid. Nothing to hide.

"Gareth doesn't do favours. Never has done. He might convince you an idea is a favour, for the wider benefit, but you can bet your backside he'll gain from it somehow."

"You don't seem to have a lot of faith in your brother. How long has he been CEO of Dickens And Sons?"

"Oh, I have every faith in him. But Dickens and Sons is a dying cow. I have every faith he'll milk that cow until it falls down dead."

"But he won't be sharing the milk with the poor sods working on Christmas Day?"

"You're getting the picture," Thomas said. "He'll share the milk. Just not the cream. He's my brother, and I love him, of course. But you know how it is."

"I think they call that a love-hate relationship," Charles said.

"Something like that," Thomas agreed.

"What about Janice? Do she and Gareth share a love-hate relationship?"

His laugh was brief and quiet, almost involuntary.

"Similar," he said. "But without the love part. Even when we were kids, they were always at each other's throats. It's the little things, you know? She'd wind him up and he'd retaliate. He'd usually take it too far, and then they'd both end up in Mum's bad books."

"What about your dad? Didn't he get involved?"

"Dad? No, Dad was always working. And if he was home, we knew better than to upset him."

"I get the impression he has a temper," Charles said. "Would you say that's a fair assessment?"

"Actually no," Thomas replied. "I mean, he's only human, and there is a limit to how much he can tolerate. But he has a way about him. Most of the time he can get his message across with just a look." He relaxed in his chair, just as Charles had hoped he would, crossing his legs and resting his hands on his jeans. "We were terrified of him when we were kids. Not because he'd lose his rag or anything, and he never hit us, before you ask. Not all of us anyway."

"I wasn't going to ask."

"It was his presence more than anything," Thomas continued. "We didn't dare put a foot out of place when he was around. If he got home and Mum told him about something we did, he'd just stare at us, then tell us to go to bed."

"Which you did?"

"Of course. We didn't need telling twice," he said. "Well, most of us didn't."

"Oh?"

"Gareth always pushed his buttons. He never knew when to quit. He always had to have the last word."

"And did he get it?"

"Never," Thomas said. "And he paid the price for trying."

"Your dad hit him, did he?"

Thomas sighed, averted his eyes, and thought hard about how to respond.

"Gareth is a product of his own doing. He pushed my dad too far, and like I said, he paid the price," Thomas said. "So what you see now—"

"Gareth's anger?" Charles said, for clarification, and Thomas nodded.

"Is his own doing."

"A vicious cycle," Devon said.

"That's the way it was back then," Charles said. "You could get away with it then. Not these days. But when I was a boy, everyone got the slipper or the belt. Unless you were out, of course, in which case you'd have your trousers pulled down in front of everyone and your backside slapped until you behaved."

"Brutal," Devon said. "If I misbehaved, I was forced to miss pudding, and before you say it, yes, I probably should have misbehaved a little more, but then I wouldn't be me, would I?"

The comment added nothing to the narrative, except to demonstrate to both Charles and Thomas that she was comfortable with her appearance, and rightly so, and also give a little back in return for the depths of conversation that Thomas was being asked to delve into.

Charles imitated Thomas's posture, aware that his grubby, old shoes were not fine leather and that his tatty trousers needed pressing, unlike Thomas's crisp jeans.

"Talk to me about Jeffery," he said. "From how I understand things, Gareth is the wild one and you seem to be the calm, reasonable one. Where does Jeffery fit in?"

"Jeffery? He's my dad," Thomas said, matter of factly. "If you understand my dad, then you understand Jeff."

"I don't understand your dad," Charles replied. "Help me, will you?"

Thomas let his head fall back, puffing out a breath of air as he considered how to phrase an explanation.

"You're right," he said, sitting up straight. "I'm calm, collected, and, I like to think, reasonable."

"From what I've seen so far, I'd have to agree," Charles said.

"I'm also terrible at business," he added. "I just don't care enough about it. I'm not driven by success or power. I just want to enjoy my life."

"That's not a bad thing."

"It is when you have two older brothers," Thomas said. "Gareth is the complete opposite. He's angry, he's driven—"

"To impress your father?"

"Perhaps," Thomas said. "He's also very good at business, and he cares about success and power and those things. The short version is that he's my grandfather."

"Bit of a loose cannon, is he? Your grandfather, that is."

"He was," Thomas corrected. "He died when I was young. But yes, he was one that got the firm through the seventies when, according to my dad, the whole country was on strike."

"And so Jeffery is somewhere in the middle of you both, is he?"

"He's not quite as laid back as me, but yes. He's got a good head on his shoulders, and he knows how to control his temper."

"He's your father," Charles said.

"He's my father," Thomas agreed. "Although, those lines have been blurring these last few years." Charles gave him an inquisitive look, hoping for an embellishment on the statement. "Since Dad retired, his patience seems to be slipping. He's much quicker to react these days. He's a lot more like Gareth these days. Not quite so bad, but he's getting there."

"He's becoming his own father," Charles said, looking for an acknowledgement that he was understanding the family dynamics more, and Thomas gave a curt nod. "I'm afraid that we humans aren't like a fine wine, Thomas. We all tend to regress a little as we age. And Janice? What's she like?"

"Janice is a free spirit," he told him. "She unshackled herself from the family as soon as she was able to marry."

"But she still works for the family business?"

"Only because Mum convinced her to stay," he said. "But she keeps herself at arm's length from Gareth. It's a bone of contention that she stood no chance of taking over from Dad. She'll get no higher than HR Director. It's a sad fact."

"Was the position up for grabs, then?" Charles asked.

"Not really. Gareth has been groomed for the role since he was a kid. There was no doubt that he'd take over eventually."

"It sounds to me like Jeffery would have been well-positioned for the role," Charles said.

Thomas leaned forward again and lowered his voice.

"If that's what you think, then you've understood every word I've said."

Again, Charles mimicked Thomas's posture, leaning on the desk so that their faces were only two feet apart.

"It sounds to me like Janice and Jeffery could both hold a grudge against Gareth," he said. "Is that an accurate statement?"

"I suppose," Thomas said, then tried to brush it off. "But nothing serious. I mean, they would never do anything to hurt each other."

"No, of course not," Charles said. "But you have to admit. It's interesting that your brother's boy was killed and now your sister is missing."

"You call it interesting," Thomas said, and for the first time, there was more than a hint of malice in his tone. "I call it devastating. In fact, it's more than that. If we're not careful, this episode is going to tear this family apart."

"I understand," Charles said. "And please forgive me. I didn't mean to—"

"I don't think you do understand, Inspector Cook. My brother lost his little boy today. He's already lost his wife. The family is held together with fraying string," Thomas said. "If we lose Janice, then..."

He paused and, as if he was unable to even imagine the scenario, squeezed his eyes closed to dam the emotions.

"Then what?" Charles said, sensing a weakness in that dam that might just let the truth flow.

Thomas took a moment to wet his lips and link his fingers, then raised his head. The jovial, carefree expression that singled him out from his siblings was gone.

"It would kill my mother," he said. "And then our whole world would come tumbling down."

CHAPTER 27

"You took your time," Gareth said, from where he was sitting in one of the armchairs. The comment had little effect on Thomas, who closed the door behind him and made his way over to where his father kept a decanter of whiskey with matching cut-crystal glasses on a silver tray.

Susie felt Jeffery's hand reach for hers and gave it a squeeze, as if to say, *don't worry. It's just family stuff*, and she reciprocated weakly before removing her hand and placing it on her lap.

"I had a lot to say," Thomas said, with his back to the room as he poured himself a drink. The glass clinked as he replaced the decanter lid, and he turned, ignored Gareth, and squeezed his mother's shoulder. "You okay, Mum?"

She reached up and touched his hand gratefully, offering an accompanying weak smile.

"Dad?" he said.

"I'm fine," Abbott grumbled.

"What about me?" Gareth asked. "Aren't you going to ask me? You know I lost my boy today, don't you?"

"We lost *our* boy," Elizabeth said quietly, and Gareth fell silent.

"He was *our* boy, not just yours. He was one of us, Gareth. You're not alone in this. We're all suffering."

"I might as well be alone," he said. "All you've bloody well spoken about is Janice ever since you got that box. It's like Harry didn't even matter."

"Because Janice is alive, Gareth," Thomas said. "She's out there somewhere, minus a finger." He shook his head softly like he deeply regretted giving his brother the news. "Harry's dead mate. He's gone. I'm sorry, but he is. If we could turn back time, then we would. But we can't. None of us can."

"Thomas is right," Abbott grumbled, his stare never venturing from the flickering fire. "Janice is out there somewhere. Our Janice. And the people who killed Harry are with her, doing God knows what."

"Abbott don't—" Elizabeth started.

"It has to be said," he replied, raising his voice just enough to get his point across. "I might have stepped away from the business, Gareth, but while there's breath in my body, I won't sit by and watch them tear this family apart any more than they already have."

"Dad, listen—"

"No, you listen, Gareth," Abbott said, retaining control of the room with what Susie could only describe as effortless calm. "Your mother and I raised four children and four children there will be on the day that I'm buried. I'm not as callous as you might think. Just because I'm hard on you all doesn't mean I don't love every one of you, and that includes my grandchildren."

"Even Janice's?" Jeffery asked.

"Even Janice's," Abbott replied, turning to look at him briefly before staring over to Gareth. "Our family has lived through every tragedy, disaster, and pandemic the world has thrown at us—"

"Oh not this again," Gareth started.

"Yes, this again, damn you," Abbott said, his face turning a heated pink and his eyes bulging from their sockets, until he took a few breaths and regained his composure. "You seem to forget, my boy, you are no longer living your life the way you see fit. You're carrying the torch now, and I'll be damned if you think I'm going to sit here and watch you drop it."

"I'm not going to drop the torch, Dad."

"No, you're bloody well not if I have anything to do with it. But if you..." He paused then corrected himself. "If we fight amongst ourselves at home, then how on earth do you expect to steer the company?"

"Ah, and there it is," Thomas said.

"What's that supposed to mean?" Abbott replied.

"Nothing. Except that while our nine-fingered sister lies in a cold, dark room somewhere, and just as I thought you of all people had turned a corner and somehow realised there's more to life than Dickens and Sons," Thomas said, "you show your true colours. It's not about the family, is it? Little Harry wasn't a grandson to you, was he?"

"Thomas," Elizabeth said, sounding more disappointed than cross. But Thomas ignored her.

"He wasn't though, was he? All Harry was, was the next male in line to be groomed for a life in the service of the Dickens family business."

"I think you're letting your emotions get the better of you, Thomas," Abbott said, with a warning in his tone.

"I am. And you know what? I don't bloody care, Dad," he replied. "You know, for a moment there, when you were talking about your four children being alive when you're buried, I really thought this whole thing had made you realise how important family is. How much you loved us. But all you're interested in is your own bloody legacy. You want people to remember you when you're dead. You want them to look at Dickens and Sons in fifty years' time and speak of how great *you* were."

Abbott inhaled long and hard, his eyes never wavering from Thomas, who, at the door to the hallway, stopped.

"Janice stood here last night," Thomas said, pointing at the floor beneath his feet. "In this very spot." He shook his head again sadly. "And everything she said now somehow makes sense."

"Thomas," Elizabeth called out.

"Goodnight, Mum," he replied, as he opened the door and left the room.

The Dickens parents shared a look, one of contempt and the other accusing, but neither said a word. They were too old and experienced in marriage to air their dirty laundry, Susie thought.

"I think I'll go and check on Arthur," Gareth said, shoving himself out of his chair. "I'll say goodnight."

He was about to follow Thomas when the doorway was suddenly filled, and in walked the two police officers.

"I do hope we're not intruding," Inspector Cook said. "I thought we should probably leave you in peace for the time being. I thought I'd just check to see if there's been any developments."

"No and no," Gareth said, answering both of the questions at once. "But you are right about one thing. You probably should leave."

"Thank you, Chief Inspector," Elizabeth said, offering a sympathetic half-smile. "I'll call you as soon as we hear anything."

"It doesn't matter what time it is," Cook said. "I want to know the moment they make contact."

"What about this specialist team that you spoke of?" Gareth asked. "Or are they busy tending another hostage crisis somewhere else?"

Cook stepped past Gareth into the room, where he made a point of addressing Elizabeth and Abbott. He faltered for a moment as if he were searching for the right words.

"You should know," he began, with a quick glance at his colleague, who squeezed past Gareth to stand by Cook's side. "We'll be handling the investigation. We won't be handing over to another team. Hopefully, you find that reassuring."

"Reassuring?" Gareth said. "That an old codger who can't even find my son's killer, and his—"

"Gareth," Abbott snapped, and he glared at his eldest son, conveying enough of a threat that any angry rant could have. He eyed the chief inspector and then checked his wife's expression. "That is reassuring. Thank you."

"Is there any reason why?" Elizabeth asked. "I mean, they are taking this seriously, aren't they?"

"I can assure you that this investigation is of the highest priority, Mrs Dickens," Cook said. "I, that is, we have a good understanding of the family now. The last thing you need is to relive the past couple of days any more than is needed."

"But what about experience?" Gareth said. "I mean, okay, I can get my head around you having to deal with murder cases on a monthly basis—"

"Weekly," Cook corrected him.

"Weekly, then. But this is entirely different. This is, I mean, surely this can't happen too often?"

"More than you think," Cook said. "There was something in the region of seven thousand kidnapping offences last year. Sadly, the number grows each year."

"This isn't just kidnapping, is it?" Abbott said. "She's a hostage."

"Not yet she's not. They haven't made any demands."

"What type of sentence are we talking about here?" Abbott asked. "For kidnapping? How long will these people get?"

"That all depends on the degree of planning involved. If say she was snatched on a whim by some desperate man or men, then they might receive as little as a twelve-month sentence."

"But if it was planned?"

"Up to twelve years," Cook replied. "Twelve hard years. Again, it all depends on the planning. Rather like murder."

"And can I presume my boy's death would add some weight to that sentence?" Gareth asked dryly.

"Of course," Cook said, looking over their shoulder at him. "But unless we can prove Harry was murdered with intent, then I'm afraid they might face a manslaughter charge."

"Manslaughter?" Gareth said, bewildered by the word. "They mowed my poor boy down."

"And it's my job to prove otherwise," Cook said, raising his voice enough to retain his manners but assert his position. "Now, unless there's anything else?"

"There's nothing," Gareth said and held his hand out towards the door. "I'll see you out."

Cook made to follow his lead but stopped to finish what he had to say.

"We'll spend the morning at the station," he said. "So you'll have the morning to yourselves."

"I do hope you don't have a dozen other cases to work on," Gareth said.

"No. Like I said, this is the highest priority. But the station has resources and space for us to work," he said. "We'll be back in the afternoon to finish off the interviews. Unless you hear anything, of course, in which case we'll be here immediately." He stopped and gave each of them a kind but sincere look, lingering longer on Susie than she had hoped he would. "Well then, I'll see you all tomorrow, I hope."

"Chief Inspector," Abbott called out, and Cook faced him once more. "What are our chances here?"

"Are you looking for odds, Mr Dickens? Because I'm not a gambling man."

"I'm not a gambler either," he replied. "But I am a realist. Do you think we can get her back?"

Cook thought for a moment before answering.

"I think we can, yes," he said. "But like I told you before. It's going to depend on you all as much as the men who have Janice."

"That's what I hoped you'd say," Abbott replied. "And you do have experience in this sort of thing, don't you? What I'm trying to say is, I very much hope my daughter's life isn't in the hands of somebody who hasn't dealt with this type of thing before."

The eyes of the room bore down on the detective, but he wore the attention well.

"Mr Dickens, I'm sure you'll agree that when you get our age there are very few new experiences to be had," he said, and Abbott agreed with a slow and definite nod. "Now I bid you all good night. Try to get some rest."

CHAPTER 28

Their doors closed simultaneously, and Devon pulled her seatbelt across her, clicking it into place in silence.

Cook did the same, then fumbled for the button to start the car. The lights came on automatically, illuminating the house and the thin mist that was creeping in from the low-lying fields around them.

"Do you want to tell me about it?" she said, and he slotted the car into drive, refusing to meet her stare.

"Not really," he said, confirming that he knew she was referring to the experience he spoke of. "It was a long time ago." He let the handbrake off and the car rolled forward, tires crunching on the loose gravel beneath them. "Besides, there are a hundred other things I'd rather discuss."

"Like Gareth Dickens?"

"Like Gareth Dickens," he confirmed, finally glancing in her direction. "And his band of brothers."

"Go on," she said, as he drew the car up to the end of the drive. It was close to seven p.m., pitch dark, and the only lights they could see were distant glows in the mist – farms, remote houses, and the largest of them all, Lincoln City, a soft patch of light on the horizon like a distant fire.

He turned out of the drive, then almost immediately turned left into Acredyke Lane, flicking the headlights to full beam and leaning forward in his seat, cautiously guiding the car along the narrow, single-track road.

"One of them is lying," he said.

"We've only spoken to one of them," Devon said. "Officially, anyway."

"One of them is hiding something then," Cook said, his eyes never leaving the road. "Devon, how long will it take you to get to the station in the morning?"

"What?"

"How long does it take?" he said. "Door to door."

She shrugged.

"Thirty minutes, or so. Maybe less."

"So, you need to leave at six-thirty tomorrow."

"Six thirty? You want me there at seven?"

"We've got a busy day," he said, seeming to relax a little as they came to the end of the road. He turned out of the lane onto the much wider Fen Road, heading towards Lincoln. "And before you ask, you can book the overtime."

"I'm not fussed about the overtime, guv."

"Well, book it anyway," he told her, then looked across at her. "Otherwise, I'll look like I'm lying when I submit mine."

She laughed and it felt good, and a car heading in the opposite direction illuminated the first signs of a smile on his face.

"What do you have planned?" she asked.

"Coffee." He said. "Always start with a coffee. It's not like the Dickens have made us welcome with drinks, is it?"

"Probably a good thing," she said, and he looked at her slightly bemused. "You don't trust them, right?"

"I don't trust one of them," he corrected her. "I just don't know which one."

"So? What are we doing?" she asked. "After coffee, that is."

"Well, first thing's first, I want a full debrief from our uniformed friends. Then, I want to check in with CSI to see if they identified the finger."

"I doubt they've even looked at it, guv. In my experience, they need to stare at it on a shelf for a few days."

"It's worth putting the pressure on," he replied. "Then comes the hard part." He gave her a nervous glance before his eyes found the road again. "I need to expand our team."

The words felt like a blade in her gut. Her heart. Like she imagined a break-up would feel.

"Expand, guv?" she said, doing her best not to sound needy but failing miserably.

At the end of the road, he indicated, although there was no other car in sight in any of the three possible directions.

"We need help, Devon," he said. "We can't do this alone. I'm going to try and get DS Hannaway on board. I'll need to clear it with Collins, though."

"We don't need help. Look at what we've done so far."

"I want somebody to investigate the shops that were open on Boxing Day. Newspapers shops. Remember?"

"I can do that. I said that I would."

"I also want somebody to visit every one of the Dickens's properties."

"Again, I'm happy to get involved."

"No," he said, eventually pulling out towards Washingborough but saying nothing else. She waited until they had passed through the village and were navigating the roundabout at the junction of the new bypass before she said anything.

"I haven't disappointed you guv, have I?"

"Disappointed me?" he said, with a laugh.

"Should I have left you at the house and done the newspaper shop thing?" she asked. "I would have. But you said I could stay."

"No," he told her, emphasising the response with a shake of his head. "No, you have not disappointed me, Devon."

"Well, what then?" she said. "I don't get why we need to bring anyone else in on this. Not yet anyway."

He pulled the car over to the side of the road, close to the water treatment plant, and yanked the handbrake up.

"Sorry," she said, closing her eyes and hating herself. "I ask too many questions. I know I do. It's a flaw of mine. I have many, and that's one."

"You should have more confidence in yourself," he told her, softly but leaving scant room for argument.

"That's another flaw of mine," she said. "Sorry, I just want this—"

"Tomorrow, I will be visiting Dickens and Sons," he said, cutting her off and then turning his face from the headlights of an oncoming car. He released his squint and stared at her. "And I want you with me, Devon."

"Me? Not Hannaway? I mean, surely he's got more experience than me."

"Well, maybe I'll call him and ask him what he wants to do. Visit every shop within a few miles of Branston Booths, or come with me to tear this investigation wide open."

"Okay, yeah. I want it," she said. "Sorry. I just..."

"Go on," he said.

"Nothing," she replied, turning to stare into the gloom outside.

"Devon?"

She faced him, finding him unmoved, clearly not going to let it drop, and she sighed.

"I'm just enjoying myself, guv."

"You're what? You do realise this has escalated from a hit-and-run manslaughter to a kidnapping?"

"I know, I know. Not that. I mean, I'm..." The words played out in her head, and she cringed at even thinking about them. "I don't often enjoy working with somebody, guv. Or rather, other people don't often enjoy working with me."

"Are you the last to be picked for the football team, Devon?"

"If that's how you want to put it, yes."

"Same," he said. "In fact, when I was at school, I remember a time when the teams were picked and I was left standing there."

"The last one?"

He nodded.

"And they left me there," he said with a laugh. "Even the side that ended up with me didn't want me. How about that for a disappointment?"

"Brutal," she said. "Listen, I don't usually open up. It's actually a bit weird. I'm usually on my own doing the stuff nobody else wants to do."

He sat back, making it obvious that he had no intention of moving off anytime soon.

"How old are you, Devon?" he asked.

"Wow," she replied. "Are you even allowed to ask that anymore?"

"How old are you?"

"Twenty-eight," she said.

"How long have you been in the force?"

"Officially?" she asked, and he nodded. "Four years."

"And you haven't gone for sergeant yet? Why not?"

"Because nobody knows I exist, guv," she said. "Except for the ones that turn sideways when they pass me in the corridor."

"People do that?" he asked, and this time, she nodded. "Does it bother you?"

"No. I mean, it did at first. But it's something you kind of get used to," she said. "When you're like me, you learn to embrace your other qualities, and you hope that out there somewhere is somebody that will appreciate them so much, they might look past everything else and like me for who I am."

He said nothing, and all hopes of him coming up with some sort of wise saying, or even cracking a joke to rouse a smile, faded.

He put the car into drive again and then indicated. But he didn't pull the car onto the road. Instead, he just sat there, the bright light casting an intermittent orange glow in the mist.

"Devon?" he said, and she wiped her eye before pulling her gaze from the window.

"Guv?"

He didn't look at her. Instead, he chose to focus on the empty road ahead of them, as if he was formulating a plan.

"It's fair to say that you have been noticed. By me," he said finally, and then he smiled to himself as he eased the car onto the road. "I think we should create our own team."

CHAPTER 29

December 27th

The digital clock on John's bedside table was still blurry when Penny placed a mug of tea down for him. He squinted at the lights and rubbed his eyes.

"It's six," she said. "You need to be up."

"I am up," he replied, to which she simply ran her eyes down the length of his body.

"Funny looking up," she said. "Come on. I'll get some toast on."

"Are the kids up?"

"Not yet. And I plan on keeping it that way. So shower quietly."

He flopped back down onto his pillow.

"How the hell does anyone shower quietly?" he said as she left the room.

He flung the covers off and swung his legs down, slipping his feet into his slippers. The chair beside the bed was home to the clean washing he had yet to put away and last night's clothes, all of which tumbled to the floor when he dragged his dressing gown out from beneath the pile.

The toilet seat was cold, the water in the shower was tepid, and by the time he stepped into the kitchen, his toast was too cool to even melt the butter, and it broke when he tried to spread it.

He abandoned the toast, leaving a carpet of charred crumbs on the chopping board, and selected a packet of biscuits from the cupboard that Penny's Mum and Dad must have left behind. They were his favourite, too. The shortbread type with raisins and a dusting of sugar. He tore open the packet and grabbed three just as he heard Penny's footsteps on the stairs. Stashing the opened packet in the cupboard, he quickly dunked the three of them together into his tea, waited a moment, and then stuffed them into his mouth.

But much like the toilet seat, the shower, and his toast, his tea was far from warm and the biscuits took far more chewing than he'd anticipated. With a mouth full of biscuits, he stamped on the pedal bin and swiped the charred toast remains into the waste just as Penny entered the kitchen.

"All right, love," she said, to which he simply pointed to his full mouth and then gave her a thumbs up. "Toast all right, was it?"

He swallowed hard, far before the biscuits had had time to soften, and the sharp shortbread edges tore at his gullet.

"Grand," he croaked finally.

"You okay?"

"I'm fine," he said, washing the remains of the biscuits from his tortured throat with a mouthful of cold tea. He set the cup down on the side, eyed the kitchen worktop for any evidence of his cheat breakfast, and then leaned in to kiss her. "I'll see you tonight, then."

"Don't be late, will you? I said we'd pop over to Maggie and Dave's tonight."

"Maggie and Dave's?" he called out, pulling on his coat. She leaned through the kitchen door into the living room.

"Yeah, you remember? I told you. We're going to do a games

night. Give the kids a bit of a break from these four walls. Don't tell me you've forgotten."

"No," he said. "No, it's fine. I remember now."

"Seven p.m. So, we need to leave here at six-thirty, all right?"

"I'll be home by six," he said, offering a weak smile. "Have a good day."

"I love you," she called out, as he was closing the door, and he pushed it open a few inches to call back.

"Love you, too."

The car was, as he had predicted, freezing. Thankfully, the morning sun had cleared his windscreen of frost, but it had done little for the temperature inside. He started the engine and sat back, giving it a moment to warm up while he closed his eyes and collected his thoughts.

But his thoughts were far from positive. Perhaps the onslaught of disappointments he'd experienced during the thirty minutes he'd been awake had jarred his nerves because from whatever angle he considered his predicament, the risks were becoming greater than he could handle.

His stomach lurched this way and that, which then fed through to his heart, racing as if he'd run a hundred-metre stretch. Finally, a layer of cool sweat formed on his forehead and along the length of his back.

A hand slammed onto the driver's window beside him, and he was pulled from his thoughts like a young child being dragged from the icy depths of a frozen lake.

Outside, with her hand holding the collars of her quilted coat together, Penny smiled down at him, until she saw the look of terror on his face, which he tried to conceal, but failed.

"John?" she said.

"Hi, dear," he replied. "Is everything okay?"

"Are you going to wind the window down?"

"I should get going," he called through the glass.

"Aren't you forgetting something?" she said. "Open the window, will you?"

"I gave you a kiss, didn't I?" he began, and then stopped when she held up a handful of sandwiches wrapped in a used bread bag.

"Your lunch."

"Of course," he replied and then fumbled for the switch to lower the window. "How stupid of me."

She laughed it off, but there was something about the way she looked at him that was unsettling.

"What?" he said, and she contemplated an answer, resigning to an unconvincing shake of her head.

"Nothing," she said, and then smiled one of those smiles that could brighten anybody's day. "Have a good day."

"Do I get another kiss?" he asked, and she bent down to kiss him. But he'd taken it too far. With her face just inches from his, she peered at him quizzically.

"You're sweating."

"I'm fine–"

"Are you feeling okay?" she said. "You've not been yourself these past few days."

"I'm grand," he said, but she could tell when he was lying. It was a gift she had always had and one which he was reminded of every time he tried to hide something from her.

"Are you going to tell me what's wrong?"

"Nothing's wrong, dear."

"Do I need to cancel tonight?"

"No, of course not."

"John, you need to talk to me," she said, then realised that her voice was far too loud for six-thirty in the morning, and she lowered it accordingly. "You've been acting strange for a few days now, and don't tell me you haven't. Even James has noticed it."

"James? What has he said?"

"It doesn't matter. The point is that…" She hesitated. "We're worried about you. You're working far too hard."

"Someone has to pay for Disney World, don't they?"

"Disney World? Is that all this is about? Because if it is—"

"It's not," he said, hoping to calm her down. "Sorry, I don't know why I said that. Look, I'm fine, love. I'm just tired. I'm bloody annoyed that I don't get to spend as much time with you all. But I'm going to change it. I'm going to make this better if it's the last thing I do."

"I don't want it to be the last thing you do, John," she said. "None of us does. We just want you to be happy. If you're happy, then we can all be happy."

"Well, then let me try and be happy," he said and glanced down at the clock on the dashboard. "Speaking of happy. I know somebody who won't be if I don't make a move."

His explanation had been weak, but it had done something towards her demeanour, and she stood, beaming down at him as he put the car into first gear. But then he hesitated and looked up at her.

"Penny?" he said, and she cocked her head in waiting. "You know I'd do anything for you, don't you?"

"Of course—" she began, but he cut her off.

"I mean it," he said, as he began to lift the clutch, and looked directly into her eyes. "There's nothing I wouldn't do for you."

CHAPTER 30

December the twenty-seventh started well for Jack Hannaway. In four days' time, the world would be celebrating the new year, and for the most part, people across the globe were dwelling on their regrets, vowing to change their habits in the form of ill-conceived resolutions.

Today was another shift on time and a half. Today was a day away from his wife and child, a day that he didn't have to spend with his mother-in-law, and a day in which he could catch up on his admin, discuss the football with Forsythe, and drink as much coffee as he wanted without his wife commenting on how his heart would suffer, and that she wanted him to be around to see Briony marry one day.

"Morning, ladies, gentlemen, and you, of course, Forsythe," he said when he burst into the incident room. "And how was everybody's Christmas? Joyous, I hope?"

He took his seat at his desk and hung his coat over the back, tapping on the space bar of his computer to wake it up.

"You're in a good mood," Forsythe said. "I take it your wife finally saw sense and moved back to her parents' house?"

"No such luck," he replied. "But there's always next year. I've started writing my letter to Santa already."

"Does she know you talk about her like that?" Chalk said, leaning over the back of her chair to talk to him.

She was what his father would have called vertically challenged, and looked like she could do with a few decent meals, but in her short time on the team, she hadn't put a foot wrong and had proven to enjoy a little friendly banter, which placed her far higher than a few senior officers Hannaway could think of.

"Only if she reads my letter to Santa before she posts it," he said with a wink. "Now then, what do we have today?" He flicked through a small stack of folders on his desk, puffing his cheeks and exhaling while he decided which of them would be the easiest.

"I need your sign-off on the report I wrote for the Co-op robbery," Forsythe said, tossing another folder onto his desk. "And Chalk needs some help with the arson job on Monks Road."

"What do you need help with?" he asked her.

"Oh, just the order of events," she replied.

Hannaway glanced over his shoulder to make sure no senior officers were present, lowered his voice, and then leaned over to her.

"You mean, you're confused about when exactly I arrived on scene?"

She nodded, appearing a little nervous.

"I arrived with you both," he told her. "That's what happened, isn't it?"

"If you say so."

"I do," he said. "And one day when you're in a jam, you'll know where to come." She nodded again and then turned to get back to work. "We stick together here, Chalky. No one upstairs has our backs, so we need to have each other's. Is that clear?"

"I'm glad to see you're indoctrinating DC Chalk with the correct protocols, Sergeant Hannaway," a voice said from the doorway, and he turned in his seat to find DCI Cook standing there in a suit that appeared to have come from a box in the back room of a charity shop back in nineteen seventy-five.

"Well, what do you know? It's the ghost of Christmas past," he muttered under his breath, before feigning occupational bliss. "Good morning, Chief Inspector Cook. I see you've brought the weather with you."

He glanced over to the huge windows at one end of the room, onto which an entire quota of December's rain pelted. Cook shook the water from his jacket before hanging it on a wall hook and then dumped his satchel, which appeared to be at least twice as old as his suit, onto a spare chair.

"How did the misper go?" Hannaway asked.

Cook, fastidious in his habits, prepared his desk, aligning his notebook, pen, and folders before even looking in Hannaway's direction.

"The misper became a hit and run," he said.

"Oh dear," Hannaway replied. "I bet that put a spanner in your Christmas party."

"The hit and run then developed into a kidnapping investigation."

"So you clocked up some overtime," Hannaway said. "It couldn't have happened to a nicer officer, guv. I suppose you need to write your reports now, do you?"

"No, as it happens, the hit and run remains unsolved, as does the kidnapping," Cook replied. "Which is why I'm here."

"I'm not following, guv," Hannaway said.

"Meaning, I need bodies."

"Bodies, guv? Well, you're the one on homicide. We're just plain old CID."

"Specifically, young bodies, eager to gain experience and learn," Cook said, clearly recognising the humour but lacking in adequate personality to appreciate it. Instead, he eyed Chalk and Forsythe with curiosity.

"Oh no," Hannaway said. "You can't take them."

"Oh, can't I? I thought I was the detective chief inspector, and you the sergeant?"

"Sorry, guv. It's just that they've got reports to write. Everyone knows how important it is to be on top of admin. You said it yourself the other day."

"Quite right," Cook said with a heavy sigh. "Quite right indeed."

"Thanks for understanding, guv."

"Absolutely no problem at all," Cook replied taking his seat. "Just let me know when you're ready."

Both Chalk and Forsythe turned to stare at Hannaway with equally bemused expressions on their faces.

"Sorry, guv?" he replied. "What do you mean, when you're ready?"

A little irritated, Cook set his pen down and took his time to turn in his seat to meet Hannaway eye to eye.

Slowly, he kicked out the seat adjacent to him.

"You mean, you want me, guv?" Hannaway said, with a nervous laugh.

"You said it yourself, Sergeant Hannaway. DCs Chalk and Forsythe are far too busy completing reports, and unless you expect me to interrupt the team in the next room, that leaves only you."

"You need my help, guv?"

"I do."

"On the hit-and-run investigation?"

"And the kidnapping," Cook replied. "They are linked. It could be good experience for you. Robberies and TDAs are a daily occurrence, but kidnapping, especially of this magnitude," he said, shaking his head, "are as rare as rocking horse droppings."

Hannaway looked at the pile of folders on his desk, and then at his two friends, who chose to bury their heads in their paperwork.

"All right," Hannaway said. "All right then, I'm in."

"Good," Cook said with a smile, as he collected his pen from the desk. "I'll have a sugar in mine, if you don't mind. Oh, and milk in last please, not first. I can't stand my coffee too milky."

Behind him, the incident room door opened and DC Devon sidled in with a takeaway coffee cup in each hand and her bag hanging from her elbow.

"My, my," Hannaway said, enjoying her expression alter when she saw him standing beside Cook. "We are all early birds this morning, aren't we?"

"Here you go, guv," she said, setting one of the cups down in front of Cook. "I didn't know how you like it, so I just got you a black coffee." Cook looked at her, seemingly impressed. "Thought you could add some milk if you wanted it, but you can't take it out, can you?"

"That was very considerate of you, Devon. Thank you."

"Well, that saves me a job," Hannaway said, watching as the nervous creature that was DC Devon tentatively took the chair that Cook had kicked out from beneath the desk and hung her coat over the back of it.

"Right, before we begin," Cook said, then halted and looked back at Hannaway. "Do sit down, Hannaway. You're making me feel uneasy."

"Yes, guv," he replied and drew out the chair opposite Devon, and watched as the two of them sipped at their coffees.

"Devon, Sergeant Hannaway will be joining us for the time being. As I explained yesterday, we need another pair of hands."

"That's right, guv," she said. "I think it's a good idea."

"Right, well, I suppose we ought to bring you up to speed, Hannaway."

"You can call me Jack if you like, guv," he replied. "I mean, while we're in here. Not in front of the customers, of course."

Cook contemplated the statement, and at first, Hannaway thought he was going to spew some rubbish about all the protocols and hierarchies that would break. But he looked thoughtfully at Devon for a moment and then spoke to him.

"All right, Jack it is."

"Good, and what should I call you both?" he replied. "Charles? Or are you a Charlie? No, no I've got it. You're a Chaz."

"You can call me, Detective Chief Inspector Cook, guv, or sir," Cook said. "As for Devon, I'm sure she knows her mind enough to inform you of what she might like to be called."

"Right," Hannaway said, and his eyes rolled over to Devon, his eyebrows raised in question.

"Just Devon," she said shyly.

"This is going to be a barrel of laughs, isn't it?" Hannaway muttered, and Cook responded by dragging the whiteboard closer to where he was sitting.

"Harry Dickens. Eight years old. Spent Christmas Day with his dad, grandparents, aunts, and uncles at the grandparent's house in Branston Booths."

"Not the Dickens family?" he said. "As in Dickens and Sons?"

"That's right," Cook replied, then continued before Hannaway could add any more of his thoughts. "Harry was found dead on Heighington High Street at approximately seven-thirty a.m. on Boxing Day. The FME suggested he'd been hit by a car, suffering massive internal bleeding which the pathologist agreed with."

"Jesus. Merry bloody Christmas," Hannaway said.

"Not for them," Devon said.

"No," Cook agreed. "It hasn't been a pleasant Christmas for any of them."

"I was just being..." Hannaway started, then relented. Clearly, he'd have to make adjustments while he was working with these two.

"We have an eyewitness. Male, early forties, lives down the road from the paper shop outside of which Harry Dickens was found."

"He saw the whole thing?"

"From a distance," Cook said. "He heard a loud diesel engine, then moments later, when he turned the corner, he saw a grey Audi reverse into the young boy and then speed off."

"For God's sake," Hannaway said, taking it all in. "ANPR?"

"One thing at a time, Hannaway," Cook said. "The MISPER I received when I was here last was the boy. His father, Gareth Dickens, eldest son of Abbott Dickens and current CEO of Dickens and Sons gave us a positive ID."

"Right, so who owns, the Audi? I presume the witness—"

"John Gregory," Devon added.

"Right. I presume he got the number plate?"

"He didn't need to," Devon said. "CCTV from the newspaper shop gave us an image of the woman with young Harry. The family have confirmed her as Janice Dickens, the only daughter of Abbott and Elizabeth Dickens, and that she was driving an Audi."

"Blimey! She mowed down her own nephew?"

"Wrong again," Cook said.

"Later that day, when we attended the house to conduct interviews, we discovered a box on the doorstep. Six inches square, wrapped in the day's newspaper, and tied with a bow."

"Any message?" Hannaway said, sensing something awful was going to follow.

"Bah humbug," Cook replied, which immediately tickled Hannaway's darker sense of humour and raised a wry smile.

"Bah humbug?"

"Is that funny?"

"If their name wasn't Dickens, then maybe not," he said.

"Well, it's not the inference to the writer that caught our attention, it was the contents of the box," Cook said.

"The contents?"

"A finger," Devon said, and Hannaway felt a cold chill run the length of his spine.

"Janice Dickens's finger?"

"It's being analysed as we speak," Cook said, although Elizabeth Dickens suggested the ring on the end of it resembled one which she bought her daughter for her twenty-fifth birthday."

"I can see why you need help," Hannaway replied, sitting back in his seat. "Have we found the car?"

"Not yet," Cook replied.

"Any cameras nearby that might have caught the delivery person?"

"Nothing," Devon said. "We had a team of uniformed officers on that yesterday."

"What about the newspaper? You said it was that day's paper?" Hannaway said. "There can't be too many shops that were open on Boxing Day."

"I can see we picked the right man for the job," Cook said, seeming impressed. "We also learned that the Dickens family have a number of properties which they rent out."

"A property portfolio? I suppose with the interest rates the way they are, bricks and mortar is the best place to keep your cash. Banks aren't exactly going to double your money."

"We've interviewed the youngest brother and a..." He took a moment to refer to his notes. "Susie Fraser. Girlfriend of the middle Dickens brother, Jeffery."

"Was she there?" Hannaway asked.

"She was, and to a degree she's impartial, so I wanted to speak to her while the memories were fresh and before anybody had a chance to fog her perspective."

"Fog her perspective? Why would somebody want to..." Hannaway began. "Do you think one of the Dickens is behind this?"

"Well, let's just say that it's not happy families inside the Dickens household," Cook replied. "The box containing the severed digit was wrapped in newspaper articles. One of them was about recent cutbacks at Dickens and Sons."

"So?"

"And future cutbacks," Cook said quietly. "Cutbacks that only the senior management team knew about."

"And only the Dickens family are on the SMT?" Hannaway said, to which Cook nodded. "So, you think that, unless one of the Dickens family told an outsider, then our culprit is a Dickens. But surely they did tell somebody if the local rag ran a story on it."

"I thought about that," Devon said. "But the incident during which Harry was run down and Janice was taken took place very early. Too early for somebody to buy the paper, read the story, and then formulate a plan to kidnap Janice."

"What if there was no plan?" Hannaway suggested.

"Two people?" she said. "Which means that one of them would have had to convince the other of their plan. What time do paper shops open? Six a.m.? That gives somebody less than an hour to buy and read the paper, hatch a plan, and then convince somebody to help him. On Boxing Day nonetheless, when everybody has families staying or kids to entertain."

She had a point, although it pained Hannaway to admit it, even to himself.

"Do you have transcripts of the interviews?" he asked.

"Not really. We conducted them in a private room at the Dickens house," Cook said.

"You did what? Is that even allowed?"

"They were voluntary and informal," Cook said. "I can assure you if I feel the need to rely on what they have to say to build a case, then we'll have them in here and we'll go through the proper channels. But given that they lost a young boy that morning and their daughter had potentially been kidnapped, I felt it was the more compassionate route. Besides, I was under the impression a specialist team would be drafted in."

"I take it we are now the specialist team?" Hannaway said.

He pieced the narrative together in his mind, identifying possible lines of enquiry to develop. He knew what he'd do. But Cook clearly had a plan, and given the rather fractious mood of the meeting, he felt it best to wait to hear what Cook had to say.

"Which leaves us with a few areas to cover," Cook said finally. "Which is where you come in. I want to visit the Dickens and Sons factory and offices this morning, but we still need the CCTV from any paper shops that were open on Boxing Day, and we need to get in touch with the property management firm to coordinate visits to the Dickens properties. We can't obtain warrants for every one of them, but if they are empty, then we shouldn't have a problem."

"Right," Hannaway said, nodding. "So, how about you and I pay a visit to the factory, while Devon works with the property management firm and the local shops? We can meet back here later on today to compare notes."

Cook reached into a binder and produced a clear, plastic envelope which he slapped down on the table.

"I like what you're thinking, Jack," he said. "Except, I'll be taking Devon with me. She's more familiar with the family and at this stage, my main priority is to keep the family's emotions stable. We don't have time for you to play catch up on this one. I need an individual experienced enough to pick it up and run with it."

"What?" Hannaway said. "You want her with you? But she's–"

"A detective constable," Cook said. "Yes, I know. And a damn fine one at that."

He slid the clear envelope towards Hannaway.

"Addresses and details of the property management firm they use," Cook said, checking his watch and then studying Hannaway's face. Hannaway was experienced enough to know that it was times like this that people in Cook's position perceived a great deal about an individual. It was like the opening of a camera shutter, and the image embedding itself onto the film roll was almost impossible to change once exposed.

"All right, guv," Hannaway said. "I get it. You want me to run with this? No problem."

"It's a lot of work for one officer," Cook said, leaving a door open that Hannaway knew to wedge his foot into.

"I'll work with the property management firm, guv," he said. "I can get the other two on the paper shops."

Cook studied Chalk and Forysthe at the far end of the room. Chalk was typing while reading her notes. Forsythe was a one-finger typist and only effective at that if his tongue was poking between his lips. After a moment's appraisal, Cook nodded.

"They don't need a full debrief. Just give them the task," he replied. "But I thought you said they had important reports to write?"

"They do. But like you said, guv," Hannaway said, as he stood from his chair, collecting the clear envelope and tapping it on the desk for good measure, "robberies and TDAs are two a penny. Kidnappings are as rare as rocking horse—"

"Thank you, Sergeant Hannaway," Cook said. "Call me when you're done."

CHAPTER 31

The security guard on the gate at Dickens and Sons uttered not a single word during the entire transaction. From the moment Charles lowered his window and greeted him with a pleasant, "Good morning," he behaved as if arriving unannounced was akin to insulting the man's sainted mother. Charles followed up with a friendly, "I don't have an appointment, I'm afraid," to which the guard simply leaned through his cabin window, handed him a clipboard with a wad of signing-in forms and a pen, and then dropped out of view, presumably into a seat of some kind, or a bed, judging by the redness of the man's eyes.

It took no more than a minute for Charles to complete the form, adding Devon's details to the last section, and then he held the clipboard out of the window.

"All done," he said, and the guard emerged again, collected the forms, and then handed him two visitor passes on green lanyards. Charles had considered asking the man where he might find the management office but thought better of it. Besides, the whole site seemed to have been laid out chronologically, with what looked like the ruins of an old farmhouse and barns at one end, the Victorian red brick factory in the middle, and a huge glass structure of some kind at the other end. "Well, I doubt Gareth Dickens and his brothers have offices in the tumbledown farm," he said and peered across at Devon.

"The big greenhouse?" she suggested, to which he nodded, and guided the car to a spot as close as he could get, which, due to another barrier blocking the entrance to the little VIP car park, was some way off, closer to the old factory than the offices. "At least I'll get my steps in."

They climbed out of the car and Charles thought about what she had said while they walked.

"Steps?" he said.

"What?"

"You said you'd get your steps in."

"Yeah. Ten thousand steps."

"You've lost me," he said, bracing again the cold wind that seemed to flow from the river.

"Ten thousand steps a day, guv," she said. "It's a health thing. Like, running every night or whatever. My watch tells me when I've done it."

"When you've done what?" he said, wishing that he'd never asked in the first place.

"Ten thousand steps, guv," she said, pulling her hands from her deep pockets and dragging her sleeve up for him to see a smart-looking digital watch. "It recognises how many steps you've taken in a day. Pretty good."

"And then what does it do?"

"What do you mean?"

"Well, what does it do when you've done ten thousand steps?"

"Well, nothing. It just sort of... Well, it tells you that you've done it."

They spoke while they walked, and as confusing as the conversation had been, it was nice to get inside her head, to understand what made her tick.

"And does that make any difference to you?"

"Well, I suppose. I mean, it's not like I need to buy a new wardrobe anytime soon, but..."

"Does it make you feel good?" he asked, as they reached the glass building, and he held the door open for her.

"I suppose so," she replied. "It's good to know I'm not just sitting on my backside."

"Well, if it makes you feel better about yourself," he said, "then I'm all for it. After you."

The ground-floor reception was sparsely furnished with only a couple of small couches for visitors and a glass coffee table with a spread of periodicals and newspapers. There were three doors leading off to a small kitchen, plus the men's and women's restrooms. To their right, an open staircase led up to the first floor, a journey adorned by a series of old photographs, presumably of the Dickens and Sons site throughout the ages, so that by the time the visitor or potential customer arrived at the first floor, the evidence of family heritage already had them fingering their pen lids ready to sign the cheque book.

Beyond the coffee table, the space opened up into a large, open plan area filled with desks, printers, and all manner of office paraphernalia not too different to the incident room, only larger.

From inside the large space, a printer whirred into life, and both Charles and Devon made their way toward the noise. There must have been twenty-odd desks in the room, collated in groups of fours or sixes, and even an eight. But only three of the desks were occupied, the closest of which was on their right as they passed through the door.

"Excuse me?" Charles said to a lady who leaned on the printer waiting for a sizeable document to be spewed into a pile. She turned and seemed quite surprised to find them there.

"Can I help?" she said, quite politely, with a hint of the mellow Lincolnshire accent rolling the ends of the question.

"We're looking for Gareth Dickens," Charles said, to which the woman's response was exactly as he had expected it to be.

"I'm afraid I haven't seen him. His brothers are here though. Their cars are outside, anyway, so I presume they are."

"And where will I find them?" he asked.

She was about to respond, but it was as if she was suddenly suspicious, and she left her post at the printer to close the gap between them.

"Might I ask what it is you need?" she said. "Do you have an appointment?"

Reluctantly, Charles slipped his warrant card from his pocket, and after a quick check to make sure neither of the other two workers were watching, he held it up for her to see.

"It's a private matter, but we rather hoped to find him here."

She studied them both for a moment, deliberating on the best course of action.

"Up the stairs," she said. "See the executive receptionist. She'll let them know you're here."

"Much appreciated," Charles said, just as the printer spat the last sheet of paper onto its tray and then fell into silence. He glanced over at the thick stack of A4. "I would have thought a place like this would insist on printing both sides."

"What?" she said, and he nodded at the printer.

"The document. It's one-sided printing. Not very efficient, is it?"

"You clearly don't know the Dickens family," she replied, then gestured back towards the reception. "Her name's Victoria. Tell her Gwyn sent you."

"I will," Charles said, then with a wave of his arm, invited Devon to lead the way. They were just heading back when he noticed a pair of glass doors on their right. "What's this? A lift? The building only has two floors."

"Maybe it's for disabled access," Devon suggested, which seemed plausible, but given the elaborate attention to detail the designer had given to the place, it was doubtful the elevator was anything but a shameless display of opulence and wealth. "I wonder if old age chief inspectors count."

"You're not serious, guv?"

"Of course I am," he said, pushing the button. The doors opened immediately to reveal space for at least two wheelchairs and a couple of people standing. Again, he invited her to enter first, then followed and hit the button for the first floor.

"What?" she said suddenly.

"I didn't say anything," he replied as the elevator began its ascent.

"You're smiling though," she said. The grin on his face broadened and it felt different, nice somehow. "What is it? Is my jacket inside out?"

She checked her clothing and then sought a shiny part of the elevator to check her reflection, but she found nothing out of place.

"You look fine," he told her, hoping to put her mind at ease.

"Well, what then?"

He gave a sigh and the elevator jolted to a halt.

"You didn't argue my comment about my age."

"Your what?"

"I said that perhaps the elevator was for old age chief inspectors, and you said nothing."

"So?"

"It's funny, that's all."

"Sorry, guv, how is it funny?"

"Only that most people in your position would have said something even if you felt it untrue. Something like, oh you're not old, guv."

"Did you want me to?" she said, her eyes widening.

"No, not at all," he replied. "In fact, I find it quite an admirable trait."

The doors opened with a swish and then rattled into their holes like guards allowing a visitor entry.

"Guv?" she said. "I'm not following."

On the far side of what appeared to be an even more stylish and opulent reception, a pretty young lady watched them inquisitively.

"You're genuine," he told Devon. "There are no airs and graces. No feeble comments to make me feel good about myself and perhaps sway my opinion of you. It means that what you say carries weight, and I respect that."

He left her there in the elevator to muse over what he had said and stepped into the reception.

"Good morning. Can I help you?" Victoria said, closing a few files on her desk just as Charles might have done had he been working on something sensitive.

"We're here to see Thomas and Jeffery Dickens," he replied, approaching the desk.

Her nails were immaculate and far too long to be practical, more of her thighs were exposed than her short black skirt could cover, and it looked as if she'd stuffed two large pieces of fruit down her blouse. And if all of that hadn't been enough, there was something unnatural about her lips, cheeks, and eyebrows.

"May I take your names, please?" she asked, her claws loitering tentatively over her keyboard.

"If you could just tell them that Charles Cook is here to see them, they'll know who you mean."

If the work she'd done to her face and body seemed self-obsessed and immature, her professional tone and mannerisms told a far different story.

"If you'd care to take a seat," she said, but neither Charles nor Devon made a move.

She collected the phone handset from her desk, hit two buttons, and then waited, averting her eyes as she did. A few moments later, she replaced the handset and tried another number which produced the same result.

"I'm afraid they must be out of their offices," she said to them. "Would you like some coffee while you wait?"

"Their cars are here," he said. "I'm sure they're around, aren't they? It's important that I see them."

"Well, I'm afraid..." she began, but Charles made his way over to the corridor, from which there were several doors to the left and right, plus one large set at the far end. "You can't go in there."

"Oh, it's okay," he said. "I'm sure they'll be pleased to see me."

"No, but..." she said, finding her route to block him far longer than his journey to the corridor. He stepped into the corridor, immediately hearing the brothers' excited voices coming from the room on their right. The door was marked with a stainless plate bearing the name *Janice Dickens, HR Director*, and before Victoria had time to reach them, he pushed open the door to find both Thomas and Jeffery rifling through filing cabinets and Janice's desk.

It was Thomas who looked up first.

"What the bloody hell—"

His remark caught Jeffery's attention, who followed his gaze and found Charles staring back at him.

"Morning," Charles said cheerfully.

"Sorry, Mr Dickens," Victoria said from behind Charles. "I tried to stop him."

"It's okay, Victoria," Jeffery replied, his eyes fixed on Charles's. "We were expecting Mr Cook. We'll take it from here."

The receptionist slipped back to her desk, leaving a leathery aroma in her wake. It was a masculine scent that somehow suited her.

"What are you doing here, Chief Inspector? You should have told us you were coming."

"I could ask you both the same question," he replied, stepping into the room to surreptitiously study the titles printed on the folders he was holding. "This is Janice's office, isn't it?"

"So?" Jeffery said, sliding the folding cabinet door closed. "It's business. We have access."

"Oh, I'm sure you do," Charles replied. "It's just that you both seemed to be quite excited when I arrived. Frantic, even. Dare I say it."

"We have a lot to do," Jeffery said. "Janice should be here doing this."

"I see," Charles said, looking at Devon for her reaction but finding only an impassive expression. "I was rather hoping for some of your time."

"Time is one thing we don't have a lot of," Thomas said.

"That's a shame," he replied. "I was hoping for a tour of the grounds."

"You don't think she's here, do you?" Jeffery said. "And don't you need some kind of warrant or something?"

"If you refuse me entry, then yes, I do need a warrant," Charles agreed. "It would be a shame to have to take a more formal route. I find the presence of our uniformed colleagues can be ever so disruptive."

The brothers exchanged glances.

"You do realise that we're victims here, don't you, Chief Inspector?" Jeffery said, and he marched over to Charles, stopping so close that Charles could smell the coffee on his breath. "Our sister is out there somewhere, while our mum sits at home wondering if she'll ever see her again."

"Which makes it even more imperative that I look around the grounds, Jeffery," he replied. "Especially given that I found you two grieving brothers ransacking her office. Now, if you want to be back before lunchtime, then I suggest we make a start."

CHAPTER 32

They were a funny-looking pair, the property managers. From the driver's seat of his car, Hannaway observed them with much amusement, likening them to a contrasting comedy duo. The first of them was tall. Taller than most men. Close to six foot five or thereabouts, by Hannaway's reckoning. He was lean too, as if a strong wind might not only blow him over but snap him in two, unlike his colleague who was far shorter than the average man yet nearly four times larger in the waist.

And the contrasting features didn't stop there. The tall man had an untamed mop of jet-black hair and a thick moustache, while the shorter of the two was as bald as a coot and clean-shaved.

Tall wore a grimace, what Hannaway's father might have called a resting bitch face, while Short appeared to be cheerful and care-free, or at least ignorant of the trials of life.

The only common factor tying the pair was their choice of clothing – neat, dark suits with white shirts and matching blue ties and pocket squares.

As they emerged from the office in Bracebridge Heath, the

taller man caught sight of Hannaway. He nudged his friend's shoulder and then nodded at the car.

That was all the signal Hannaway needed. He climbed from the car, bracing against the strong wind. He held his coat together with one hand while searching his pockets for his warrant card with the other.

"Now then," the shorter of the two said as they approached. "Help you?"

"Detective Sergeant Hannaway. I'm looking for Roy Pierce and Robert Pierce."

He held out his warrant card for them to inspect, then snapped it closed and tucked it into his pocket.

"You found them," the shorter replied, holding out his hand. It wasn't often an individual was so welcoming, especially after they had learned of his occupation. So, he shook the man's hand, and then the next. "I'm Roy. This is my brother, Robert. What can we do for you?"

"I understand you work for the Dickens family," Hannaway said.

The two of them stared at each other briefly, then turned back to Hannaway.

"No," Robert said, his voice lighter in tone than his brother's. "We don't work for them, but they are a client of ours. Elizabeth Dickens. That's who we deal with. Mostly, at any rate."

"I see," Hannaway replied, as a particularly strong gust of wind took hold and nearly unbalanced him. "Do you think we could talk inside?"

Again, they exchanged glances, as if the two of them could communicate through eye contact alone.

"We've just locked up," Roy said.

"We're heading out, you see. We have a busy day ahead."

"Well, I'm afraid that busy day of yours might just have gotten a little busier," Hannaway replied. Then he gestured at the office behind them and held out his hand. "Shall we?"

"So, this is the factory, is it?" Charles said as he scanned the vast expanse of machinery before them. The space was so large it could have been an aircraft hangar or a railway station if it wasn't for the lathes, the presses, the saws, the welders, and the rest of the machines Charles didn't recognise. "What is it you make here?"

"Fabricate," Jeffery said. "We fabricate, not make."

"Okay then. What is it you fabricate?"

"Machinery," Jeffery replied. "Mostly farming machinery. Cultivators, subsoilers, sideknives, and the like. We have a range of tine fittings and sweepers that do well."

Charles watched the man's lips move but understood nothing of what he had said.

"Some of those can be pretty technical," Devon said. "You must have a large team. I mean, they have some serious technology. You know? So that the tractor or combine driver can control them from inside the cab."

"The fabrication is done in here," Thomas said. "From here, the units are taken to be sprayed down the end there." He pointed to the far end of the space just as a spray of sparks shot up into the air and the sound of a grinding wheel filled a cavernous workshop. "After that, the control boards, hydraulics, and wiring looms are fitted. Want to take a look?"

Charles watched the various individuals going about their jobs, some of them wearing goggles, ear defenders, and fireproof overalls, grinding, welding, or operating the heavy machinery, while others carried out the more menial tasks, sweeping up, moving boxes, and generally looking busy in the presence of two of the Dickens brothers. A huge gantry spanned the width of the building on runners, allowing the hoist to take units from one station to another, accessing almost every inch of floor space.

The place was an engineering marvel in itself, let alone the items that were fabricated inside.

"How often do you come in here to see how things are going?" Charles asked, shaking his head at the invite.

"Not often," Thomas said. "We prefer to keep our visits to a minimum."

"Besides, that's what middle management is for," Jeffery said and then smiled at Charles's intrigued expression. "They're kind of a bridge between us. A way of showing the workers that there is a ladder."

"You have a class system?" Charles said.

"A hierarchy," Jeffery explained, then sighed. "Listen, if we came down here every day to see how things were going on, there would be a clear us and them system in place. But if we create a bridge between us all, the rest of the workers can see that if they work hard, there's a way up. Don't you see?"

"I'm afraid the force operates slightly differently," Charles said, turning on his heels to leave the building through the huge sliding doors. He checked to see that they were all following and then shoved his hands into his pockets. "There's a way up, but every rung you climb makes you realise how comfortable the rungs below are. The force is quite transparent, you see? You get to see where you could go, but the fog only clears as you near your goal."

"It sounds to me like you're an unhappy employee, Inspector," Thomas said.

"No, not really. You can be loyal and honest at the same time. The two are not on opposite poles," Charles replied, then looked about the grounds before him. The Victorian building was behind them, the glass monstrosity to their right, and their left were ruins of some old, stone buildings. "What's over there?"

Jeffery made a point of being indifferent to the old ruins.

"Oh, that's where it all began," he said. "Dickens Farm, or what's left of it."

"That's where your ancestors lived and worked, is it?"

"It is, or at least it was," he replied, taking a few steps forward to admire the old scene. "You can see them better from the offices. You can see the layout of the farmhouse and the barns. Even the outhouse."

Charles laughed.

"We had one of those," he said. "And I must admit, I don't have fond memories of the experience. Do you think I could see it?"

"The outhouse?" Thomas said, a disgusted look spreading across his face.

"No, the farm. The whole thing."

"Like I said, Inspector," Jeffery said, and he pointed up at the glass offices, "you can see the entire thing from up there."

"And what's past that? Is that the river?"

"It is," Jeffery told him. "There's a gate that leads down to the end of Five Mile Lane, where the train station and the little chain ferry used to be."

"Is there anything left?"

"The station burned down years ago. A footpath runs along there now," Jeffery said, looking to his brother for any insights. "Besides, you can't get to it from here. Not by car. You'd have to go down—"

"Five Mile Lane?" Charles said, and Jeffery nodded again. "And what about all the land?" he asked, peering away from the factory and the river into a thick mass of vegetation.

"That's our contribution to The National Trust," Thomas said, with more than a little pride.

"It was the farmland, I suppose?"

"It was," he replied. "Most of it was sold off, but our grandad wanted to keep some for nature. There are close to one hundred acres left for wildlife to reclaim. The National Trust gave us a grant for it, but Dad used to donate that to charity."

"One hundred acres? That must be worth a fortune," Devon said.

"It is, to the right person," Thomas replied. "Developers have come sniffing before, but we don't need the money. Dad prefers to honour Grandad's wishes and let nature do its thing rather than let somebody turn it into an ugly housing estate."

"I must say that surprises me," Charles said. "In a good way, of course."

"We're not all bad," Thomas said. "Despite what you might think."

"Have you seen enough, Chief Inspector?" Jeffery asked.

"No, I'd like to have a look around the farm," he replied.

"It's a heritage site," Jeffery said. "We can't go inside. Not without the appropriate PPE anyway. Plus, I'd have to go and get the keys to the gate."

"I can wait," Charles said. "Oh, and while you're fetching them. I'd like to see a full list of employees."

"What on earth for?" Jeffery said.

Charles turned his back on the farm and faced the brothers, searching every twitch of their facial muscles for some kind of sign.

"The same reason I want to see the old farm, Jeffery. Because you said yourself that nobody knew about the cutbacks except for the family. Yet the newspapers obviously know."

"So, go ask them," Jeffery replied. "Isn't that what you do? You investigate. Ask them who told them about the cutbacks."

"If you think my time would be well spent trying to convince a journalist to give up his or her source, then it's a good job you're in manufacturing," Charles said. "Besides, if we go to the newspapers, they'll print a story about how inefficient the force is, or how we're scratching for clues."

"Which you are," Jeffery said, and Charles saw more than a hint of victorious glee in his eyes.

"Your sister is missing and your nephew is dead," Charles said.

"And somebody knows who is behind it all. And if that person isn't a Dickens, then they damn well work here."

"And if they work here," Devon said, "then they have access to the farm."

"Get the keys, Jeffery," Charles said.

"What? She can't be in there. It's a pile of bricks. There's only a couple of buildings still standing and they don't even have roofs on."

"It shouldn't take long then, should it?" Charles said, and he took a step towards the brothers, keeping his hands in his pockets. "She could be in there right now. We already know she's hurt. Why wouldn't you want to find her?"

"Of course I want to find her," he hissed.

"DC Devon will accompany you," Charles said, then glanced across at Thomas who had barely uttered a word. "You can wait with me. Perhaps you can fill me in on more of your rich family history while we wait?"

The office was welcoming only in the fact that it protected them from the fierce wind outside. The walls were painted a dull magnolia with framed prints of sports stars, most of which Hannaway had seen before in various shops. They weren't even signed, but he had to admit, the monochrome images suited the rather bleak decor of the old, converted cottage with its exposed beams and rough-finished walls.

"You want to do what?" Robert said. "Every property?"

"Only the unoccupied properties," Hannaway said. "We can visit the rest of them later."

"We can't just walk into people's homes. There are rules, you know?"

"I fully appreciate—"

"I mean, how would you feel if somebody just turned up at

your house and demanded to look around? You wouldn't let them in, would you?"

"That all depends," Hannaway replied.

"On?"

"On whether or not the individuals in question, i.e., you two, were respectable property managers, and whether or not I had something to hide. Personally, if I had nothing to hide and wanted to aid a serious police investigation, and the men who managed my property were decent blokes, then I'd have no problem." Hannaway watched the pair internalise their arguments. "But like I said, we'll begin with the unoccupied properties. Perhaps we can provide the residents with some kind of advanced notice while we search the empty places?"

"We need to give twenty-four hours' notice," Roy said.

Hannaway checked his watch.

"Can we do that now?" he said. "We're talking about more than twenty properties. How many of those are empty?"

"Three," Roy said. "But can I ask a question?"

"Of course," Hannaway replied.

"What's all this about? You said this is a serious police investigation, and I get that you're withholding information, but can we at least know what you're looking for? We might even be able to help."

Hannaway ran a hand through his natural curls, taking a moment to consider his response. The two seemed like good men, they were clearly trusted by the family, and all their objections had been to protect either the residents or the Dickens family.

"How well do you know the family?" he asked, to which Roy shrugged.

"We've worked with them for years. Why?"

"Because they're going through a particularly hard time," Hannaway explained, and the shorter of the two's eyes narrowed thoughtfully.

"Not that young lad yesterday?" He glanced across at his

brother briefly and then back at Hannaway. "The hit and run. They were all talking about it in the pub last night. It wasn't little Harry, was it?"

"I'm afraid so," Hannaway said.

"But what does that have to do with the houses?" Robert asked. "What are you looking for?"

"Not what, who," Hannaway replied, then gave in. It was obvious if he was to get the unlikely pair on board, he'd have to provide some sort of explanation. "Janice Dickens went missing shortly afterwards. Her car was seen leaving the scene of the crime."

"Janice? No way. She wouldn't do that. Not to her own bloody nephew anyway."

"It may surprise you to learn that we agree. Myself and the senior investigating officer are anyway."

"So, what then?" Robert said. "I really can't see the link here."

Hannaway stared up at the huge beanpole of a man. Every part of his expression formed a picture of genuine, grave concern.

"It's easier to understand if you see it as the events unfolded," he said. "The boy was hit. Janice's car was seen leaving the scene of the crime. She hasn't been home. Her husband hasn't seen her and her car has vanished."

"Haven't you got access to those cameras?" Roy said. "You know? The ones on the traffic lights and whatnot."

"ANPR. Yes, of course. The car hasn't passed through a single camera, and believe me, it's almost impossible to go a few miles without being picked up these days, let alone leave the county," Hannaway said. "Which led us to believe that Janice Dickens somehow accidentally knocked her nephew down and then fled. In cases like that, the culprit usually faces up to the truth. Not many people could live with themselves after such a terrible accident."

"But?" Roy said. "I'm sensing a but here."

"Since then, we've been convinced that Janice wasn't altogether to blame," Hannaway said with evident reluctance. "In fact, we're quite sure she's not to blame."

"So, who is?" Roy asked.

"Somebody with a grudge against the family. Or at least a grudge against the family business."

"Right, so you're investigating half of Lincolnshire then, are you?" Robert asked, sarcastically.

"No," Hannaway said. "In fact, we're only investigating a handful of people. You see, we believe Janice Dickens has been kidnapped."

"You what?"

"I know," Hannaway said. "It sounds like something from a film, but I can assure you, if you knew the details, you'd agree."

"What are they demanding?" Roy asked. "I presume they're making some kind of demand?"

"And what about the boy?" Robert added. "Why was he involved?"

Hannaway held his hands up in defence.

"We're still building the facts," he said.

"And who are the people you're looking into?" Roy asked, to which Hannaway cleared his throat and prepared to deliver the punchline.

"The family," he said.

"You what?"

"The family," he repeated. "You see, we believe that whoever is doing this is doing so because of a decision the firm has recently made."

"I don't understand," Robert said. "What decision?"

"I can't go into details, but suffice to say that only the family knew about this decision."

"Hence why you want to look at the properties," Roy said, piecing the parts together.

"That's right," Hannaway replied. "If a member of the family *is* behind this, then it seems plausible that they might arrange for Janice to be kept in one of the properties."

"They can't have. We'd know about it."

Hannaway grinned back at him.

"Precisely."

"Jesus," Roy said, and he dropped into a nearby seat.

"So?" Hannaway said, unwilling to let the momentum wane. "Are you willing to help us?"

"We are," Roy said quietly. "But can I ask one thing?"

"Go on," Hannaway replied.

"Is she alive? Janice, I mean. Is she still alive?"

Hannaway watched the concern on the man's face and admired the hope in his eyes.

"We believe so," he said. "And thank you for your help. I'll make sure the family hears about it. Hopefully, that'll put you in good favour."

"Thank you," Robert said, and Roy nodded his agreement.

"You said there were three empty properties?" Hannaway said, and though distracted by their imaginations, they both confirmed. "Which means there are twenty-two occupied properties. Is that right?"

"It is," Roy said.

"I'm going to need to see twenty-two live rental agreements," Hannaway said and gave them an apologetic look. "It's just so I can demonstrate that every vacant property was searched."

"I can do that," Robert said, and he made his way towards a set of three old, steel filing cabinets. He pulled open a drawer and puffed out his cheeks. "Why don't you two make a start on Sleaford Road? I'll collate the paperwork and meet you there."

His brother nodded and then pushed himself from the chair.

"There is one more property that we don't manage, of course," Roy said, and Hannaway stopped to read the troubled expression on his face.

"Roy?" his brother said from the far side of the room and gave him an accompanying warning look.

"Dickens Farm."

"Dickens Farm?" Hannaway replied. "That's not on the list. Why don't you manage it?"

"Nobody does," Robert said, from the far side of the room. "It's derelict. Fallen down, mostly. The family don't like people to know about it. Last time I went down there, you couldn't even see it, the place was so overgrown."

"There are a few buildings still standing. Just about, anyway," Roy added. "It's not very safe."

"You're really selling it," Hannaway said.

"Well, I wouldn't want to live there, and thankfully I don't have to present it to prospective residents," Robert said. "But if you wanted to hide somebody, it would be perfect."

CHAPTER 33

"It's perfect," Cook said, once they had pushed through the overgrown bushes and had begun walking across the fallen stones. Devon cast an eye across the site, looking for a sign that somebody had been there recently, and then looked up at him.

"What's that, guv?" she said.

"I said, it's perfect," he replied, stepping around a charred spot, where a vagrant or some kids had built a fire. "Anyway, you took your time getting the keys. Procrastinating, was he?"

"I don't know. I waited downstairs," she said. "Besides, Gareth's car was in the car park."

"Gareth?" he said, in disbelief, then lowered his voice to a hiss. "What the hell is he doing at work? You'd think he'd be bloody mourning the loss of his son."

Devon said nothing, hoping her face would say it all.

"And you preferred not to engage with him?" he said, then agreed. "I don't blame you."

She gave him a look to signal that he was right, but that it was perhaps for the best if they didn't discuss the topic while the brothers were in earshot. Then she cast an eye about the place, taking in the derelict farm.

From ground level, she began to wonder if there had been some substance in what Jeffery Dickens had said about seeing the site from above. From where she stood, only a few of the lower courses of stonework could be made out, and many of those were rather dubious on account of the piles of local limestone bricks lying where the weather, wind, and gravity had decided. In some cases, the walls were still half standing, whilst in others, perhaps because of their sheltered positioning, they remained upright, although Devon dared not stand beside them. The hardhat and high visibility vest that she and Jeffery had fetched would do very little to protect her against a crumbling wall.

"Perfect for what, anyway?" she said.

"Sorry?"

"You said the place was perfect. Perfect for what, guv? It's like a scene from Time Team. I keep expecting Tony Robinson to pop his head over one of the walls. Nobody has been here for years."

"Oh, I wouldn't say that," Cook replied, as he fingered the broken limb of a hawthorn, then eyed the ground.

"What is it?" she said, but he was far too preoccupied to respond and pulled an irritated face to support his silence. He traced a path through the rubble, then disappeared around a corner. Both Thomas and Jeffery followed, leaving Devon to bring up the rear, stopping first to inspect the hawthorn.

She couldn't begin to know how he'd seen it, but it was there. A thin limb had been pushed back, snapping the protective bark to reveal a glimpse of pale wood inside. Not being a horticulturist, Devon had no idea of how long such a wound would remain so vivid in colour, but she trusted Cook's observation, and given that he had spouted the Latin name for the plant near the pond at the Dickens house, she was sure he would know.

She followed the three men, being mindful not to twist an ankle on the smatter of stones, rounding a corner and following the brothers' bemused voices as they sought a response from Cook.

The outhouse they had spoken of seemed to take pride of place in a clearing between the ruined barns and sheds, the tumbledown farmhouse, and one of the more resilient of structures. The clearing was like a courtyard in appearance, with the buildings forming a kind of horseshoe shape around it, and she imagined people emerging from the farmhouse doorway in all weathers to use the facilities. She wondered if she would have managed such a feat during one of those long, dark winter nights, or if she might have held on until the morning.

"Devon," Cook called out, and she was torn from her imaginings back to reality. There was something in his tone that suggested urgency and she found herself scrambling over crumbled stonework in pursuit of his voice. She found them in one of the barns, having forced the old, weathered door.

The look on Thomas and Jeffery's faces supported Cook's urgency, and as she manoeuvred past them, she saw the cause.

A layer of dust had settled on the grey paint, but still, against the centuries-old backdrop, the Audi appeared like some kind of time machine, and Cook, donning a blue, latex glove, the curious ancient, testing the temper of this strange and alien thing.

He glanced up at Devon as he moved round to the back of the car and she edged past the brothers to join him.

The rear bumper bore a slight dent in the centre, made noticeable by a tiny smear of dried blood. Cook shook his head, suggesting they keep that little gem to themselves for the time being.

The lock clicked when his thumb depressed the button and they each held their breath in anticipation of what they might find. The opening of the boot lid turned the interior light on to reveal the black carpet through the crack. The wider he opened the lid, the more of that black carpet they saw, expecting at some point for the view to be marred by a pair of bound feet or a mass of straggled hair.

Eventually, Cook went for a bust. He let the lid open of its own accord and they stared down at the contents with mixed emotions.

"Well?" Thomas said, a slight quiver in his voice. "Is she..."

Unable to finish his sentence, he stared across at them, silhouetted against the backdrop of the Lincolnshire sky so that the only features that defined him were the glints of his wet eyes.

Eventually, Cook shook his head.

"Thank god," Cook said, tugging the glove off and stuffing it into his pocket. He paced a few steps and then returned to Devon's side. "I want CSI down here within the hour."

Whereas Devon might have thought the two brothers would embrace with renewed hope of their sister's fate, she found they'd barely moved, as if the whole ordeal had scared them stiff.

It was only Jeffery's phone that broke the spell that bound them, and he reached into his pocket to answer it.

"Mum?' he said, turning away to talk outside, in private.

"As I was saying," Cook continued. "I want CSI down here, uniformed officers on the gates, and most of all, I want to know how that car came to be here." He looked up at Thomas, who was watching his brother through the open barn door. "Thomas, is there another way in?"

"There's only one gate for vehicles," he replied, looking back over his shoulder to where his brother was on the phone.

"Have the area cordoned off, Devon," Cook said, as she created a list of tasks in her notepad. "Nobody is to touch that gate." Again, he sought information from the youngest of the brothers. "Where does it lead? How do you get to the gates from outside?"

"There's a track across the fens," he replied. "Off of Five Mile Lane. But nobody ever uses it. The gate's been locked for years."

"Well, somebody has used it," Cook replied, just as Jeffery re-entered the barn, the dim light revealing enough of his expression to reveal the news wasn't positive. "You look like you've seen a ghost, Jeffery. What is it?"

"It's Mum," he replied, quietly, and then after a moment of staring at the car, he looked directly at Cook, the way a child might look to his father. "They've called her. The people who have Janice. They've made contact."

Devon watched in horror as the three men each sought some kind of answer in the other's expressions, each coming up short until Cook took stock of the situation.

"Jeffery, did you get me that employee list?" he said.

"No, I couldn't find anything that isn't confidential. We do have to protect personal data, you know?"

"I think we're way beyond worrying about GDP regulations, Jeffery," Cook replied.

"I suppose you could use the health and safety register in Janice's office," Thomas said. "I saw it earlier. That should include everyone who has access to the site."

"Thank you, Thomas," Cook replied. "Would you mind getting it for me? Devon, you stay here until the circus arrives. Get CSI to work, tell them about the gate, and then see if one of them can drop you at the house."

"I'll wait for you if it helps," Thomas said. "I can bring her."

"I would have thought you'd want to be with your family, Thomas," Cook said.

"What I want, Inspector," he replied, "is for my sister to be found and for this whole sordid affair to be finished with. And if that means I need to stay behind and give your colleague a lift, then so be it."

"Devon? Are you okay with that?"

"Yes, guv," she said. "It might take a while, though."

"That's okay," Thomas said. "I've plenty to be getting on with. Come and find me at the office when you're ready."

"Right, well, that settles it," Cook said and turned to Jeffery. "You can ride with me."

CHAPTER 34

To Charles's surprise, Susie was still present when he arrived at the Dickens house, following an overly panicked Jeffery into the living room, who dropped to his knees beside his mother and held her hand.

Susie looked up at him and then shied when she read the expression on his face. Just as before, Abbott was on the bench outside. In fact, aside from Thomas and Gareth not being present, the only real difference to the scene was the addition of young Arthur, who was nestled into his grandmother with tear-stained eyes.

"Mrs Dickens," Charles said, and she looked up at him, shocked as if she was seeing him for the first time. But then the tautness in her face softened. "Are you okay?"

"I'm far from okay, Inspector Cook," she replied, though her tone was far softer than her words.

"I'm sorry," he replied. "That was a poor choice of words." She gave a slight shake of her head as if dismissing the topic, and Charles stared through the window at Abbott. "And your husband?"

"Abbott needs time to think," she said. "That's his place. It's where he decides on the best course of action."

"And by taking himself away he prevents himself from saying something he might later regret?" Charles asked tentatively.

"He hasn't always done that," she said. "There was a time when he wore his heart on his sleeve. Life has hardened him, I think."

"With the ailments of age comes wisdom," Charles offered.

"Let days speak and many years teach wisdom," she replied, as if she knew he was going to say that, and to which he had a ready response.

"The book of Job," he said, and she smiled at his understanding. "We need to discuss the call. Perhaps it would be for the best if..." He nodded at the boy.

"Arthur knows what's going on," Jeffery said.

"Even still."

"He stays," Jeffery said, his glare daring Charles to argue.

"Then, perhaps you could provide an account of what happened," Charles said to Elizabeth. "And of course, what was said."

"I'll take him," Susie said, rising and straightening her clothes. "This is a family thing."

"And you are family," Jeffery interjected.

"Not quite," she said, after a moment or two of thought. She held out her hand to Arthur. "Come on. How about you show me the new toys you got for Christmas?"

The boy seemed so small in the nook of his grandmother's arm, and he peered up at her for permission. Slowly, she relented, letting him go with obvious reluctance and watching with sadness as Susie led him from the room. Charles waited for the sound of Susie's voice to fade, then cleared his throat.

On the bench outside, Abbott watched them all, making no effort to come and join them, and neither did his expression offer any sort of indication as to his plans or thoughts.

Charles stepped slowly over to the couch that Susie had vacated.

"May I?" he said, and Elizabeth nodded curtly.

"Of course," she said. "I should make some tea."

"Not on my behalf," Charles said, seeing her own half-filled cup on the coffee table.

"Well, Jeffery then. You'd like some, wouldn't you?"

He moved from his crouch to perch on the edge of the sofa beside her.

"Just tell us what they said, Mum. What is it they want?"

She sat back, for the first time her shoulders seeming to relax. Then slowly, she let her head rest on the cushion behind her, closed her eyes, and took a deep breath.

"Chief Inspector," she said, whilst in an apparent trance-like state to control her emotions. "You told us you had an idea of what they would demand." Her eyes opened, and she looked directly at him, but she said nothing more, waiting for him to respond as if it had been he who had made the demand.

He felt Jeffery's inquisitive stare, penetrative, accusing, and unrelenting.

"Chief Inspector?" Jeffery said, using his full title for the first time, perhaps because of his mother's presence. "You also said you have some experience of this type of thing. We'd very much like to hear what you have to say."

"The way I see it, this family has enjoyed a position of power for many years. You have earned a healthy respect from many of the locals," he said. "But let's not forget that communities are subject to opinion, bias, and even swayed by perception."

"This is not the time for a cryptic crossword," Jeffery said.

"Okay then. Do you imagine that the entire population of North Kesteven votes conservative?"

"What?" he said. "No, probably not."

"So you agree that, although we share a sense of pride in where we live, we do not all share the same sense of what is just and unjust. Not everyone here will be a fan of the Dickens family, with your wealth and perceived power."

"Probably not," Jeffery said. "Especially with the cutbacks we've been making."

"And there you have it," Charles said. "The cutbacks. You see, when governments or management make difficult decisions for the greater good, those who fall foul of the plans, whose lives are made harder, often feel hard done by. Resentful even. It rather reminds me of Thatcher's decisions not to bail out the steel and mining industries in the eighties, and we all know what happened then."

"No," Jeffery said. "Some of us were just kids in the eighties."

"There were riots," Elizabeth explained. "The whole country was falling apart."

"Not falling," Charles said. "It was being torn apart. Falling suggests the country was being impacted by natural events." He shook his head to convey the gravity of his words. "Whereas, in fact, it was being torn apart by individuals who felt wronged by Thatcher's decisions. Individuals who were in positions of power, or influence, and who created mass hysteria. They even made an attempt on her life."

"The Brighton bomb?" Elizabeth said, nodding slowly. "I remember it."

"They tried to force her to step down. Members of her cabinet turned their backs on her. She was alone. Right up to the end, she was alone until she had no choice but to concede."

The front door slammed, and moments later, Gareth rushed into the room. He didn't hurry to his mother as Jeffery had done. Instead, he slowed when he saw the three in discussion, saw his father outside on the bench, and then lowered himself into the armchair.

"What's happening?" he asked, then looked at his mother. "Mum?"

"The good chief inspector was just likening us to Margaret Thatcher in the eighties," Jeffery said.

"What?"

"Whoever is doing this wants one thing, Gareth," Charles said. "They want to see the Dickens empire come to an end, and they'll go to any means to achieve it."

"Mum?" Gareth said, but she said nothing, choosing instead to let Charles embellish his comment.

"They want the business to close," Charles said. "Do that, and they'll release Janice."

"They want what?" Gareth said, again, looking to his mother for some kind of contest to Charles's theory.

"He's right. We're being torn apart," she said.

"And just like Thatcher's government," Charles added. "You're being torn apart from the inside."

"From the inside?" Gareth said, looking to his brother for some kind clue as to what he was talking about. "You mean…"

"I mean that I believe whoever is behind all of this, whoever constructed Janice's kidnapping, whoever is responsible for your son's death, Gareth, and whoever wants to bring Dickens and Sons down," Charles said, "is a member of this family."

"What rubbish," Gareth said. "None of us want to destroy the family business." He snatched up Elizabeth's phone and scrolled through the list of calls. "They withheld the number," he spat, tossing the phone back onto the coffee table. "Bloody cowards."

"Elizabeth?" Charles said, ignoring the hot-headed outburst.

"They said that Abbott is to make a statement by midday tomorrow," she said.

"A statement? You mean, a press statement, Mum?" Gareth asked, but she ignored him and seemed to cling to Charles's stare.

"Or?" Charles said quietly.

But she just shook her head, unable to speak those terrible words.

CHAPTER 35

"Let's have two of you on the front gate, two on the gate to Five Mile Lane, and two here on the old farm. Would that be all right, Sergeant?" Devon asked. "CSI are pulling prints and DNA from the car inside that barn over there."

"Righto," Sergeant Hammond said, pulling his bright yellow jacket onto his broad shoulders. He pulled his hat on and then slammed the boot of the liveried car. He called to two of the officers who were waiting for instructions and was about to get to work when Devon tugged on his jacket.

"Sergeant?" she said, and he stared down at her hand on his arm. She let it drop to her side and smiled an apology. "It goes without saying that the press should be kept away. I don't think DCI Cook would want them seeing anything."

He cast his eye across the strewn stones and few remaining buildings, then up at the glass offices and brick factory beyond the thick wall of thorny vegetation.

"The Dickens are having a rough time," he said, then grinned at her surprise. "They were in the paper the other day. Something about redundancies."

"We can't speculate on–"

"You've got the crime scene lot on a derelict farm owned by the Dickens family. The good DCI Cook is embroiled in family affairs. You can't tell me they're not linked to the redundancies."

"How did you know?"

"Oh, people talk, Devon. People talk," he said, seeming to enjoy the elevated position he held. "Especially when the topic of conversation is the richest the people in the area and the unlikeliest duo in the entire police force. People talk."

"What else have they said? These people."

"Oh, nothing much. Only that Cook seems to have taken a shine to you," he said, then leaned back to give her a visual appraisal from head to toe, and seemed far from impressed. "I bet you'd swallow an old man like Cook whole, wouldn't you? Especially if it meant getting a little helping hand towards becoming sergeant, and I'm sure lonely old Cook's hands would have plenty to hold onto."

"You pig," she hissed as one of the uniformed PCSOs joined them.

"Sergeant?" one of them said, waiting for Hammond to give them an instruction. He looked awkwardly between them as if he was aware of interrupting something.

Hammond continued to stare at Devon for a moment longer, daring her to create something more from the interaction, with a witness to hear her response.

"I'll let you get on," Hammond said to her. "You wouldn't want to disappoint the old man now, would you?"

He made a gripping motion with both of his hands and she turned her back on him, disgusted by the blatant inappropriate behaviour. She was always hearing of reports of misconduct, but so often the victims were far prettier, smaller, and even younger.

She stumbled over a pile of stone, rather than walking around it. Anything to get away from him as fast as she could, but only to hear the malice in his laugh, which of course then encouraged the younger PCSOs to join in. Thankfully none of them called out, and she ducked behind the cover of the old barn to regain some composure. She pressed herself flat against the old, stone wall, acutely aware that it was one of few walls still standing and that it could come tumbling down at any moment. But, to hell with it. There was no way she could let that pig of a man see her as upset as she was.

It was only as she stood there, alone in the near silence, that she could truly imagine life as it had been. The skeletal remains of buildings and even the smaller structures that barely had a single course of stonework left, all added to the illusion.

Or was it an escape? Was the scene she pictured just an escape from the cruel world in which she lived?

Through the mass of tangled branches and thorns that encircled the old farmyard, the glass building in the distance appeared almost ghostly, reflecting the blue winter sky and the distant landscape like it was a gateway to somewhere very different. It was, of course, a different world, a view of which she absorbed while she cast Sergeant Hammond's foul tongue to some dark corner of her mind. She watched as the arm of the barrier on the front gate rose and fell to allow a lorry through. And then she saw it. Atop a tall pole beside the main entrance. A camera. A camera that, had the Audi passed through the main gate, might have captured the face of the driver.

She shoved off the wall, just as a figure stepped into view to her left, and she startled before realising it was one of the crime scene investigators, a tall blonde with a figure that Devon would have given her right arm for. She lifted her goggles to sit on top of her white hood and then pulled her mask down to answer her phone.

"Michaela Fell," she said, then looked up and waved at the driver of the lorry that had come to a stop on the far side of the surrounding thicket, where the car park ended. She stood on a small pile of stone to make herself taller, and the driver flashed his lights. "No, we couldn't get our little van through, so I doubt you'll get that thing across the rubble," she said. "There's another gate off of Five Mile Lane. You'll have to go back out of the main gate and through Washingborough." She paused a moment to listen to the driver talking and then told him she would see him in a few moments. It was only when she had pocketed her phone and was pulling her mask back into place that Devon spoke.

"Is that the lorry that will take the Audi away?" she asked, which came as a surprise to the blonde.

"Oh, hello. I didn't see you there," she said, tucking a clear folder under her arm so she could fish a fresh pair of gloves from her pocket. "Yes, it is. Sadly, my colleague, Pat, didn't tell the driver about the rubble all over the track. But not to worry. We're all done here. There's nothing much more we can do until we get the car into the workshop and the samples in the lab."

"Have you managed to find anything?" Devon asked.

The tall blonde handed Devon the clear A4 envelope in her hand.

"This was on the back seat. We've taken prints from the plastic already," she said. "Any use to you?"

Devon took the envelope, opened it carefully, and fingered through the few sheets of paper inside, each of them printed on Dickens and Sons headed paper. It was the title of the second sheet that caught her eye.

"2023/24 Redundancy Schedule," Devon read aloud, then scoffed at the red text beneath it. "Confidential."

"Is it linked?" Michaela asked. "The layoffs, I mean. Do you think it's got anything to do with all this?"

She gestured to the barn with a nod of her head.

"We think so," Devon replied, closing the envelope. "Anything else?"

"A few prints on the car, but nothing on the steering wheel, door handle, or gear stick."

"Nothing at all? Wiped clean, maybe?"

"Most likely. But like I said, we won't know anything until we're back at the lab."

"What about the blood on the bumper?"

She smiled beneath her mask and shook her head.

"Nothing concrete. Not yet," she said. "And before you ask, give me twenty-four hours and I'll have something for you. Forty-eight hours and you'll have a full report."

"What about the box and its contents?" Devon asked

"We should have something for you today. It might have been this morning if we hadn't been called out."

"You know DCI Cook will want to fast-track this one, don't you?" Devon said.

"Don't you all," she replied. "I don't think any of you have ever told me to take my time on this one, or said, in your own time, Michaela."

"Well, this one is no different. If anything, it's even more critical," Devon said, then read the inquisitive expression Michaela adopted. "We think the car is involved in a kidnapping incident. We're hoping that what you find in the car will help us find the victim."

"Are they still alive?" she asked, her manicured nails fingering the rolled rim of a latex glove.

"As far as we know," Devon said. "Forty-eight hours is a big ask though. They've been missing for longer than that."

"We'll do our best," the investigator said. "Consider it fast-tracked. You'll have some news today. Maybe not a full report, but I'll give you what I can."

"Thank you, Doctor Fell," Devon replied.

"Call me Michaela, please," she replied, then removed her goggles again. "Are you quite okay? You look a little peaky."

"Do I?" Devon said, suddenly embarrassed enough to avert her eyes. "I'm afraid peaky is my go-to complexion."

Michaela smiled, but her intelligent eyes suggested she neither believed Devon's excuse nor did she dare press for answers.

"Well, leave it with me then," Michaela said, finally snapping her glove into place. "I'd better go and help Pat wrap up. With any luck, we can get out of here without that Sergeant Hammond seeing us." Devon cringed at the mention of Hammond's name, which the intuitive investigator seemed to pick up on. "He hit on you as well, did he? What a grease ball."

"Something like that," Devon replied. "Anyway, I'd better be off. I said I'd stay until you were done, and, well, you're pretty much there, aren't you?"

"We are," Michaela said. "Either myself or Pat will be in touch. Now get out of here before Hammond comes back."

Devon left the ruined farm in a daze, and as soon as she was clear of the bushes, she looked up at the office block in dismay. She blinked a few times in case her vision had been marred by the tears that had threatened to fall.

Hurriedly, she made her way over to the offices, skirting around the edge of the car park to avoid the noisy factory. She pulled her phone from her pocket, found the list of recently dialled numbers, and then called the first on the list.

Her heart thumped while she waited for the call to be answered, and for a moment, she thought it might ring out. But eventually, a tired voice coughed once and then spoke.

"Hello, Devon," Cook said. "How's it going down there? I thought you would have been out of there by now."

"I was hoping to be leaving right now, guv," she said. "But Thomas isn't here. He was supposed to wait for me."

"What do you mean?" Cook asked. "Have you checked the office? Is his car there?"

"No, guv," she said. "He must have left without me. His car's gone."

CHAPTER 36

It was that time of year when the lights in the street windows reminded John that Christmas had only been a few days ago. It was a time of limbo when nothing seemed to move forward. When everything you hoped to achieve had to wait until the new year had been celebrated and life began to return to normal.

He closed his car door, locked it, and then leaned on the roof for a moment to catch his breath, compose his thoughts, and prepare the narrative that Penny would no doubt want to hear.

He rummaged in his bag and pulled out the bag of sandwiches Penny had given him earlier, and deeming the car the only real place to stash them, he unlocked the door, slung them onto the passenger seat, and then, just as he locked it again, he noticed the dust on the knees of his trousers.

"You're early," somebody said from behind him, in that voice he both adored and dreaded to hear. He brushed the dust as best he could, and then turned to face her. "And you're dirty."

"We had a bit of a clear out," he said. "You know, while the office is slow."

"They got you in over Christmas only for you to have a clear out? Do these people think you don't have a life? Do they even know you have children? Do they even know it's Christmas?"

"Of course they do," he told her, as she stepped in closer and began brushing more dust from his shoulders.

"You're filthy, love," she said. "What on earth have you been doing?"

"Like I said, clearing out. The filing room can get a bit dusty. Nobody really goes in there."

"So why keep them? Why not just digitalise everything?"

"We have to keep hard copies for ten years or something," he replied. "Some kind of legislation. I don't know." He put his arm around her, smiled, and then led her towards the house. "Come on. Let's get inside. You haven't even got a coat on."

But something caught her eye, and she slipped from his grip to peer into the car.

"You haven't eaten your sandwiches," she said, looking confused and a little hurt.

"Oh, you know how it is, darling. I don't always get the time."

"And what's that?" she asked, shielding the windows from the sun as she peered into the back of the car. Her expression altered somewhat, to convey a look of utter bewilderment. "Is that your old tool bag?"

"My tools?" he said, feeling his heart plunge to the depths of his stomach. "Oh, that's right. I said I'd bring them in case we had to move stuff around."

"What's the other bag?" she asked, trying the door handle but finding it locked.

"Babe?"

"John, what's going on?" she asked. "That's the weekend bag I got you a few years ago. Why's that in there?"

"It's nothing."

"John," she said, in a tone that left very little room for manoeuvre. He stared at her, unable to find any words that would help in the slightest. "Open the car door."

"Oh, come on—"

"Open the door, John," she said. "Now."

"Leave it, Penny. The kids are inside. Let's just—"

"The kids are at Mum and Dad's," she said.

"Your mum and dad's?"

"They offered to have them, and I said yes."

"Without asking me?"

"Don't try to turn this around, John. Open the car door, please."

"You sent the kids to your parents' house without running it by me? I thought we always checked with each other before—"

"Open the *bloody* door," she snapped, loud enough to send delayed ripples through a few of the neighbours' curtains. Then she lowered her tone to a veritable hiss. "You've been acting odd all week. Going out at night. Not saying where you're going. Working every hour under the sun."

"I just want to make—"

"Some memories, John. Yes, I know. So you keep saying. But the only memories we've made this Christmas are of me and the kids and you and your bloody lies."

"I'm not lying," he told her, matching her volume but caring enough to lower his voice. "I can't believe you sent the kids off to your mum and dad's. I came home to spend some time with them."

"Well, you might have told us. Honestly, John. You said you'd be home at six."

"I've been working my backside off all bloody week."

"You've done no such thing," she said, her voice loud enough to carry down the length of the entire street. She'd won the match for the loudest voice, and now they did battle with locked stares.

"What did you say?" he said, and with obvious shame, she averted her gaze to stare at the ground.

"I said, you've done no such thing," she repeated. Then with her expression wrought with regret, she looked up at him as if it might be for the last time. "I know."

"You know what?"

"I know," she said. "I called your office."

"You did, what?"

"I called your office, John. I spoke to your boss."

"Janice? You spoke to Janice Dickens?"

"No, she wasn't in. I spoke to Gareth."

"You did what? He's the bloody CEO."

"Oh, he was very accommodating," Penny said. "In fact, it was like he was going out of his way to be helpful. Not the impression I originally had of him, but he was nice enough to check the rota for me." It was as if every one of John's muscles and organs had suddenly been wrenched downward, and the bile in his gut rose under the pressure. "You haven't been in the office for a week. It appears that you applied for annual leave back in November."

"Oh, Penny—"

"Where have you been, John?" she said, folding her arms, apparently oblivious to the cold.

"I can't say," he told her. "Honestly, babe—"

"Don't," she said, holding a hand out before her. "Just don't lie to me, please. Not anymore."

"Why don't we talk about this inside?" he suggested, to which she shook her head.

"No. No, I want to be on my own."

"Oh, Penny don't do this."

"Who is she?" she asked, somehow managing to keep her voice flat and calm so much so that she almost lost her Lincolnshire accent.

"Who's who?"

"The other woman," she said. "Who is she?"

"What other woman?"

"Is it Janice? Is that who it is?" she asked.

"No, of course not."

"You spend enough time with her. It was only last month that you said you found her crying in her office. No doubt you comforted her. Did it lead on from there?"

"Nothing led on from anywhere, Penny. You've got this all wrong."

"But you did comfort her?"

"What? Yes, of course I did. Just like I would hope somebody would comfort you if I wasn't there."

"Then what is it, John? What is it? What have you been doing all week? Where do you go when you go out at night? And how come we're suddenly well off enough to pay for bloody Disney World?"

"Would you believe me if I said there was nothing to worry about?" he said quietly, knowing that she would scoff at the idea. "Would you just let me tell you in my own time?"

Their stares clashed again and he held her gaze hoping that she might love him enough to believe him, or believe *in* him at least.

"In your own time?" she muttered, sounding as if she might cry at any moment. Then she nodded and took a few steps towards the house, where she turned to face him. "You can come home when you're ready to tell me."

"Babe?" he said and ran after her only to come face to face with the closing front door. He slammed his hand against the wood. "Penny, come on. Open the door. Penny, please."

But he knew her well enough to know that she was as stubborn as she was beautiful. He turned and pressed his back against the door as he heard the bolts slide into place on the other side.

"Penny, you've got to believe me."

But she didn't reply and his adrenaline waned. The cold air seemed to feed off of his fear. The street during the Christmas limbo was quiet enough for him to hear her sobs from inside, and he closed his eyes to block the noise, pulling his coat tight around him.

He dropped to a crouch, plucking his phone from his pocket, only to read the single message with equal measures of hope and dread.

It's done, the message began. *Meet me there.*

CHAPTER 37

"I left him there," Gareth said, and he locked stares with Charles. "He got something from Janice's office and then left. He should have been here before me."

"He said he was going to wait for DC Devon," Charles said. "But his car wasn't there."

"No, he left with me. I followed him out of the gate," Gareth said.

"So, you followed him home?" Charles asked.

"Not exactly. I dropped Victoria off in Waddington. She wasn't sure if the buses were running."

"The receptionist?" Charles said.

"I'm not a monster, Chief Inspector. I'm not going to make her get the bus when it's just a five-minute detour for me."

"Even when your mother has received such a terrible call?" Charles said. "It looks like I had you all wrong, Gareth."

"But what does all this mean?" Jeffery said. "They can't expect us to close the business. I mean, that could take months."

"They want a statement," Elizabeth said. "They want us to announce that the business will be winding down."

"A statement?" Gareth cried out again. "That's enough to sink us. The other shareholders will pull out. We'll be in liquidation by the time the bloody New Year fireworks go off."

"Elizabeth?" Charles said. "Can you tell me exactly what they said?"

"Just that," she replied, then turned to face her eldest son. "We've got until midday tomorrow to make a statement."

"But how the bloody hell are we going to do that?" Gareth said. "Don't they just want money or something? I thought all this was just some attempt to make somebody else rich."

"This is far from such a thing," Charles said. "Does the company have somebody who manages your PR? A marketing team or something? Maybe a member of middle management?"

"We don't have a marketing team," Gareth said. "We've been around longer than anybody has been alive. Most of the businesses that need our services already know about us. Why the bloody hell would we advertise?"

"So you don't have any links to the press?" Charles said. "I thought I heard somebody mention the opening of your new office building. Who organised that?"

"Oh, well, we've got phone numbers of course. Thomas does all that. He uses an agency, I think."

"Thomas?" Charles said, waiting for the rest of the room to make the connection that he had.

"Yes, Thomas," Gareth replied, then his head cocked to one side when he saw Charles's expression. "Hang on. You don't think—"

"I've made no attempt to mask my true thoughts since my first visit, Gareth," Charles said, then turned his attention to the mother. "I'm sorry, Mrs Dickens. But we have to be realistic."

"Thomas isn't capable of it," she said softly, although not without an element of doubt in her tone.

"Thomas was one of the few who knew about the cutbacks. He has access to any files he might need, and now we learn that

Thomas is the one who would have access to the press and media."

"Why don't we contact the newspaper?" Jeffery suggested. "Surely all you need to do is call them, speak to the reporter who wrote the article, and ask them if it was Thomas who told them."

"And what do you think that would achieve?" Charles asked, and Jeffery stood, turned his back, and paced the few steps to the window where he stared out at his father.

"Well, you're obviously ready to lock Thomas up and throw away the key," he said. "Perhaps we could attempt to clear his name before you add a notch to your belt." He turned away from the window and stuffed his hands into his pockets. "Or are you tired of all this? Are we keeping you from your family, Inspector?"

"Jeffery, I feel I should remind you that your nephew has been killed and your sister apparently kidnapped, and the only potential motives I can deduce from everything I have learned these past few days is that either somebody is unhappy with the way they have been treated, or they are unhappy with the way others have been treated. Now, given that the decision to make cutbacks was only known to members of this family, then I can only deduce that one of you is unhappy with the way in which others have been treated. Somebody with a heart. Somebody who has a relationship with the press."

"You could at least talk to the reporter before you throw away the key, Inspector."

"And say what?" Charles said. "Ask them if one of the family has been in touch. Or who told them about the cutbacks?" Charles shook his head. "The media will never give up their sources, and even if they did tell us, all we would do by getting in touch would be to light the fuse. Before you know it, you'd have reporters from all over Lincolnshire camped on your doorstep." Jeffery opened his mouth to respond, but Charles was far from finished. "And as for throwing away the key, if I had my way, Jeffery, I'd have the lot of you down at the station being questioned. But given the devastation you've all been through, I've decided not to venture down that path just yet. Don't, for heaven's sake, tempt me to reconsider my sympathies."

"All my brother's saying, Inspector—" Gareth began.

"That's enough," a new voice said, as a cold breeze found Charles's thin socks. Abbott Dickens stood in an open bi-folding door, his presence far greater than his stature. "Chief Inspector Cook has explained himself. He's clearly shown us a great deal of respect. Let's not give a reason for him to make this any harder than it has to be."

"But, Dad, have you heard what he said about Thomas?" Gareth said. "Have you heard what he wants us to do?"

"There's not much I'm not privy to, Gareth," Abbott told him. "Perhaps you should take a leaf out of my book and gain some perspective somehow before you show your hand in its entirety."

"Dad, he's accusing Thomas—"

"I told you to shut up, Gareth," Abbott said, his face turning beetroot red. "Just shut up and let me think."

It wasn't only Gareth who silenced after Abbott's outburst. The room hushed, and only the crackle of wood in the log burner could be heard.

"Dad," Jeffery began.

"Don't push me, Jeffery—"

"I'm not. I was just wondering what we going to do about the demand."

Abbott closed the door behind him and then waved his hand for Gareth to vacate his seat. Once in his armchair, the old man seemed to consider his words before speaking, and when he did, they were aimed solely at Charles.

"Chief Inspector, it seems to me we have a decision to make," he began. "Either we make an announcement and begin to wind down the business, or what? What are the consequences? Do you think they'll really hurt her? Or..."

He stopped there, not willing to voice the alternative before his already distraught wife.

"I know as much as you," Charles replied. "Until we learn who these people are, we have no idea of the lengths they will go to."

"But you said that kidnappings occur more often than we think," Abbott said. "How do they normally come to an end?"

"I think your case is quite unique, Mr Dickens," Charles replied.

"But you said that you've had some experience of this type of thing. How did that end?"

It was as if Charles had been standing at the end of a dark tunnel, in which he could hear the train coming but was still surprised when it emerged and had scant time to avoid being hit.

"Badly," he said. "Very badly indeed."

He hoped his sombre expression would deter the old man from pressing for more information, but men such as Abbott Dickens rarely let matters of the heart get in the way of the truth.

"Somebody died, did they?" he asked.

Charles stared across the room at him, feeling his stomach turn at the memory of a terrible time in both his life and career.

"What will you do, Mr Dickens?" Charles asked. "Or does this decision belong to Gareth as the current CEO?"

"My son may be the current chief executive, however, I am the majority shareholder," Abbott replied. "The decision lies with me."

"Dad?" Gareth interjected.

"I said the decision lies with me, damn it," he said, then returned his attention to Charles, regaining a hold on his emotions save for the break in his voice. "Do we lose everything my family has built over the past century, everything we have around us, and everything I had hoped my grandchildren would inherit? Or do I lose both a grandson and a daughter, whom I love so very dearly?"

"You'll want some time, Mr Dickens," Charles said.

"We don't have time," Gareth said.

"I disagree," Abbott said. "Dickens and Sons has been the centre of this community for centuries."

"Oh, here we go," Gareth said.

"Will you be quiet?" Abbott said, his face flushing once more. He waited a moment for his words to truly sink in until Gareth turned away in embarrassment.

"Dickens and Sons has survived world wars, epidemics, famine, economic downfall, and much, much more, Chief Inspector," the old man said. "It has been the lifeblood of this community. Without it, Heighington and Washingborough wouldn't even be on the map."

"That's a bold statement, Mr Dickens," Charles said.

"It might sound arrogant, but it's true," he replied, and he took a deep breath, seeming to relax into the armchair to continue his fireside narration. "We began as farmers, back when farming meant something when the name Dickens was on a single signpost and the only people who knew of us lived within a mile or two. But we are Dickenses, are we not? When the farm burned down, we built another. A bigger and better farmhouse with bigger and better barns. When the industrial revolution struck and the workers left for the cities, we evolved. And when the economy crippled us, we started over. We began engineering. We had the land. We had the know-how. And we had a name that people trusted. That was my grandfather's time. That was when the Dickens and Sons you see today was born. We may no longer be farmers, Chief Inspector, but we are still Dickenses. And know this. It will not be my generation of Dickens who sits by and watches the flame be snuffed out."

"But what about Janice?" Elizabeth said. "For God's sake, man, she's your only daughter."

"Dad," Gareth said. "Let's discuss this. There has to be a way."

"I've made up my mind," Abbot replied in a tone that even

Charles was silenced by. "If one of my own boys is responsible for this, then I'll be damned if I'll let him beat me."

A gentle knock on the door was all the excuse Charles needed to escape the room before a family battle took place.

"I'll get it," said Charles, and he made his way through the large hallway. A figure showed through the opaque glass, short and squat, and he sighed a breath of relief at what he hoped would be a friendly face. "Devon, you made it."

He leaned out of the front door, expecting to see a retreating liveried police car but saw only an old diesel estate with the name of a private hire company on the driver's door. He stared down at her questioningly, but then followed her gaze to the doorstep.

"Guv?" she said and then retrieved a fresh pair of latex gloves from her pocket.

"No, leave it, Devon," he replied, checking over his shoulder to make sure none of the family was nearby, and she stooped to study the package. "Don't touch it."

"It's the same type of box, guv," she said, reading one of the articles on the side. "Shouldn't we open it?"

"I said to leave it," he replied. "Call CSI. Call them now"

"What's happening?" a voice said, which by its very depth and tone could only belong to Abbott Dickens. He came to stand beside Charles, looked down at Devon, and then the box, and then let his mouth fall open in horror.

Devon pulled her phone from her pocket and her thumb danced across the buttons far faster than Charles could have managed.

"Michaela, it's DC Devon," she said, standing from where she had crouched and turned her back to the wind to hear the phone call, and her voice faded as she began to pace.

"Is it..." Abbott began.

"I don't know," Charles told him, then looked across at the tired, old man. "Are you still sure you're making the right decision?"

CHAPTER 38

She had seen the house on Washingborough Road many times. In fact, she couldn't remember ever passing it without having a quick nosey, especially since John had worked at Dickens and Sons. She had always admired the size of the home his boss had enjoyed and wondered if she had any idea of the conditions her employees lived in. It was the type of home Penny had seen on the TV, with an open kitchen diner, a huge lounge space, and an en suite. There was probably a dressing room too. The sort with his and hers wardrobes with lights that turned on automatically to reveal a range of clothes sorted by type, on identical hangers. Not crammed in like Penny's were.

When she was twenty or thirty yards from the large, open driveway, she began to panic. What if she had everything entirely wrong? What if there was some explainable and even commendable reason for John's behaviour?

But it was only when she was at the foot of the driveway that her concerns really took hold, like an iron grip in her chest, forcing her to open the collar of her coat despite the strong, cold wind that followed the path of the road as if it was a river.

She stopped there, trying to clear her mind, panting slightly with the rage that was building like molten lava beneath the surface of the earth, searching for a weak spot to break through, indiscriminately destroying anything in its path. Although, the focus of Penny's wrath was well and truly fixed in her mind as she battled with her fervid imagination depicting a wild range of potential outcomes – from the woman opening the front door to her only for Penny to unleash hell, to the less belligerent but equally as the pleasurable battle of the tongues, in which Penny was sure she would gain the higher moral ground.

A deep breath, released slowly through puffed-out cheeks, was what it took for her to take the first few steps, after which adrenaline carried her, creating a momentum that led her all the way to the large double doors, where she found herself poised to push the doorbell. The doors were ornate, expensive-looking, modern doors designed to mimic those found on an old hall or manor house, and she half expected to hear the ringing of a distant bell instead of the familiar ding dong that rang out from inside.

And then, it was done. Too late to turn back. Too late to pretend she hadn't done a thing. All that remained was for her to keep her lashing tongue in check and remember that the goal was to walk away with her head held high. Or else the long walk had been for nothing, and she might do more damage than had already been done.

A full minute had passed, so she rang the bell again. The car was on the driveway. Penny recognised it from the time she and John had bumped into her in the supermarket car park. Even then, Penny had wondered about her. With her knee-length boots, tight jeans, and expensive coat, she looked like nothing more than a high-class slut.

Perhaps she had seen Penny walking up the drive or standing outside on the road. Perhaps she was standing at a window looking down at her. Penny took a few steps back to stare up at the windows, and for a moment, she thought she saw movement. She ran back to the front door and slammed her hand against it.

"Janice?" she called out. "Janice Dickens. I know you're in there."

She stopped just long enough to listen for approaching footsteps, the closing of a door perhaps.

But she heard nothing.

"Janice. Open the door. I know you're in there. I know what you've done."

She rang the bell a few times more, then continued to bang the door with the flat of her hand. But still, nobody answered.

"You bloody coward," she yelled, vaguely aware of a pair of elderly women who had stopped their afternoon stroll to spectate. "What are you bloody looking at?" Penny screamed, then stepped back onto the drive to look up again. "Come on, you cow. Open the bloody door. You can't hide, you know. I'll find you."

Nothing moved, not even a curtain. Even the clouds reflected in the windows were motionless, hanging there in that deceitfully blue sky, in awe.

But there was a calm in that sky. A calm that somehow penetrated her mind, dissipating the rage that bubbled and frothed there until she was spent. She let her head fall back and closed her eyes, feeling the cold for the first time.

There was nobody home. All the banging and ringing in the world wouldn't open the door. She didn't look up again, finding herself turning on her heels, dejected, and making her way back to the road, where the two elderly women made as hasty a retreat as they could muster.

But the two gossips were far from Penny's mind. If Janice wasn't home, then perhaps she was with John. Perhaps they were talking about her right now, making plans. Maybe it was one of those deep, hushed, post-coital chats as they lay in each other's arms.

It was as she was walking past the Volvo SUV with the 2023 number plates that Penny found her hands emerging from her coat pocket, clutching her bunch of keys. It was as if somebody else had temporary control of her mind and her limbs as she stepped closer, involuntarily, and then ran the tip of her house key along the length of the shiny bodywork, leaving a deep scar in the metal.

When the tip of the key slipped from the end of the car's wing, she stopped to admire her work and pondered the analogy. A scar, deep and unmistakably carried out with malice.

"Oy," somebody called out, and she turned to find a man at the open front door. "Oy, stop that. What the bloody hell do you think you're doing?"

She stumbled backwards as the man ran down the driveway, tucking his shirt into his jeans along the way. He stopped at the car as Penny almost tripped onto the footpath.

"What the bloody hell have you done?" he said, glaring at her, and then he stepped towards her, his hostile expressions almost cartoon-like. "Why did you do that?"

"You're him, aren't you?" she found herself saying. "You're her husband. You're Janice Dickens's husband."

The bitterness in his eyes softened as he studied her but clearly failed to recognise her face.

"Who are you?" he said slowly as if he knew what she was going to say and why she was there.

"My name is Penny Gregory," she told him flatly, her heart thudding like the pounding pistons of a steam engine. Her chest rose and fell, but she no longer cared to conceal her angst, and she took a deep breath, swallowing hard to moisten her throat. "Your wife is having an affair with my husband."

Time stood still for those few short seconds.

"Penny Gregory," he said calmly. "You're John's wife?"

"I am," she told him.

He seemed confused as if she'd just explained that the world was flat after all and that she had irrefutable proof.

"My wife? Having an affair with John?"

"I'm sorry," she said. "I didn't mean for this. What I mean is that...well–"

"You didn't expect to see me?" he suggested. "You hoped you would speak to my wife? Or maybe, do something else?"

"I don't know. I don't know what I was thinking. I wasn't really. Thinking, that is. I wasn't thinking."

"How long have you known?"

"An hour or so," she said. "I worked it out this morning. He's been acting oddly, you see. Not at all like himself."

"Explain oddly."

Now that he had asked, she found it hard to put her thoughts into a comprehensible sentence. The ideas, the clues, or whatever they were, seemed to spill from her as if there were an excess of vulgarities inside.

"Staying out late," she started. "Lying. Unusual behaviour, of which I couldn't explain if you paid me to."

"Lying?"

"He's been going to work this week. All over Christmas."

"Well, I'm afraid my brother-in-law is the one to blame for that."

"I've spoken to Gareth," she explained. "He's the boss, right?" He nodded and silenced. "John was supposed to be on annual leave. He had no cause to go in. Then this afternoon, he came home early."

"Even the Dickens let their staff go early on special occasions."

"He was dirty. Covered in dust. On his knees, his elbows, even in his hair. Like he'd been rolling around in God knows what. And there were things in his car. A bag of clothes. Tools. His weekend bag. I know it was because I bought it for him."

The news hadn't sent him reeling as Penny had thought it might. He seemed to be taking it in, then applying it to some theory in his wife's defence, or as if he was finding a way to prove Penny wrong.

"And then there's the tickets," she continued. "To Disney World. He got them for the family. Four of them. Must have cost a bloody fortune, and, well, I'm not ashamed to say that we don't live in a house like this. We don't have spare money. We could barely afford to buy Christmas dinner this year. If it wasn't for my parents, the kids wouldn't have had... Sorry, I sound self-important."

"No, no, not at all," he said, genuinely eager to hear what she had to say.

But it was all she could do to shake her head and fight back the tears.

"I know it's her," she said. "I know it. Before Christmas, she was all he ever spoke about. It was Janice this and Janice that. Honestly, he's always been such an amazing husband and he's a bloody good dad, too. We've never had much, but I always thought we had our sincerity. You know? I never thought he'd do this."

"But why Janice? Why do you think it's her?"

"I don't know. He kept saying that things will be different this year. That it's going to be better for us, as if he'd come into money or something," Penny explained, then realised the entire conversation had been one-sided. "I'm sorry. But do you... I mean, has Janice been acting out of sorts? Have you ever suspected her?"

"No," he said. "No, I wouldn't have said she was acting any differently than normal."

"Well, has she given him any money? Do you have a joint account?"

"Well, I not sure if I'm going to discuss–"

"Of course not. Sorry. But I need to know if it was her who paid for the tickets to Disney World."

He gave her question some thought, giving her time to reflect on her poor presentation, and she lowered her face, hoping he wouldn't see her reddening cheeks and shame-filled eyes.

"I would have noticed if that kind of money had gone from

our account," he said, softly. "Listen, go home. Talk to your husband."

"You think I'm being silly, don't you?"

"Listen, Christmas is a hard time. Especially for parents. Trust me. I've spent the past few days with my and my mum and dad. I often wonder which of them is more challenging, the kids or my parents."

She laughed a little, but it wasn't a laugh. It was nothing more than an acknowledgement of his attempt to raise a smile.

"So, Janice isn't behaving oddly at all?" she asked, to which he simply shook his head. "And you've been with her, have you? Over Christmas, you've been with her all the time?"

He stepped forward and gently took her by the arms, offering a reassuring grip until she looked up and met his stare.

"I can't speak for your husband, Penny," he began. "But if he is playing around, then I'm quite certain it's not with my wife."

She felt her shoulders sag like a weight had been lifted from them, only to be replaced with a new, much heavier burden.

"I see," she said, searching for a sign of deceit in his eyes, but finding none. "So I *have* been stupid. I was wrong about her."

"I'm afraid so," he said, and she stared at the long scratch along the length of his car. "I'm so sorry. I'm so terribly sorry."

"Don't worry," he told her. "It's just as scratch. I'm sure the garage down the road can fix it."

"I'll pay," she said. "Let me give you my details."

But he held his hand up and shook his head, and sighed.

"Not all of us Dickens are monsters," he said. "I'll get it fixed. Nobody needs to know."

"Not even Janice? Won't she ask questions?"

He smiled and tapped his nose.

"Go on," he said. "Go and talk to your husband. I'm sure there's a reasonable explanation behind all of this."

He waited while she digested the information, and had the two been more familiar, he might have even offered a hug. But they were not familiar, and she found herself alone once more, staring at her feet as she walked slowly off the driveway onto the footpath and then turned to head back towards Heighington, his words playing over and again in her mind.

She hadn't taken more than a dozen steps when she stopped, turned, and then called out to him.

"You're sure, aren't you?" she said. "You're sure Janice and him..."

She couldn't bring herself to finish the sentence without bursting into tears, and thankfully, he seemed to know what she was going to say.

"I'm sure," he said, plunging his hands into his jeans pockets. "And if makes you feel any better, I've been with her every day over Christmas."

CHAPTER 39

"Would you look at that?" Cook said. He was standing at the incident room window looking out at the City of Lincoln. As usual, whoever was in charge of the building's heating had set the thermostat to tropical, which made leaving all the harder. "Sometimes I think the sun goes down earlier each year."

"It *is* winter, guv," Devon replied, as she emptied her bag onto the table. The idea had been to ride the momentum of evidence in the office, so they could make a plan, yet he had seemed lost in his own thoughts since they had left the Dickens house. "Shouldn't we go through all this before the others get here?"

It took a moment for the question to penetrate whatever his cloud, but penetrate it did, and he turned to her thoughtfully.

"Have you called them all?" he asked.

"I called Sergeant Hannaway," she replied. "I asked him to contact the others. I called him from the car, guv, remember?"

"Oh," he said, seeming reluctant to be pulled away from the view. "Well, I suppose we'd better get on with it." He pulled a chair from the table, dropped into it, and then seemed to sag like an overfilled sack of potatoes. "Why don't you prepare a summary for the others?"

"Me, guv?" she said, suddenly anxious at the idea of leading a briefing.

"You are more than capable," he said. "And you need to believe in yourself more. Besides, if our little team is to become a quintet, then I think we should begin as we mean to go on. I want the others to know that you have my support. You never know, it might just help them up their game."

"Guv," she said, by way of acknowledgement, but heard the doubt in her tone.

"When was the last time you led a briefing, Devon?" he asked, to which she bit her lower lip despite trying to appear confident. "I see."

"I did stand up once in front of everyone at uni," she said.

"To make an argument?"

"No. Not really. I answered a question on interpersonal interactions," she told him. "It was my psychology class."

"But you felt you held it together?"

"I did," she said, then heard her voice quiver. "But only because I knew the topic. I'd not long read about it."

"Then I suggest you brush up on where we are," he said, checking his phone, and then slipping it into his pocket when he caught her watching him.

"Guv?" she said, and he averted his eyes. "Guv, why don't you call her? I'm sure she'll understand."

"Because she won't answer, Devon," he said, a little more aggressively than she had expected, which he clearly recognised. "I'm sorry. I just know she won't. When she called me on Christmas Day, that was the first time she'd called me, the first time any of them had called since..."

His regretful expression suggested he'd said too much.

"Since when, guv?"

He said nothing.

"Nothing, it doesn't matter."

"No, come on," she said. "Listen, you got me to open up,

somehow. I hope you don't think I tell *everybody* about my own personality flaws."

"You don't have personality flaws, Devon. If people behave badly to you, or if they're cruel, then that's their problem. Don't for one minute blame yourself for other people's flaws."

"And is it your fault that your daughters don't speak to you?" she asked.

"I already told you it is. I put my work before them. I put everything before them."

"That's rubbish," she told him, which judging by his almost angry expression, shocked him. But now was not the time to sit there and appraise his reaction. She had to continue. "Children don't stop talking to a parent just because they work too hard."

"They're not children. They're adults."

"Are they? Are they really adults, guv?" she asked. "I'm sorry if what I have to say comes across as impertinent, but I can't sit and watch you tear yourself up."

"I'm not tearing—"

"Look at you, guv," she said. "I'm sorry, but if we're going to work together, then there needs to be honesty." She waited for an argument, or even for him to tear his stare from the window to look her in the eye. But neither came. "Do you know what I think? I think that the reason you work hard is because you have nothing else."

"Excuse me?"

"What time did we leave the Dickens house last night?" she said. "We pulled a fourteen-hour shift, guv."

"The Dickens family are going through hell, Devon."

"Yes, they are. But that's not the reason you stayed there, is it? That's not the reason you worked late, and it's not the reason why you missed the chance to see your daughter."

"What the bloody hell would you know?"

"I don't think you ever intended to meet her."

"Devon, you're sailing very close to the wind."

"I think you used the family as an excuse. You had to have. God knows they've hardly made us feel welcome, have they? They're hardly appreciative of what we're trying to do. So don't tell me you care about them. Don't tell me that you're pulling fourteen-hour shifts because you care for them, because that's rubbish, and you know it is."

He pulled his gaze from the floor slowly, as if his eyes were weighty, and he stared at her, saying nothing.

"I think you're afraid of something, guv. I don't know what it is, but you're afraid of something. I think you want to talk to your daughter. In fact, you'd give anything to talk to her, if you could just be reassured that whatever happened more than a decade ago wasn't the topic of conversation. I don't know what happened, guv. It's none of my business. But you can't do this to yourself. Just speak to her. You'll feel better for it."

Again, he said nothing. Even the anger he had shown a few moments previously had dissipated, leaving behind an impassive gaze reminiscent of those worn by soldiers returning from battle.

A silence ensued, which Devon felt the urge to break, but she knew that he must be the next to speak. She'd had her say. She'd laid her cards on the table, and now she had to wait to see his hand.

But the opportunity for him to respond came and went, and before Devon could prompt him, the incident room door opened behind her.

"Afternoon all," Hannaway said, tossing his bag onto the chair beside Devon. He dropped into another seat, set the envelope of addresses on the table, and then prepared his notepad. Eventually, he looked up at them both only to find that neither had moved an inch. "Well, aren't we the happy bunch? Shall I get some cake and balloons, so we can make a real party of it?"

It was a young PCSO who severed the awkward mood, pushing the door open and leaning into the room as if she daren't touch the floor inside.

"Guv?" she said, her voice loud enough to be heard, but timid in nature. Cook looked up at her, eyebrows raised. "Got a fella downstairs. Says he knows something about Janice Dickens?"

The news brightened Cook's face for a brief moment, and he shoved himself out of his chair as Forsythe and Chalk edged past the young PCSO, apologising for being late as they joined Hannaway at the table.

"Guv?" Devon said, standing to join him as he made his way towards the door. But he held his hand up.

"No. No, you stay, Devon," he said flatly, and then cast his eye about the room. "Brief the team, will you? I want Thomas Dickens found, and I want him found fast. Preferably before his mum and dad receive another little box."

"But, guv?" she started.

"Unless of course, you're not up to the job, Devon?" Charles said, pausing at the door long enough for him to see the dejection in her eyes. "I thought as much. Now, get to it. I want to see your plan when I get back."

CHAPTER 39

Of all the people Charles had expected to find in the interview room, Richard Dickens was not one of them. The last time Charles had seen the man had been at his house on the outskirts of Heighington, but now that he thought about it, the visit came as no surprise.

"Mr Dickens," Charles said, extending his hand for him to shake. "I'm afraid there's a been a few developments since we last spoke."

"Developments?" the man replied. "What developments? The last time we spoke, you hinted that Janice had done a runner after knocking little Harry down."

"Yes, I'm afraid at the time we had very few lines of enquiry."

"But you're saying that that isn't the case?" he said, which seemed rather odd to Charles.

"Mr Dickens, have you spoken to any of the family recently?"

"Me?" he said with a laugh. "Talk to the family? You have got to be kidding, haven't you?"

"I'm sorry, I don't quite see—"

"Have you met them? They're not exactly what I would call my type of people."

"But Richard, your wife has been missing for nearly three days."

"Which means she'll be home in a day or so," he said. "Maybe."

"That's a curious thing to say," Charles said. "Are you suggesting that she does this regularly?"

"Not regularly. Only when we argue. She always comes home."

Charles stood from his seat and paced a few steps away from Richard while he gave the news some thought. Then once he'd assembled his thoughts into a fresh line of questioning, he turned on his heels.

"Mr Dickens, why didn't you tell me this when we came to see you?" he asked, to which Dickens gave a heavy sigh and leaned on the table.

"She's my wife. What do you expect me to do, hand her over so you lot can lock her up? She might be a pain in the backside, Chief Inspector, but I can assure you the kids are better off with her around."

"You mean, you're better off," Charles said.

"Look, I've been calling her number for days now only to find her phone switched off every time."

"Right?"

"So yesterday I called Thomas, her brother."

"And?" Charles said.

"Switched off," Dickens said.

"Did you try any of the others? Gareth or Jeffery?"

"Gareth is a ticking time bomb, in case you hadn't worked that out for yourself."

"Jeffery?"

"Jeffery is the veritable definition of bipolar, Chief Inspector. He is all the best bits of Thomas and the worst parts of Gareth. If I'm honest, I can't stomach either of them, so if I can go without speaking to him, then I will."

"Her mum then, perhaps?" Charles said. "She seems fairly straight."

"Oh, give me a break. She's the worst one of them all. Calling her would be an invitation for her to blame Janice's behaviour on me. It's not my fault she's spoiled, is it? I didn't bloody raise her. All I did was marry her, and if I'd known the family a little better back then, maybe I'd have cut my losses. I tell you, that family–"

"We found her finger, Mr Dickens," Charles said, enough to stop him mid-sentence. He stared across the table, clearly wondering if he'd heard correctly. "Her little finger. Left hand. Packaged in a box and left on your in-laws' doorstep."

"Her finger? Janice's finger? I'm sorry, I don't understand. Why would she..."

He stopped mid-flow, while the reality of what Charles had said hit home.

"Since then, the family have received a call from the perpetrators," Charles said, then offered a little more of an explanation. "Demands."

"Demands? Bloody hell, you mean, she's been–"

"Kidnapped, Mr Dickens. It would appear that your wife hasn't been home because she's been kidnapped."

He searched Dickens's face for any sign of guilt, or at least feigned horror. But every instinct Charles had honed over the years told him that the man's reaction was genuine. He shook his head in disbelief and then gave a little laugh.

"Do you have any idea how ridiculous that sounds?" Dickens said. "Kidnapped?"

"I'm well aware of how it sounds, Mr Dickens, and believe me, I battled with the idea for some time until I finally saw sense."

The words were designed to offer both reassurance and sincerity and after a few short moments, they did just that.

"What do they want?" he asked. "Whoever this is, what do they want?"

He asked the question calmly but with obvious emotion, the

way men often do when presented with challenges of the heart, and as men so often do when facing challenging questions, Charles deferred.

"You said you had some information on where we might find Janice," Charles asked.

"You didn't answer my question."

"I realise that," Charles replied, and he leaned on the back of the chair opposite Dickens. "Today we received another box."

"Another..."

"It's with our forensic team now, but as you can imagine, we're keen to bring this to a close. We're keen to bring Janice home."

The man's chest rose, filling the woollen sweater, and then deflated, and his shoulder sagged in unity.

"Somebody came to see me today," he said. "A woman. Her husband works with Janice. He's kind of her assistant, he's the HR manager, but I get the feeling he does a lot of the work."

"And?" Charles asked. "What did she have to say?"

"Only that she was under the impression that her husband and my wife were up to no good."

"She's having an affair?"

"Not that I know of, Chief Inspector," he replied. "But then, what else could she have been doing? Perhaps I've been burying my head in the sand all along?"

"It's not an easy conversation to have, Mr Dickens," Charles said. "But have it, we must."

"I told her that she was wrong about her husband. I told her I'd been with my wife all over Christmas."

"Why did you do that?" Charles asked, to which he shrugged.

"I don't know. To protect Janice, I suppose," he said. "And to protect her, as well. The woman. She seemed quite upset." He snorted a restrained chuckle and looked up at Charles. "Upset enough to run her key along Janice's Volvo, anyway."

"Oh dear."

"It's nothing," he said, waving it off. "Nothing a bit of paint and a few days in the garage won't fix." He leaned back in his chair, a different man to the one whom Charles had first encountered. "So, let me get this right. You no longer think she had anything to do with Harry being hit?"

"No, I believe that was down to one of the individuals who carried out the kidnapping," Charles said.

"So now, instead of her being a suspect, she's the victim. Is that right?" Dickens asked. "And whoever is behind all of this has now cut off another finger?" Charles nodded gravely and Dickens stared at the wall while he thought. "It's the cutbacks, isn't it?"

The comment piqued Charles's interest and he lowered himself into the seat, studying every twitch of every muscle in the man's face.

"You knew about the cutbacks?" Charles said. "The family seem to think it's a close secret. Have you told anybody?"

"Me? No, of course not. I learned a long time ago not to get involved in the Dickens family business."

"But Janice could have told somebody? I mean, if she told you, then perhaps she told somebody else?"

"I would imagine so," Dickens replied. "Janice is capable of anything when given enough motivation."

"What does that mean?" Charles asked.

"It means, that it's wise not to divulge any secrets to her," he said. "In case you ever fall foul of her temper. She's got a tongue as sharp as a razor."

"Mr Dickens, who was it that came to your house?" Charles asked. "What was the name of the husband? Can you remember?"

"Of course I can remember," he replied. "He lives down in the village and works with her every day. John, his name is. John Gregory."

CHAPTER 40

"John Gregory," Cook said, as he burst into the incident room, moving faster than Devon had even seen him move before. He pointed at one of Hannaway's officers. "You. What's your name?"

"Me?" she replied, nervously. "Chalk, guv. DC Chalk."

"Good. Are you familiar with PNC?'

"The national computer? Well, yes, guv," she replied. "I use it every day."

"So, get to it. John Gregory. Heighington. His full address should be in Devon's notes."

He pointed at Devon's notebook and clicked his fingers twice. The move could have been considered rude or derogatory, but given the man's sudden energy, she put it down to his busy mind working overtime. She flicked to the page in her notepad and slid it over for Chalk to copy.

"Guv, we've developed a plan to find Thomas—"

"Forget the plan," Charles said, as he scribbled the new name onto the whiteboard, then tapped the scrawled writing with the end of the pen. "This is him. This is our lead. I've just had Janice Dickens's husband in the interview room downstairs. Apparently, John Gregory's wife, Penny Gregory, went to his house earlier, keyed his car, and accused Janice Dickens of having an affair with her husband."

"That's the witness, guv," Devon said. "We've already spoken to him. His wife has already confirmed that he was home all morning until he went to the shops and saw the Audi drive off."

"Ah, but we know there are more people involved, don't we?" Charles said. "We know whoever is masterminding this travesty has one or two others working for him or her. We know that somebody drove the Audi while somebody else drove the van." He tapped the name again. "I want to know everything about John Gregory."

"We can start with his HMRC records to find out where he works," Devon said, to which Hannaway nodded his agreement.

"No need," Cook said, and he added a line from John Gregory's name to Janice's. "John Gregory is the HR Manager at Dickens and Sons, would you believe it?" The tip of his tongue emerged from between his lips as he wrote the title beneath John Gregory's name, and then he moved to Janice's. "And we all know Janice's role in the organisation, don't we?"

"HR Director," Devon said, which came as a surprise to Hannaway, and the cocky yet jovial expression that he wore so naturally was replaced by intrigue. He leaned forward, apparently doing what Cook had asked and catching up on the run.

"Which means that John Gregory very likely knew about the cutbacks," Cook added. "Don't you see?"

"If anybody knew about the cutbacks, you'd think HR would," Hannaway said, but something else was nudging Devon's shoulder. An idea that drew her hand to the folder Michaela had found in the Audi. She dragged it towards her and flicked it open while Cook and Hannaway discussed the potential routes they could take to build a greater picture of John Gregory.

"Guv?" she said, holding a list of names out in front of her. But Cook was in the flow and clearly had yet to forgive her earlier impertinence. "Guv?" she said, a little more forcibly, and the two men stared at her, one with curiosity and the other with nothing less than contempt. She slid the piece of paper across the desk, then sat back, linking her fingers across her lap.

"This is a list of the employees for the next round of cutbacks," Cook said, to which Devon simply shoved the folder in his direction.

"And in the folder are rounds two, three, and four," she said. "But that's the one of interest to us. Round one."

"Good Lord," he replied when his eyes had reached the midway point. He handed the A4 sheet to Hannaway, then looked across at Devon with renewed respect.

"John Gregory," Hannaway said. "He's being made redundant."

"And he worked alongside Janice Dickens," Cook said.

"And he had those tickets," Devon added. "The Disney World tickets."

"Life will be better for them next year," Cook said. "Penny Gregory said that her husband kept talking about them having a better life next year. She said it to Richard Dickens this afternoon."

Cook did that thing that Devon had noticed he did when he was battling with facts. A few paces in one direction, a pause, and then a turn on his heels like a sergeant major.

"The redundancy is the motive," he said. "And his working relationship gave him the means to access the information."

"But instead of trying to find an opportunity, all we have is an alibi. An alibi that his wife and kids could support. He was at home with his family until the morning when he popped down to the shops."

"He was hiding in plain sight, guv," Devon said.

"Here we go," Chalk called out from her desk on the other side of the room. "John Gregory. I've requested a warrant to check his financial statements, which might take a while to be approved. But I have found a tenancy agreement on a property in Washingborough."

"Heighington," Cook said. "His house is in the next village. Heighington."

"I know, guv," she replied. "But this says Washingborough. Five Mile Lane. It's a commercial property."

"A commercial property?" Cook said. "But the man doesn't have two pennies to rub together."

"I'm just telling it as it see it, guv," Chalk replied. "It's a three-year lease which started last month."

"Five Mile Lane leads to the derelict farm, guv," Devon said. "In fact, it's the only way in for a vehicle."

She would have continued, but her phone screen lit up and the little vibrations set the phone into a gentle spin with every buzz.

Cook turned away, beginning another of his curious paces, while Hannaway led Forsythe over to Chalk's computer to see what else she had found.

"DC Devon," she said into the phone, as she watched the team, which, until a few moments ago, had various fractious veins running through it and now suddenly appeared to be coming together.

"Devon, it's Michaela Fell," the voice said, in an articulate southern accent, not posh, but educated and polished.

"Have you got the report?" Devon asked. "That was quick."

"Not yet," she replied. "I'm afraid the latest request has thrown quite a large spanner in the works."

"Oh dear," Devon said. "Any more spanners and we'll have a full set."

"I'm afraid we've got the full set and more," Michaela said. "In fact, we've got the entire toolbox."

Cook turned, apparently oblivious to Devon and lost in his own thoughts.

"Could you explain?" Devon said, keeping her voice calm so as not to gain any spectators. "I'm not quite following."

"The finger in the second box," Michaela said. "I don't need a DNA analysis to know it doesn't belong to Janice Dickens."

"Sorry?"

"It's not Janice Dickens's finger, Devon. Judging by the size of the digit, I would say it belonged to a male. I can't give you a full report yet, but I can give you a head start."

"Go on," she replied, and Michaela sighed into the phone.

"Male, middle-aged, probably an office worker, and quite definitely wealthy."

"You can get all that from a severed finger?"

"Not without help from a database of fingerprints. We've got a match," Michaela said, and Devon could hear the smile in her voice. "The finger belongs to Thomas Dickens."

The sensation that Devon experienced when hearing those last six words was akin to being a child and having her father spin her round and round until she was quite dizzy. It was all she could do to remove the phone from her ear and set the call to loudspeaker for the others to hear.

"Devon? Are you there?" Michaela asked.

"I'm here, yes," she replied. "Sorry, I was just putting the call onto loudspeaker." She caught Cook's attention with a brief wave of her hand and then pointed to the phone. "Michaela, could you repeat what you just said to me, please?"

"The part about being male, middle-aged—"

"No. No, the last part," Devon said, and Cook cocked his head, finishing his pace close to where Devon was seated. "I have DCI Cook with me, now."

"I see," Michaela replied. "Well, we've identified the finger in the second box, Chief Inspector."

"You mean, it's not Janice's?" he said.

"Definitely not," she replied. "The finger belongs to, or belonged to, I should say, Thomas Dickens."

"Thomas Dickens? Are you sure?"

"We haven't had time to run any DNA analysis yet, but apparently he was involved in some kind of investigation last year so his prints were on the database."

Cook studied Devon's expression as if he were checking to see if her thoughts mirrored hers.

"Thank you, Michaela," he said. "We appreciate your call."

'There is one more thing," she added. "I'm not sure how helpful it will be, but the first finger seems to have been removed with bolt croppers or some kind of cutters. The cut is clean and the flesh was cut from both sides, which would indicate a large cutting implement such as a bolt cropper. The second finger, however..."

"Was removed by some other means?" Cook suggested.

"That's right," she said. "The removal would have been far more brutal, a chisel or a knife. One-sided against a flat surface, perhaps. We need to spend more time on it to be sure, but—"

"Thank you, Michaela," Cook said. "Thank you very much indeed."

Devon ended the call and the team stared at the phone for a few minutes.

"Didn't you look in the box?" Hannaway said with a look of utter incredulity. "I would have thought you would at least—"

"You would have thought nothing," Cook told him. "All we would have done is compromise the evidence and if that's the approach you would have taken, then I'll consider that the next time I send you out. As it stands, maybe this is what we need. Some focus."

"John Gregory?" Devon said, to which he nodded. "Are we bringing him in?"

"Not without a plan," he replied, more to himself than to anybody else. He looked up from the table at Devon. "That plan of yours to find Thomas Dickens. Talk me through it."

CHAPTER 41

"Thomas Dickens, guv?"

"Tell me about it," he said, nodding his confirmation. "How are we going to find him?"

"Well, the plan was based on Thomas being a suspect," she said, and a moment of uncertainty flashed within her eyes.

"The plan was to find Thomas Dickens, was it not?" he said, and she inhaled, her broad chest filling every spare inch of her blouse.

"It was, guv," she said, and then he sensed the rest of his team of cast-offs listening in. He clapped his hands and gestured for them all to join them, and as they did, he beckoned Devon to begin. "Well, first of all, his car is a late model 2023."

"That was my idea," Hannaway said. "You see, many late model cars, especially high-end—"

Charles held his hand up to stop him mid-sentence, then looked to Devon.

"I want to hear it from Devon," he said, and that uncertainty he'd seen seemed to blossom into something new and fresh.

"Trackers, guv," she said. "It's a 2023 BMW, so we need to get in touch with the local dealership."

"Who can pick this up?" Charles asked, but nobody spoke, perhaps due to his blunt reaction to Hannaway trying to steal Devon's moment. He clapped his hands again, loud enough to fill the room. "Come on, people. There are two people out there with missing fingers, one dead boy, and a family business that has been running for over a century that's about to be shut down as a result. There are five of us. Five. No more, no less. So I need someone to pick this up and run with it."

"All right," Forsythe said, raising his pen. "I'll take it."

"Good man," Charles said, then looked to Devon for her to continue. "What's next?"

"Phones," she said. "If the tracker doesn't give us anything, then maybe his phone is still on?"

"I'll take that too," Forsythe said, which both surprised and impressed Charles.

"Next on the list is the camera on the security gates at Dickens and Sons," Devon continued. "When I was there, I noticed a camera on the gates. Maybe it caught Thomas leaving, and if it did, then maybe it'll show if he turned left towards his parents' house or right towards Lincoln."

"I like it," Charles said. "Are there any more cameras on the site?"

"There are, but sadly not on the office block. It looks like the key areas are the factory and the gate. There's almost nothing on the office."

"No doubt the family are more interested in monitoring employee attendance than theft," Charles said. "Who wants it?"

"I'll take that one," Hannaway said.

"What happened with the property developers? I thought you were spending the day with them?"

"Been there, done that, guv," Hannaway replied. "Nothing to report, I'm afraid. I mean, don't get me wrong, I wouldn't mind living in any of the three empty properties, and I'd love for us all to go to the last one I saw. Hot tub in the garden, en suite bathrooms in two of the five bedrooms, a kitchen to die for, and a living room the size of this room."

"I think we have other priorities right now, Sergeant Hannaway," Charles told him.

"That's what I thought," he said. "Other than that, they said the only other vacant property they have is Dickens Farm. But I figured you guys were covering that."

"Were all three houses like that?" Devon asked. "High end, I mean."

"I suppose so, yeah," Hannaway replied. "I was talking to Robert and Roy about it, and apparently the family go for long-term lets, wealthy families. That's their target market. The properties take longer to rent out, but at least they don't have to redecorate every time."

"Agreed," Charles said, and he turned to Forsythe and Chalk. "What about you two? How did you get on?"

They looked at each other in conference, and Forsythe eventually accepted the responsibility, reaching for his notepad and flicking through to the correct page.

"Only three of the seven outlets were open on Boxing Day," he began. "One of them had their CCTV installed at about the time King John signed the Magna Carta, but the other two were part of the Co-op chain, so we've reached out to the head office. Apparently, they store the video footage on a centralised cloud server."

"A what?" Charles asked.

"He means that all the data is sent to a cloud server, guv," Hannaway added, but still the use of the word cloud was throwing Charles off. But never one to let a technicality stem an investigation's momentum, Charles feigned a general understanding and pushed on.

"So, when do we get that?" he asked, and Forsythe checked his watch.

"Probably tomorrow," he said.

"Probably?"

The confidence with which Forsythe had accepted the responsibility suddenly waned, and he began to panic a little. It wasn't a showstopper, but if Charles was to bring the young man onto his team, then his ability to handle difficult situations would need to be developed.

"I'll call them again," he said.

"We got there in the end," Charles told him. "Chalk, work with Forsythe. Divide the tasks between you and update me every hour."

"Guv," she said, by way of acknowledgement.

"Right then," Charles said, checking his watch, and then scooping up his whiteboard marker. "It's three p.m. We have two missing persons, minus a finger each. We have one suspect with a clear motive and obvious means. We need to know who he speaks to regularly. Who has he spoken to in the last few days? Where has he been? If John Gregory really was just a bystander, who were the two individuals who kidnapped Janice Dickens and knocked an eight-year-old boy down?"

"We can see if the network provider can give us anything on John Gregory's phone," Forsythe suggested. "We've got to call them anyway to discuss Thomas Dickens's phone."

"Good," Charles said, pointing the pen at him, then turning it on Devon. "Get downstairs and talk to Sergeant Barrow for me. I want six uniformed officers and transport enough for at least three suspects."

"We're going to raid the rented property, guv?" Devon asked. "Shouldn't we build some kind of case beforehand?"

"Given that we have twenty-one hours until Abbott Dickens has to make a statement, we don't have that luxury," he told her. "I'm going to call Detective Superintendent Collins now. Hopefully, he can help me get CPS on board. If he agrees, then I want to hit the property before four p.m."

"What about if Sergeant Hannaway talks to Barrow, guv?" she

suggested. "He's a sergeant. He's more likely to get what we need."

Charles stared at her but she averted her eyes, choosing to look at the others around the table.

"Is there some kind of problem, Devon?" he asked. "You can lead a meeting, and develop a plan to find a suspect, but you don't want to go downstairs and relay a direct instruction from a chief inspector?"

"No guv," she replied.

"Good. Get to it," he said, retrieving his phone from his pocket and looking at each of them in turn. "I want to be on the road in under forty-five minutes."

CHAPTER 42

It was as if he'd been waiting for her, watching through the custody suite window so he could open the door just as she reached for it, unbalancing her so that she stumbled into him.

"Bloody hell, Devon," Sergeant Hammond said, as she recovered her balance. "You want to be more careful. You could have knocked me across the room."

The insult was well buried behind a veil of concern, so that, should anybody have heard, it would have seemed quite innocent.

"I'm sorry, Sarge," she said. "I didn't see you there."

"Try not to let it happen again. This afternoon is important. We can't have you stumbling through the doors before we've managed to break them in. But then again, perhaps you can help us force entry."

She said nothing. There was nothing to say. Nothing that would do anything to expedite the end of the conversation.

"You looking for Barrow?" he asked.

"I am, yes."

He twisted his hips to face the custody desk and peered through into the back office.

"Service," he called, and Barrow looked up from his desk. "I'll leave you to make the arrangements. Just take a bit more care in future, eh?"

Hammond edged past her, leaving Devon standing in the doorway, numbed from the experience. It was another of those comments that she could have reported. But that would have resulted in yet more cold shoulders, nasty comments, and, who knows, maybe even another transfer.

"Here she is," Barrow said, emerging from the back office to stand at the computer behind the custody desk. He made a show of using the computer, but Devon couldn't see the screen. "The woman of the hour. How's your sugar daddy?"

"Chief Inspector Cook is not my sugar daddy, Sergeant," she replied. "In fact, he asked me to pop down to see you."

"Oh, really? Now that does surprise me," he replied, clearly unimpressed. He glanced up at the clock on the wall. "Three-fifteen. It must be nearly time for his afternoon nap. Tell me, does he ask you to tuck him in, or read him a story, perhaps?"

"We're hitting a commercial unit in Five Mile Lane," she said. Then for the purposes of clarity, she added, "That's in Washingborough."

"I'm quite familiar with Five Mile Lane, Detective Constable Devon," he said. "We were there this morning if you remember?"

"This isn't Dickens Farm. This is a commercial unit near the main road."

"Variety is the spice of life."

"We're going to need half a dozen officers, plus transport enough for three suspects."

Again, he checked the clock on the wall.

"And when do you need all of this, pray tell?"

"DCI Cook wants to be out of here by three forty-five."

It was the first time that Barrow had actually stopped working for long enough to look up at her. The smug expression he wore was replaced by mock confusion.

"Tomorrow, you mean? Surely?"

"Today," she said. "In half an hour, to be precise. What should I tell him?"

He puffed out his cheeks and made a show of checking the resource planner, then smacked his lips.

"The best I can do is three bodies and an Astra."

"We need six and a transporter," she told him. "It's an instruction from DCI Cook."

"Well, then perhaps when you take him his hot chocolate you can tell him that I've left my magic wand at home, and unfortunately, I simply cannot pull the resources from out of my backside."

"Sergeant Barrow, I don't wish to—"

"Three uniforms and an Astra," he said. "Take it or leave it. It's the best I can do."

She gave it some thought. His tone and body language suggested that should she argue further, the chances of even securing the limited resources he had offered would reduce, and no doubt he would spout some rubbish about her taking too long.

"I'll take them," Devon replied, and then turned away. She stopped at the door, finding it difficult to walk away without giving him something to think about. "I imagine DCI Cook will have something to say about this."

"I imagine he will," Barrow replied, as Devon shoved open the doors and almost knocked Hannaway over. "Oh, sorry, Sergeant Hannaway."

"Look where you're going, Devon, for God's sake. You could have broken my foot if you'd stepped on it."

Another comment. Another cheek turned. And he stared at her, daring her to retort. It was an odd sensation. In the incident room, he hadn't exactly been friendly, but he certainly hadn't been nasty. But now they were alone, his true colours were beginning to show as if his behaviour in front of Cook had just been a show.

"Sorry, Sarge."

"Are we all set? The guv is on a call with Detective Superintendent Collins. Doesn't sound like it's going too well."

"Kind of," she replied, referring to his question.

"Kind of? What does that mean? We're either set or we're not."

"Three uniforms and an Astra. It's all we can get," she replied, feeling the burn of blood rising through her blushes. She backed away. "I should tell the guv. I'll see you outside."

She nearly ran towards the stairs to the first floor, where the incident room was located, but before she reached the doors, Hannaway called out.

"I'd be careful if I were you, Devon," he called, and she stopped, not daring to turn to face him. Instead, she gripped the cold, brass door handle to calm her nerves. "You don't know him like I do. He might seem like a nice, old man, but you know what they say about him, don't you? You've heard the rumours, I suppose?"

He waited for her to respond, but she refused to even look his way despite being more than twenty metres away, safely out of reach.

"Ask him about his family, Devon. His wife and daughters. Ask him where they are and why he doesn't see them," he said. "And then ask yourself if a man like Cook truly wants to help a young officer like you, and if he does, then what's his motive?"

"Like me? What do you mean?" she asked, and then slowly gazed the length of the corridor to where he was standing, leaning against the custody suite doorframe, staring back at her with a cruel grin forming on his face.

"Ask him about Maggie Ryder and the restraining order," he said, then winked and backed through the doors. "I'll see you outside, Devon."

"Sir, I really think we can handle this," Cook was saying into his phone when Devon entered the incident room. He had his back to the door, so she slipped inside quietly, keeping her distance, listening, watching, and unable to shove Hannaway's words from the forefront of her mind. "Well, for a start, I've expanded my team. DS Hannaway and DCs Forsythe and Chalk. The three of them have worked together for some time, so that should make the integration simpler."

He paused while Collins spoke, letting his head drop backwards to stare up at the ceiling.

"Sir, I agree, under normal circumstances we'd have a negotiation team involved. Somebody more practised in this type of crime. But let's face it, this isn't exactly the Iranian Embassy, and yes, of course, I can deal with it. A suspect, sir? Yes, we have. A John Gregory. He's a local man who works alongside Janice Dickens performing the role of HR Manager for the company business, which means he would have had access to information regarding the cutbacks the firm was planning. Add to that the fact that it was he on the list we found in Janice Dickens's Audi, he's taken out a lease on a commercial property less than a mile from Dickens And Sons, and he's the only witness to the hit and run. And, well, all roads lead to him, sir. If we go in and get him, we can have this wrapped up by tomorrow, and I'm sure the last thing you want to do is to hand an investigation over to Nottingham, especially when budgets are being scrutinised."

He pulled the phone from his ear and let his head drop forward. The man was tired, he was working hard, and all he had to help him was Devon, who'd had no experience in kidnapping, Hannaway, who clearly held some grudge against them both, and then Forsythe and Chalk, who had both been out of uniform for a matter of weeks.

"That's right, sir," he said. "Leave it with me. Very good, sir. Of course, I'll keep you informed."

He ended the call, seeming to stare out of the window at the city beyond the LNER stadium, home to Lincoln City Football Club. Aware of her predicament, and that he'd almost certainly perceive her presence as sneaking or snooping, she opened the door quietly, let it close with a bang, and made a show of entering in a flurry.

"All set, guv," she said, avoiding eye contact when he turned to face her. She began collating her papers and files, and he watched her with interest. It was only when she banged the stack of papers on the table to straighten the pile that he spoke.

"Are you ready for this, Devon?" he asked, and she took a deep breath.

"I am, guv. Yes." She gestured at the phone in his hand. "Have you spoken to Collins?"

"I have," he replied and averted his eyes to stare at the whiteboard. "I'm afraid we're on our own. He feels that if we were to hand the investigation over to a specialist team from Nottingham, then we'd be admitting incompetence."

"Surely it's not about being incompetent, guv," she said. "It's about getting Janice and Thomas Dickens home, isn't it?"

"That's what I told him, Devon," he replied. "That's what I told him. But I'm afraid he seems to be more interested in securing next year's budget. The good news is that he's given me the all-clear to second our three friends."

"I thought he'd already okayed that?"

"Sometimes it's better to ask for forgiveness than permission, Devon," he said with a smile. "Now then, are we set?"

"Set?" she said. "Oh, that. Well, sort of, guv."

"Devon?"

"Oh, it's okay. Nothing to worry about. Sergeant Barrow said he could only give us three uniformed officers and an Astra, and if I'm honest, we're lucky to get those," she said. "But we'll have Hannaway, Forsythe, and Chalk, so we should be fine."

"Devon, I explicitly told you we need six uniformed officers and a transporter. That's two officers per suspect, leaving you and I to pick up any stragglers if there are any."

"I told him the instruction had come from you, guv," she said.

"Well, perhaps you'd better work on your communication skills," he said, pacing three steps away and then immediately turning on his heels with his index finger raised. "In future, when I ask for resources, I expect resources. It is not at your discretion, Devon, to negotiate with the custody sergeant."

"Yes, guv," she said quietly.

He checked his watch, then closed his eyes while taking a deep breath.

"If this goes wrong, Devon," he said, but left the remainder of the threat to her imagination, and then marched out of the door.

She caught him up on the stairs, but with the folder and envelopes in her arms, she struggled to keep pace and just about caught the door into the corridor with her foot. Two uniformed officers were manhandling a young man toward the cells, and she had to turn sideways to let them pass, doing her best to ignore the prisoner's intrusive glare as he passed, and then his cackle as he was led away.

By the time she reached the custody suite, Cook had already gone through, and she backed through the doors, being careful not to bump into anybody.

"Ah, Chief Inspector Cook," Barrow said, his tone far more jovial than it had been not ten minutes earlier. He made a show of finishing something on his computer with a flourish and then smiled at the older man. "All present and correct, guv. They're bringing the transporter around now. Shouldn't be too long."

"The transporter?" he said, turning to glare at Devon, and then back at the duty sergeant.

"That's right, guv," he said, then continued his charade by referring to his notepad. "Six officers and transport enough for three suspects. That is correct, is it not?"

"That's correct," Cook said, and as he turned to visually

display his disappointment to Devon, Barrow winked at her over his shoulder.

She looked Cook in the eye, lost for words, except to state the facts. "But he said we could only have three officers and an Astra."

"An Astra?" Barrow said. "Sorry, Devon, but you're not going to get three suspects in the back of a Vauxhall Astra. No, what you need is a transporter."

"But you said–"

"I said, what?" he said, daring her to accuse him of anything but following an instruction.

"Devon?" Cook said.

"Sorry guv. My mistake," she replied. "I must have misheard."

He thanked Barrow and left by the car park door, leaving Barrow to enjoy a smug and winning smile aimed solely at Devon as she followed. She pulled her coat around her and fastened the buttons with one hand while holding the files and folders with the other. Hannaway was enjoying a cigarette with the half a dozen officers assigned to them at the far end of the car park, and he nodded at them both from a distance, signing to Cook with two fingers that the transporter wouldn't be long.

"Let's wait in the car," Cook muttered, and Devon followed in silence, still reeling from the trap she'd fallen into.

Both doors thudded closed, and whereas outside, the air had been cold and the breeze biting, inside the atmosphere was close enough that she could smell the age of his cheap suit.

"I want you to take a back seat on this one," he said. "Let uniform gain entry, Hannaway will follow, and then you and I can bring up the rear."

"Guv," she said, then mused on the distance he was creating. It was like she was at the cusp of hauling a weight up a mountain, only for it to slip from her grasp yards from the summit. "I get the impression that you're disappointed in me."

"No," he said sharply, as if he had expected her to say something along those lines. "Don't blame yourself. If anybody is to blame, it's me. I asked you to run before you can walk."

"But guv—"

"Let's not make a big deal of it, shall we? We all make mistakes."

"Guv, if this is about what I said earlier, then I'm sorry. I spoke out of turn. It's none of my business what happened to your family."

"What do you mean, what happened to my family?"

"I just mean that, whatever reasons you have, it's none of my business. I shouldn't have spoken out like that."

"No, no you shouldn't have."

"I just felt we were getting on well, that's all."

"We were, Devon," he said. "We were. But there's a lesson in there for both of us and forward we must move."

Through the windscreen, she saw the transporter swing into the car park. It came to a stop beside the group of officers, where the uniforms climbed inside, leaving Hannaway, Forsythe, and Chalk to ride in Hannaway's Volkswagen Golf. Cook flashed his lights once, signalling for Hannaway to lead the way, then held his hand out to the transporter driver to follow. Then slowly, he eased his Jaguar out of the car park to pick up the rear.

The moments before a raid were typically tense. Most officers involved would be going through the brief, focusing on the dos and don'ts, checking equipment, and picturing the suspects. But Devon found that her nerves were not related to the raid at all. In fact, for the first time, she actually felt quite calm about what was in store. Not quite nonchalant, but another matter was taking precedence.

"Guv?" she said quietly, once they were on the main road toward Washingborough. "Can I ask you something?"

"Does it concern my family?" he asked, his eyes never leaving the road.

"Not really," she said. "It's just…"

She couldn't say it. It was there, on the tip of her tongue, but she couldn't bring herself to say it. They stopped at the lights beside the cemetery, and he eased the car into park before looking at her, his brow furrowed.

"What is it, Devon?"

"You mentioned the other day that you had some experience of negotiating, but you didn't explain," she said.

The lights changed and the convoy set off slowly, turning left at the junction.

"Well, if I haven't explained, then it's for a reason," he replied. "What was the real question you wanted to ask?"

"Guv?"

"The real question," he said. "What were you really going to ask me?"

She thought she had covered herself well, but somehow, he'd seen through her facade and left her no room to manoeuvre.

"People have been talking, guv. That's all."

"Ah, I see," he replied, driving as a driving instructor might with his hands never wavering from the ten-to-two position. "And?"

"I just wanted you to know that I don't care what they say," she said, which seemed to catch him off guard. "You've been nice to me. Nicer than most anyway. Whatever it was that happened, whatever the reason for your daughter not talking to you for all that time, and whatever the reason for people talking about you, that's all in the past. The DCI Cook that I know began life on Boxing Day in that grubby, little newspaper shop in Heighington."

Regardless of his mood and the disdain he had demonstrated, her words had struck a chord that resonated and sustained. His eyes shone and he cleared his throat, gripping and re-gripping the steering wheel as if the emotions he withheld were forced through his limbs in search of an outlet.

They stopped at a small set of lights by a railway bridge where the road was too narrow for traffic to pass, and habitually, he nudged the car into park.

"I assume you expect some kind of reciprocation?" he said.

"Guv?"

"Well, if we're going to live in the now and not in my past," he said, "then I assume you mean to dissuade me from delving into your own past, Devon."

"My past, guv?" she said. "I don't have a past." His cheeks rose and his lips formed a smile, but there was only regret and disappointment in his tired face. "So? Are we okay, guv?"

The lights turned green and he set off behind the transporter, guiding the long saloon beneath the bridge and onto Fen Road.

"The first part of burying your past, Devon, is admitting that you actually have one to bury," he said. "Let's talk again when you're ready to be honest with me."

CHAPTER 43

"Does anybody have anything to say?" Jeffery said to his family.

The fire had been lit an hour before and the glowing embers were fading. Yet nobody felt compelled to add more wood. Nobody had really moved. It was as if the news of Thomas being a possible suspect in the crimes that were set to tear the family apart had seriously unbalanced them.

"What's to say?" Abbott said eventually. "The inspector told us we would hear from him when he knew more, so wait we shall."

"You can't honestly believe Thomas had anything to do with it, surely?" Jeffery said, but when his father remained silent, he turned to his mother. "Mum? What do you think? Don't you think we should be out there looking for him? He could have been in an accident or something."

"If I told any of you what I think," she said. "I'm afraid we would never be the same."

"We're not though, are we?" Gareth said. "We're not going to be the same. I've lost my boy, and my sister, and now whether Thomas is guilty or innocent, I've lost him too. If he's not involved in all of this, then he's probably been taken by the same people who took Janice. How can you expect me to ever be the same?"

"We haven't lost Janice or Thomas," Elizabeth said. "Not yet, we haven't. Where there's hope, we must cling to it, and as the bible tells us—"

"Oh, don't quote that bible rubbish at me, Mum," Gareth spat. "If there was a God at all, this wouldn't be happening."

"Do not speak to your mother in such a tone!" Abbott said, and he rose from his chair as a younger man might, his eyes narrowed and every muscle in his face taut. His low voice seemed to penetrate the very walls around them and rose in volume as he stood. "How dare you? After everything she's done for you. After all, we've been through."

"Dad, you're all sitting here like he's either condemned or dead already. What do you expect me to say?"

"I expect you to demonstrate compassion. Some restraint," Abbott replied, his face reddening and his large chest swelling. "I expect you to demonstrate strength and leadership, Gareth. I expect you to—"

"You expect me to what, Dad? To be more like you? To be more like Grandad? Because everyone loved him, didn't they? Everyone always said how much like him I am. Is that a disappointment? Or are you jealous of being a failure in his eyes? Maybe if he'd had a son more like me then I wouldn't have inherited the business. Maybe Grandad wouldn't have had to work up the day he died if he'd had a son he could have trusted, a son he could rely on to be strong. Maybe I wouldn't have to be laying off staff left, right, and centre if I had inherited some kind of stability."

"Gareth, just stop," Elizabeth said, and she rose to stand beside her husband who absorbed the words as if the blow had been physical.

"Oh, leave off, Mum. Everyone is looking at me like I'm some kind of monster. Just because I'm having to make some difficult decisions. Decisions that, had he done the right thing when he was running the show, or Grandad when he was in charge, I wouldn't have to be making. I don't want to lay people off. I don't want people to cross the street when they see me, or turn their backs when I walk through the factory. But that's exactly what they do. And do you know what? The only reason I bloody well do it is to keep the business going. We all know it should have closed years ago. Had we sold it when we had the chance, we'd still be financially stable. And everyone out there..." He pointed towards Heighington, his face a contorted sneer. "They'd look at us with respect. They wouldn't cross the street when they saw us. They'd remember the good times. They'd know we did everything we could and that we suffered just as they did."

"Get out," Abbott said, but when Susie looked his way, she saw that he no longer stood tall. He was defeated, growing breathless with bitter disappointment.

"I should leave you to it," Susie said, and she made to stand, but Jeffery held her down.

"No. No, stay," he said.

"I really shouldn't be here."

"I said, stay!" he told her, rather forcibly, and she succumbed to the anger in his tone.

The distraction had done little to ease the burden on Abbott, and with help from his wife, he lowered himself back into the armchair.

"This family has been through much," he said, quiet enough that the rest of the room hushed to hear him. "Dickens and Sons has borne every tragedy the world has thrown at it for nigh on three centuries. Famines, disease, world wars—"

"Yeah, and it's profited from them too," Gareth muttered, which earned him a glare from his father, with far more effect than any words might have had.

"Susie, perhaps you'd better go upstairs for a while," Elizabeth suggested.

"No, she can stay. She might as well know," Gareth said. "She might as well be in on the family secret."

"Gareth," Abbott said, but his warning tone had little effect.

"What? Don't tell me you're ashamed, Dad," he replied. "After all these years, you're finally ashamed of who we are and of how we managed to survive all those tragedies you speak of."

"I'm warning you."

"How your great-great-grandfather raised the prices of the crops while the rest of the county was flooded? Or maybe we should talk about the real issue here?"

"Gareth—"

"With the blood of children," he said, and Susie gasped. "There. There, I said it. What are you scared of? Are you scared she's going to tell everyone that Dickens and Sons isn't the caring company that we make it out to be? How our donations to charities and that we give land over to the wildlife are simply a means to help us all sleep at night?"

"You've gone too far this time," Jeffery said, then turned to Susie. "Don't listen, babe. He's just blowing it all out of proportion."

"Oh, am I?" Gareth said. "Am I really blowing it all out of proportion? Tell me, Jeff, how did our family survive when everyone left for the cities?"

"Oh, for God's sake, Gareth. It's old money. They were different times."

"And that makes it right, does it?" Gareth asked. "It makes it right that our ancestors led everyone to believe that they were good, honest people. That they helped children out of the kindness of their hearts, to save young lives whose parents had died, when the truth of it all is that they sent those children into fields and when they dropped down dead from the cold and malnourishment, or when they died from their injuries, they just tossed the bodies into the river like they were nothing more than industrial waste."

Abbott hung his head, and even his wife's comforting arms couldn't reconcile the fire inside him.

"I want you to leave," Abbott said. "I want you to go upstairs, pack your bag, and get out," he said, taking a breath for each part of the fragmented sentence. He looked up finally, his eyes red and aggrieved. "I don't even know who you are anymore."

"I'm your son, Dad," Gareth said, almost amused at his father's words. "I'm you. I'm Granddad, and like it or not, I'm the next generation of Dickens."

The two were in a stalemate, neither one of them willing to let the other have the last word.

"I have seen," Abbott growled, seeming to struggle with his breath, "over the last few days, the very best of Thomas. He has shown himself to be a kind man. A man who, until now, I was proud to call my son. A man who isn't afraid to stick up for his sister, even when his two brothers take sides, and who has never uttered a word I deem to be shameful."

"That's because he couldn't care less about the business, Dad. It's not like he ever helps us make a decision, is it? He never gets involved. How on earth would he ever say anything to disappoint you when he doesn't have any passion for it?" Jeffery said. "All Thomas has ever wanted is a healthy bank balance and home-cooked meal every now and again. Thomas cares for Thomas, and that's it."

"Jeffery, just stop," Elizabeth said. "Everyone just stop this, please."

"Just as I have seen the best of Thomas," Abbott said, ignoring his wife's plea for peace. "I have seen the worst of you two. I see it now. I see Thomas for who he really is. He's me. And whatever he may or may not have done lies with you, Gareth. Thomas is me forty years ago before I bore the burden of what my father handed to me. And I see you both. I see you, Jeffery, for who I am now, and you, Gareth, for who my father was."

He moved away from his wife, stepping into the light of a window which revealed his pale grey face.

"And, if now is a time for revealing truths, then know this. I despise what I see before me. I despise myself for bringing you both into this world, I despise my father and his before him." He took another step, having to hold on to the back of the sofa for balance. "But most of all, I despise…"

He stopped mid-sentence and grimaced as if in pain. His grip on the sofa gave way and he stumbled forward, dropping to his knees and clutching at his chest.

"Abbott?" Elizabeth screamed, and she rushed forward to ease him to the floor. "Abbott, what's wrong? Abbott, Talk to me. Please, darling, talk to me."

But the old man said nothing. The agony of each short, sharp burst of breath was evident in his downturned mouth, tightly closed eyes, and balled fists.

"Do something!" she screamed at her sons, and Susie looked at them both in turn, finding each of them frozen to the spot. "Don't just stand there. Call an ambulance."

"There's no time to wait for an ambulance," Susie said, shoving herself off the sofa to kneel beside Abbott. She loosened the old man's collar, then looked up at Jeffery who remained wide-eyed. "Car. Get the car started."

As if he'd been slapped in the face, Jeffery suddenly stood, and after a few moments to collect his thoughts, he suddenly ran from the room.

Susie put her hand on Elizabeth's shoulder.

"You'll need to go with them," she said. "Can you pack him a bag? Just the essentials and any medication he's on."

Perhaps it was the maternal instinct, the quiet calm that many women seemed to call upon in times of need, but Elizabeth stroked her husband's forehead once, then leaned down and kissed him on the forehead.

"You're going to be fine, Abbott," she said. "You're going to be just fine. Just hang on, okay?"

His hand groped for hers and he gave it a squeeze, before letting it fall to the floor again. Then Elizabeth made for the stairs.

"What's wrong with him?" Gareth asked quietly, clearly unable to put the argument to one side long enough to help his ageing father.

"I don't know," she told him, hearing the venom in her voice.

"You're a nurse, aren't you? Can't you tell?"

"I'm a pain specialist, Gareth," she snapped. "Not a bloody doctor."

He seemed to sense her anger and was silent while she monitored his father's pulse.

"What can I do?" he asked eventually, as Jeffery came back into the room, bringing a blast of cold air from the open front door with him.

"You can carry him to the car," she said, as Elizabeth appeared in the doorway behind them holding a small bag with Abbott's essentials and little Arthur's hand in the other. "And you'd better pray to God you get a chance to make peace with him."

He ran past her to his father. Gareth joined him, and as they prepared to lift the old man from the floor, she said something. There was very little thinking involved. Very little of anything, except being tired of the whole affair.

"Jeffery?" she said, and as with his arms hooked beneath his father's shoulders, he looked up at her, for the first time showing genuine fear. "I'll be gone when you get back."

CHAPTER 44

Five Mile Lane was a dead end, single lane track connecting the main road through Washingborough to the River Witham more than a kilometre away. Ahead of the car, Charles saw Hannaway's car enter the small business park followed closely by the transporter. He eased back, letting the two primary vehicles take up position, before parking out of the way near the entrance.

"Remember what I said," he told Devon, as he eased himself from the car, then waited for the thud of her door to close. "We'll let them go in first, and then follow."

She said nothing, either sulking or scared to say something wrong. Either way, it pleased him. Now was not an ideal time for unwelcome distractions.

The leased unit in question was identifiable only by the lack of signage and a numbered sign to the right of a large sliding door which was big enough to fit a lorry through. The buildings were all similar in appearance, differing only in size, and with the abundance of green, sheet metal cladding would be deemed an eyesore to those who clung to natural beauty, yet crucial to the employees of the various businesses.

Hannaway took control of the uniformed officers, sending two of them around the back of the large, green building, two of them to the main business park entrance, and two of them to prepare the ram – a handheld, steel cylinder weighty enough to break open the pedestrian doorway situated to the right of the vehicle entrance.

From where they were standing, Charles heard the clammer of radio chat from Devon's pocket, which he assumed to be the two pairs of officers stating their positions and readiness. Hannaway glanced once at Charles, who then nodded his approval for the chaos to begin.

As it turned out, the ram was an unnecessary addition as the pedestrian door was unlocked. The uniformed officer pushed it open, then looked to Hannaway, who in turn glanced back at Charles.

"Aren't they going to call out, guv?" Devon asked. "Surely we need to announce our presence?"

"We have a warrant from the magistrate, Devon. This is a police raid, not a birthday party."

"I know, but under normal circumstances–"

"Would you call these normal circumstances?" he said. "Hand me the radio, will you?"

She delved into her inside pocket and held it out for him, which he accepted without looking her way. Then he turned the power switch to off and handed it back, again without meeting her disappointed stare.

He caught Hannaway's attention and motioned to go in with a sweep of the flat of his hand.

"Follow me, Devon," he said, making his way towards the door.

The two remaining uniformed officers entered first, followed by Hannaway, Forsythe, and Chalk. The pedestrian door opened into a small, industrial looking hallway with doors leading to the two restrooms, and a single door at the end which opened up into the main space.

The scene was scarily familiar – an overhead crane running on steel beams along the length of the unit, a line of lathes, drills, welding machines, and saws, in addition to a plethora of benches. The only difference to the factory at Dickens and Sons, other than the scale of operations, was the smell. The factory at Dickens and Sons had smelled of decades of oil, grease, paint, and sweat, whereas this place smelled only of new. The machines were unmarked, unscratched, and free of the scars of fabrication. To their right was a set of steel steps leading up to a mezzanine floor with a single office door, which was closed.

"What the bloody hell is this?" Devon whispered.

He ignored her, still unwilling to enter into any kind of pretence.

"Hannaway," he said quietly. "Check any fire exits in case they saw us coming."

He led the uniformed officers away along with Forsythe and Chalk, leaving Charles alone with Devon. Eventually, he stared down at her, noting the wanting expression on her face, like a puppy that wants its owner to throw the ball.

"The door was unlocked," she said. "Somebody must be here somewhere."

She was right, of course, and they both peered up at the mezzanine office.

"Stay behind me," he said, then started towards the set of stairs to their right.

"Guv?" she said, in a hushed whisper. From the bottom of the stairs, he finally caved and turned to her. "I'll tell you. Not now, but I will tell you. I just need time."

He nodded. There was a truth in her eyes, her tone, and in the way she seemed to plead with him for some kind of forgiveness.

"Stay behind me," he told her, and started up the stairs. He was halfway up when he peered out over the factory. He could see the two uniformed officers, and after a moment, he placed the other three moving about in the near darkness. He was about to say something to Devon when he heard something from inside the office. It was faint but familiar. The type of sound that stops a person in their tracks.

"I heard it," she hissed, and she stepped closer, urging him forward. At the top of the stairs, they each took a side of the door, pressing their backs to the wall giving them a view of the entire factory. It was Chalk who saw them first, and through a series of hisses and motions, she caught Hannaway's attention.

And then they heard it again. A scream. It was muffled, but damn, it could be nothing else. A female. Struggling. Heavy breathing. Sobbing.

Only when Hannaway was at the foot of the stairs did Charles move. Slowly, he turned to face the door and Devon reciprocated. She nodded, as if he had asked if she was ready, or if she was okay, but his attention was not on her wellbeing. It was on that scream.

The door handle was stainless steel, the round type that required a twist instead of a downward shove. He reached for it, adjusting his grip to ensure a smooth entry, and then took a few deep breaths. The handle didn't squeak or squeal and was loose enough that he felt the mechanism reach its zenith.

But before he could push the door open, Devon placed a hand on his.

"Let me, guv," she whispered, with sincerity colouring her eyes. He stared back at the young officer who had already proved her ability yet demonstrated a severe lack of control over her mouth. But there was something about the way she looked at him. A fire. Determination. "You follow me."

He paused for a moment and her grip on his hand tightened on the handle. She wasn't letting go. He shoved the door and then stepped back out of the way.

"Police, nobody move," Devon announced as she entered.

And then there was silence.

A greenish light spilled from inside the room, and as Devon

moved further inside, it spread across the mezzanine floor, flickering as if the connection was loose.

Had there been danger, he would have known in an instant and would have called Hannaway and the team up the stairs. But there was nothing except an odd sensation similar to thinking he had known how a magician had performed a particular trick only for his theory to be dashed at the last minute.

Hannaway waved at him from the shop floor, a confused look on his face and he did that internationally recognised gesture meaning, *what the hell is going on?*

But Charles ignored him, not having a suitable answer to give, and instead took three steps into the room, then turned on his heels to face the source of the light.

"Can I help you, Inspector?" John Gregory said from where he was sitting on a desk chair with his feet up on a brand new desk. Another scream sang out from the laptop on his desk, muffled, yet it could be nothing but a woman in trouble. "Is this about the accident?"

Devon was calm and was still taking in the scene, searching the corners of the space for another door. But there was none. Charles knew that. He'd been in dozens of units like this one and they all followed a similar template. A guilty man may have tried to run, or at least showed signs of panic. But John Gregory retained his composure, despite the obvious surprise.

"Where is she?" Charles said, and hearing the thuds of boots on the stairs outside, he put his hand up to stop five more officers from bursting into the room. "Where's Janice Dickens?"

"Janice?" he said, and leaned forward to tap a button on his laptop, pausing the film he had been watching mid-scream, leaving a greenish glow across his face. "I've been wondering the same thing, Inspector."

CHAPTER 45

"Okay, let's start again," Cook said. "For the benefit of the recording, I want you to tell me everything you told me at your commercial property on Five Mile Lane. Start from the beginning. Take it slow."

The interview room was cool with garish lights and showed no signs of the festive period save for the Christmas songs an old drunk was singing at the top of his voice in his cell, although the accuracy of the lyrics was dubious.

"Am I still under arrest?" Gregory replied.

"You are, and if you'd like to call a lawyer, or wait for a legal aid, then that's fine. But I must press the urgency of the matter."

"You still haven't explained what's going on," he said. "What's happened to her? What about my family? Do they know where I am?"

Devon watched as Cook deliberated for a moment, then as if the two men were old friends, he leaned on the table and spoke sincerely.

"If you are waiving your rights to have a solicitor present, John, then perhaps I can offer you some advice?"

"Go on," he said, slightly unsure of what was to come.

"Speak truthfully. Leave no detail out, and if you are innocent as you say you are, then it'll be fine," Cook said. "You have been arrested on suspicion of conspiracy to the kidnapping of Janice Dickens. Your family is, as far as I know, unaware." He checked his watch then pulled his sleeve down over his wrist. "We can detain you for a further twenty-three hours. Do as I ask, and I'll see to it that your wife pays you a visit."

"I doubt it," he replied, then shook his head dismissively when Cook showed interest in the comment. "You said Janice has been kidnapped. I don't understand. Why would somebody do that?"

"To quote yourself, Mr Gregory," Cook said, "I've been wondering that myself. The fact of the matter is that the young boy you saw being knocked down was Janice's nephew, Harry."

"Harry? As in, Gareth Dickens's boy?" He looked to Devon for confirmation as if Cook might have just made it up. "That little boy was Gareth Dickens's?"

"That's right," she said. "And the Audi you mentioned belonged to Janice's husband. They had swapped cars so he could take their children to their grandparents for Christmas."

"Jesus," he said, clearly shocked. "So, Janice ran her own nephew over? Sorry, I'm still not following. This is all a bit sudden."

"We believe that Janice was abducted moments before you rounded the corner," Cook explained. "In your previous statement, you mentioned hearing a loud diesel engine before you saw the Audi."

"That's right. It sounded like a van," he said. "Sounded like the driver was putting his foot down."

"We don't have much to go on at this stage, I'm afraid. But if that van was involved, then it's likely that Janice was taken away in it, while somebody else removed the Audi from the scene."

"Knocking down Gareth's boy in the process?" Gregory asked.

"Exactly," Cook said, then sucked in a long breath through gritted teeth.

"But why? What do they want? Money?"

"No," Cook said, and waited a moment for Gregory's shifting eyes to still. "They want the family to announce the closure of Dickens and Sons."

"They want what?" he said. "Close the business? It's been going for years. Since my dad was alive, at least."

"Longer," Devon said. "The Dickens family have worked that land in one way or another for centuries."

"And they want it closed? Why? Hundreds of people rely on them for employment."

"We believe it has something to do with the planned redundancies, Mr Gregory," Cook said, and Devon handed him the clear envelope found inside the Audi, which he opened and then withdrew the sheet of paper with the list of employee names on. "Do you recognise this, Mr Gregory?"

He slid the sheet of paper across the desk.

"Of course," Gregory said, sliding it back to Cook. "I typed it."

"You? You typed it out?"

"I'm the HR Manager," he said, with a shrug, then licked his lips. "Am I right in assuming that you believe whoever is behind Janice's disappearance is one of the names on that list?"

"We do," Cook said.

"And that person is me?" he said.

"Look at it from our point of view, Mr Gregory. Your name is on that list. You worked alongside Janice. We know you were aware of some redundancies, but we've just learned that you not only knew that the company was going to make you redundant, but in fact, you typed the list up," Cook said. "Do you mind if I ask about your financial situation?"

"My what?"

"I don't need specifics, Mr Gregory, but would you say that you live a comfortable life? That you have no major financial concerns?"

He mulled the question over, not perhaps wondering about what his answer should be, but whether or not Cook had the right to ask it. And if Devon was honest with herself, she was wondering it too.

"I'm not judging you, at all, and by no means do I wish to be invasive."

"But?"

"But you just bought your family tickets to Disney World," Cook said. "Florida. Expensive."

"So?"

"The type of expense that you could do without in light of your redundancy. If that were me and I had a family to take care of, I'd be looking to tighten my belt, not spend five figures on a holiday."

"I see," Gregory said, and he leaned back in his chair. "So, you think that perhaps I'm bitter about my redundancy and that, were it me behind all of this, I'd looking to gain some kind of financial advantage. Something to make the next few months a little easier."

"Something like that, yes," Cook replied. "I'm sure you've heard of an MMO? It's what we use to evaluate the validity of a suspect in a particular crime."

"I've heard of it," Gregory said.

"Good, well then, you might know that it stands for means, motive, and opportunity. The three factors that guide us. You see, in most cases, an MMO provides evidence that a suspect could be guilty. Not *is* guilty. *Could be* guilty. There's a huge difference. You see, let's take this investigation as an example. You have the means to illegally detain Janice Dickens."

"My factory?"

"Exactly. One of the hardest aspects of a kidnapping is finding somewhere to keep the victim for lengthy periods of time."

"Right?" Gregory said.

"And of course, you have a motive."

"The redundancy," Gregory said, nodding. "I'd agree with that. I mean, that's not an admission of guilt, but I think I can see why you'd think that, at least."

"Good," Cook replied. "Then there's the opportunity, and that's where this gets interesting. You see, I can place you at the scene of the crime. It was, after all, you who called us to report the tragic hit and run incident."

"But then, you can also place me at the scene of the crime for the period after the accident," Gregory said. "I waited for the police to arrive. I gave a statement. I showed my ID and I made myself available when you came to visit me, what, an hour afterwards?"

"Which crushes any MMO," Cook replied and he too sat back in his seat. "Unless of course you had two accomplices. Because you would have known that you would be questioned, because you knew your name was on the list of redundancies." He turned to Devon. "Can I see his phone?"

"My what?" Gregory said, as Devon retrieved the phone that had been found in his pocket when he'd been processed. "You can't go through that."

"Oh, I think I can, Mr Gregory," Cook said, then handed it back to Devon. "Help me out here, will you?"

She took the phone back off him and then navigated to the recent calls, finding one number in particular with no associated name.

"Who does this number belong to?" she asked Gregory, presenting the screen to him.

"I can't remember," he replied, and she navigated to the messages app.

"Guv?" she said, showing him the phone. Cook leaned sideways to get a closer look and began reading the previous few messages out.

"It's done. Meet me there," he said, then looked up at Gregory. "What's done, John?"

Gregory said nothing, and so Cook continued to read the messages aloud.

"I'm out. Meet me there," he said, then looked up at the man opposite. "Who are you meeting, John? And where?" Again, Gregory said nothing. He closed his eyes and laid his hands flat on the table. "You're up to something, Mr Gregory. Who were you messaging? It's not Janice's number. You knew you were being made redundant. You knew about all the redundancies."

"Because I typed them out."

"And because of your working relationship with Janice Dickens," Cook said. "So, in this instance, we may not have a qualifying MMO. However, we have reason to believe that more than one individual was involved."

"The van and the car," Gregory said.

"Which, in the eyes of the Crown Prosecution Service, negates the need to provide evidence of an opportunity."

"Hence why the charges against me are only conspiracy to kidnap, and not just kidnap."

"You're good at this, Mr Gregory," Cook said, and he leaned forward. "So, hopefully now you understand why you're sitting here with us."

Gregory looked across at Devon. It was an odd sensation. Many of the suspects she had interviewed had either been hostile from the beginning or turned defensive when faced with the evidence abasing them. But John Gregory was different. He was clearly an intelligent man, slight in stature, yet confident in his abilities and his morals.

"I can give you more, if you want," he said finally, and his eyes flicked back to Cook. "Check Janice's phone records. You'll find a hundred calls to and from my number in the past few months.

You could even check to see where the phones have been. I'm sure I've seen it done on the telly. You can place Janice and me together on most days."

"I'm not interested in extra-marital affairs, Mr Gregory."

"You've been talking to my wife," he said, after a short pause long enough to enjoy a smile.

"No. No, we haven't," Cook said. "We've spoken to Janice's husband. He told us that Penny had been to see him earlier today."

"Ah. I'll bet that was awkward?"

"Not really. But he did say that she was emotional enough to run her key along the length of Janice's car," Cook said.

"She can become quite fiery when she gets going," Gregory said. "Sorry about that."

"Mr Gregory, whilst I appreciate both your cooperation and your candid attitude, I'm afraid your apathy is doing very little to convince me that you're not involved in this somehow."

"How do you expect me to be?" he replied. "What do you want me to say? What should I do?"

"Convince me," Cook said. "Convince me that despite the insurmountable evidence growing against you, we should drop our investigation into you and look elsewhere."

Gregory listened and nodded but remained impassive, offering not a clue as to his thoughts. Cook, however, was showing signs of frustration, signs that Devon had yet to witness, proving that the man she had come to respect in the last few days did indeed have cracks in his armour.

"I'm not a rich man, Inspector Cook," Gregory began. "You were right about my financial status and you were right to question the cost of those tickets. They seemed like a good idea at the time. But as poor as I might be, and although I might spend every penny I earn on my family, keeping them safe, keeping them warm, and putting food in their bellies, I do have something I can put to good use. Something to better my situation. An attribute I can use to do better than my father did, and his before him. That's what we strive for, isn't it? That's what we try to do. We try to do better so that we can be proud of our achievements, and so that others might respect us."

"Some do," Cook said. "Others just want to get by."

"I have a mind, Inspector Cook," Gregory said. "It's just that, until recently, I've never had an opportunity to put it to good use. I never knew what to do with it. It's funny how, when we're faced with pressure, we find ways out. Those abilities we've harboured or internalised for so long somehow seem to have meaning."

"Mr Gregory, might I remind you that we are on the clock here?"

"What would you have done, Inspector?" he replied flatly. "What would you have done if you learned, not only of your own redundancy, but that of dozens of people you worked alongside? People you respect. People with families. People you deem to be the best in their field."

"I'm not following," Cook said slowly, as if he had an idea but wanted clarification.

"Okay, I'll rephrase it. What would you do if you knew what I knew and had access to somebody in Janice's position?" he asked. "A woman with wealth, a woman you respect and most of all, a woman you trust."

It was the first time Cook looked towards Devon, and she stared back, hoping he was thinking the same as she was. But then he nodded at her, allowing her the chance to decipher Gregory's cryptic response.

"You hired them," she said to Gregory, and he smiled, but there was something in the way he stared at her that suggested there was more to it than that. "You started a business using Janice's capital. You hired the best of the redundancies."

"No, it was Janice and me who compiled that list," Gregory said, stabbing at the sheet of paper with his index finger. "Every one of those names is the best at what they do, and every one of them will be working for us within three months."

"And customers?" Cook asked.

"Who would you rather deal with, Gareth Dickens or Janice Dickens?" he said. "You see, it doesn't matter to me whether Dickens and Sons is still running in six months' time or ten years from now, because anyone who is any good at their job will be working for us, and any customers worth having will be buying from us."

He sat back in his chair, not exactly with a smile, but there was a smugness there that Devon had to admit, he'd earned.

"And the messages?" Cook asked. "Who were you speaking to?"

"Like I said, we needed Janice's contacts. We needed men experienced in managing property fit-outs, contractors–"

"The Pierce brothers?" Cook said, to which John Gregory gave a weak smile.

"It's done," Gregory said. "He was referring to the extraction unit in the spray booth. It needed signing off before it can be used."

"Who else knows about this?" Cook asked.

"Nobody. Only the names on that list, Janice, and our lawyer," he replied. "We had to involve him to make sure we weren't in breach of any contracts."

"Your wife?"

He shook his head slowly.

"Not even Janice's husband," he replied. "So, in six months' time, when the business is in operation, my wife, my kids, and I, will be enjoying overpriced burgers in Florida. We'll wash them down with overpriced soft drinks, and my wife will regret she even considered that I was having an affair. But it's okay. I'll forgive her. In fact, I'm quite proud of her tenacity."

"And Janice?" Cook asked. "Can you still do all of this without her?"

"Here's the thing," he replied. "Without Janice, none of this is possible. Without her contacts, her money, and her influence, I'm in a lot of financial trouble." He laid his hands flat on the table again, face down, and spoke as frankly as he could. "So, do you still think it's me, Inspector? Do I still tick all of your little boxes?"

CHAPTER 46

He regretted throwing the file the moment it hit the whiteboard and spilled the contents to the floor. A wide-eyed Chalk bent to pick up the mess, but Charles caught Hannaway's reflection in the window and saw him shake his head telling her not to, not yet anyway.

It was dark outside, and the view over the lower half of the city was marred by low cloud. The stadium was aglow with some event or other taking place. Hundreds or even thousands of people blissfully unaware of what was happening to the Dickens family and what Janice and Thomas could be going through right now.

"Hannaway?" he said, catching his eye in the reflection.

"Guv?"

"Talk us through the facts. Let's start from the beginning."

Charles watched as Hannaway spread his own files out on the table. Forsythe and Chalk moved back to give him some room, but Devon remained where she was, helping him sort the papers into individual piles.

"Boxing Day morning," Hannaway began, and presumably he

was about to provide the narrative given to them by the Dickens family and John Gregory, but Devon spoke up.

"Shouldn't we start before that?" she said, and Charles twisted to see her. She flicked through her notepad searching for a page, then flattened it on the desk. "It started before that. We just assumed it began with the abduction."

Hannaway looked up at Charles, as if he was waiting for him to tell her to shut up, and he might have if he didn't believe the young DC might have a point.

"Go on, Devon," he said, and she seemed to sneer at Hannaway, like a sibling gaining an advantage somehow.

"When we first spoke to the Dickens family, guv," she began. "We originally thought that she'd taken Harry Dickens because of an argument that took place the previous night. Do you remember?"

"I do," he said. "She was bitter. She went to her room."

"The argument was with Gareth," Devon explained. "Or at least with the company, which is basically Gareth's decision making."

"Right, so?" he said, and she faltered, seeming to struggle with her words. "If this was merely a case of getting revenge over a few bitter words, then why go to the trouble of kidnapping her? Why not just write her out of the family business, or something?"

"I don't know," she mumbled. "I was sure I had something."

"Well, the next time you have something Devon, you might want to keep it to yourself until you've given it some serious thought," Charles told her, then nodded at Hannaway for him to continue.

"Janice woke up before anybody else," Hannaway continued. "And it appears that she popped down to Heighington to get some greetings cards and a newspaper. She didn't take her bag, but she did take little Harry Dickens with her. The theory is that he was up early and wanted to go with his aunt."

Chalk raised her hand. Not as a schoolchild might, but enough to gain Charles' attention.

"Go on," he said, pleased to see one of the two less experienced officers engaged.

"Newspaper, guv?" she said. "Forsythe and I spent an entire day driving around the area trying to get CCTV footage showing anybody who bought a local paper that morning."

"Whoever abducted Janice Dickens had the paper already," he said, and she nodded. "Janice bought it. Why the bloody hell didn't we see that?"

"We were too busy searching for Janice, guv," Devon said, but Charles chose to ignore her.

"Carry on, Hannaway," he said, and although Devon tried hard to disguise her disappointment, it was clear by the way her shoulders sagged.

"That's where John Gregory's account comes into play, guv," Hannaway said. "According to his statement, he heard a loud diesel engine like that of a van's, and then as he turned the corner onto the high street, he saw the Audi knock the lad down, and then speed off. Gregory ran to the boy and called an ambulance."

"And that's where the plan went wrong," Charles muttered to himself.

"Sorry, guv?" Hannaway said.

"Nothing," he replied. "Carry on."

Hannaway puffed his cheeks and exhaled, searching for his position.

"At that time, yourself and DC Devon believed that Janice Dickens had knocked him down accidentally, and then panicked. This led to a search of the family's property portfolio, which proved to be less than fruitful."

"Another wasted day," Charles said, again to himself, and he caught Hannaway and Forsythe exchanging concerned looks. "Then what?"

"Then you found the box, guv," he said. "The first one with Janice's finger."

"Wrapped in newspaper," Charles said, acknowledging Chalk's earlier comment with a nod of his head.

"This then altered the investigation. According to DC Devon's notes, the pair of you conducted interviews with Susan Fraser and Thomas Dickens."

"They were informal," Charles said. He crossed his hands behind his back and took a few paces back to the window, using the reflection to remain connected to the conversation. "We were just buying time before Detective Superintendent Collins sent a specialist team in. To be honest, I wanted to handover as much information as we could get. But the interviews did give us a good insight into the family. We learned that Thomas couldn't care less about the business. He's more interested in living the playboy life."

"Don't forget about Susan Fraser, guv," Devon added. "She said the family were so toxic that she was going to call it off with Jeffery. She doesn't want to be involved."

"That's what she told us," Charles said. "But she was still there the last time we visited, wasn't she?"

"She was, yes."

"Well, then perhaps we should put that down to emotions. The family had just lost Harry. The tension in that house was awful. People will say all sorts of things when they don't quite have a grasp on their emotions."

She was astute enough to understand the message buried within the statement, but defiant enough to press her point.

"Thomas and Jeffery left," she said, then dropped to the floor and began sifting through Charles's files. "Here. Here it is, look." She held up a single sheet of A4 paper. "This is the timeline you and I put together while speaking to Susie. As soon as we left the house, Abbott Dickens called a meeting with him and his sons.

After that, Gareth met us to identify the body, while his two brothers went to the office. They were gone for an hour."

"What does that mean?" Charles said. "What's your point? We spoke to them about that. They had business to attend to while Gareth was preoccupied. What is your point, Devon?"

Again, she faltered.

"I just think that..."

"Do you recall what I said a moment ago?" he asked her. "About developing an idea before wasting my time?"

"Yes, guv," she said quietly. "Sorry. I was just sure—"

"Just like you were sure about the argument between Janice and Gareth Dickens?" he said, then watched her sink into a sulk. Once more, Charles beckoned for Hannaway to continue, but before he had a chance, a thought struck Charles. "The original call to Elizabeth came in while we were conducting the interview with Susan Fraser."

"Right," Hannaway said, clearly not following where he was going.

"We found the car at the old farm," she said. "That's when the second call came in. A day later."

"That's right, guv," Hannaway replied. "I was with the property management company. You and Devon were at the farm and Forsythe was with Chalk running around the newspaper shops."

"And we've checked Elizabeth's phone records, have we?"

"I have, guv," Devon said. "It was a pay-as-you-go number. Unregistered, but if you want, I can—"

"Hannaway, don't you think it's odd that we weren't around when either of the calls came in?" Charles said, cutting Devon before she hashed out another ill-executed theory.

"I suppose so," he replied.

"The second call came in, just as we found the car," Charles said. "That was nearly a day after the first call, and the first thing I did was rush to the house, leaving Devon to wait for the CSI team and uniforms to keep the place secure."

"What are you getting at, guv?" Hannaway asked, and Charles stared at him, pleased that somebody had the gall to speak frankly and not tread on eggshells.

"They didn't want us to find the car," he said.

"Of course they didn't."

"No, I mean, they knew we were close to the car. They knew we were close, and they knew that if another call came in that we'd drop everything and go to the house."

"They wanted to get you two away from there," Hannaway said, to which Charles nodded.

"Why would they want to get us away?" Charles mused, more to himself than anybody else.

"The redundancies, guv?" Devon suggested, and he clicked his fingers. Finally, she had contributed something. "The redundancies. They were found on the back seat."

"If they could get us away from the car for a while, they could have removed them."

"But they didn't get a chance," Devon said. "Because you asked me to stay. I was with the car until CSI took it away."

"And who was waiting in the office for us to leave?" Charles said.

"Gareth," Devon said. "You're not suggesting it was Gareth? His son was killed."

"I think at this stage, we would be foolish to focus on a single one of the Dickens," Charles said, then addressed them. "I want everything we can get on them. Phone records, movements, financials. Everything. One of them is involved in this somehow."

He was about to start dishing out specific instructions, when Chalk raised her hand again.

"What is it?"

"I've got a hit, guv. On Thomas Dickens's car. I made the request to the dealer before we raided John Gregory's place. They've sent me a link to the tracker."

"Where is it?" Charles asked, feeling the temperature in the room rise a degree or two.

"It's down by the river at the end of Five Mile Lane," she said, then looked up at him with wide eyes. "It's been there since midday."

CHAPTER 47

The shift in Cook's mood had filtered down to whatever neuron or whatever part of his brain it was that controlled driving. His hands were at the ten-to-two positions, as they normally were, but he was far more aggressive with the accelerator. Occasionally Devon leaned forward to make sure Hannaway was still behind.

"You okay, guv?" she asked, doing her best not to sound like a scolded puppy.

"I'm fine," he replied, after a moment.

"I feel like you've lost confidence in me," she said. "I'm sorry if I sound needy. I don't mean to. But ever since we had that chat–"

"You mean, ever since you analysed my life after knowing me for less than twenty-four hours?"

"Right," she said. "Since then, it's been different. Is that why? Is it because you thought I had analysed you? Because I didn't mean to–"

"Have we tried Thomas's phone?" he said, as he slowed for the red light at the railway bridge. He didn't stop the car. He edged forward cautiously, watching for any oncoming traffic, and then put his foot down the moment he saw the route beneath the bridge was clear.

"I tried it before we left, and again as soon as we were on the road," she replied. "Look, guv, if you no longer trust me, then just say. Just say, and I'll—"

"You'll what?" he said.

Washingborough was a blur of Christmas lights and fog, and at the speed they were travelling, the view through the windscreen wasn't too different to the view from the bridge on the Starship Enterprise, with the stream of little, coloured lights becoming a series of dashes in her peripheral vision. But before she could think of a suitable answer, he steered her away from the topic.

"What about the gates to Dickens Farm? Do we still have any uniforms on the gates?"

"They all left once CSI had finished, guv," she said. "All six of them."

Her final comment had caught his attention, and he glanced at her from the corner of his eye. Just briefly, but she had noticed.

If the blast through Washingborough had reminded Devon of the view from the Starship Enterprise powering through the galaxy, then Five Mile Lane was a black hole. Regardless of the fog and the dark, Cook slowed only a little, manoeuvring around potholes when he saw them, wincing when he didn't and the car absorbed the brutal bumps. Behind them, Hannaway's headlights jolted up and down as he too fought the same battle.

They passed the little track that led across the fen to the gates of Dickens Farm, continuing down the single-lane track where, as they drew closer to the river, the fog grew ever thicker. It grew so thick, in fact, that Cook was forced to slow down, his keen eyes peering into the bleak night.

"You haven't made any friends since transferring to Lincoln, have you?" he asked when they saw the little parking area ahead of them, beyond which was the footbridge across the river. "In fact, would I be right in assuming that you've made a few enemies?"

"I've made one friend, guv," she replied. "Well, I had, until I analysed him." She gave a little laugh. She hadn't meant to. It just sort of came out, and she found herself clearing her throat to rid her voice of any weakness. "I'm not sure why. I just seem to rub people up the wrong way."

"You do no such thing," he told her.

"Well, then I must be an easy target," she replied. "I don't know why. Maybe because of..." She stopped and presented herself with a wave of her hands.

"What?" he asked.

"You must have noticed that I'm not exactly a size-six supermodel, guv. People aren't drawn to me."

"Does size matter?"

"Money only matters when you don't have it," she said. "Size matters when you have too much."

He drew the car to a stop in the little parking area and checked his mirror as Hannaway pulled alongside them.

There was no sign of Thomas's car, but a little bridge provided access to the riverbank a hundred metres away. Cook leaned forward, lowered Devon's window, and called out to him.

"You lot check the riverbank. We'll be right behind."

Hannaway eyed Devon and she turned away in case he had seen the redness of her eyes. The last thing she needed was to give him any more ammunition.

And then it happened. She just came out with it. She verbalised the thoughts that had poked and prodded her mind for nearly a year. The thought that she had tried so hard to push to one side. Memories that were there when she opened her eyes in the morning and there when she closed them at night. They even woke when she opened the fridge door for one of her midnight snacks, taunting her, and teasing her into making another sandwich.

"I was bullied at Newark Station, guv," she said, but he said nothing, and she felt obliged to say more. It was like those words had been the initial trickle of water spilling over the riverbank, loosening the topsoil to make it easier for the next wave to break free. Ahead of them, Hannaway's rear light disappeared from view. "We should go."

"No," he said. "No, carry on."

"But, guv—"

"One thing about being old, Devon, is that you have the benefit of experience," he told her, the dashboard lights casting a blueish hue across his face, accentuating the lines in his forehead. "You get to recognise what's important with far more clarity."

"You mean like not putting work first?" she said, but he didn't reply. "Okay," she said tentatively. "I get it. I'm working you out. I'm not analysing you, but I am working you out."

"The negative side of age is that you become a grumpy old so and so every now and again."

"Is that an apology?"

"No. No, it's more of an observation. If I apologise, then you'll hope it doesn't happen again," he said, and he settled into his seat, making no show of going anywhere fast.

"I tried to take my own life," she said, then stared out of the window. "It was stupid. I don't know what I was thinking. I'd just had enough. I was this close to giving it all up," she told him, holding her finger and thumb an inch apart.

"Was there somebody you could talk to?" he asked. "Somebody to report it to?"

"I tried that the first time," she said, shaking her head. "That just made life worse. The insults didn't stop, they just became quieter."

"And the whole thing became so bad that you..." There was no need to complete the sentence. The fire behind her eyes was inextinguishable and it was all she could do to look away and fight the sensation that was lodged in her throat.

"You have no idea what it's like, guv," she said, hearing her voice rise in pitch. "I didn't join for this. I signed up for the National Detective Program to get away from all of this. I thought I'd be working with good people. People who could see past what I look like on the outside. But they're just the same. Worse, if I'm honest."

"Did you receive support from the force? Counselling, I mean," he asked, to which she shook her head.

"I just took compassionate leave. I suppose that was what saved me really. Sitting at home on my own. You'd think being alone is the last thing somebody who had done what I... What I mean is that depression can be quite coercive. You surround yourself with people, work all the hours you can to avoid being alone, and all the while there's a voice in your head. It reminds you that you don't want to be there. That you'd be better off at home on your own. But then, when you finally are at home on your own, it convinces you that you're no good and that things will never change. That people will never see past my size. That people will never see me for who I really am."

She had surprised herself. Never before had she voiced that particular reflection. Even when she had come to understand the process of how depression gets a grip, there had been no ah-ha moment. Only tears. But somehow she could talk to this man. This man who had gained her trust. Who had reached down to offer his hand, then turned his back just when she thought she was climbing from the darkness.

"That's when I started to wonder how. You know? How I'd do it."

"And what did you come up with in the end? What method did you deem most suitable?"

"Oh, guv. Really?"

"Really," he said. "I want to know."

It took a moment for her to summon the courage to venture into that particular dark corner. It was the darkest of all the corners she had found, and even she hadn't rummaged through its contents very often.

But she was here now and the light was getting brighter.

"I suppose it's different for everyone," she began. "I didn't want to make a scene. You know? Make a statement. I just wanted it to be over. I just wanted the hurting to stop. You hear all sorts of rumours, don't you? Theories about death and their intricacies. But none of us know. Not really. We don't know what hurts, which is the fastest, or how we'd be when somebody finds us. We don't know any of that. It's like the final frontier, and when we do eventually learn, it's too late to share. We all have to learn in our own way."

"That's very reflective," he said softly. "I suppose I agree."

She inhaled, preparing herself to shine that light once more. For the last time, she hoped.

"I took pills," she said. "Painkillers. An entire box of them."

He said nothing. Perhaps he was picturing the scene. Perhaps he was thinking about Thomas Dickens's car. Or perhaps he was wondering how on earth she was sitting there beside him.

"I made the wrong decision," she said. "I doubt that will come as no surprise to you. But I didn't think it through. You see, without going into detail, the method I chose gave me time to think about what I'd done. Time enough to crawl to the front door. Time enough for somebody to find me. A neighbour. And time enough for an ambulance to be called."

He nodded his understanding but remained silent, and if she was honest with herself, there was very little he could say on the topic.

"Do you feel better?" he said eventually, which was a risk-averse option.

"For telling you my darkest secrets?" she said. "I'm not sure."

"For being honest," he said, and he reached for the door handle, putting an end to the conversation as if they had been discussing the weather.

She wiped her eyes and climbed out into the evening, feeling the cold wind's bite lick at the tracks of her tears. She caught up with him as he headed down to the riverbank, and they heard Hannaway's muffled voice not too far away.

"Guv?" she said, and he slowed as she approached. "Guv, I just told you everything."

"I believe you have, yes," he said to her amazement.

"But you're acting like it's nothing. Like you're not at all shocked."

"Because I'm not," he replied.

"Guv?" Hannaway called out. "Over here."

Through the fog, they could make out the man's form standing beside the rough outline of a large saloon.

"What do you mean you're not shocked? I just spilled my guts—"

"I'm not shocked, Devon," he began. "Because I already knew."

She was stunned and she stopped walking, letting him move on without her for a few steps before he too came to a halt.

"You knew?"

"I read your file, Devon. I read it the day we met. Collins sent it to me. And before you jump to conclusions, it wasn't a flagrant disrespect for personal data, it was a management decision to ensure you receive the support that you need."

"The support I need?" she said. "You just made me relive the worst time of my entire life."

"I know," he replied. "And you feel better for it. You said so yourself."

"But, guv—"

"And now we can move on," he said, pressing onward to the car. "Now we're being honest with each other, we can move on."

She was speechless. A part of her wanted to scream or lash out at him somehow. But another part of her, the reasonable element of her persona, found some warmth in there, and even in the darkness and fog, as he stopped beside Hannaway and the orange glow from the open boot washed over them, she saw him in a whole new light.

"Devon?" he said, but she was still reeling. "Devon, come here. You need to see this."

She knew what she would see. But why on earth he insisted on her seeing it, she couldn't quite understand.

Thomas Dickens was lying in the foetal position, fully dressed. His eyes were closed and a thick, dark trickle had run from the top of his head somewhere beneath that playful mass of curls and dried like an estuary of blood.

"Excuse me," she said, turning away for breath, and leaving the two men gazing at the corpse. But just as a beam of torchlight flicks from place to place, so too did Cook's eyes, and she felt its heat somehow, watching her.

To do nothing at such a time would only welcome a bitter comment from Hannaway, and so she moved round to the side of the car out of his line of sight. The passenger door was already ajar, and carefully, she nudged it open enough to lean inside, being careful to touch nothing. The inside of the car was showroom clean, the level of cleanliness only an individual with time on his hands could maintain. There were no empty drinks bottles, no items of clothing, hats or gloves, and no discarded wrappers.

But there was something far less tangible.

"Guv," she called out and backed out of the car to find him peering around the boot lid. He must have read the urgency in her eyes, as he left Hannaway's side and joined her, taking a moment to glance inside, then looking back at her quizzically.

"It's empty," he said.

"Get in," she replied, and slowly, he leaned inside the car, just as she had. She stepped close to him, watching his face from over his shoulder. "Now tell me what you smell."

CHAPTER 48

The roads were getting busier as, for most people, Christmas became a memory and lives began that gradual descent into normality, broken only by the minor interruption of the New Year celebrations. Christmas lights still hung in gardens and from gutters while the fog pressed down like cold breath on candles.

"Get Chalk on the phone, will you?" Charles said, and he handed Devon his phone while he drove. "Use mine. It'll route through the Bluetooth thing."

He waved his hand at the dashboard, roughly pointing to the stereo.

"The Bluetooth thing. No problem."

She swiped at the phone and it presented her with a digital number pad.

"You'll need to unlock it, guv," she said, holding the phone out for him. "I don't know the code."

"It's two three zero one nine nine," he said, which she entered, found Chalk's number in the recently dialled list, and made the call. She must have been at her desk, as Chalk answered the call on the first dial.

"Guv?" she said.

"CCTV," he said, with no greeting or introduction. "Dickens and Sons main gate. How's it looking?"

"That's next on our list, guv," she replied. "We're just on hold with the network provider."

"Well, leave Forsythe on hold and open the video file for me, will you?" Charles said as he turned onto the new bypass road that ran around Lincoln.

"Sit tight," she said, and they heard the clatter of fingers on her keyboard.

"Devon, what time did you call me earlier? When you noticed Thomas's car was missing?"

"Hold on, I'll check my phone."

"I'm just opening the security portal now," Chalk said.

"We 're looking for today's file," Devon told her as she searched her call history. "I made the call at one-fifteen. We're looking for the thirty minutes or so before one-fifteen p.m."

"Twelve forty-five," Chalk said, and her exhale rasped across the phone's microphone. "Got it."

"Right, we're looking for a black BMW. Thomas Dickens's car. The number plate should be in the main file."

"The what?" Chalk said.

"The one on the floor," Charles added, and he caught Devon looking away, choosing not to reflect on his little tantrum.

"Here we are," Chalk said. "I'll just speed up the video a little. Bear with me."

"I don't get it, though," Devon said. "I can't see a motive."

"Are you thinking out loud, Devon?" Charles said, as he navigated a roundabout, took the exit, and then straightened out.

"No," she said. "I just can't see it."

"I'm sure everything will become clear in the next hour or so," he said. "How long until Abbott Dickens has to make the statement?"

"They said midday tomorrow," she said, checking her watch. "Sixteen hours. We've got sixteen hours to either convince Abbott

Dickens to shut the business down or find Janice. But I still can't see how this is linked."

"Here we go," Chalk said, reminding Charles that they were still on the call. "I've got it. Black BMW. Registration matches. He left the factory at twelve forty-five turning left onto the main road towards Washingborough."

"Thirty minutes before I made the call," Devon said.

"Hang on," Chalk added. "It looks like Gareth Dickens followed him out less than a minute later."

"And he turned left as well?" Devon asked.

"He did, yes."

"That doesn't mean anything," Charles said. "They'd need to turn left to get back to their parents' house. Chalk, can you rewind it?"

"Rewind, guv?"

"Yes, go back a bit. To the point where his car goes through the gates."

"Okay," she replied, sounding a little unsure as to why. "Okay, I'm there."

"Can you zoom in?" he asked, as he approached the final roundabout on the bypass and indicated right. "Tell me who's driving, Chalk."

He glanced across at Devon, whose mouth hung open in anticipation and his eyes widened when Chalk finally spoke.

"Bloody hell, guv," she said. "It's not Thomas Dickens, that's for sure."

"Send Devon a photo," he said.

"A photo?"

"Yes, a photo. On the WhatsApp thing," he said, gesturing wildly in the air. "Whatever the quickest way is to send a photo."

It took around thirty seconds for the image to come through on Devon's phone, and she sighed with relief when she stared down at it.

"Well?" he said, then winced at his own impatient tone.

She held the phone up for him to see and watched as he inspected the photo while he drove.

"You were right," he told her, then addressed Chalk. "Thank you, Chalk. I want a focus on Gareth Dickens. Phone calls, text messages, his car, his credit cards, anything you can get on him. I want it all in a file when we get back."

"It's going to be a late one then, is it?" Chalk said.

"Late, early, whatever label you want to give it, Chalk," he replied. "The clock is ticking on this one and I don't intend to stop until we find Janice Dickens. The alternative is not an option."

The address that Chalk had found for them led to a house on a newish housing estate on the edge of Bracebridge Heath. It wasn't a large property, but it was tasteful, and the street seemed both respectable and affluent enough for there to be an abundance of Christmas lights and nodding reindeer on neighbouring lawns.

Charles parked the car on the road, blocking the driveway on which a two-year-old Range Rover Evoque had been reversed. Its tailgate was open and the light from within spilled onto the block paving.

"Guv," Chalk said. "Forsythe wants a word with you before you go. You're on loudspeaker."

"Go on," Charles said. "I'm listening."

"We've gained access to Gareth Dickens's phone records," Forsythe said. "I'm just waiting for his bank statements to come through. According to the log, the magistrate sent the warrant half an hour ago."

"Good. Progress. That's what I like to see," Charles said.

"Phone records show that Gareth Dickens made several calls to the same number during the days before and after the abduction."

"Okay," Charles said. "Do we know who the phone belongs to?"

"Robert Pierce, guv," Forsythe said. "He's one of the property managers."

"I knew it," Charles said, slamming his hand down on the steering wheel. "I bloody knew they were involved."

"Gareth Dickens's bank statement is in," Chalk said.

"Come on, then," Charles said, feeling that pang of excitement coursing through his bones the way it did when all the facts started coming together. It was like navigating a maze and glimpsing the exit. There was still work to be done to escape, but they knew which direction to walk.

"Oh, Jesus, guv," she said.

"Just bloody tell me, Chalk," he said, then winced again. "Sorry. Can you just tell me?"

"One hundred thousand pounds," she said. "Transferred from Gareth's savings account to an unknown account number two days before Christmas."

"Unknown?"

"We can do some digging," she offered.

"Do it," he said. "Dig. Bloody well dig through the night if you have to. He's unlikely to require legal aid and I think it's fair to say that whatever lawyer he uses is going to be no slouch, so we need absolutely everything we can get our hands on."

"All right," Chalk said. "Leave it with us."

"What about the Pierce brothers?" Forsythe asked. "Should we bring them in?"

"No," he said. "No, if they're the ones holding Janice somewhere, then we'll need to give them some freedom. The last thing we want is for every suspect to be locked inside a cell. The poor lass will starve to death."

"We'll need a warrant for their bank accounts, but we could take a look at their phones, guv," Chalk suggested. "It shouldn't take long."

"What about their car?" Devon asked.

"It's a van," Chalk said.

"It's a what?" Charles said.

"A van, guv," she said. "Sergeant Hannaway said they had a van."

"Can we get an ANPR alert set up in case it gets picked up?" Charles asked. "We might at least get to see where they go to in this van of theirs."

"Agreed," Charles said. "Chalk, Forsythe, can you handle all that?"

"We can," she replied, and there was a smile in her voice as if she was enjoying the sudden burst of activity.

"Also," he said. "Sorry to add to your woes, but we've left Sergeant Hannaway on Five Mile Lane waiting for CSI and the medical examiner to arrive. He should have some uniformed support by now. Can you ask him to send a unit to the address you just gave us? I have a feeling we're going to need an extra pair of hands."

"Will do. We'll call you when we've made progress," Chalk replied, and Charles leaned forward to end the call.

"Before we do this," Devon started. "Can we just go through the whole MMO thing? Just so we're both on the same page."

"I think his MMO at this stage is not our primary concern, Devon, given the CCTV and the phone calls, which he didn't tell us about, I might add. Not to mention the money. One hundred thousand pounds? A hundred grand? Who has that kind of cash in his savings accounts?"

"I just can't see what motivation he would have to shut the family business down," she said. "Why would he have his own sister kidnapped? He's the CEO. If he wanted the business shut down, surely he could convince the shareholders to do so?"

"His father is the majority shareholder, Devon," Charles said. "I'm not sure if he could be convinced to shut the gates for a few minutes, let alone close them forever."

"I just don't get it," she said. "It's not right. We're missing something."

He sat back and peered past her at the house to make sure they were still alone.

"Do you know how many investigations I've closed where I've gone into a final interview and been one hundred per cent sure I had all the facts?"

She shrugged and shook her head.

"None," he said. "Of course, it's none. You never have all the facts. You think you might, but during the course of the interview, information comes out. Evidence that appeared to be fragmented and disjointed suddenly comes together. And by the time you read the suspect their rights for the last time and walk them down to be charged, you're bloody sure as hell. Well, at least you'd better be sure." She smiled her appreciation for the words but still remained unconvinced. "Listen," he said. "What does your gut tell you?"

"My gut?"

"Your gut?" he repeated. "Forget logic. Forget evidence. What does your gut say?"

"It says that if it's one of the brothers, then Gareth is the most likely. But it still doesn't make sense. It just doesn't add up."

"Are you prepared to give this one a chance?" he asked. "Do we trust each other now?"

"I don't know, guv. Do we?"

He grinned, enjoying the stronger Devon that had somehow emerged from the chrysalis he had met two days ago.

"We do," he told her, then shoved the car door open. "Come on. Let's get this done. It's going to be a long night."

They said nothing as they climbed from the car, and although he had expected Devon to quiz him on the line of questioning he would take, she seemed to be taking it all in and was thankfully unfazed by the task.

The front of the property was suited for professionals with

either very little interest in gardening or very little time for it. The block-paved driveway that filled the space was clean and sprawling with not a grain of soil to be seen, let alone a climber or two, or a shrub to break the straight lines. He peered into the back of the large SUV as he passed, noting a few bags that had been hastily tossed inside.

Devon rang the doorbell and stepped back, mirroring his efforts to retrieve his warrant card from his pocket. They heard somebody running down the stairs inside, then pause, and a dark shape in the hallway stooped to peer through the frosted glass, then backed away almost immediately.

Charles rang the doorbell once more, then stepped back to stand beside Devon, who was about to call out, until he held up his hand to stop her.

"Never give them a head start," he muttered, and he offered her a wink. "If we tell them who we are, they'll be out the back door in a heartbeat, and I don't know about you, but I'm not much of a runner."

Eventually, the front door opened a crack and a dark-haired girl peered out at them both, recognising them immediately.

"Ah, Victoria. How are you?" Charles said, holding up his warrant card, and then nodding at the Range Rover's open tailgate. "Going somewhere, are we?"

CHAPTER 49

No news of Abbott had arrived, and in the family's wake, the house was cold and lonely. Twice she had tried to restart the fire only to watch the glowing embers fade. Susie had resorted to pulling on her fleece-lined leggings, a pair of thick socks, and her thick Arun cardigan. She had considered the jumper that Jeffery's parents had bought her for Christmas. It was a lovely thing. Cashmere wool with a turtleneck which no doubt would have really finished off her country look had she worn it with the knee-length boots and quilted Barbour jacket that Jeffery had bought her. But it hadn't seemed quite right to wear it. Not when she had no intention of staying.

Tea, the only reliable source of heat, had been her saving grace since they'd left. She'd had three cups now and the thought of another was alluring, but not enough to justify another visit to the washroom with the promise of its ice-cold toilet seat, which seemed to undo any good work the tea had done in the first place.

With her arms wrapped around herself, and her hands tucked into the soft, woolly cardigan, she paced the walls and the furniture, studying the family photographs. There had been so much talk of Jeffery's grandfather that she wondered what he might look like. She bet herself that he was a stern man. The type that held his head high and never showed an ounce of emotion in his entire life. In her mind, he dressed well. Thick, woollen suits, as were popular in the day, a weighty moustache like a walrus, and maybe a pocket watch on a chain.

Susie carried that image with some amusement as she ventured on her journey through the Dickens family history. With nobody to explain who was who, she made her own judgement on the identity of those she didn't recognise.

There were images far older than Jeffery's grandfather could have posed for. Some of them appeared to be Victorian or thereabouts, monochrome images of lean men standing beside their seated spouses. Even in the images of daily life, the men wore suits. Only in one photo did somebody dare to remove his jacket and roll up his sleeves, and that was perhaps the oldest image of them all. It was grainy and the man was almost unrecognisable. Had the image been taken with a modern camera, she had no doubt his skin would have been a glorious brown. Instead, he simply appeared to be grubby and unwashed as he walked behind a plough or some device pulled by two huge horses. The farm buildings were in the background. The type she had seen in a hundred different photos over the years, with walls of stone and few windows. She imagined the winters there to be as cold inside as she was then, and was grateful that the toilet was inside the house and not at the end of a courtyard as the one in the image appeared to be, barely larger than a phone box.

Another image showed a much younger-looking Gareth with Harry, Arthur, and who Susie assumed was his wife, Marie. She had been pretty. It was now obvious where Harry and Arthur had got their good looks from. Gareth wasn't bad-looking, but he certainly wasn't handsome.

But then, neither was Jeffery really. They were a hardy-looking lot, the Dickenses, with square jaws, bright eyes, and noses which appeared to be slightly small for the faces they adorned. At least

Janice had escaped the unfortunate genetics, no doubt inheriting her mother's more feminine look.

She checked her phone again, wondering if she had, by chance, missed a call or a message from Jeffery, but there was nothing. Having performed a complete tour of the living space, inspecting every photo it had to offer, she found herself wandering into the hallway.

For all the faults she had found in the family, she had to credit Elizabeth. Her taste in furnishings was second to none. Even the little ornaments had been placed just so. Not too many and not too few with a range of complimenting textures that softened the great entrance – glossy porcelains against the natural fibres of cut pampas grass reaching out of a stoneware vase, and wrought-iron brackets holding broad, hessian-wrapped candles.

She found herself at the door to Abbott's study. Her hand reached for the handle automatically while her conscience provided a weak argument against such an invasion of space. But her conscience was no match for her intrigue, and the door opened with minimal effort.

It wasn't the first time she had been inside, of course. But the interview with the two detectives had been far more harrowing than she had realised, leaving no mental space to appreciate the room.

He was a paradox of a man, who clearly strived to be like his ancestors. Carrying the flame was a phrase she had heard him say. But there was a sensitivity there too. He had taken himself away to his bench in the garden to deal with his emotions, but he hadn't hidden.

His desk was fastidious, the furniture glorious, and the ambience of the room one in which a man could find peace in a house where three young boys and their sister must have run wild.

She was about to open the desk drawer closest to her when she heard the crunch of tires on gravel, and she ran to the hallway, where she stopped and stared at the front door, preparing to greet the family with as grave an expression as she could muster.

She heard the footsteps on the gravel and the low rumble of a man's voice. But the door didn't open. Instead, somebody knocked on the hardwood. Three firms knocks. Loud enough to be heard from deep inside the house.

Slowly, she crept to the door wondering if she should open it, or if it would be better, given the circumstances, to wait until whoever it was had left. What if it was the men who had called Elizabeth? She stepped back from the door at the thought. What if they had come to cause trouble? What if they grabbed her and stuffed her into a car like they had done with Janice?

They knocked again, this time with far more vigour, and she saw the handle move. Part of her wanted to reach out and slide the chain on, but then they would know she was inside. Then they wouldn't go away. She could run upstairs. But then what?

The door eased open and she found herself backing away, her hands groping for the wall behind her.

The figures were nothing more than dark shapes in the foggy night. They stilled when they saw her, and eventually, the taller of the two stepped into the light.

"Oh, it's you," she said when she recognised the man. She could have dropped to the floor her knees were so weak.

"Susie?" he said, that soft Scottish accent a lullaby after such a nightmarish fright. "Susie, are you okay?"

"I am now," she replied, laughing at her own stupid imagination. "I thought it was... Never mind."

"We're looking for Gareth," he said. "Is he home?"

She shook her head slowly as the little, squat lady stepped in and stood beside him. She was a funny-looking thing who reminded Susie of a girl she had gone to school with. Her intelligent eyes did little to mask a distinct lack of confidence, her clothes were plain, as if she dared not draw attraction to herself, and her hair reminded Susie of one of the ladies in the old Victorian photos on the living room wall.

"Haven't you heard?" she said. "They're at the hospital."

"The hospital? Whatever for?" the inspector asked.

"It's Jeffery's dad. Abbott. He had a heart attack."

"Oh Christ," he replied. "Are you alone here?"

"I am, yes," she said. "I didn't think it right to go with them. Besides, what if somebody came? One of the men, I mean. What if there was news of Janice and Thomas?"

"I see. Well, perhaps we'll catch up with them there," he said, and he turned, inviting his colleague to lead the way. He stopped in the doorway and turned back to her. "I'm surprised to find you still here, Susie. The last time we spoke you were keen to break it off with Jeffery."

"I was," she said. "That is, I am. I just haven't found a good time, what with everything that's happened."

"But you will? Or are you having doubts?"

"I will go. I have no doubt," she said. "No doubt at all. But before I do, there's something I need to tell you."

CHAPTER 50

The Resus ward at Lincoln County Hospital could be accessed through a set of automatic doors, allowing critical patients fast access from the ambulance to emergency care. The space was large. The size of two tennis courts, with a central station for nurses and doctors, and more than a dozen cubicles around the edges, although in Devon's opinion, they were far larger than mere cubicles. The two she had passed on her way to the nurses' station had been twice the size of her bedroom, at least, with equipment that wouldn't have looked out of place on the international space station.

"Are you looking for somebody in particular?" a nurse said. She was a small woman of Asian descent with kind eyes that narrowed suspiciously until Cook discreetly presented his warrant card.

"We're looking for Abbott Dickens," he said quietly.

"He's in six," she replied, with a glance over her shoulder, but then stepped into their path. "You can't go in, I'm afraid."

"It's not actually him we want to speak to," Cook explained. "We're looking for his son. Gareth Dickens."

Devon peered past the nurse and saw an occupied cubicle at

the far end of the room, and Elizabeth Dickens fussing over a sheet-covered mound on the bed.

"I think they're all waiting in A&E," the nurse explained. "We couldn't have them all in here. Not until he's stable, that is."

"Was it a heart attack?" Cook asked.

She glanced back at Elizabeth Dickens and then gave one of those regretful looks and shook her head.

"I can't really discuss it unless you're family."

"Could we have a word with his wife?"

"I think it's best if you let her focus on her husband."

"Chief Inspector," Elizabeth said as she stepped from Abbott's cubicle, and the nurse sighed with frustration.

"I won't keep her long," Cook said, as Elizabeth approached them.

"I'm glad you're here. I meant to call," Elizabeth said.

"We popped by the house. Susie said we'd find you here," Cook said. "How is he?"

"Alive," she said, in that tone that often accompanies a woman's strength under strenuous circumstances. "The doctors have run some tests, but I'm afraid he'll be here for a few days. They've given him something to help him sleep. So now we wait."

"Well, here is the best place for him," Cook replied softly.

"It may be," she replied. "But I'd sooner have him home. Is there any news? About Janice or Thomas?"

He opened his mouth to speak and Devon prayed that he'd leave it.

"The nurse was right," he said. "You should focus on your husband right now. We're doing what we can."

"But time..." she said, and stilled her mouth, though a slight tremble remained in her jaw like she was suppressing the urge to burst into tears. "It's running out. My babies. My..."

"Mrs Dickens—"

"Oh, Inspector," she said, leaning into him and clinging to his arm. "What's happened? What's happened to my family? I told him to give it up. I told him all those years ago."

It was ill-advised in nearly every rulebook and protocol to comfort a family member, especially in a male-to-female environment, when there were so many British police officers being investigated for sexual abuse and exploiting their positions.

But Cook was old-school and so was she. They came from a time when such precautions hadn't even been conceived. Better times, he might have said, and he held her. Something in the way he looked down at Devon suggested he knew he shouldn't, but he made no attempt to pull her away.

"I want them back," she mumbled into his chest. "I just want them all home and safe again. I want it to be over, Inspector."

He said nothing, at least. It would have been easy for him to mutter a promise he couldn't keep in the moment, just to make her feel better. But he didn't.

He took a deep breath and squeezed his eyes closed, signalling for Devon to take a step away.

"Elizabeth, there's something I have to tell you," he said, his mellow Scottish accent somehow softening the statement. The sobbing stopped for a moment, and slowly, she pulled her head away from him. It was as if they were old friends, yet they had barely spoken in the few days they had known each other. "I'm afraid Thomas isn't coming back."

Her hands fell from his arms to her sides and hung loosely. She stared into his eyes with disbelief, or hope at least. The two were almost identical in such times.

"We found him this afternoon," Cook added, shaking his head apologetically. "I'm so sorry, Elizabeth. I'm so, so sorry."

"My boy?" she whispered, and Cook caught her as her knees gave way. Instinctively, Devon reached for a nearby chair beside the nurses' station and helped Cook lower her down. It was all she could do to peer over at Abbott's bed, and despite being a woman with four children and four grandchildren, she was all alone in the world. She sobbed into her hands and Cook dropped to a crouch to hold her hand.

"Fetch a nurse," he said to Devon, and she immediately walked over to where the nurse they had spoken to before was loitering.

"I'm afraid Mrs Dickens has had some rather bad news," she said, and the nurse looked across at where Cook and Elizabeth Dickens were holding each other again, and then she glanced across at Abbott's bed. "It's not her husband," Devon added. "Is there anything we can do for her?"

"Mum?" a voice called out from the far side of the room where a corridor led to the A&E waiting room. "Mum? What's going on?"

Gareth marched across the room, leaving Arthur with Jeffery.

"Mr Dickens," Cook said, slowly rising to his feet, but he wasn't fast enough. Gareth took hold of Cook's arm and pulled him from his mother.

"Get off her," he cried out. "What the bloody hell do you think you're doing?"

"Gareth!" Elizabeth said, her voice thick and teary.

But Gareth held onto Cook's coat and he began dragging him away until Devon aimed a well-placed knee behind his, catching him off-guard and he dropped in front of her. It took a few seconds for her to twist his arm behind his back and force him facedown onto the floor.

Cook straightened his jacket and dropped to a knee beside them, leaning in close to speak into Gareth's ear.

"If you want me to arrest you for your brother's murder right here in front of your mother, then you just carry on fighting, Gareth," he hissed, and Gareth's struggling ceased. His head was laid flat against the floor and he peered up at them both. "That's it. Stay calm, and we can save her that little heartache at least. God knows she's been through enough for one Christmas."

From out of her pocket, Devon withdrew a pair of handcuffs

and slipped them onto his wrists, giving each bracelet an extra squeeze for good measure.

"Where are you taking him?" Elizabeth cried out, as Jeffery and Arthur ran to her side.

With Cook's help, Devon dragged Gareth to his feet, offering him one more chance to see his father lying still on the bed in the cubicle.

"Take a good look, Gareth," she told him. "It might be the last time you see him."

"Daddy?" Arthur called out from his grandmother's side. "Daddy, where are you going?"

From beside his mother, Jeffery pulled the boy close, keeping hold of her hand just as he had at their house.

"Look after him for me, will you?" Gareth said to his brother, and then as much as Devon would allow, he leaned towards his son. "And you take care of Nanny, okay?"

"Where are you going, Daddy?"

"I love you, boy," he replied, as Devon pulled him away and began leading him towards the exit as he began to struggle against her grip. "I love you, Arthur. Don't ever forget that. I love you."

CHAPTER 51

The recording issued a prolonged buzz to signal that the recording had commenced, a design to eliminate the possibility of officers losing the critical introductions which could then be disregarded in a court of law.

"Interview commenced at nine-fifty eight p.m., December twenty-seventh," Cook said when Devon gave him the nod. "Those present are myself, Detective Chief Inspector Cook, Detective Constable Devon, Victoria Hughes, and her legal counsel..." He stopped and gestured for her lawyer to introduce himself.

"Steven Bowen," he said. "Hawkins and Co LLP."

"Good, let's begin," Cook said. "Miss Hughes, you are under arrest on suspicion of being an accomplice in the murder of Thomas Dickens. You do not have to say anything. But it may harm your defence if you do not mention when questioned something which you later rely on in court. Anything you do say may be given in evidence. Do you understand?"

She nodded and then glanced across at her solicitor.

"For the recording, please?" Devon said, and she nodded once more, her eyes wide with fright.

"I understand."

"Can you please explain where you were today from eleven a.m. to one p.m.?" Cook asked, without looking up.

"At the office," she replied.

"By which, you mean at Dickens and Sons on Washingborough?"

"I do, yes."

"And what time did you leave?" Cook asked, to which she hesitated and then responded slowly, speaking more to her lawyer than to Devon or Cook.

"Around midday," she said. "Gareth... That is, Mr. Dickens said I could finish early seeing as it was quiet."

"That was good of him," Cook said. "Does he often do that?"

"No. No, I nearly always get the bus. I don't drive very often, you see. I quite like the bus ride. My mum's the same."

"I meant, does he often let you go early?" Cook said.

"Oh. Oh, no. Not often, anyway. He's usually gone by the time I finish."

"But today he took you, did he? In his Mercedes? Is that right?"

"I'm not sure what car it was," she replied. "I'm not very good at cars. But yeah, we left together."

"In the same car?" Cook said. "Just to be clear."

She looked at them both in turn.

Then nodded.

"For the recording, if you will," Devon said again.

"Yes. Yes, we left in his car."

"And just to be clear, Miss Hughes, whose car was that on your driveway? The one you were loading with bags when we arrived at your house."

"The big one? Oh, that's my mum's," she replied. "She lets me use it when she's not home."

"And can I ask where you were planning on going to?"

"Going? Oh, yes. I was just going down to see a friend. In London."

"You had quite a few bags. Was it to be a long trip?"

"Only until the new year," she replied. "She has a place out in Essex, so it's nice to see the fireworks in town and then we get the train back to hers. So much cheaper than hotels, especially at this time of the year. We did it last year."

"And if we were to talk to this friend, she would corroborate this, would she?" Cook asked.

"Of course. I doubt she remembers much of the night, but she'll certainly remember me staying. We had matching onesies."

"I meant, she would corroborate your plans to visit her this year, would she?" Cook said.

"Oh. Well, I don't know. I was going to surprise her, you see?"

"So, you were heading down to London to see your friend who didn't know you were coming?"

"It wouldn't have been a problem," she said, and she glanced at her lawyer again.

"May I ask where you're leading with this line of questioning?" he said, his pen poised ready to note down the response.

"Oh, it's quite simple, Mr Bowen," Cook replied, and he fished a printed photograph out of his blue folder but kept it turned down for the time being. "You see, the CCTV at Dickens and Sons captured your client leaving the premises at around midday, just as she said."

The lawyer nodded his approval, but the look on his face suggested he was expecting the photo to show something to the contrary.

"However," Cook continued, "she wasn't a passenger in Gareth Dickens's car."

He turned the photo over and slid it across the table.

"This is Gareth," she said, with a slight tremble in her voice.

"Oh, apologies," Cook replied, fishing another image from the folder. "This is the one of you. He slid the second image across the table. "Do you recognise the car, Miss Hughes?"

Bowen took her hesitation to lean across and whisper in her ear, and she sucked in a deep breath.

"No comment," she said.

"Does this image show you driving a car out of Dickens And Sons premises, Miss Hughes?"

The lawyer shook his head and continued to make notes.

"No comment," she said again.

"Do you know whose car this is, Miss Hughes?" he asked.

It wasn't the first time Devon had come across a no-comment brick wall, but it was the first time the evidence had been so clear. The line of questioning Cook was taking was designed to provide a jury with clear and concise answers to pertinent questions, allowing them to see the reluctance of the suspect to respond and form their own opinions as to why. If the questioning and evidence were well presented, a no-comment response did little to prove a suspect's innocence.

"No comment," she said, and Cook retrieved the images, stacking them neatly and tucking them back into his folders, from where he withdrew three more photos, the first of which he slid towards Hughes.

"Do you recognise this man?" he asked, and she baulked at the image of Thomas lying in the boot of his car. "How about this car?" Cook said, sliding the next image across. It showed a wider view of the scene with the number plate, make and model of the car, and Thomas in the boot.

"No comment," she said, turning away but unable to prevent the tears from streaming down her face.

"Last one, Miss Hughes," Cook said, sliding the final image across, showing Thomas Dickens's hand lying across his chest, with its grotesque wound clearly visible.

She forced herself to stare at the photo and then froze, unable to pull her eyes from the savage wound.

"Miss Hughes?" Cook said. "I must ask for a response."

Bowen coughed once and she turned to look his way, catching the sly, head shake.

But instead of speaking, she returned to the image, then slid it out of the way to view the other two, spreading them out so that the brutal picture could be told in one sweeping glance.

"Miss Hughes?" Cook said. "For the purpose of the recording, Miss Hughes is studying the images." He leaned forward, linking his fingers, and waited patiently. "Miss Hughes, I'm going to tell you what I think happened. I want you to stop me when I'm wrong. Is that clear?"

She said nothing and made no gesture to acknowledge what he had said, but Cook continued.

"I think there was some kind of altercation between Thomas and Gareth Dickens in the office this morning," he began, leaving a pause to be stopped if need be. "I think the altercation resulted in Thomas Dickens's death. I also believe that Gareth panicked and convinced you to help him get Thomas's body away from the office. You drove Thomas's car. You dumped it at the end of Five Mile Lane and Gareth collected you. He drove you home, where you began to make arrangements to leave."

He glanced across at Devon, seeming surprised to have not been stopped yet.

"Was any of what I just said inaccurate, Miss Hughes?"

Bowen was growing anxious, doing his best to catch her attention so he could offer advice. But her eyes never left the images. Not once.

"What I don't understand, Miss Hughes," Cook continued. "Is why you helped him. Why not simply call the police?" He left a pause for her to respond, but it was as if she was lost in the memory of the events, unable to pull herself back to the now. "What was the argument about? Can you tell me that?" he asked, his voice calm and gentle. "Why did he cut his finger off, Miss

Hughes? Or perhaps it was you? Perhaps the argument was with you, and it was Gareth who helped you?"

"No," she said suddenly. "No, it was him. It was Gareth."

The moment was marked by a softening of Bowen's eyes. It was a look of defeat, and from now on, his job would be much harder.

"To be clear, are you saying it was Gareth who hit Thomas?" Cook said as if he were talking to a child to find out who stole a bottle of milk. She nodded, and then before Devon could prompt her, she spoke.

"Yes. Yes, it was Gareth," she replied. "But I don't know why. He wouldn't say. He just called me into Janice's office. That's when I saw him. That's when I saw Thomas."

"And you loaded him into the car, did you? With Gareth?"

She nodded again.

"I did. Well, I tried. Gareth did most of it. He's better in those situations than I am."

"What situations might they be?" Cook asked, and she faltered.

"I just mean tough situations. He's good under pressure."

"And the finger?" he said. "Who did that? Was that Gareth, too?"

"I didn't do anything," she said, clearly frightened. "All I did really was drive the car. I didn't do anything. What was I supposed to do?"

"Gareth removed Thomas's finger, did he?" Cook asked. "What did he use?"

"A knife. It was a knife from the kitchen in the office."

"And where is this knife now?"

"The river," she said. "He wiped it clean, then threw it into the river. It wasn't me. I couldn't. I was nearly sick."

"So was I," Devon said quietly, and Hughes stared across the table at her. "When I saw what the pair of you had done."

Hughes held the stare before shoving the images away, unable to look at them a moment longer.

"Am I going to prison?" she asked. "I didn't touch him, I swear. I just drove the car. What was I supposed to do?"

"Call the police?" Cook suggested. "That's what I would have done."

"I couldn't," she said. "I..."

"Go on," Cook said, prompting her to finish the statement. "Why couldn't you call the police? Surely if you discovered Thomas lying on the floor and Gareth standing over him, that would be your first instinct?"

She closed her eyes, leaned on the table, and let the tears run free. There was no sobbing. Only tears.

"Miss Hughes?" Cook said. "Are you in a relationship with Gareth Dickens? Are you protecting him somehow?"

She bowed her head, letting the tears fall onto the table beneath her.

"Yes," she sobbed.

"Is that why you couldn't go to the police?"

"Yes," she said, raising her head. "Yes. I couldn't call the police, because I was trapped in a bloody office with a man who..."

"Who what?" he said, with a little more intensity in his voice. "A man who what?"

She remained silent as if she was afraid of uttering another word.

"I think at this stage, it's best if we call a break," Bowen said. "My client is clearly distressed."

"I think at this stage it's best if we outline where we are in this investigation, Mr Bowen," Cook replied. "Your client has admitted to being an accessory to murder. What she hasn't told is why she's so afraid of Gareth Dickens, and if Thomas's murder has anything to do with Janice Dickens's abduction–"

"Janice Dickens's what?" Hughes said, her mouth hanging open in shock.

"Hold on, Inspector," Bowen said. "You haven't mentioned an abduction. You can't just throw that out there and expect my client to simply comply with any tertiary claims. She has been arrested on the charge of accessory to murder. I would expect an officer of your experience to refrain from using the boundaries of that charge to include any wider allegations—"

"Well, why don't we clear that up now, before we take a wee break?" Cook said. "On December the twenty-sixth, Janice Dickens was abducted. Since then, the family have received demands to close down Dickens and Sons. Now, Mr Bowen, I would expect a man of your experience to realise that contrary to what the television shows might convey, murder is a rare occurrence. Kidnapping is even rarer. So, for the two crimes to occur within the same family within three days of each other is quite remarkable. I doubt any jury in the land would believe that the two are not linked in any way."

The suspect and her legal representative exchanged glances, then turned back to Devon and Cook.

"I'd like some time to talk to my client," Bowen said.

"You can take all the time you like," Cook replied, neatly stacking his papers and photographs into the file. "But I must warn you. If your client has anything that might help us find Janice, then I would recommend a brief discussion as opposed to a lengthy debate." He checked his watch and tugged his sleeve back down. "In thirteen hours, Janice Dickens will lose another piece of her anatomy or worse."

"Or worse?" Hughes said.

"Use your imagination," Cook replied. "Interview suspended at eleven-ten p.m. He stood, then gestured for Devon to leave them to it, holding the door open while Devon paused the recording, then left the room. He was just about to let it go when a timid voice called out from inside.

"You don't know what he's like," she replied, and they returned to the doorway to find Bowen offering hushed advice, which she duly disregarded. "You don't know what he's capable of."

"So why don't you tell me what he's capable of?" Cook replied. Devon made her way back to the table to resume the recording, but he held his hand out to stop her and shook his head. "Off the record, Miss Hughes."

"I want immunity," she said. "I can tell you things, but I need to know I'm safe. I can't go to prison. I won't survive it. I know I won't."

"I can't give you immunity. Not in thirteen hours, at any rate," Cook replied. "

"I need something in return. I know things. I know his secrets. My secrets. I know everything."

"At this stage, I think it's pertinent to refer to section seventy-one of the Serious Organised Crime and Prosecution Act 2005," Bowen said, speaking with obvious caution, as if testing the waters. "You can initiate a request for immunity."

Cook pulled out his chair again and lowered himself into it, his fatigue evident in his slow movements and the tension in his shoulders.

"You have my attention, Miss Hughes," he said.

"I won't say anything else. I need to know I'm safe."

"Mr Bowen is quite correct," Cook replied. "I can initiate what's called a section seventy-one. The request for immunity isn't straightforward, however. The Director of Public Prosecutions must approve the request, as should the Attorney General, and that's even before the Crown Prosecution Service have their say."

"How long does that take?" she asked.

"Longer than thirteen hours," Cook replied. "Unless the circumstances are time-bound."

"So, can you start them?" she asked. "I won't say anything until I have immunity."

"Immunity against what, exactly?" Cook asked. "I'll need to submit a report now. It should be accurate on the first draft, providing every detail of the specific crime for which immunity is being requested."

"Murder," she said quietly. "I want immunity from being charged for murder, or accessory to murder, or whatever it was you said."

"Are there any other crimes for which we should be claiming immunity?" Cook asked. "Abduction, for example?"

She shook her head. "I don't know anything about Janice Dickens. Honest, I don't."

"Murder then. I presume you're referring to the murder of Thomas Dickens?" he said, and Devon watched as he studied her body language, seeming to take delight in the information being drip-fed. "Like I said, we need to be clear from the outset."

"Thomas Dickens," she said with a nod, balling her hands on the table and then looking up at him with more courage than Devon had given her credit for. "And somebody else. Another murder."

CHAPTER 52

"Gareth Dickens," Charles announced as he entered the incident room with Devon close behind him. Hannaway, Chalk, and Forsythe all looked up from where they were sitting, surprised by the outburst. Charles stomped over to the whiteboard, circled Gareth Dickens's name, and then with an adjoining name, wrote Marie's name. "I want everything we've got on him."

"We've already looked into him, guv. He's in custody, isn't he?" Chalk said, and she began tapping away at the keyboard.

"More," he replied. "I want more. "He's behind all of this, and we've got one chance to nail him. So let's get our heads together."

"Is there something we should know, guv?" Hannaway asked. "You seem a little excited, dare I say it."

"That's because I am excited," Cook told him, and he turned on his heels to look him in the eye. "I'm very excited, Sergeant Hannaway. In fact, I am so excited that I'd like to invite everybody to work through the night."

"What?" Forsythe said, then looked at the rest of the blank expressions. "Work though the night guv?"

"Is that a problem, Forsythe?"

"Well, no. Only that my brother was coming over with his kids. You know?"

Charles checked his watch again.

"Twelve hours and forty minutes," he said, "until the fate of Janice Dickens becomes clear. Tell me, Forsythe, how well do you think you'll sleep at night if you go home now and we fail to find Janice before the deadline?"

Forsythe held his hands up.

"Okay. Sorry. I wasn't thinking. It's been a long day, that's all."

"It *has* been a long day," Charles agreed. "So how about some coffee?"

He stared at Forsythe.

"Alright, alright," Forsythe said. "I get the hint."

He stood and left the room without argument, which Charles noted.

"Here we go, guv," Chalk said. "The only records of Gareth on file are related to his wife, Marie Francis Dickens. Born nineteen seventy-nine." She mumbled quickly through the less relevant facts until she reached the part of the file that interested her. "It looks like her car was found in a dyke just outside of Washingborough last year. The investigating officer suggested she lost control and came off the road." Chalk looked up from the report at Charles. "CSI later discovered a suicide note down by the river. It was addressed to her boys."

"Suicide?" Charles said. "But no body was found?"

"Guv, perhaps if you told us what you're looking for—" Hannaway began, but was cut off by Chalk.

"There's more," she said. "A small dent was found on the car's bodywork with some red paint. But there was no confirmation that the damage was new. It says here that police searched the local area and even dragged the river, but never found her."

"I've got something here, guv," Devon said, looking up from her laptop. "The family made a statement a few days after the accident. They said that Marie's disappearance was sudden but that she had been suffering with mental health for some time, and in the interest of the two boys, Harry and Arthur, they requested the media to give them some time to come to terms with their loss."

"Guv?" Hannaway said, sounding a little frustrated. "What on earth is all this about?"

Charles glanced briefly at Devon, hoping that she could relay what they head learned while he tried to piece together the news.

"Victoria Hughes is in a relationship with Gareth Dickens," she told him.

"Who the bloody hell is Victoria Hughes?" he asked in a tone that he wouldn't dare use with Charles, but for some reason deemed it suitable to use with Devon.

"She's the executive receptionist at Dickens and Sons," she told him. "Which you'd know if you bothered to read the reports I've been typing up."

"I did try," he said. "Perhaps you should add a summary at the beginning of each one so the rest of us can stay up to date without reading *War and Peace*. Anyway, is that who you two were interviewing?"

Charles watched the interaction between the two in the window's reflection and even caught the embarrassed expression on Chalks' face, who then returned to her work.

"It was," Devon said quietly. "She's requested a section seventy-one."

"A what?"

"A section seventy-one," Devon repeated. "Immunity from prosecution."

"I know what a section seventy-one is," Hannaway said.

"In which case, why then did you question it?" Charles said, speaking to him through the reflection. But Hannaway gave nothing but the response of the guilty – silence. "It turns out that Miss Hughes knows about a murder in addition to that of Thomas Dickens. If we use that information wisely, we might be able to back Gareth Dickens into a corner." He looked across to Devon who was clearly riled by Hannaway. "The other murder that Victoria spoke about. Are we going with Marie?"

She gave it some thought for a moment.

"It does strike me as a coincidence, guv," she replied. "The wife goes missing, a suicide note, no body found. Victoria wants immunity because she knows what happened to Marie."

"Immunity? We've got twelve and a half hours, guv," Hannaway said.

"He's right," Devon said. "Shouldn't we get on and write the report for the Director of Prosecutions? They're going to need some convincing."

"There's no rush for that," Charles told her. "We can't waste time working on a year-old murder case. Not when Janice Dickens is still alive."

"But don't we need her to open up. If we're going to prosecute Gareth—"

"No. She's said all we need to know for the time being," he said. "Gareth Dickens was responsible for the murder of Marie and Thomas Dickens. Convince me he isn't responsible for what his sister is going through. Or better still, convince me she isn't dead already."

"As it happens, Forsythe did have some luck while you were out," Hannaway said, standing to walk over to Forsythe's desk. He returned holding a few sheets of paper held together with a paperclip, and then handed them to Charles.

"Are you going to provide a summary, Hannaway? Or am *I* to read *War and Peace*?"

Charles tossed the paperwork onto the table and waited for an explanation.

"Gareth Dickens transferred one hundred thousand pounds from his personal bank account to..." Hannaway said, making no attempt to conceal the scornful look he gave Devon. "The Pierce brothers. Two days before Janice went missing."

"Two men," Charles said, snatching up his whiteboard marker. "And they have a van."

He found a clear spot on the board beneath Gareth Dickens's name and began to write, narrating as he did.

"Phone calls to and from the property managers. One hundred thousand pounds transferred. Argued with Janice Dickens on Christmas Day."

"Motive?" Hannaway said, and Charles stabbed a full stop on the whiteboard following the lines of enquiry. "He's the CEO of the family business," Hannaway explained. "Why on earth would he kidnap his own sister and force his father to close the business? It doesn't make sense."

"Ah," Charles said. "That's where you're wrong. Devon?"

She took the cue and spoke to Hannaway with the respect his rank deserved but far more than the man's manners warranted.

"According to Susie Fraser, Gareth Dickens told his father to shut the business down," she said.

"He did what?"

"Apparently, when they were discussing the demand, the family had an argument. Gareth voted in favour of closing it down. His father refused."

"And his father has the deciding vote, I suppose?" Hannaway said. "Being the majority shareholder. But why? Why would he want to give it all up? Every one of them has a seven-figure bank balance. Why give that up?"

"Something to do with shame and children," Devon said. "Susie didn't quite understand it, and she was sent out of the room before they discussed it in full. But all she heard was that it had something to do with the family's history and some kind of orphanage."

"An orphanage? What orphanage? There's no orphanage around here."

"That's what she said. Apparently, the family used to take in children from the church to give them a start in return for a hard day's work."

"That's not an orphanage," Hannaway said. "I don't know what you'd call it, but that sort of thing was rife a couple of hundred years ago. I saw a documentary about it once. The kids go to the church for help, and the church hands them onto local farms or mills or factories. Whatever business the rector got his annual kickback from. I wouldn't call it an orphanage though. Kids used to go missing all the time back then, but there were never any records, so if they died, nobody had to explain anything. Bloody awful business if you ask me."

"Maybe the Dickens refer to it as an orphanage to somehow ease their shame," Charles told him. "I doubt if the locals would hold them in high regard if they knew about their family's past. And as for what it is called, it is nothing but downright child abuse, exploitation, manslaughter, and in most countries, it is false imprisonment. Either way, it sounds a little far-fetched for a man as unscrupulous as Gareth Dickens to feel guilt or shame about something his ancestors did, given what we now know about him."

"It's a motive though, guv," Hannaway said as Forsythe reentered the room carrying a tray full of coffees. He set them down on the table and looked around at them all, hoping for somebody to fill him in.

"I think that, while Janice Dickens is still missing, accusing the Dickens family of manslaughter for something that happened more than a century ago would be foolish no matter how true, Sergeant Hannaway," Charles said. "No, a man like Gareth Dickens is motivated by one of two things or both. Money and power."

"He already has both," Devon said.

"Ah, but not enough," Charles replied, the narrative revealing itself as he verbalised his thoughts. "He might be the CEO, but we all know who has the power in that family."

"His dad?"

"Aye, his dad," Charles said. "And as for money, yes, he might, as you said earlier, have a seven-figure bank balance, but is that enough? Is that enough for a man like Gareth Dickens, who has lived such a privileged life? Whose family has toiled for what they have? Is that enough?" He shook his head. "No. My guess is that it's not enough. He wants the real money. He wants the capital in the business and the only way he'll get his hands on that is if the business shuts down while he's CEO and while he has a large stake."

"They're making redundancies," Chalk offered. "Maybe the firm is in trouble, what with Covid and Brexit and the rest of it."

"Aye," Charles said again. "That's it. The sooner the business shuts down, the more it'll be worth. It's got nothing to do with what the family did a century ago. Gareth Dickens wants the money from the business and the only way he'll get it is if his father agrees to shut it down. Now, tell me, Devon. How would you convince a man like Abbott Dickens to shut down the family business after centuries of hard work?"

She sat back in her seat, pulling her cardigan around her to cover herself from Hannaway's scrutinising eye.

"Hit him where it hurts," she said. "Family."

Charles nodded.

"Family. Destroy the family from the inside, just like Margaret Thatcher's cabinet did to her in the eighties. He's giving his father no alternative but to surrender."

"What's all this about Thatcher?" Forsythe asked, as Charles took a sip of the dreadful coffee and set it back down on the tray.

"Nothing and everything," Charles replied. "I'll let Sergeant Hannaway give you the history lesson," he said. "Meanwhile, I am going to drink my coffee. After that, Devon and I will go downstairs and lay our cards on the table. It's time Gareth Dickens did some talking."

"What about us, guv?" Hannaway asked, and once more,

Charles turned to face the window, finding the curly-haired sergeant in the reflection.

"Whatever way we look at this, the Pierce brothers are involved," he replied. "Find them. Follow them. Don't let them out of your sight."

CHAPTER 53

Charles waited for Devon to begin the recording and for her to announce the date and the time before he introduced them both, and then waited for Gareth and his solicitor to follow suit.

"Gareth Dickens," he said, sounding bored with the process already.

"Trevor Gardner," the solicitor said. "Partner at Gardner and Gardner Law."

"Very good," Charles said, and briefly studied the man's sharp suit, twinkling cufflinks, and whiter-than-white shirt, before turning his attention to Gareth. "Gareth Dickens, do you understand why you are here?"

"Not really," he said, as an adolescent might respond to an enraged parent.

"Well, I'll be happy to reiterate," Charles continued. "Gareth Dickens, you have been arrested under suspicion of the murder of Thomas Dickens, your brother. You do not have to say anything. But it may harm your defence if you do not mention when questioned something which you later rely on in court. Anything you do say may be given in evidence. Do you understand now?"

Gareth shrugged, sighed, and then leaned on the table, his cuffed wrists preventing him from doing much else.

"I still don't understand why I'm here," he said.

"I must say, Mr Dickens, for somebody who only hours ago lost your brother, you don't seem very upset."

"What do you want me to do? Cry? Do you want me to fall to the floor and roll around in hysterics?"

"The only thing I want from you is the truth," Charles replied.

"In the past week, I've lost my son, my sister has been kidnapped, my brother is dead, and my dad is in hospital after suffering another heart attack," Gareth spat. "So you'll forgive me if I'm all out of emotions, right now. It's been a bit of a rough week."

"That's understandable," Charles said. "As for forgivable, well, the jury is out on that one, isn't it?"

"Listen, I just want to go and see my dad," Gareth said. "My family need me."

"Ah yes. Family," Charles said. "The one thing we all try to protect. The one thing that, no matter how resilient we make ourselves, can break us." He thumped his chest with his fist. "Gets you here, doesn't it?"

"Do you know what it's like to lose a child, Inspector?"

"It's Chief Inspector, and aye, I do," Charles said. "I know what it's like." The fiery sneer on Dickens's face faded a little and a questioning frown grew from the embers. "I know what it's like to lose a child, to lose a wife," Charles said, shaking his head as the suppressed memories came to life once more. "I know what it's like to lose everything. So let's not hide behind all of that, Gareth. Let's lay it out. Let's talk about it for what it is. For what I believe you did."

"Which is?"

Charles mirrored Gareth's posture, leaning on the table and linking his fingers.

"Did you kill your brother, Gareth?" He asked. "Did you kill Thomas?"

His eyes were calculating and intelligent yet revealed nothing tangible, and he only broke the fixed stare to glance at his lawyer, who simply shook his head.

"No comment," Gareth said, his voice quiet and hard.

"How did it happen?" Charles pressed. "Did you mean to do it?"

"No comment."

"Why kill him? What did Thomas know? Did he know about Janice? Is that it? Did he find out where you hid your sister?"

"I think we should keep the line of questioning to the charges at hand," Gardner said.

"Well, maybe I'll save that one for another day," Charles replied, returning his attention to Gareth. "Because there will be another day. In fact, there'll be plenty of days." He glanced around the bland room. "You'd better make yourself comfortable, Gareth. Because like it or not, you're going to be spending a lot of time in here."

"If you have evidence that my client was somehow involved in the death of his brother, Chief Inspector, I suggest you present it. Because until now, you have provided me with nothing."

"Evidence?" Charles said. "Oh, I can show you evidence alright. I can provide CCTV footage of Thomas Dickens entering Dickens and Sons premises in his car, and I can provide evidence of Victoria Hughes driving the car out again. I can provide evidence of your client, Mr Gardner, leaving the premises less than twenty seconds later, following in his car. I was there when your client returned to his parents' house, and I saw his reaction when he learned that Thomas hadn't come home, and I must say, if he wasn't the CEO of the family business, then I'd suggest a career on the big screen."

"That hardly constitutes grounds for arrest."

"Aye, I know," Charles said. "I know. But do you know what

does constitute grounds for arrest? Finding Thomas's body stuffed into the boot of the same car Victoria Hughes was seen leaving in, at the end of Five Mile Lane."

"You'll need more than that, I'm afraid," Gardner said.

"Alright then. How about a statement from Victoria Hughes herself?" he said, to which Gareth suddenly paid attention. "Aye, Gareth. She's a lot to say has that lass."

"It's her word against mine," Gareth said. "I had nothing to do with it."

"Aye, well, we'll have to see about that, won't we?" Charles said. "It's probably worth mentioning that she's agreed to tell us everything."

"Everything?" Gareth said, the colour of his face paling.

"Everything," Charles said slowly, being sure to pronounce every syllable clearly. "And she's requested a section seventy-one, too. Pretty serious stuff."

Gareth looked to his solicitor, who laid his pen flat on his file.

"Immunity," he explained, at which Gareth's eye widened a little.

"Immunity from what?" he asked.

"From prosecution. I mean, if she helped you to get Thomas's body into the car and then drove it out to Five Mile Lane, she'd be an accomplice to murder for sure," said Charles. "She'd get somewhere between five and fifteen years depending on the jury and her counsel. But I'd settle for putting you behind bars, Gareth. It's worth mentioning at this point that we have our forensics team preparing to enter your offices. The car is already at the lab. And Thomas's finger? Well, we'll get to that one in a minute, shall we? Have you anything to say before we move on?"

"It sounds like you've already made your mind up," Gareth said.

"Oh, you know how it is. I have to remain impartial. It's not for me to pass judgement. I just call it as I see it. And what I see is a conniving, manipulative, and selfish man whose lies and deceit have finally come to a head. Your life is over, Gareth. Your world is about to come crashing down."

"It already has," he said, his voice breaking a little. "My life came crashing down when Harry was knocked down. Are you forgetting that? Are you forgetting that I lost my boy in all of this?"

"I have to admit, seeing what happened to your wee boy is a memory I'll struggle to forget. In the same way that I'll no doubt find it hard to shake the image of Janice's finger in a box. Thomas's too, come to think of it."

"So how about giving me a break, eh? How about listening to my side of the story?"

"I'm all ears, Gareth. I'm all ears," Charles said. "But first of all, why don't I tell you what I think happened, and perhaps you can tell me if I'm wrong. We are, after all, on the clock here." He checked his watch. "In less than twelve hours' time, one of two things will happen. Either your father will announce the closure of Dickens and Sons and your sister will be released, or he won't make the announcement and she won't be released."

"Unless, of course, my dad miraculously does make the statement, but Janice still doesn't get released," Gareth said. "In which case, no doubt, you'll be looking at me."

"You can't release her in here, can you?"

"I can't," Gareth agreed. "So let's hear it then. Let's hear what you have to say."

"All right," Charles said. "But, Mr Gardner, I should warn you, I do have to venture off-topic to make my point. I'd appreciate it if you could save your arguments for when I'm done. Let's not waste any more time, eh?"

"As you wish, Chief Inspector," he replied, readying his pen.

Charles stood from his seat and paced the few steps to the door, where he stopped, turned on his heels, and cleared his throat.

"I want to begin with your wife, Gareth," Charles said, and

caught the faintest of movements in his eyes before he gained control of his reactions. "Marie Dickens."

"I remember her name. Oddly enough."

"Well, it was more for the recording, really," Charles explained. "I'm sure you do remember her name." Gareth's eyes tracked him as he paced behind Devon and came to another stop. "I think anybody who kills their wife would remember their name."

"I object," Gardner said.

"You can object all you like, Mr Gardner," Charles said. "I told you I would need to venture off-topic. So if you could hear me out?"

"There's off-topic and then there's wild accusations."

"Did she catch you, Gareth?" Charles asked. "Is that what it was? Did she catch you and Victoria in a compromising position? Is that what it was?"

"You have no idea," Gareth said, shaking his head as if taunting Charles.

"Oh, I have ideas alright. I think she caught the pair of you. In your office, probably. I think she caught you and you chased her. And when she drove off in her car, you went after her. What did you do? Cut her off? Or did you force her from the road?"

"No comment," Gareth said.

"There, you see? The coward's response. You were responsible for Marie's death and Victoria bloody well knew it. So when you hit Thomas and he went down, the only person you could ask for help was Victoria. She was your accomplice the first time and she helped you again, didn't she?"

"No comment," he said again, as if he was daring Charles to make further accusations.

"It's all getting out of control, isn't it?" Charles said. "How much money are you losing, Gareth?"

"What?"

"How much money are you losing? The firm is going down.

You're making redundancies. Sell it now and you'll all walk away with a decent profit. Wait much longer and the value will be through the floor."

"Is that what you think this is? A plot to extract money from the business?"

"That's exactly what I think this is. You withdrew one hundred thousand pounds from your personal account. The Pierce brothers deposit twenty thousand into theirs. Where's the rest of it? Sitting in a briefcase somewhere until the job is done? Or are you holding back because of what they did to little Harry? You see, I believe you facilitated the whole thing. I believe you paid the Pierce brothers to grab her and to hide her somewhere. It was all your plan. One of them drives the van with Janice in the back, the other gets rid of her car. Harry wasn't even supposed to be there. And if it wasn't for Janice being a loving aunt, then he wouldn't have been, would he?"

Gareth glanced briefly at his solicitor, who shook his head.

"No comment," he said.

"Nobody was meant to die, were they? Least of all Harry. But you're in it now. It's too late to stop. You had to go through with it. The only way your father would give the business up is if his family were threatened. But he didn't, did he? He refused. He refused, and Thomas saw through your ridiculous argument that the family should be ashamed of what they had. All that rubbish about the children. You don't care about some children your family exploited a century ago. I know that, and Thomas damn well knew it."

"No comment."

"He came to you, didn't he? When we were at Dickens and Sons, Thomas found you in the office and he told you what he knew, what he'd worked out, and the only way to shut him up was to lash out. But he hit his head, didn't he? He hit his head and he didn't get up. So what did you do? What did the almighty Gareth Dickens CEO of Dickens and Sons do? You panicked. You panicked and called on the only person you could trust. The only other person who had something to lose. Victoria. If you go down, then she goes down."

Gareth stared across the table, his eyes narrow and glistening.

"Help me, Gareth," Charles said. "Help me out here. Tell me where Janice is. Let me take her home to your mum."

"I don't know where she is," he said, despite Gardner's shake of his head. "I had nothing to do with Janice's kidnapping. You're right. I transferred one hundred thousand pounds from my personal account to Roy Pierce. But it was for a property. A flat. A rental property for my boys. It was so that they could grow up with their own money. So they weren't forced into the bloody family dynasty."

"And Thomas?" Charles said. "What about him? What about Marie?"

He laid his hands on the table, closed his eyes, and took a deep breath, exhaling through flared nostrils.

Then finally he opened his eyes.

"Every aspect of your theory is wrong," he said. "I didn't kill Marie, and I certainly didn't coordinate the kidnapping of my own sister."

"But you were responsible for your brother's death?" Charles asked. "Is that what you're saying?"

"You said a forensics team is going to my office?" he replied.

"That's right."

"Tell them to look in Janice's office. That's where it happened. I hit him. He went down. He hit his head. Just as you said."

"Are you protecting her, Gareth?"

"You'll find a bag containing the clothes I was wearing in the skip behind the office building."

"Gareth, are you protecting Victoria?" Charles said. "Did she help you at all?"

"No," he said, after a brief pause. "No, it was all me. I did it alone."

Charles leaned on the back of the chair opposite Gareth and shared a concerned look with Devon.

"Gareth, in a moment, I'm going to ask my colleague to escort you to the custody desk. You'll be charged with the murder of your brother," Charles said softly.

The time for being hard on the man was over. He'd confessed to one crime. The rest would follow in time.

"Before that happens," Charles continued, "is there anything you want to tell me? Is there anything you could tell me that might help us find Janice?"

"I do have a question," he said, his voice flat and emotionless as if the fight in him had run its course. He looked up at Charles, his eyes now red and beginning to stream. "You said you were a father and that you know loss."

"That's right," Charles said, unwilling to embellish the statement with detail.

"Can I see him one more time?" he asked. "My boy. Arthur. I want to see him before they send me down. He needs to hear it from me."

"Why don't you tell me where Janice is, Gareth?" Charles replied. "Tell me where I can find her and I'll see what I can do."

The man who had, until now, remained upright, strong, and defiant, slumped in his seat, letting his cuffed hands fall into his lap.

"Tell him that I love him," he said softly. "Do that much for me, will you?"

CHAPTER 54

"It's utter rubbish and you know it is," Cook said as he drove, forcing Devon to remain silent in the passenger seat. In the little time she had known him, she had never seen him so riled up. Even when she had overstepped the mark and given her opinion on his actions, he had remained fairly calm. But now? Now he was like a different man altogether. Now there was a rage. A rage that she didn't want to be on the receiving end of.

And then something struck her. Something Hannaway had said.

Ask him about the restraining order.

"He bloody well knows where she is and he's just too cowardly to admit it," Cook continued, ranting to himself. Even his driving had become aggressive, jerking the steering wheel to make turns, not stopping to let the oncoming traffic come through when the road narrowed or a parked car blocked their way. "Manslaughter. That's what he'll get. Bloody manslaughter. Ten years, of which he'll serve five."

So, this was the man his wife and family escaped. This was the man beneath the facade of gentle calm. A frustrated, aggressive animal without control of his emotions.

"He knows we'll never find Marie," he continued. "He probably dumped her in the river as soon as he forced her car off the road. She was probably in the North Sea before her car had even been found. And as for Janice, god knows what he's done with her. She's probably in the same place."

"Do you want to arrange a dive team, guv?" said Devon.

"No. No, I don't want you to arrange a bloody dive team. What's the point? We don't even know if she's dead yet. We know nothing. That's the point. Nothing. The man's a conniving bastard. He deserves to rot in a prison cell, and what's more, the public needs to know about this. They need to know that the man behind the treasured family business is nothing but a murdering monster. But no doubt that smarmy Gardner will manage to cover it up somehow, or keep the family name out of the public eye, at least. It makes me bloody sick, Devon. Sick, I tell you."

"At least we have him in custody now."

"Aye, we have him in custody, which gives us even less chance of finding Janice. No doubt she'll be found in six months' time in a poxy shipping container somewhere. Either that or she'll wash up on the coast of Holland."

He slowed just enough to take the turn into Acredyke Lane, a single track with more potholes than tarmac, and even the attempts to repair the holes appeared to have been carried out by a four-year-old with Play-Doh.

"We also still have Sergeant Hannaway and the others bringing in the Pierce brothers. They might give us something."

"Aye, right. With the promise of another eighty grand, I doubt they'll say anything but no comment. I mean, did CSI find their prints on the car?"

"No, guv. It was wiped clean," Devon explained. "We got the full report through while we were in the interview."

"Bastards," he said, slamming his hand on the steering wheel. "Anything else?"

"Nothing we didn't already know or at least guess," she

told him.

The report had been comprehensive, but thankfully Katy Southwell had provided a summary of the findings, saving Devon from having to read through the technical jargon.

"The blood on the rear bumper was definitely Harry Dickens's. The car was wiped clean. The first finger, the smallest finger on the right hand, definitely belonged to Janice Dickens. The second, the smallest finger on the left hand, was definitely Thomas's. The main differences between the two are that Thomas's finger was removed post-mortem with a single blade, such as a chisel or a sharp knife, whereas Janice was still alive when her finger was removed with some kind of tool, like bolt croppers or large wire cutters."

"That doesn't mean anything," Cook said. "Whatever he used to remove Janice's finger could still be wherever he's keeping her."

"There are also difference in the boxes the fingers came in. The newspaper articles on Thomas's box appear to be random and even the way they were glued on was different."

"As if it was done in haste?" Cook asked, and Devon nodded.

"Unsurprising, eh?"

"Aye, he was panicking. He'd have been better off dumping Thomas in the river along with his car rather than letting us find him."

"Maybe he wanted us to find him," Devon said, and let the statement hang there in the thick atmosphere inside the car. He pulled onto the long driveway that led up to the Dickens house, and then parked beside the row of cars belonging to the family. A light was on inside the house, and another came on when Cook turned the engine off. "Somebody's home and awake."

"Aye, well. It's not like any of them are going to be sleeping anytime soon, is it?" he replied.

"Speaking of sleep, guv," she said tentatively. The light from the house cast one side of his face into shadow, revealing the deep lines beneath his eyes and the drooping lids.

"Do you need a nap or something, Devon?"

"Not me, guv. I was talking about you. You look ill, if you don't mind me saying."

"Me?" he said, with a feeble stab of laughter. "I can't sleep. I won't sleep. Not until all this is done."

She waited a moment, watching his eyes as they flicked across the house and then to the beginnings of dawn on the distant horizon.

"So what's the plan?" she asked.

"The plan?" He shrugged. "Tick boxes, Devon. We tick boxes. We go through the motions, you know? Search his belongings. See if there's something, anything at all, that might lead us to Janice. If we can prove he knows where she is, he'll be looking at a twenty-year concurrent sentence or more, instead of the five-year holiday he's currently looking at."

He let his head fall back onto the headrest and Devon waited, not wanting to be the one to instigate any kind of action. His mood was fractious. The decisions had to be his.

"Listen, Devon," he said. "I'm sorry, eh?"

"Sorry, guv? What for?"

"For..." He gestured wildly then let his hands fall back onto the steering wheel. "For whatever that was a while back. My rant. It's not me."

"It's okay, guv," she replied.

"No, I mean it. It's not me," he explained. "It might have been at one time. A long time ago. But not now. I mean it."

"I get it, guv," she said. "It's fine."

"It's just that... Well, you don't deserve it. That's what I'm saying. You deserve better. You shouldn't have to put up with that. It's the kind of behaviour I'd expect from Hannaway. But not me. All right? Not me. I don't want you treading on egg shells around me."

"Okay, okay," she said, and the effort he'd put into explaining himself deflated, leaving a void. "Can I ask you something?"

He turned his head to look at her and those heavy eyelids barely revealed the shiny eyes beneath them.

"What about?"

"It's personal," she said. "Of sorts."

He paused for a moment.

"Do I have a choice?"

"You do," she replied, to which he said nothing. He just stared at her, waiting for her to continue. "Who's Maggie Ryder?"

Barely a muscle in his face moved, and even his breathing seemed to halt for a moment.

"Who told you about her?"

"People talk," she replied. "And I was honest with you."

"Ah, but I had the advantage of HR on my side," he told her. "I already knew most of what you told me."

"Correction. You knew what the forms tell you. You knew the information in the little boxes," she said. "I told you how I felt. There aren't any little boxes to write that stuff in."

"True," he said.

"And I told you."

"And now you want me to tell you?" he asked. "Now you want me to give up my secrets?"

"Not give them up," she replied softly. "Just fill in the blanks. The spaces between the boxes, as it were."

He sighed heavily and stared out into the darkness.

"Maggie Ryder?" he said, as if there could have been some kind of mistake.

"That's the name I was given," she replied, and he nodded, taking a deep breath before he spoke.

"Now there's a name I haven't heard for some time," he mused, and then stared up at the house. A third light had been turned on and he glanced back at her, hopefully.

"Like you said, guv," she told him. "Whoever's home isn't going to be sleeping any time soon."

CHAPTER 55

"DC Maggie Ryder," he began. "That's who you're referring to. She was a lot like you in many ways. Competent. One of the good ones, you know?" he said, but didn't seek a response. Instead, he seemed to slip into a memory. "Aye, she was one of the good ones." He sucked in a breath as if was about to speak, but then hesitated. "I was a DS back then. A sergeant. Christ, that feels like an age ago. I remember we had this DI we both reported into. Finch, his name was. A right bastard. I think that's why we both got along, Maggie and me. We both hated the bloke. Good copper. There's no doubt about that. But his leadership skills might have been better suited in the army. Like a bloody sergeant, he was. Gave Maggie a hard time, which meant that the rest of the team gave her a hard time. I was probably the only one who saw her for what she was."

"What happened?" Devon said, gently coaxing him back onto the tracks from the tangent he was venturing down.

He smiled at the comment, recognising its purpose.

"We'd been after this gang," he said. "Bearing in mind that there was no real SOCO back then. It was before I'd been moved into the serious stuff. Gangs, drugs, robberies. You know how it is. The day-to-day stuff. Anyway, this gang had been having bundles of drugs dumped into the sea just near the estuary – heroin, coke, you name it. Fishermen picked it up, they distributed it to the small guys, and then started over. Bloody thousands of pounds worth, Devon," he said, shaking his head. "You'd never seen anything like it. Anyway, for every bundle we intercepted, another two would get through. We just couldn't get what we needed to get the case over the line. This went on for months. Then one day, we had a breakthrough. Some small-time dealer blabbed in the hope of getting some leniency. He gave us a place. A block of flats on the other side of the city. You have to remember that we'd spent hours – no, days – on this. Sitting in my car watching people. Out all night long sometimes, just in the hope of catching a break. And then it all seemed to happen at once. Finch gave us the all-clear. Gave us uniformed support, the works. I remember it as clear as yesterday. The dogs. They were chomping at the bit to get up the stairs. I remember the door being put through. A dozen officers piling into the flat. Top floor, mind. I was bloody knackered. We made the arrests, well, most of them. One guy had climbed out of the window and onto the roof. Lunatic, he was."

He stopped for a moment.

"You went after him?" Devon said.

"Me?" he said. "No. I couldn't do another set of stairs if my life depended on it. Not at pace, anyway. No, Maggie went after him. Cornered the fella, too. I went up afterwards with the rest of the team. You'd think that at times like that, people would come together. You know? An officer is an officer. It doesn't matter where they're from. It doesn't matter about the colour of their skin."

"She was a person of colour, you mean?"

"She was black, aye," he said. "Which to most people doesn't matter, right? But back then, she stood out like a sore thumb. Made her an easy target, if you know what I mean?"

"People can be so cruel."

"They can, aye," he told her. "And this lad. The suspect."

"A person of colour?" she said, and he nodded.

"So what do Finch and his boys do when they find her on the roof with this young man cornered?"

"Go on."

"They make comments. Racist stuff, you know?"

"I can imagine."

"Can you?" he said. "Can you? Because until then, I didn't realise just how bad it was. I didn't realise the type of stuff they were saying. I mean, he was up on the wall. One step backwards and he was a goner. She was right there with him, and they were telling him to jump and to take her with him. That there'd be two less of them in the world. Imagine that? These people are supposed to be on her side. They're supposed to serve, not judge. We don't judge, right? That's not our job."

"I believe that's the general idea," she said.

"Right. Anyway, he made a move. Saw his chance and took it. Knocked her down to the ground and made a beeline for the door. Finch and his lot all got him. Didn't stand a chance. They were like ants. I mean, police brutality type of stuff, aye? Shocking, it was. They carried him off, well, dragged him off. I argued. I told them to go easy. That they'd got him and there wasn't need for it, but I suppose the adrenaline was going. Pack mentality and all that. They were too busy saying that she'd let him go. That because of the colour of her skin, Devon, that she'd bloody let him get away."

"And Maggie?" she said, to which he looked away, turning his head so she couldn't see his face. "Was she okay?"

"I found her on the wall. Right where the lad had been standing. All alone and gazing out at the city." Charles must have felt Devon's stare, because he looked at her, eyes glistening in the dawn light. And just as he must have felt her stare, he must have sensed the question on her lips. The question she dared not speak. "I talked her down," he said. "It was close, though. At one point, I mean, I thought she was going to go. But I did it."

"How?" Devon asked. "What did you say?"

"I don't know," he replied. "Honestly. I have no idea what I said. The truth, I think. I hope. What do you say to somebody in that frame of mind? The truth is that I don't know what I said and it no longer matters. What matters is that poor girl came down. Nobody needed to know about it. Nobody had to know. I wouldn't have told a soul, and I haven't," he said. "Until now."

"Surely you had to write a report?"

"DC Maggie Ryder hung up her uniform for the last time a few days later. Once all the rumours had begun. Rumours courtesy of DI Finch, of course."

"What type of rumours?"

"What type do you think? Racist rumours. Sexist rumours. Lies. All of it. Lies. Drawings on the wall in the bathrooms. Her on her knees with a chain around her neck, and me, naked, holding the other end."

"No wonder she quit."

"Aye, well, sadly rumours like that tend to gain momentum. They develop a kind of gravity of their own. Before you know it, rumours become the truth. Gospel. It didn't matter what I said, as far as everybody else was concerned, Maggie and I were...you know?"

"Lovers?"

"Aye, that," he said. "Bloody rumours. Started by some coward who clearly realised he'd been in the wrong and needed to build some kind of defence mechanism. That's what they do, you know? They try to get people on their side. Convince them of their lies, and then what chance do you stand, eh? Everyone you see, all the people you've worked with for all those years suddenly believe you're some kind of sicko. A pervert preying on junior officers. Abusing my rank."

"Jesus, guv," Devon heard herself say.

"Jesus indeed, Devon," he replied. "Jesus indeed."

"Not everyone, surely?"

"Everyone who mattered," he replied. "Finch wasn't stupid. He got word to the top brass, he got word to the new recruits, and he got word to my wife."

"Your wife?"

"And my kids," Cook said. "And that's when things went very wrong."

"Oh my God, is that why she left you?"

The question caught him off-guard, and he stared at her but stopped himself from reacting.

"I cannot prove it. I can't prove anything. But the day that Maggie didn't show up for work, I decided to pay her a visit. You know? To see if she was okay."

"Right, that's the decent thing to do."

"Aye, that's what I thought," he continued. "But to do that, I had to go radio silent. I had to disappear for a wee while."

"Okay?" she said, not liking the sound of where the tale was going.

"Which meant that when my wife called the station to tell me a person of colour had taken one of my girls from outside her school, I wasn't there to hear it. I was with Maggie. I was trying to convince her to get back to work. I was trying to convince her that the colour of her skin didn't matter. That she was a bloody good officer. And all the while, some bastard that Finch had tipped off had my baby girl."

Devon was speechless. It was like a TV drama unfolding before her eyes. One in which she thought she knew how it ended, but there was still another episode to go, so she would be okay for the time being.

But it wasn't a TV drama and the ending came early. No twist. No final act of bravado. No happy ending.

"Whoever it was demanded that his friends be released."

"The men that you'd caught a few nights before?"

"Aye, them," he said. "Like I told you, it was some serious organised crime stuff. I didn't realise how serious, but I knew enough not to let my identity get out there."

"You really think Finch did that? But why?"

"Oh, I doubt he meant it to go as far as it did. I doubt he thought anything would happen. But it did happen," Cook said. "By the time my wife had told me what had happened, time was already running out. I tried to negotiate," he said flatly. "I offered them everything. My house, my savings, the lot. But there was nothing more I could give. I had nothing in my power to offer and nobody who would take me seriously. I was supposed to go in and release them, but you know how hard that would have been. I wasn't supposed to tell anybody. I was supposed to release them and then wait for a call."

"But you didn't, I'm guessing?"

"I told Collins. He was a DCI back then. But nothing happened. He just told me that he'd been looking for me. The suspects had been moved. They were being held on remand in Lincoln nick. He said that he'd tried to get me on the radio, but—"

"But your radio was off."

"Aye. I was with Maggie. I was being the good guy. I was doing my bit for humanity. I was doing what I thought was right. Sod the rumours. I could handle *them*. What I couldn't handle was seeing a good cop, no, a good friend, at the end of her tether. I couldn't handle seeing a mate of mine, someone I respected, wake up in the morning and have to make the decision to see the day through or to call it quits. That's what I couldn't handle."

"Guv," she said, for want of anything that might do his emotion justice.

He wiped his eye discreetly and took in a breath. The pause seemed like an eternity. But she couldn't hurry him. She couldn't hurry the ending. He controlled the timing. It was his story.

"She was dead before I got home," he said flatly. "Her body

was found in the same block of flats. In the elevator, to be precise."

Devon gasped. She felt her mouth hanging open but could do little to close it. She just sat there staring at the man beside her explain how his daughter had died.

He reached for the door handle and coughed to clear his throat.

"Guv," she called out, before he could climb out. He turned to face her, but said nothing. "What was her name?"

He smiled again, a distant sun through a veil of cloud.

"Rebecca," he said softly. "Her name was Rebecca."

CHAPTER 56

The wind off the fens was biting and heavy clouds threatened rain. But none of that mattered. Not like it would have done before Cook had relayed his story. Devon wished she hadn't pressed him now. She wished that she'd just minded her own business. She wished that she hadn't seen the kinder side of him. That she could somehow dislike him enough to not feel the tearing empathy.

But how could she not? How could she not like him? How could she not feel for him, even if the consequences of that terrible day resulted in another side of him showing its face?

That's what must have happened, she told herself, as they stood there at the Dickens's front door waiting for somebody to answer. The rumours reached his wife. She must have found out where he was when she tried to reach him. She must have somehow believed that he was up to no good with Maggie Ryder while his family was falling to pieces. That his radio was off for reasons way beyond the good he was trying to do.

That would be enough to destroy any marriage, true or not. And how could he argue? What could he say to convince her otherwise? Who would believe that he was with a woman he was rumoured to be having an affair with trying to help her get back on her feet?

The door opened and Cook spoke, though his words were lost to Devon's thoughts. It was a silent movie. He spoke and Elizabeth Dickens put her hands to her face. He stepped into the house and she fell into his arms.

And he held her.

Like a good man, he held her.

Like a man who knew loss, he held her.

She pictured the days after the event. The days when he had to find somewhere to live. The days when his family ignored his calls or didn't answer the door. She pictured him raging, frustrated at not being heard. Infuriated that, for the kindness of his own heart, he'd lost it all. He'd lost everything.

How long had he tried? How difficult had it been for him to control his temper? To watch the people he loved more than anything in the world turn their backs on him?

And the funeral.

God, the funeral.

She could picture it. The truth that his wife had believed would have been relayed to friends and family. He would have attended. Of that, she was sure. He wouldn't have missed that. He'd have wanted to say goodbye. But he would have done so alone. He would have been an island of suffering amidst the glares and reproach. The cold shoulders, the looks of disgust. It would have been enough to send him mad.

But he was tenacious. You had to be in that job. You can't give in. You can't just give up. That's why it had taken months to finally make a breakthrough on the drugs investigation. Because of his tenacity.

Elizabeth led them into the living room, which was empty and cold. Through the tall windows, the sun was peeking over the distant horizon.

But still, Devon heard nothing. Still, she imagined Cook's life falling apart.

She imagined him banging on the front door to the place he had once called home. She imagined him following his daughters to school and his wife to work. He imagined them being told to ignore him. Not to talk to him. That he was bad. That he was selfish. That he hadn't been there.

That their sister's death was all his fault.

She imagined the hearing that must have followed. A restraining order. Not a prosecution, but a restraining order. Prosecution would follow should he breach the order.

And so his long path into loneliness would begin. The long road to nothing. She could see it now. It was written in his face. His story weighed heavy on those bags beneath his eyes. It was as if every line and crease in his skin was his tale, written in a language few understood. Maybe only her. For she had the code. She could decipher him now.

And she pitied him.

"Devon?" he said, rousing her from her thoughts.

"Eh?"

"Devon?" he said again.

"Guv?"

He nodded sideways towards the kitchen island.

"Kettle," he said, and he flicked his eyes at Elizabeth, who was settling into Abbott's old armchair; a broken woman.

She nodded and made her way into the kitchen area of the huge open-plan space, still reeling from what he'd said, and battling with what she imagined had taken place afterwards.

"But why?" Elizabeth said, as Cook sat down on the sofa close to where she was sitting. "Why would he do that?"

"It's not something that any of us can understand," Cook told her. "I wish I could have come with better news, but I can't. For what it's worth, I don't think he intended to do it. It sounds very much like they argued and Gareth lashed out. We have reason to believe that Thomas hit his head as he fell."

"Oh my God," she said, and began rocking backwards and forwards in her seat. "My boy. My poor baby boy."

"And there's more, I'm afraid," Cook said, as Devon ignited the hob and placed the kettle down as quietly as she could. "I believe Gareth was responsible for Marie's death."

"No," she said, more of a breath than a word.

"And I believe he's behind Janice's kidnapping."

"My Gareth?" she said. "He can't be. He wouldn't do that. Not to his sister. Not to us. His family."

"I might remind you, Mrs Dickens, that Gareth has given us an account of what happened to Thomas. He's taken responsibility for his death. I'm sorry to say this, but I believe a man that could do that to his brother, well, he's capable of anything. I think he's acting out of desperation. I don't believe for a minute that he ever intended anybody to get hurt. I believe things have just..."

"Just what?" she said, and Cook looked up at Devon before returning his attention to Elizabeth.

"I believe things have just got out of control, Elizabeth. I think he wants to shut the business down. He knows it's going under. He knows it's only a matter of time before it's worth nothing, and he knows that your husband wouldn't shut it. Not unless there's a damn good reason."

"Family," she said shaking her head. "Even family wouldn't convince him to close it down. Do you know something, Inspector?"

He waited for her to continue, rather than answering. Maybe from fatigue. The man had been working for nearly twenty-four hours. Or maybe it was more because there was very little to say to a woman whose world was tumbling at her feet.

"I should be defending him, shouldn't I?" she said. "He's my boy. He's my flesh and blood. Any decent mother would be defending him. A good mother would have kicked you out the moment you uttered the words."

"But most good mothers haven't already lost one son," he said. "And most good mothers wouldn't be in the position that you're in now."

She nodded slowly and the kettle made a gentle whistle, signalling that the boil was close.

"Is there something I can do, Inspector?" she said. "Surely I can speak to him?"

"Gareth is playing the game," he told her. "He'll be tried for murder, but his counsel is good. He'll be looking at a manslaughter charge."

"What does that mean?"

"It means he'll be out in five years, give or take," Cook said. "If that was his only crime, do you think you could find it in your heart to forgive him?"

"For Thomas, you mean?"

"He didn't mean to kill him. Of that I'm sure, Elizabeth."

"Eventually," she said, and offered a weak smile. "Or at least move on. I'm not sure if I could forgive him, but..."

"But you can't risk losing another son. When we lose a child, we tend to cling to the ones we have left, Elizabeth," Cook said, to which she nodded.

"I am a mother, after all."

"I think he knows that. I think he's counting on your forgiveness," Cook said. "Something that even the most compassionate of mothers couldn't do if he admitted to something far worse."

"Janice?" she said, and he nodded. "I think he's arranged for her to be hidden somewhere. I think he'll take that to his grave if it means that you'll forgive him for Thomas."

"And meanwhile, Janice is left to rot somewhere? Is that what you're saying? Is that what you think of my boy?"

"It's not a conversation I ever envisaged having, Elizabeth. I'm sorry if I sound a little harsh. But the reality is that a desperate man will do things that you and I never thought humanly possible. There's no explanation I can give. All I can do is say how I see it. I'm trying to get your daughter back. I'm not trying to make this any harder than it already is."

"You're saying that he's a monster."

"I'm saying that he's desperate," Cook said. "Right now, there's a small chance that in five years' time, he'll be out. There's a chance that in five years' time, he'll be able to rebuild his life. There's a chance that he could still watch Arthur grow. He could still be a dad to him. He could still be loved, eventually. When enough time has passed. Is he really going to risk that chance? Could you?"

"But Janice pays the price?" Elizabeth said, as the whistling kettle began to shake with fury. Devon turned the hob off and removed the kettle, and Elizabeth stared up at Cook. "What if I spoke to him? He might tell me. What if told him I'd love him no matter what? He might open up."

"And would you?" Cook said.

"Talk to him? Or love him?"

"Both," Cook replied, and eventually she nodded.

"I'm a mother, aren't I? I'm *his* mother, and as you said, I've already lost one child. I can't lose another."

Devon opened the fridge to get the milk and they both looked up at her. It was a fleeting break, but it served to be the distraction they needed to pull themselves from the irrepressible gloom.

"I don't suppose Abbott has changed his mind about making a statement?" Cook said, to which she shook her head slowly.

"The business is everything," she said, and then gave a little laugh. "You'd think after what we've been through, after what he's been through, you'd think he'd see sense, wouldn't you? We don't need the money. We don't need the business. Not anymore."

"It's a pride thing," Cook said.

"It is. He's a stubborn, old fool."

"Have they said when he'll be released?"

"Oh, I don't know," she replied dismissively. "He's awake now, at least. He's stable. I think they just want to keep an eye on him for a while. I said I'd bring him a few things. But if I'm honest, I walked through that front door and I just began to wonder. I began to wonder what all of this is about. A few days ago, we had a family. Dysfunctional, it may have been, but it was a family. It was my family." She held her hands to her face and stilled as Devon placed her tea on the coffee table. Cook gestured for Devon to give the woman some space, and as she did, Elizabeth spoke once more. "Let me talk to him. Let me talk to Gareth. I just want my daughter back. I just want whatever scraps of my family I have left to be home and safe."

Doing her best to keep out of the way, Devon busied herself with the framed photographs that were dotted among the now cheerless and defunct Christmas decorations.

Marie Dickens appeared in a few, and on the outside, she looked as healthy as any woman should be. But there was something in her eyes. A sadness maybe. Or was that just some unconscious part of Devon's mind planting doubt, given what Chalk had found about the woman's mental health?

She moved to the photos on the wall. The first was a professionally taken portrait of Abbott and Elizabeth. They were dressed well, her in a floral dress with a band of pearls around her neck and him in a three-piece, tweed suit. They looked happy. Content at the very least. Not sad. Not unhappy. Not like they would be for the foreseeable future.

"Why don't you go and freshen up?" Cook said to Elizabeth, and Devon glanced over at him. He checked his watch. "It's seven-thirty. That's four and a half hours until we need the statement."

"Until they kill her, you mean?"

"It's four and half hours, Elizabeth. Four and a half hours. A lot can happen in that time."

She sipped her tea and briefly nodded her appreciation at

Devon, who averted her eyes, choosing instead to move to the next photo. It was an old image, ancient, in fact. A monochrome snapshot of a time long ago, grainy and faded. It was so old that Devon could imagine the man behind the lens, ducking beneath one of those old sheets to block the light.

But that image was nothing compared to the man before the lens, the man in a tweed suit not dissimilar to the one Abbott was wearing in the previous photo. He was standing in a field, and his shadow stretched out behind him across the stubbled crop where two children, each dressed in the Victorian garb Devon had seen in old TV shows, stood. They were far from the camera, and clearly not intended to be part of the image, but the girl wore a white cap or bonnet with a long dress, and the boy, who was larger in size, wore heavy trousers and an old, dirty shirt. A farmhouse formed much of the background, with Lincoln Cathedral poking up from behind it – that iconic and ancient monument to times gone by.

"Do you think he'll talk to you?" Cook said.

"Maybe," Elizabeth replied. "But I have to try. Like you said, we have four and a half hours. I have to try."

"Then let's try," he replied. "Go and freshen up, eh? Make yourself feel a bit more human."

Slowly, Elizabeth stood and walked across the room, stopping briefly to look at Devon, who looked back at her in time to see a weak smile. And then she was gone, her footsteps trudging heavily up the stairs.

"We should check Gareth's room while she's getting ready," Cook said, and she heard him moving towards her. But there was something about that old photo. That old testament to time. "Devon, did you hear me?"

"Guv," she said, ignoring his question, and she turned to him, feeling her heartbeat increase in speed as hope roused its weary head and emerged from the shadow. "Guv, I think you need to see this."

CHAPTER 57

There was life in Charles's hands, in his fingers. Electricity raced through his limbs and his thumping heart beat a helpful rhythm. Hope. There was hope. It was written in the sunrise before them, the winter crops in the fields on either side of Five Mile Lane, and in the expression on Devon's face as she gripped the Jaguar's dashboard.

"You're sure about this?" he said.

"No," she said, almost immediately. "No, I'm not sure at all. But do you have a better idea?"

He drew the car to a stop at the rear gates to the sprawling Dickens estate, and she turned in her seat.

"Can I see it?" she said, and Elizabeth, who had remained silent for much of the short journey, passed her the framed photograph. Immediately, she shoved open the door and held it up to the old ruins a few hundred metres away. Leaving Elizabeth in the car, Charles joined her, where she began explaining her theory. "Look, guv. I noticed it when we were here last. When we found the car." She stabbed a finger at the ruins. "You can see the shape of the farm buildings. They're in a kind of horseshoe shape. There's a courtyard in the middle of it all with the privy and all the outbuildings." She held the photo up again. "Now look at this."

"It's just an old farmhouse."

"Exactly," she said. "Do you remember what Abbott Dickens said about the family's ordeals? He said they'd survived famine and wars, and even when the farm burned down, they rebuilt. They started again. They didn't give up."

"This isn't the original farm?" he said.

"No, *this* is the original farm. *This* is the farm that burned down." She stabbed her finger at the photo. "This is the one they built to replace it. This is later. Look, in the photo, Lincoln Cathedral is sticking up from behind it." She ran a few steps to her left, holding the photo up until she was in the right spot, and the cathedral was aligned. "It's nothing like it, guv."

"Which means—"

"It's in the trees," a voice said from behind them and they turned to find Elizabeth standing beside the car. "She pointed into the mass of trees, the land that Abbott Dickens had given over to the National Trust for wildlife. But her face didn't convey the excitement that Charles felt and that Devon must have been experiencing. She looked ashamed. Broken.

And it was in that silence that Charles heard something, connecting the final piece of the puzzle.

"Listen," he said to Devon, and just faintly, the sound of construction could be heard, carried on the same cold, winter breeze that tugged at Charles's coat tails. "Construction."

Somewhere, amidst the housing development that lay on the borders of Washingborough, machinery thumped a monotonous tune.

"Dance music?" he said.

"Thomas said that most of the land had been sold to developers," Devon replied. "He said there were hundreds of acres, but that his father wanted to keep this part for nature. Just this part."

"Like he was doing the world a favour," Charles said.

"He wasn't doing anybody any favours," Devon replied.

"He was keeping the family secret," Charles said, and he took the photo from her. "The children."

"They all burned," Elizabeth said. She walked slowly towards them, unafraid. With nothing left to lose. The wind caught her coat, which flapped wildly, but she made no effort to fasten it. It was as if the cold breeze was cleansing her. Like it was tearing the secrets that she had sworn to keep from her very soul. "Every last one of them."

"The fire?" Charles said, and she nodded.

"It wasn't an accident," she explained. "It was the only way. Times were changing. The country was becoming organised."

"The Victorians," Charles said. But she made no effort to agree or disagree.

"Families like the Dickens, who worked in partnership with the rectors and the parish, could no longer do what they had been doing," said Elizabeth. "They couldn't get away with it. Child labour. Those poor children were set to work for nothing but a roof over their heads and a slice of bread in their bellies. They were doing the work of men. Dangerous work. And when they were injured, they were cast aside to make room for another."

"This is horrific," Devon said, more to herself than anybody else, but Charles heard the compassion in her tone.

"The authorities were coming down hard on families like the Dickens," Elizabeth continued. "On men like Abbott's great grandfather. If it wasn't the farms, then it was the factories, and if it wasn't the factories, then it was the church, or laundries, or shipyards. All manner of industries had exploited the children for too long. It was the beginning of human rights. It was the beginning of equality." She shook her head sadly. "They swept through the country like a plague. Men were jailed, families were ruined, and those who weren't jailed were named and shamed. But what could the family have done? They couldn't set the children free, and they certainly couldn't pay them, which is how many businesses managed to continue."

"They could have just the kids go."

"What, and have them tell the world about how poorly they were treated? About what happened to the children who were injured? Who'd had limbs torn off by machinery they should never have been using. Children who, on paper at least, didn't even exist."

She stepped closer and reached into her pocket, retrieving a folded sheet of stationery, which she then handed to Charles.

"Read it," she said, and he unfolded the note, and then read it aloud.

"To Dickens and Sons," he read. "With immediate effect, please accept this letter as formal notice of my resignation. I find I can no longer pursue a career led by an individual who demonstrates such a twisted sense of right and wrong, and for a business so buoyant on what can only be described as a river of blood."

"A river of blood," Charles said. "They–"

"Threw them into the river," Elizabeth finished for him, her face screwing into a disgusted sneer. "How do you think the families around here would treat us if they knew how we came to be? With respect?" she said. "Do you think a farm within a hundred miles of here would buy from Dickens and Sons?" She shook her head slowly. "The truth is, Chief Inspector, that Dickens and Sons should have been shut down more than a century ago. It's only Abbott's pride, and his fathers' pride, that have carried it this far."

The forest before them was imposing. From the outside, it was an impenetrable mass of wood and thorns. But those were just the defences. The armour. The protective moat guarding an ancient secret.

Elizabeth made no attempt to stop them when Devon pushed open the gate. It swung open with a squeal, then hung there, as if it was daring them to pass through.

They left her near the car, watching them as they sought an entry into the wild mass.

"Over here," Devon called out, and for a girl who, in her own words, was not a size-six supermodel, she was agile enough to find a pathway, ducking beneath the long reaches of brambles and stepping down on huge mounds of stinging nettles, flattening the way. She stopped to make sure Charles was following, and she caught his eye. "Someone's been through here. Recently."

He peered past her, just able to make out the faint path.

"Keep going," he told her, and she did.

She kept going like a train forces its way along snow-covered tracks, bullish in her approach, unrelenting and unperturbed by thorns and spikes and stings. And when her foot caught on the tendril of some hidden plant, she kicked through it. When the branches of the trees reached down to snare her hair, she pulled back in defiance.

And then they saw it. Through the tangle of undergrowth and shielded by the canopy of trees, they saw it. If it had been a beast, then the broken windows were its sad eyes. The rotted front door that hung by a single hinge was its tongue hanging limp. And the ivy that clung to nearly every brick was the veil that covered its shame.

He held up the photo for the last time, and she watched him.

"This is it," he whispered.

The form that lay beneath the veil of ivy was wide – fifty or sixty feet, by Charles's reckoning. It seemed to watch him as they approached, with those saddened eyes. He stepped over the broken front door and peered inside. It was as he had expected. Not unlike the image his mind had conjured when he had first imagined the building. A fireplace dominated the space with the remains of its long-spent embers strewn across the terracotta hearth. The rotted remains of an old kitchen table stood crippled on its two remaining legs with its quarry of crockery in various states of repair laying where they had fallen nearby.

Glass crunched beneath their feet, and they stopped to listen.

"Janice?" he called out. "Janice Dickens. Are you here?"

Aside from the main door through which they had entered, the large room boasted one other. He imagined it newly painted. White with a brass handle. The round type that one had to grip and twist.

It was as if Devon had read his mind, as they both stepped cautiously towards it.

"Janice?" he called out again. "Janice, are you here? It's the police. Call out if you can."

He stopped by the door and fetched a tissue from his pocket, which he used to cover the door knob, protecting any finger prints it might bear, and any secrets it might hold.

And then slowly, he turned.

Dim light filled the black void as the old door creaked open, spreading across the old plastered walls like a cancer invading the darkness, intrusive and invasive.

The room was long and windowless. A hallway perhaps. So long that even that cancerous light couldn't grace its deepest depths. But it did reveal a table or a stool just a few feet in. An old thing with turned wooden legs. The type an old milk maid might have sat on to fill her pail. He shoved the door open further to reveal a dark stain across the surface. Half-a-dozen empty water bottles sat in the shadows. The plastic type that washed up on beaches around the world. He gave the door a final shove and gave a heavy sigh.

Two eyes stared up at him, glowing white in the dimness of that dank and stale place. Two eyes of a face that was but bound and gagged with a mass of filthy hair hanging down, like the ivy on the bricks.

He didn't say anything. Not at first. He savoured that relief in her eyes, prominent in the absence of any other facial features. They spoke words that no language could describe. A story that no author could pen.

She sat upright. Unable to move into any other position. Her ankles were bound to her bloodied hands and wrists, which in turn had been tied to an iron ring that had been fixed to the wall, no doubt to hold some tool or other way back when a long-dead Dickens had called the place home.

"Janice?" he heard himself say. "Janice Dickens?"

She blinked twice, her face almost vanishing into the darkness each time.

And then she turned her head to peer into the darkness behind her, as if beckoning him to follow her gaze.

"Get me a torch," he said quietly to Devon, who stood beside him.

She fumbled with her phone, which then emitted a bright light, and she handed it to him. Cautiously, he stepped inside, as Devon bent to release the gag around Janice's mouth. He heard her gasp of air. He heard the anguish in her breath.

The hope.

But the light from Devon's phone had revealed more secrets. The floor beyond her was strewn with papers, bright now that he was close, glowing white at the touch of the torchlight. He bent to pick one up and then held the phone above it.

"It's a diary," he said, bending to collect more. He turned to Janice who simply stared at him, her head rocking gently as Devon fought to release her bindings. "Whose diary is this?"

But she said nothing. Shock presented itself in strange ways, and her wide eyes implored him to read on.

"Arthur Abbott Dickens," he read aloud. "December twenty-first, eighteen seventy-eight."

He tried to read more but the scrawled writing, poor light, and his shaking hands proved it too much of a challenge.

"This is your ancestor's?" he said to Janice, shaking the pages at her. "This is what your father wanted hidden?"

But still, she continued to stare up at him until he could tear his eyes from the pages to stare at her, and then she gazed into the darkness once more.

"What?" he said. "What is it?"

He shone the light further into the void. But aside from the papers, there was nothing to see.

"Talk to me, Janice. What's there?"

She seemed to be ignorant of her newly freed wrists and ankles. Perhaps she had been in that position for so long that movement would take time.

He shone the light into the hallway once more and took a single step, only to find an uncomfortable sensation as the sole of his shoe failed to find the reassuring flat floor he had expected.

Then he turned the light to the floor, reached down, and carefully peeled the discarded pages away.

"What is it, guv?" Devon asked, to which he said nothing. Not until he knew for sure. "Guv?"

He stood from where he had crouched and stepped back to where the floor was flat. And then he turned to her.

"Guv?" she said again, and he peered down to Janice, who was sitting on the floor just a few feet from him. "Guv, talk to me," Devon said.

"It's her," Charles replied quietly, searching Janice's eyes for a sign that he was wrong but finding only a sickening confirmation. "It's Marie Dickens."

CHAPTER 58

December 28th

A full day had passed. A full circle of day and night, and with it had come sleep. Good sleep. Dreamless sleep. The type Charles hadn't known for far too long. He welcomed it like an old friend and parted with it along with the hope they would meet again.

Let's not leave it so long next time, he thought.

The drive to work had been slow. Traffic had passed by, as if in another world. A world in which things mattered. A world in which people faced troubles and kept secrets.

But, not in Charles's world. In Charles's world, the sun shone brightly. In Charles's world, there were few shadows and lies. In Charles's world, there was hope.

No, not hope, he thought, as he climbed the final step to the first floor. *Certainty*.

The thought roused another old friend as he shoved his way through the incident room doors. A smile. A smile which seemed to grow in response to the applauding few. Chalk, Forsythe, and even Hannaway, all made their appreciation in a show of solidarity.

And then there was Devon. She was sitting alone, but that was okay.

"We're not done yet," he said, when the few had finished their clapping. He remembered DI Finch used to say something similar, as if he enjoyed watching the joy and enlightenment fade to disappointment before he dished out the remaining tasks. He slapped a new file onto the table. "But we've got the bastard," he said, jabbing a finger at the folder. "Pathology report. Gareth Dickens is going down for a very long time, boys and girls. Pat yourselves on the back, eh?"

"What about his sister? Did she say who it was?" Hannaway asked.

"She said she didn't know. Whoever it was pulled something over her head," he replied. "But what she did say was that there was only one of them. A man. She didn't hear his voice."

"So, she has no idea who it was?"

"Nope," Charles said. "Not a clue."

"But surely it's her brother. I mean, if he hid his wife's body there?"

"That's exactly the angle I'm going to present to Crown Prosecution," Charles replied. "We've got him for Marie's murder. We've got him for his brother's murder, although I'm sure he'll get manslaughter for that. All we can do is pray a jury sees through his lies."

"Is she going to testify?" Hannaway asked. "Against her brother, I mean? Is she willing to take to the stand?"

"She is," Charles replied, and then a thought struck him. "I thought I asked you to watch the Pierce brothers."

"Couldn't find them," Hannaway said. "We looked all night. They're not at home and they're not at work."

"They've done a runner?"

"I've got ANPR set up," Chalk said. "As soon as their van passes through a camera, we'll have them."

It was a blow, but not severe enough to cast a shadow on Charles's day.

"Anything else?" he asked, directing his question at Devon,

who until now had said nothing. She slid a report across the desk, but still stayed silent. "What's this?" He opened the file and found a few neatly typed paragraphs, presumably summarising the wad of papers beneath.

"Forensics hit the farmhouse yesterday morning," she explained, as he lifted the summary sheet up to the light and read the second paragraph.

"Six bodies?" he said, and she nodded. "Six?"

"Children. Nothing but charred bones, really. But enough to identify four boys and two girls between the ages of six and nine," she said. "They found them under the house. Under the footings, to be precise."

"They were hiding them. They were hiding the bodies. So, when Abbott Dickens gave the land to National Trust," Charles said, mimicking quotation marks with his fingers in the air, "he was just protecting the family. He knew a developer would tear the house down. He knew the remains would be found. All that tosh about giving it over to nature," he said, shaking his head.

"And the children's charity," Devon added.

"Aye, Jesus," he replied, and then jabbed an index finger her way. "That's guilt, that is. Nothing but guilt and shame."

"Yeah well, it didn't do them much good in the end, did it?" Devon added. "Do you know who I feel sorry for? Elizabeth. She's lost a grandson and a son, and she won't see Gareth for a while."

"Speaking of Gareth," Charles said, collecting his files from the desk. He gestured for Devon to follow him, then singled out Hannaway with a double click of his fingers. "Find me those brothers, Hannaway. They can't have got far."

"Will do, guv," he replied, as Devon followed Charles through the door.

"I thought you'd like to see this," Charles told her, when they were descending the concrete stairs.

"The nail in the coffin?"

"Aye, the nail in the coffin," he said with a little laugh. "It's funny, eh? All we need is for him to confess to the kidnapping and we'll have him banged up for twenty-plus years. Him and the Pierce brothers."

"You really think they're involved, then?"

"Ah, come on. Who else could have helped him? All that cash flying about," he said.

"It's pocket change for him, though, guv."

"Aye, it might be pocket change," he replied, as they reached the bottom of the stairs. He held the door for her. "But look at it this way. If he doesn't give them up, then all he'll be doing is letting them get away with the death of his own boy."

"Hmm," she said quietly. "I never thought of it like that."

"Confess and get justice for his boy. Or say nothing and let them get away with it," Charles said. "Not much of a choice, I'll admit. But I know what one I'd take."

"Before we go in, guv," she said, as his hand rested on the handle. He stared at her, eyebrows raised. "I wonder if I could ask you something."

"Business or otherwise?" he asked.

"Otherwise," she replied, without hesitation. "I just need to say something."

"All right," he said, and his hands found the loose change in his pockets. "What do you need to say?"

This time, she did hesitate. But it was coming. She had done the hardest part.

"The restraining order, guv."

"Ah, I see."

"Listen, I just wanted to say that it doesn't matter to me. I don't care what you did. Honestly. Like I said before, the DCI Cook I know was born on Boxing Day five days ago. We all react to the things that go on around us, and, well, if what you told me is true, then I don't see how anyone could blame you if you behaved poorly."

"Behaved poorly, eh?"

"I don't mean to be impertinent," she said. "I just wanted you to know that, well, I think the bloody world of you, guv. Really, I do."

He could have let the comments get to him. Perhaps, even, he should have. But there was something in her eyes. A sincerity.

"Well, I appreciate it," he said. "If I'm honest, it's an episode I'd like to put behind me. We all have them, you know?"

"We do," she replied with a smile.

He swept his hand through the air to present the custody suite doors.

"Shall we charge Gareth Dickens or should we stand here all day?"

"There's one more thing," she said, and he did his best not to appear irritated.

"Personal or otherwise?"

"Personal," she said, and then waited for him to relent. "There's going to be fireworks up at the castle on Sunday night. You know, for the new year."

"Right?"

"I was wondering if you'd like to go, guv," she said. "With me, I mean."

"Me? Go and watch fireworks?"

"That's right, guv. With me."

Every part of his mind, body, and soul told him to say no. To turn her down. Tomorrow was New Year's Eve. He'd probably be on a call with Iain for most of the night. That was how he usually saw the new year, with a glass in his hand and his only friend on the other end of the phone.

"We'll see, eh?" he said softly, then shoved through into the custody suite to find Sergeant Barrow positioned behind the desk and Sergeant Hammond in front, both of them leaning on it as if conspiring against the world. A radio was on in the background, and when Barrow saw Charles's expression, he leaned into his office to turn it down.

"Good morning, Chief Inspector," he said, returning to his desk. "I hear you had a result with your hit and run."

"Not quite the result I was hoping for, Sergeant Barrow. But a result is a result. I'll take them when they come my way."

"It sounded like it went well," Barrow said. "We just heard Old Man Dickens on the radio."

"Sorry?"

"The old man," Barrow said, jabbing his thumb back at the radio in his office. "He was just on the local station. We've got his boy in the cells, haven't we?"

"Aye, you do."

"So we figured it's linked."

"You figured what's linked, Sergeant? For God's sake, make some sense, will you?"

"He's shutting it down, guv. I thought you'd know."

"Abbott Dickens?" Charles said. "He was on the radio? You're sure it was him?"

"Yes, guv. I told you. He sounded like he was on death's doorstep, if you ask me. He's shutting the company down. Said something about the family being there for centuries. He said they've survived–"

"Wars, famine, and fires?" Charles suggested.

"Yeah, that's it," Barrow said. "That's what he said."

"Did he say why?" Devon asked, to which Barrow said nothing. Instead he waited for Charles to react.

"Did you hear her, Sergeant Barrow? DC Devon here just asked you a question."

"Right, yeah. No. No, he didn't give a reason, only that there were some things about the family's past that aren't quite aligned with who the family are now. He said it was time to close the book on their terrible past and take time to reflect on what's important."

"Close the book on their terrible past?" Charles repeated, and he looked at Devon for some sort of clue. But she just shook her head, unwilling to voice her opinion in front of Barrow and Hammond.

"Anyway, what can I do for you?" Barrow asked, being overly nice, and much to Hammond's amusement, he was clearly ignoring Devon at Charles's side.

Charles let the news sink in. It was news to the local people.

"I wonder if you could fetch Gareth Dickens from his cell, please," Charles replied. "Bring him through to interview room two, will you? And you might as well organise transport for him. I want him held on remand until his trial."

"Will do, guv," Barrow said, again with that winning smile. "He'll be with you in a jiffy. Should I break the good news to him, guv?"

"No. No, you can leave that little gem to us," Charles replied. He held the door for Devon, but just as she was about to go back into the corridor, he stopped her. "Oh, and one more thing," he said to both sergeants. "Seeing as I've got you both here."

"Guv?" Hammond said, and Barrow waited expectantly.

"I've heard a terrible rumour going about the place."

"A rumour, guv?" Barrow said.

"Aye. A rumour. Apparently some poor sod is getting bullied by some senior officers."

"Bullying, guv?"

"Aye, bullying. Playground stuff, you know," he said dismissively. "The type of thing you'd expect from younger officers. I've no idea who it is but it sounds me to me like they're not holding back."

"Not holding back?" Hammond said. "Sorry, guv. I'm not following."

"Aye, they've taken it to the top. Apparently they have a few good friends in high places. Detective Superintendent Collins is raging about it, and believe me, when he finds out who it is, heads will roll," Charles said. "Anyway, I thought you should both know. So you can keep an eye out, you know?"

"Righto, guv," Barrow said.

"We'll be sure to keep an eye out," Hammond added.

"Good," Charles said, adding his own version of a winning smile. "Personally, I'd string them up. I can't stand bullies. Bloody cowards, I tell you. If I got my hands on them, their feet wouldn't touch the ground. They'd be up on a charge before they knew what had hit them."

"Right," Barrow said, nodding slowly.

He let the words sink for a moment, then found that smile of his.

"Well, I'd better not keep you. I imagine you're both busy men," Charles said, and winked at them. "Have a good day, eh?"

"Yeah, you too, guv," Barrow replied, sharing an awkward glance with his friend.

"Oh, I will, Sergeant Barrow," Charles said, as Devon made her way past him. "I know I will."

CHAPTER 59

December 31st

The castle walls were not employed, on that occasion, to keep invaders out as they might have done a millennium ago. Just as the Victorian prison that sat inside the walls was not employed to prevent escape.

Not on that night.

Not on New Year's Eve, when those impenetrable, ten-foot-thick castle walls were aglow with the full spectrum of dancing lights. When stalls offered doughnuts, sausage rolls, pasties, coffee, hot chocolate, and a whole array of alcoholic drinks, and music filled the medieval arena to create a vibe quite different to that of yesteryear.

Families stood in packs, with wired children running amok, drunk on sugary delights, while the parents clutched hot drinks in cold hands. Young adults huddled together sampling the variety of local ales and gin, and all the while, standing at the end of a long barrier designed to keep visitors from the grass, Charles waited.

Groups of people filed in through the east gate. A few filed out in search of somewhere to bide their time. There was still an hour until the clock struck twelve, and each individual that passed through the gate, unbeknownst to them, passed under Charles's scrutiny.

Such a public event was not his most comfortable surroundings. Self-consciousness had set in mere moments after he had found his little pocket of peace, tucked against the wall out of the way, with his hands in his pockets. And then out. Leaning on the barrier and then standing straight. It was a cycle he was familiar with and continued to endure until he recognised one of the many faces that were slowly filling the castle grounds.

She came through in the wake of a large group, walking so close to those families that he nearly missed her. Dressed in a long coat and a woolly hat, and with her hands plunged into her deep pockets, the only sign she was not one of the group was when everybody laughed except her. That was when she stopped and stepped to one side so as not to block the flow of foot traffic.

He watched her with interest. The way in which her pocketed hands seemed to pull her jacket around her. The way she buried her chin behind her furry collar. How her nervous eyes flicked between the hundreds of people.

Until she saw him, and any tension in her posture deflated. She pulled her jacket from her face and beamed at him, then, checking both ways as if she were crossing a road, she walked briskly over to the little safe place he had claimed.

"You made it," she said, sounding surprised. "For a moment there, I thought I was going to have to call you."

"Aye, well," he replied, "I found myself a wee corner out of the way. Can I get you a drink or something? There's a stall by the prison that does sausage rolls. Big ones. You know? Proper sausage rolls."

"I'm okay, thanks," she told him. "I might get a hot chocolate in a while-"

"I can get you one," he said.

"Not yet," she said, looking around at all the people. "Let's give it a while."

"Aye, if that's what you want," he replied, and he leaned on the barrier without a care in the world. No longer was he the odd-looking man standing on his own. Now he was just another bloke out to see in the new year in with a friend. "Did you hear about Gareth Dickens?"

"No," she replied, still nervously looking at all the people around them. She must have sensed he was watching her, because she turned to face him. "No, what about him?"

"He was up in front of a judge yesterday. He'll be held on remand until May. Then he'll stand trial."

"What did he plead?" she asked.

"Innocent to two accounts of manslaughter. Innocent to the kidnapping of his sister."

"Innocent to all of it? But he basically told us what he'd done. He admitted to hitting Thomas and the evidence on Marie's remains–"

"Aye, I know, I know," he said.

"But the crime scene," she said. "I spoke to Katy Southwell. She said that Janice's office walls had clear blood spatter across them. She said he fell and hit his head on the corner of a filing cabinet. The pathologist, Pippa Bell, even backed that theory up, guv."

"There's no question that he was hit, Devon," he replied. "There's no question that he went down and hit his head. But there are doubts about who hit him." He watched her disappointment rise, just as it had done with him when he had learned of the outcome. "And for God's sake, call me Charles, will you? Bloody guv this and guv that. Makes me feel old."

"But if it wasn't him, then–"

"Who else was with him? Who helped him?"

"Victoria Hughes?"

He nodded slowly.

"And who did Marie Dickens find in his arms on her last day on this earth?"

"Victoria Hughes. So he was covering for her? But why? Why not just tell us what she'd done?"

"Because then they would have to give up the body."

"And if they gave up the body, the family secret would be exposed. All those children. But it *was* exposed. Pretty soon everyone will know what the family did."

"It's convenient, isn't it? He tells us that he was responsible for the death of his wife and brother. Tells us he threw her in the river. Then we find Janice. We find Marie. And we find the children. And now all of a sudden there's no secret to keep and he pleads innocent."

"So it really could have been her? Victoria Hughes, I mean?"

"Aye, it could have been. I mean, it's pretty low to point the finger at your lover, isn't it? Even by Gareth Dickens's standards."

"So he could walk? He could be free? I mean, we don't even have anything to tie him to the kidnapping except a bag load of cash, some kind of deal with the Pierce brothers, and a pretty sketchy motive."

"It's how it goes, eh? All we can do is catch them and feed them into the system. If the system wants to spit them back out again, then it will."

"No. No, I want the system to swallow him whole. I want him behind bars. The man's a manipulating, conniving..."

She stopped herself from entering into a long-winded rant, and turned her back to the barrier beside him. He stared at the officials in bright yellow jackets as they prepared the evening's spectacle, and she watched the crowd grow larger.

"Which means that his son's death will go unsolved," he said to her.

But she didn't reply.

He glanced her way but found the space beside him empty, and once more, he was alone, awkward, and very aware of his every action. He scanned the crowds, but in that short space of time between Devon arriving and disappearing, it seemed to have more than doubled. Every woman he saw was wearing a long jacket. Many of them wore Molly hats. And a surprising number of them had buried their faces in their collars or scarves.

He shoved his hands into his jacket pockets, then immediately withdrew them and leaned on the barrier. Maybe she was getting a drink, after all. Unless he had said something to upset her. Had he?

He was recalling the conversation about Gareth Dickens and Victoria Hughes when he felt a tug on his coat.

"Ah, you're back, are you?" he said, and began to turn to face her. "Listen, if you're going to disappear like that—"

He stopped mid-sentence.

She was beaming. Her smile was so broad and her face so elated, it was hard not to notice in his peripheral. Because, of course, she was in his peripheral. The architect of something wonderful standing by to bask in the glory. She was the designer of something spectacular, just like the person who had designed the evening's fireworks show would be less than an hour from now.

Because the focus of his attention was on somebody new. A new pair of eyes that beamed up at him. A new face that was hidden behind an oversized scarf.

But there was no mistaking her. Never would he mistake that face.

"Dad?" she said, and he saw Devon bite down on her lower lip. "Dad, it's me."

CHAPTER 60

"I know," he said softly, and stood up straight. He didn't know what to do. Should he kiss her on the cheek? Should he shake her hand? Should he pull her in for a big hug like he used to do when she was nine years old?

He didn't know. But she did.

She spread her arms and wrapped them around him, like he was the nine-year-old and she the adult. He found himself tentatively reciprocating, his confidence growing with every second. For so long, she had been off-limits to him. For so long, all that he'd had was her memory. Cherished memories. Memories so overused, they were like the cassette tapes he used to play that wore thin over time until the memories they held were inaccurate. Dubious. Twisted, stretched, and warped by time.

"How did you know I was here?" he said, pulling her away to look into those big, lovely eyes.

She smiled and laughed all at once. Carefree.

"Becky told me," she replied, and jabbed a thumb at Devon.

"Becky?" he said, turning to his new friend. "As in Rebecca. You never told me your name was Rebecca."

"You never asked me," she replied.

"I'm..." he began, but found his word faltering. "I just don't know what I should–"

"Just enjoy the moment," Vanessa said.

"But how will you get home? How did you get here?"

"Never mind all that," she replied, clearly now an adult with a strong hold on her emotions.

"Listen, I'm sorry I didn't make it..."

"Becky has told me all about it," Vanessa said, and she placed her hand on his arm. "It's okay, Dad. Honestly, it's okay."

"I don't know what to say," he said, and he blinked a tear from his eye, then laughed at his reaction.

She smiled in that way that women do when men let their emotions run free.

"I'm staying up here, Dad," she said. "For a while, anyway. With you. If that's what you want?"

"With me?" he replied. "Aye, aye, I'd love it. I'd have to move a few things around–"

"All in good time," she told him, and she shared a smile with Devon. "Listen. I've had a long train ride. I'm going to get some hot chocolates in."

"No, I'll get them," he said, and made to enter the throng behind them. But she held out her hand. "I said I'll get them."

For a moment, he saw his wife standing there. They shared a strength. That same strength that Devon had adored.

"Alright," he said. "Alright, if you're sure."

"I'm sure," she told him. "I'm a big girl now, Dad. I can look after myself. I'll be back in a minute, okay?"

She slipped into the crowd with ease and confidence, and then she was lost, and all that remained was Devon's uncompromising smile.

"You did this for me?" he asked her, and she nodded. "But how? How did you know how to find her? Who she was?"

"Do you remember when you were driving and you gave me your phone?"

"The passcode?" he said, and he chuckled to himself.

"Two three zero one nine nine. Twenty-third of January nineteen ninety-nine," she said. "And I am a copper, after all."

"Great. So I need to change my passcode now, do I?" He tried to find his daughter in the crowd but it was heaving now. "What other dirt have you dug up on me?"

"No dirt, guv."

"I asked you to stop calling me that."

"Charles, then," she said. "But I wish you had told me."

"Told you what?"

"About the restraining order," she said, and he looked away again. "People talk, Charles."

"They do, indeed," he replied.

"But they don't always get it right, do they?"

"No," he said to himself.

"Why didn't you tell me the restraining order was against your wife? The whole bloody station things you're a nutter with a screw loose."

"Ah, let them think it," he told her. "Better to be the nutter with a screw loose than the nobody who stands in the corner afraid of his own shadow."

"You're weird, Charles Cook," she said. "You know that, right?"

"Aye. Aye, I know," he replied, and for the first time he felt comfortable in the surroundings. "Do you know what's funny?"

"Go on?" she said.

"When those rumours first started circulating, the ones about Maggie and me, and then the rumours that I'd lost the plot and that my wife had taken out an injunction against me, it wasn't that people were looking at me differently," he explained. "It was that they were actually looking at me."

"What do you mean?"

"They suddenly knew who I was," he said with a little laugh. "Before that, nobody knew me at all."

"And clearly they still don't," she said.

"And let's keep it that way, shall we? I don't mind the rumour mill turning if it's grinding in my favour."

A murmur began running through the crowd that there were only twenty minutes remaining. Charles scanned the crowd again, hoping to catch another glimpse of his daughter.

"I've been thinking," Devon said.

"Aye?" he replied, without turning.

"What if Gareth Dickens was actually innocent?"

"It's not our problem anymore," he said, leading her away from what could be a trail of disaster.

"But just imagine if he was innocent, if Victoria Hughes was the one to force Marie off the road, and if it was her who hit Thomas."

"He'd still be an accomplice to both deaths," he said, allowing his eyes to move in her direction, but nothing else.

"An accomplice. Not a killer. If I'm right, then the chances are that he had nothing to do with the kidnapping. He could be innocent of it all, the same as the Pierce brothers."

"But the Pierce brothers had the van."

"But what if there was no van?"

"John Gregory heard the van."

"He might have heard it, but how do we know it had anything to do with the kidnapping? For all we know, it could have been just as Gregory said, a newspaper van rushing about to make his deliveries."

"But then, who was driving Janice's car?"

She smiled up at him.

"Janice was driving the car."

"Janice? But..." He paused, and her idea, as wild as it was, began to take shape. "Janice kidnapped Janice?"

She nodded slowly, pulling a face of utter dread at what it all would mean.

"And Janice cut Janice's finger off?"

"Her right pinkie finger," Devon said.

"She's left-handed," Charles said. "It was Thomas's right finger we found in the second box. But who would cut their own finger off? Unless they were desperate to make a point?"

"What if she was leading us to Marie?" Devon asked, and Charles tapped his pockets in search of the letter, dragging it from his inside pocket. He scanned down to the line he was thinking of.

"I can no longer pursue a career led by an individual who demonstrates such a twisted sense of right and wrong," he read aloud. "She knew. She knew about Marie. She knew what had happened to her, and she knew what he'd done with the body."

"And she knew that if we found her there, we'd also find Marie, and the children."

"So, the family business closes down, Gareth goes away for a very long time, and they all live happily ever after?" He mused. "What about Harry?"

"An accident," she said. "He wasn't even meant to be there. Satish told us that he was still looking at magazines when she left. She was probably going to leave him there. At least he'd be safe."

"But he walked out of the shop just as she was making her getaway," he agreed, and gave a heavy sigh. "But what about the phone calls? Elizabeth said it was a man's voice."

"Right," she replied. "It's funny, isn't it? The kidnapper called Elizabeth. Not Gareth. Not Abbott. But Elizabeth."

"She was in on it?"

"What did she say when we were at Five Mile Lane a few days ago? The truth is that the business should have been shut down years ago."

"Something to that effect," he said. "Oh, Devon. The letter. The note from Janice to her mum saying that she was leaving."

"She was putting us off the scent," Devon said. "It was a bloody decoy. Guv, we've got to do something."

"We've got Gareth in custody-."

"Yeah, but it's not exactly a done deal, is it? We've got nothing concrete except for two murder cases, for which he'll most likely get manslaughter at best. And as for his son-."

"What's up?" a new voice said, cheery, familiar, and dreadful all at once.

"Oh nothing, love," he said. "Just work stuff."

"Oh, I see," she replied, handing each of them a hot chocolate in a disposable cup.

"Your dad is in denial."

"Oh? What about?"

"It's nothing," he said dismissively. "Forget about it. Come on, let's just enjoy the evening."

"We've arrested the wrong man," Devon said.

"Leave it—"

"The wrong man?" Vanessa said. "What have you arrested him for?"

"Two accounts of manslaughter and a kidnapping, so far," Devon said.

Vanessa's eyes widened and Charles just shook his head.

"It's work stuff, Vanessa. Come on."

"I wonder how that man is feeling now, Dad?" she said. "I wonder how it feels to be accused of something you didn't do and to watch your life fall apart as a result?"

He said nothing. She was right. She was smart and intelligent, and the young woman she had grown to be had been hardened, tempered like steel.

"Go," she said.

"Eh?"

"Go," she repeated. "I'll be okay."

"But Vanessa—"

"I said go," she said again. "You can't leave that poor man in a prison cell when he's done nothing wrong. Go. I'll be fine."

"But you'll stay here?" he said, rummaging for his keys. He

slipped his door key from the ring and handed it to her. "You remember the house, aye?"

"I've dreamed of that house since I was nine years old, Dad," she told him, and then smiled. "Now, for the last time, will you both just go?"

CHAPTER 61

January 1st

Lincoln Cathedral was lit in hues of oranges, reds, and blues, as the castle walls had been. But somehow, on the horizon, the cathedral seemed ethereal, otherworldly, as the sky above it burst into life, showering the ancient monuments with dazzling colours. The sound reached Charles and Devon, but the distant lights failed to penetrate that dark, opulent corner of the countryside.

There were no fireworks at that great house. No cause for celebration. The only lights there were the flashing blues from atop the two liveried cars that Devon had summoned en route.

But the blue lights were enough to drag the shadows away.

It was as if a veil had been lifted from the Dickens house. A veil of ivy, perhaps, that had contained so many dark secrets. And just as the promise of a display had drawn hundreds to the castle walls, the flashing blues drew just two spectators to the front door.

They stood side by side, silhouetted against the light from behind them. The shorter of the two, older and broader, reached for her daughter's hand. Her good hand. Her unbandaged hand.

And that's how they remained, for a time, at least.

"It's John Gregory I feel for," Devon muttered. They were

standing beside Charles's car, the uniformed officers nearby, just waiting for the signal to move in.

"Why's that?"

"He'll be destitute," Devon replied. "Without the money from Janice."

"Oh, I wouldn't worry about John Gregory if I were you," he said. "Dickens and Sons has ceased trading. Every farm in the county will be flocking to him, if you pardon the pun. He'll be a millionaire before you get made sergeant. Remember that."

"I suppose."

"No. No, it's the boy I feel for. Arthur. I just hope that after all of this, he can lead a normal life. That when somebody asks him about his family, he can tell them they're just like any other family."

"They'll still be rolling in money after the sale of all that land, guv," she said. "I doubt he'll be like every other kid out there."

"Money isn't everything, though, is it?" Charles told her.

"What is, then?" she asked.

"Family," he replied. "Family and friends. And he might just have a dad in five or ten years' time. I doubt Gareth will get much more for his part. Not with his legal team, anyway."

"And a grandad," she added. "I hear he's on the road to recovery."

"I'll bet they're good men deep down. Now, anyway. Now they've been steered onto the road to righteousness, as it were," he said. He exhaled and watched the cloud of breath disperse. "So we're going to reopen this, are we? Victoria Hughes was responsible for both Marie and Thomas, and Janice wasn't kidnapped after all. It was just a ploy to shut the business down and bury the secrets forever? That's the line you're going with, is it?"

"It's a square peg in a square hole. All this time, we've been trying to fit Gareth and the Pierce brothers into a plot that simply didn't make sense," Devon said. Then she took a deep breath and nodded at the two women on the doorstep. "Shall we nick them, then? Get this over with?"

"You go," he said, flicking his head at the house. "You can handle it, can't you?"

"What about you?" she asked.

"Oh, I've got something to deal with," he replied, opening the door to his Jaguar. "Something personal. You don't mind, do you?"

She smiled at him and there was happiness in her eyes.

"I might need sign off on keeping them in custody. Sergeant Barrow isn't my biggest fan. He might cause some problems," she said, which he pondered for a moment.

"Call Hannaway. Tell him I told you to," he said, as he climbed into his car. "It's about time those two took you seriously." She was intelligent enough to read the message in that last statement and she smiled shyly at the gesture. He was on her side. She would know that now. He lowered the window before reaching for the door handle, and then paused. "Are you sure you don't mind? You're definitely okay with this?"

"No, I don't mind, guv," she said, closing his door for him. "I don't mind at all."

ALSO BY JACK CARTWRIGHT

The DCI Cook Murder Mysteries

A Winter of Blood

A Secret to Die For

The Wild Fens Murder Mysteries

Secrets In Blood

One For Sorrow

In Cold Blood

Suffer In Silence

Dying To Tell

Never To Return

Lie Beside Me

Dance With Death

In Dead Water

One Deadly Night

Her Dying Mind

Into Death's Arms

Join my VIP reader group to be among the first to hear about new release dates, discounts, and get a free Wild Fens novella.

Visit www.jackcartwrightbooks.com for details.

VIP READER CLUB

Your FREE ebook is waiting for you now.

Get your FREE copy of the prequel story to the Wild Fens Murder Mystery series, and learn how DI Freya Bloom came to give up everything she had, to start a new life in Lincolnshire.

Visit www.jackcartwrightbooks.com to join the VIP Reader Club.

I'll see you there.

Jack Cartwright

A NOTE FROM THE AUTHOR

Locations are as important to the story as the characters are; sometimes even more so. It's for this reason that I visit the settings and places used within my stories to see with open eyes, breath in the air, and to listen to the sounds.

I have heard it said that each page should feature at least one sensory description, which in the age of the internet anybody can glean from somebody else's photos, maps, or even blog posts.

But, I disagree.

I believe that by visiting locations in person, a writer can experience a true sense of place which should then colour the language used in the story in a far more natural manner than by simply providing a banal description which can often stall the pace of the story.

However, there are times when I am compelled to create a fictional place within a real environment. For example, in the story you have just read, any resident of Heighington will know that no such shop exists on the High Street, and no such business occupies such a vast amount of land on Five Mile Lane.

The reason I create these is so that I can be sure not to cast any real location, setting, business, street, or feature in a negative light; nobody wants to see their beloved home town described as a scene for a murder, or any business portrayed as anything but excellent.

If any names of bonafide locations appear in my books, I ensure they bask in a positive light because I truly believe that Lincolnshire has so much to offer and that these locations should be celebrated with vehemence.

I hope you agree.

Jack Cartwright.

AFTERWORD

Because reviews are critical to an author's career, if you have enjoyed this novel, you could do me a huge favour by leaving a review on Amazon.

Reviews allow other readers to find my books. Your help in leaving one would make a big difference to this author.

Thank you for taking the time to read *A Winter of Blood*.

COPYRIGHT

Copyright © 2023 by JackCartwright

All rights reserved.

The moral right of Jack Cartwright to be identified as the author of this work has been asserted by him in accordance with the Copyright, Designs and Patents act 1988.

All the characters in this book are fictitious, and any resemblance to actual persons living or dead is purely coincidental.

All rights reserved. No part of this publication may be reproduced, stored in a retrieval system or transmitted in any form or by any means, without the prior permission in writing of the publisher, nor to be otherwise circulated in any form of binding or cover other than that in which it is published without a similar condition, including this condition, being imposed on the subsequent purchaser.

Printed in Great Britain
by Amazon